HEARTBREAK HOTEL

HEARTBREAK HOTEL

Deborah Moggach

WINDSOR
PARAGON

First published 2013
by Chatto & Windus
This Large Print edition published 2013
by AudioGO Ltd
by arrangement with
The Random House Group Ltd

Hardcover   ISBN: 978 1 4713 3915 8
Softcover   ISBN: 978 1 4713 3916 5

British Library Cataloguing in Publication Data available

Printed and bound in Great Britain by
MPG Books Group Limited

For Mark, and his town.

Cut out and keep for handy reference.

Russell 'Buffy' Buffery has been married three times.

First to **Popsi** (deceased), with whom he had a son, **Quentin.**

Then to **Jacquetta** (now married to her shrink, Leon), with whom he had two sons, **Tobias** and **Bruno**. Jacquetta already had a daughter, **India**.

His third wife was **Penny**, who ran off with a photographer. They had no children.

However, Buffy had a daughter, **Celeste**, with an actress called **Lorna**.

And another daughter, **Nyange**, with a dancer called **Carmella**.

Keep up at the back.

Or find out more by reading all about them in The Ex-Wives.

Buffy

It all came flooding back. Buffy put the letter on
the table and sat down heavily. Bridie's laughter;
her gravelly smoker's cough. She could be bustling
around him now in her stained landlady's kimono.
He remembered her veined ankles in her bedroom
slippers; the dear, massive bulk of her as she fried
bacon. The past was in his nostrils; he could smell
the lino and the cats, the woozy fumes from the
Ascot that hung above the bath. Those were the
days of eiderdowns, the gas fire popping, her
stockings drying on the fender.

Bridie ran a theatrical boarding house in
Edgbaston. Buffy had lodged there, year in, year
out, mutating from a lithe Hotspur to a portly
Falstaff, when he worked in Birmingham Rep. Age,
however, could not wither Bridie. Like most fat
people she remained the same, year after year.
Grey roots appeared in her hennaed hair, she was
given two new knees, but she still resembled the girl
he knew when he looked good in tights.

Once, when drunk, he had proposed marriage.

'Darling, not only are you married already but
I've got my family here, thank you very much.' She
sloshed more whisky into his mug. 'Lodgers are a
lot less trouble than children, even when they're
actors, and besides, they pay me.'

'There's a lot to be said for it. The deep peace of
the marriage bed, tra-la, after the hurly-burly of the
chaise longue.'

'Deep peace my foot. We'd start arguing about the guttering.'

'Actually, now you mention it, you should get it seen to—'

'Shut up, you silly cunt.'

She was right, of course. They were happy as they were. Who knew what she got up to when he wasn't there? He remembered the crocodile-skin case in which she kept her Dutch cap, a gift from a gentleman admirer. She was a warm-blooded woman with an obliging nature, and actors on tour were no slouches in the leg-over department. After all, when you'd seen a stuffed badger in the local museum what else was there to do?

And now Bridie was dead. Buffy longed to cry. He was an actor, he could do it on cue. And by God he had had plenty to cry about. But grief is fiercest when muddied by conflicting emotions— recrimination, guilt, resentment. Bridie was one of the few women about whom he felt no guilt at all. In fact, to be perfectly honest, they had rather lost touch since she had moved to Wales. That he had been in *her* mind—hence the letter from some solicitor in Builth Wells, she must have left him a little something in her will—gave him his first, and last, twinge of guilt where she was concerned. Gratitude too. Due to his advanced age Buffy had lost many friends, and one ex-wife. These snuffings-out had made it clear to him, if proof were needed, that dying was a self-absorbed business. The last thing on anyone's mind seemed to be those who were left behind. Any recognition of this would be welcome, just a token. Even something hideous, like a toby jug.

Buffy heaved himself to his feet and padded into

2

the kitchen. He had foolishly left the window open and the air was bedimmed with plaster dust. Two years earlier some Russian oligarch had bought the house next door. Since then it had been sheathed in plastic; behind this the building shuddered and rumbled as its bowels were excavated to create a gym, swimming pool and cinema in which the tycoon could watch his pornographic films.

This was happening throughout the neighbourhood. Blomfield Mansions, where Buffy lived, was a block of flats on the Edgware Road. Behind it lay Little Venice; to the front St John's Wood. Both areas housed the super-rich and perennially absent. Away on their yachts, or drilling in the Arctic, or whatever they did, they left their neighbours to suffer the major refurbishments to which they subjected their property investments. Buffy walked his dog through a babel of East European voices, past hammerings and bangings and double-parked cement mixers, past signs telling him *Hard Hats Must Be Worn*. The old neighbourhood had vanished and even his local boozer, still relatively unscathed, now served blithering Thai food, assembled in an industrial unit in Park Royal and boiled in a bag. The Scotch egg was finally extinct. Some people, of course, would say high time too.

Buffy tore open a packet of biscuits. His daughter Nyange was coming to tea. She was bound to be late. She had caught it from her mother, a Ghanaian dancer with whom Buffy had had a brief fling when he could still struggle into, and out of, 32-inch trousers. Sauntering in after he had given up hope, Nyange would explain her tardiness as AMT, African Mean Time. Something about her

3

breeziness implied that it was *his* problem, that punctuality was some vague relic of colonial oppression and plunder. It was *his* hour that she had stolen, of course, but Buffy didn't have the heart to tell her.

Nyange was indeed an hour late but this time she had an excuse.

'I can't find a fucking parking space!' her voice crackled on the intercom. She turned aside to bellow at a parking warden. 'Piss off! I'm coming!'

In the end Buffy had to admit defeat and bring the tea out to his daughter's car. They sat there, tray jammed on his knee, the plate of biscuits on the dashboard. This wasn't the first time he had had to leave his flat empty and entertain his guest in some freezing Honda Civic out in the street.

'Sorry about this,' he said. 'I'd even cleaned up the place in your honour. I'd even laid the *table*. Bloody parking warden vultures.'

'London sucks,' said Nyange. 'Kid got shot in my local offie last week.'

They were parked on a double yellow line, jammed between a delivery lorry and a large 4×4 with tinted windows. One of the windows slid open and a hand flung out an empty Badoit bottle.

Buffy sighed. 'These used to be proper shops. Butcher. Greengrocer.' He pointed to a Snappy Snaps and a Foxton's estate agents (ha ha, empty of customers). 'Oh the good old days. Have a HobNob.'

A traffic warden appeared. Nyange cursed. Tea slopping, she jerked into gear and drove round the block, past idling lorries and skips full of rubble.

'Still,' said Buffy, *'When a man's tired of London—'* He stopped. Nyange wouldn't know

4

about Dr Johnson. Besides, he wasn't quite sure of its truth any more. What was wrong with tiring of London? Everything about it was conspiring to get on his nerves. He had a vision of himself in a cottage garden, a grizzled patriarch in a panama hat, his grandchildren bringing him jam jars full of tadpoles.

Nyange came to a shuddering halt at a bus stop, the only available parking space. The biscuits slid off the dashboard.

'This is ridiculous!' she snapped. Nyange was a feisty young woman—not young, actually, almost middle-aged. He had *middle-aged children*. The thought always gave Buffy a jolt. Today she was looking startlingly businesslike. The last time they met, her hair was braided with tiny beads and buttons. Today it was cut into a Louise Brooks bob and gleamed with lacquer. Perhaps it was a wig. He resisted the urge to touch it, like an elderly perv.

On the other hand, he *was* her father. The trouble was that contact in the past had been somewhat intermittent. He remembered a low-key Christmas with Nyange and her mother, two comely near-strangers in a shawl-festooned room in Deptford. They had grudgingly cooked him a pheasant portion—they were both vegetarians— and he had broken his tooth on a shotgun pellet.

'So how are you?' she asked. 'It's been ages. I was in the district.'

'Actually, a dear friend of mine has just died,' he said.

'I suppose they're all doing that.'

'Hang on, I'm only seventy. It's the new forty.'

Behind them, a bus honked. People, shuffling past to board it, glared into the car. Nyange pulled

5

away, drove round the corner and double-parked behind a Tesco's van—*You Shop, We Drop.*

'One of your old actors?'

'A theatrical landlady,' said Buffy. 'I used to stay with her in the glory days of rep. She moved to Wales a few years ago and started a B&B.'

Put like this it sounded so bald. But why should Nyange be interested? He suddenly felt lonely in the cramped, cluttered car, in a world with no Bridie in it. No more letters in his mailbox. And nobody who knew who he was talking about except a few raddled thesps who might stagger along to her funeral.

'She was my oldest friend,' Buffy said, and suddenly—at last—his eyes filled with tears. 'Through thick and thin.' He gazed down at the tray, now slopped with tea.

'Poor Dad.' She stroked his hand. 'You must be gutted. Oh fuck it.'

The Tesco van pulled away to reveal another parking warden. He was eyeing their number plate.

Nyange leaned out of the window. 'Piss off!' she shouted. 'This old man's a cripple. He's having a seizure!'

The traffic warden ignored her and took out his notebook. Nyange snorted and started the engine. She drove down the street, accelerated through an amber light and turned right into the Edgware Road. It was heavy with rush-hour traffic. She stopped on a red line.

'This is hopeless, I'd better let you out here.' She put the biscuit plate on the tray. 'I just came to tell you I've passed my exam. I'm now a fully-fledged ACA.'

Buffy, jammed in with his tray, couldn't give her

6

a hug. Awkwardly, he turned and found himself kissing her brittle helmet of hair. It smelt of musk, the Proustian aroma of the sixties. 'You brilliant girl—woman.'

Nyange already looked the part. Gone were the cornrows and leggings; today she wore a black trouser suit and what used to be called court shoes. Buffy gazed at her with awe. Even more surprising than producing a black daughter was producing an accountant. Every other woman he knew, when changing careers, became a therapist of some sort or another. God knew who went to them when they were all therapists themselves.

'So useful to have an accountant in the family,' he said, little knowing how true that would turn out to be.

*   *   *

It wasn't a toby jug. Nor was it the framed reproduction of *Highland Cattle in the Snow* that had hung next to the payphone, and to which Buffy had had a sentimental attachment. Bridie had left him her house: her B&B in Wales.

He was still dazed with the shock of it. Unable to settle, he wandered around the flat, picking things up and putting them down again. He mislaid his wallet and discovered it in the fridge. At night he dreamed of journeys where he struggled through the rain, stark naked, and returned to find Blomfield Mansions had been demolished and replaced by a Garden of Remembrance. He woke drenched in sweat, his heart pounding.

Of course he felt gratitude towards Bridie— profound gratitude. This recognition of their

7

lifelong affection, from beyond the grave, moved him deeply. It physically pained him that he could no longer throw his arms around her in thanks.

'Why not you, you old bugger?' she would chuckle. 'Wish I was there to see his face.' He being her brother, the more obvious beneficiary, who lived back in Ireland. Apparently he was a staunch Catholic who had disapproved of his sister's rackety lifestyle. But her brother didn't need the money, having speculated during the property boom, covering County Limerick with hideous mansions, all pillared porches and marble en suites; the tumbleweed now blew through them but he didn't care, he had got out before the crash.

That Bridie had no other family, nobody closer than himself, made Buffy feel strange, his own life having been somewhat entangled on the domestic front. It had thrown their differing circumstances into sharp relief. But she had chosen to live that way, she was a free spirit beholden to nobody.

*   *   *

'I didn't even know she was ill,' Buffy told his son Quentin. 'She never mentioned it in her letters.'

'I didn't even know she existed.'

'I don't know what to do.' They were having lunch at a restaurant in Frith Street.

'Your money problems are over, that's for sure,' said Quentin.

'You mean I should sell it?'

Quentin smiled. 'I can just picture you, stuck in the pouring rain two hundred miles from Soho.'

It wasn't a smile, it was a patronising smirk.

'Why on earth not?' asked Buffy irritably.

8

'*Dad.*'

That did it. Later, Buffy saw this as a turning point. *I'll show him.* Men had gone to war for less. Of course he was used to his children's affectionate contempt. Well, their contempt. What fun to startle them.

'I'm tired of London,' Buffy said. 'I'm tired of my horrible neighbours and never having anywhere to park. Nyange and I had to have tea in her car last week. I'm tired of cyclists knocking me over on the pavement.'

'We don't cycle on the pavement,' said Quentin. He and his partner James were pious citizens, biking to farmers' markets with their jute shopping bags.

'I'm tired of everybody being so rude unless they're foreigners,' Buffy said, getting into his stride. 'I'm tired of being irritated all the time, it makes me feel so elderly—I *am* elderly. But I don't feel it, until London irritates me. It's too full of memories and too many of my friends are dead.'

'You really mean you'd *live* there?' Quentin raised his eyebrows. Were they plucked? Quentin was gay; Buffy wouldn't put it past him.

'I want a change.' As Buffy said it, he knew it was true.

Their lunch had arrived. Quentin removed the pieces of celery from his salad and put them on the side of his plate. They had both agreed, some time in the past, that celery was a pointless vegetable. It was one of the things they had discovered in common.

'So where is this place?' asked Quentin.

'Knockton. It's in the Welsh Marches, apparently.' Buffy added defensively 'almost in

9

England', as if it wasn't such a big thing to go there. He already felt the beginnings of loyalty towards this unknown town.

'So you haven't even seen it yet?'

Buffy shook his head. 'I'm going to go down there next week.'

Quentin raised his eyebrows again. An anchovy hung from his fork like a little leather strap. Since moving in with James, Quentin had thickened out. Happiness had done this. The two of them had met while window-dressing at Harrods but it had been years of *Sturm und Drang* until they had found domestic peace in Crouch End.

So many upheavals in both their lives but now here they were, he and his forty-five-year-old son, munching obscure and peppery salad leaves tossed by a celebrity chef. Quentin's greying (greying!) hair was clipped into one of those crew cuts sported by the gay fraternity in Old Compton Street.

Buffy remembered a rare family gathering, Nyange and Quentin sitting side by side, the black girl and the homosexual. Penny, his wife at the time, had gazed at them. 'Very Channel 4,' she had mused. 'Now all we need is the physically challenged.' She had glanced down at Buffy, who had ricked his back and was lying on the floor, propped up by cushions. 'Oh oh, there he is.'

'Maybe it would do you good to have a change,' said Quentin.

Buffy looked sharply at his son. He wanted to get rid of him! Out of sight, out of mind. Perhaps he was becoming a liability to his children, visited out of duty, and it would be a relief all round if he banished himself to another country, which Wales practically was. He was a querulous, doddery King

10

Lear, a part for which he had secretly prepared for years and never been offered. This was hardly surprising since he no longer had an agent. Or, indeed, a career.

However, a new career beckoned. Mine host! Luxuriantly bearded, his cheeks ruddy with claret, Buffy could take centre stage again, welcoming guests into his charming B&B in the picturesque town of Knockton, wherever that was. Log fires, bonhomie, brass beds made for lusty couplings—adulterers welcome! His Full English Breakfast, all organic of course, would become legendary. Perhaps he could even raise his own pigs.

Not for him the niminy-piminy B&Bs of his past experience—the nylon sheets, the pastel wallpaper, the framed silhouettes of crinolined ladies. The near-impossibility of any form of sexual congress in some twin-bedded room smelling of air-freshener. The doily-draped nest of tables with its *Reader's Digests*. The genteel breakfast room, the tinkle of cutlery, the cruet—cruet!—the tiny sachets of his least favourite jam, strawberry.

'*You*, running a bed and breakfast?' Quentin, hiding a smirk, pressed his napkin to his lips.

'I've seen enough of them in my time. On tour and so forth. In fact, I do believe you were conceived in one. In Kettering.'

Quentin flinched. 'Too much information, Dad.'

'Your mother and I were playing Sybil and Elyot in *Private Lives*.'

Buffy's first wife—now alas dead, God bless her—had been a lusty young woman, uninhibited by the usual constraints of paper-thin walls. He remembered the lowered eyes of the other guests when the two of them, hastily washed and

11

brushed-up, appeared for breakfast. And Quentin, a little miracle inside her, just begun.

It was no wonder that Bridie's lodgings were a liberation. In its heyday the house in Edgbaston had creaked with sex. He remembered glimpsing Digby Montague, now a Knight of the Realm, darting across the landing wearing only his socks. Then there was Hillers, a predatory lesbian and memorable Lady Bracknell, sitting at the breakfast table in a fug of cigarette smoke, fondling the knee of a blonde ingénue. Even the cats were at it, one of them giving birth to kittens on his eiderdown. Happy days.

Buffy, somewhat the worse for wear, hailed a cab home. He could afford these extravagances now. His head reeled. Had he told Quentin the truth? Could he really pack up his belongings and decamp into the unknown or was he just proving to his son that there was life in the old dog yet? He felt, as one does when drunk, that events were swimmingly fitting into place. His children were long since grown and no longer needed him, if they ever had in the first place. His rent was about to be doubled. Besides, as he had told Quentin, Blomfield Mansions had changed in character. Its mouldy, net-curtained, vaguely Jewish inhabitants—tragic widows measuring out their lives with coffee spoons—had died off. Some of them had been a pain in the arse but he missed them. They had been replaced by the rich offspring of Middle Eastern businessmen who had bought the flats as bolt-holes in case their countries went up in smoke and who partied all night and revved up their sports cars outside his window. Even the doorman, Ted, had been replaced by a bunch of plastic flowers.

12

Buffy's wives were dead or long since disappeared into their subsequent lives. He was free, for better or worse. Only his dog needed him, and his dog could live anywhere. In fact, now Buffy thought of it, Fig would prefer the country.

As night fell, Buffy walked Fig around the block. His previous dog, George, had had to be dragged along on his lead. George had looked like a hairpiece; there was something flattened and matted about him. Penny said he looked as if somebody had run over him at some point in the past. He was generally agreed to have been the laziest dog anybody had known.

His replacement, however, was just the opposite, a hyperactive Jack Russell who jumped up and down like a tennis ball and yapped at passing cars, at passing anything. Jack Russells liked hunting rabbits; they weren't really London dogs at all.

Buffy thought: If I go ahead, it'll be for Fig's sake. This seemed as good a reason as any.

2

Monica

Monica didn't go along with Dress-Down Fridays. The kids in her office were half her age, of course. Everybody in the City was half her age. They looked fine in jeans and trainers but she had a fragile sense of self—she was working on this with her therapist—and felt bolstered in a suit. That sense of authority, so dearly won, would be sapped by denim. So they considered her an old fogey.

13

Tough.

Acme Motivation ran corporate events—banquets, awaydays, bonding weekends at Cotswold hotels where bankers romped like puppies and got drunk as skunks. Monica and her assistant Rupert were organising a dinner at the Kensington Hilton for Bond Trader of the Year. Rupert, an amiable, chubby young Etonian, was speaking on the phone to their client. He wore a T-shirt saying *This isn't a Beer Gut, it's a Fuel Tank for a Sex Machine.* Of course their client couldn't see this, he was on the phone, but surely clothes affected how one behaved—why else was there a fashion industry? She herself gazed at men differently when she was wearing her Janet Reger knickers.

Monica thought: Underneath this power suit *I'm* still a sex machine. The trouble was that men no longer wanted to discover this. She was sixty-four—a fact she kept quiet about in the office—but she had always taken care of herself and today her forehead was stiff from a Botox session; so stiff, in fact, that she couldn't raise her eyebrows at Rupert's T-shirt, at its hilarious inappropriateness where he was concerned.

The trouble was, the older she grew, the longer it took to assemble herself for public scrutiny and the shakier the results. In an instant, a gust of wind could transform her from smart businesswoman to bedraggled crone, barely recognisable even to herself. In a sense this didn't matter as she had become totally invisible anyway. This was both dispiriting, of course, and a kind of freedom. Men no longer glanced at her, even briefly, in the street. Sometimes she felt as if she didn't exist at all. Monica sat at her desk, sorting out the menu

14

requirements—no vegetarian options for City boys, they liked tearing at animals. She thought: Will I ever have sex again? Was that last time the very last time?

*   *   *

It was the end of the day. Monica walked down Threadneedle Street. Outside the pubs, drinkers spilled onto the pavement. Though partial to a drink herself, Monica found it astonishing, the amount that kids knocked back. Who would believe they were in the depths of a recession? The collapse of the economy had left no mark on their shiny pink faces—nor, it seemed, on the level of their bonuses. Only a smudge remained on the wall of HSBC, where somebody had sprayed *SPAWN OF SATAN*. The banking world seemed untouched by the chaos it had caused—luckily for her, or she would be out of a job. And at her age, would she ever get another?

That was selfish, she knew. But it was a tough world out there; she had struggled hard to get where she was. Sometimes, when she was feeling shaky, it took every ounce of concentration just to keep her balance. She felt paper-thin, held together by the flimsiest of staples.

O why do you walk through the field in gloves, fat white woman whom nobody loves?

Tomorrow she would indeed end up in a field, in an undignified manner, but tonight she was strap-hanging on the Northern Line. She inspected the liverspots on her hands. They seemed to have appeared overnight, as mysteriously as mushrooms. She pictured her arthritic old claws fiddling with

15

the sheet as she lay on her deathbed, a scene from countless black and white films. Who would discover her body? She no longer even had a cat to pad up and down the bed, miaowing for food and rubbing its face against her icy cheek.

She got out at Clapham South. It had been a beautiful sunny day; she only realised it now. Somewhere a blackbird sang, the notes pouring out, rinsing the world clean. On the way home she stopped at Marks & Spencer's, a shop indeed as chilly as the grave. Her friend Rachel had once picked up a man in the Serves One section. 'Friday night's the best,' Rachel said. 'If they're eating alone then they're *bound* to be single. And A/AB socio-economic group too, of course.'

Rachel's affair hadn't lasted but at least it had put roses in her cheeks. Subsequently she had fallen for a young Croatian who came to fix her boiler. Nowadays Rachel spent her evenings in a sort of dormitory filled with his fellow citizens, somewhere near Heathrow Airport, eating cold pasta from plastic bowls.

'You just have to be up for it,' she told Monica. 'They can tell by the pheremones.' Rachel had started wearing jeans again and strode around with a motorbike helmet under her arm, her toy-boy trophy. 'We're sixty years young!'

How Monica hated that phrase, the jaunty anthem of the baby boomer; there was something suburban about it. And it wasn't that simple. Her age shifted around, she couldn't get a grip on it. At times she felt a wizened old pensioner—she *was* a pensioner. At other times she felt nineteen years old, when people could smoke in the cinema and park anywhere and rent a room for three pounds

16

a week. When buses had conductors and John Lennon was still alive. When the only frozen foods were peas and fish fingers.

Monica gazed at the shelves of Serves One meals. A man came and stood beside her. Sixtyish, abundant hair, flat stomach—a rarity in their age group. He reached for a Beef Hotpot—no wedding ring—and turned it over in his hand as if searching for an answer.

Why not? It could happen like this, it had happened to her friend Rachel. They would fall in love, a sweet autumnal romance, and go to live in King's Lynn, a town Monica had never been to and thus full of possibilities. They would wonder at this late blossoming, clinking glasses in their heavily beamed living room and marvelling at that moment in M&S, when their future spun on a sixpence.

Monica indicated the shelves; she attempted to raise her eyebrows but her forehead was set in concrete. 'So much choice it's dizzying,' she said. She wanted to add: so much choice and yet only one word for love. But that would sound mad.

'Tell me about it.' The man put the packet into his basket and flashed her a smile.

'It's like all those channels on TV,' Monica said. 'Or apps on one's phone.'

'It is a problem,' he sighed. 'My wife's a vegetarian but I can't stand rabbit food.' He reached for a packet. 'Wonder if she'd like Broccoli Crispbake?'

*   *   *

There was always Graham to look forward to. Graham from Norbury, wherever that was. Monica

17

vaguely recognised the name from a railway timetable. Graham could no doubt tell her its location when they met for a coffee the next morning; it might get the conversational ball rolling.

To be honest, she didn't have high hopes of Graham. In his profile he said he had a good sense of humour, a sure sign that he hadn't. Like them all he enjoyed both staying in beside a log fire and going out for long country walks. He described himself as both sensitive and assertive, a word that slightly alarmed her—did he like trussing women up? But he wasn't bad-looking, judging by his photo, shirt-sleeved on his patio. There was another one of him in his scuba-diving gear.

The thing was, it did give a certain zip to the weekend, this meeting with unknown men—a sort-of-date, of sorts, with somebody who was up for it. Monica could almost be nineteen again. Nowadays, she felt profoundly grateful to these males for simply being available. She was tired of being alone with her meals-for-one. She was tired of chatting to a man at some gathering, everything going swimmingly, and then some young Asian wife appearing from nowhere, lacing her fingers into his and popping a canapé into his mouth. Men her age were all married—many to a younger model, but all married. Even the notorious adulterers had hung up their spurs and returned to their long-suffering wives. It was so unfair. They were wrinkled too—a lot more wrinkled than her, in fact—but however decrepit, faithless, alcoholic, vain and self-absorbed they were—droning on about their work, their prostate problems, God forbid their golf handicap—however drooling and boring they were,

18

there was always some woman, somewhere, who wanted to have sex with them. Not just that, to love them, to care for them and to drink orange juice at parties so they could drive them home.

Monica poured herself another glass of wine. She thought: I want somebody to cook for. I want somebody to whisk the parking ticket out of my hand and say, 'Don't bother your pretty little head about that.' I want somebody to laugh with during *The News Quiz*. I want somebody to protect me against rogue plumbers. I want someone to lie with, naked in bed, their arms around me.

The phone rang. It was Graham. 'Is that, er, Monica?' he asked. 'I'm sorry, I can't make our meeting. One of my teeth has fallen out and I have to go to the dentist.'

*   *   *

Next morning Monica woke with a dry mouth and pounding head. She seemed to have finished the bottle of wine. 'Had a party, then?' her neighbour asked, when she carried out the recycling box.

Monica lowered it clankingly to the ground. Of course she didn't drink too much. She just had a stressful job and needed to unwind when she got home. It was only Pinot Grigio, for Christ's sake, hardly alcoholic at all. Besides, she was in the hospitality business, it ran on booze.

That very Saturday, in fact, after her now-cancelled coffee-with-Graham, she was due to drive to Burford to check out a new hotel. The management would no doubt wine and dine her. It was a prospect that filled her with dread.

For it was the same hotel, the Yew Tree.

Renovated, to be sure, but the same hotel. *In all the hotels, in all the world . . .*

Suddenly Malcolm was with her, his breath against her face. Day and night he dwelt with her, he was never away, and now he put on his Bogart voice, one eyebrow raised. He'd always been a rotten mimic but she didn't care . . . Malcolm, the love of her life. Malcolm, the married man.

Burford, Gateway to the Cotswolds, conveniently situated an hour's drive from London (even more convenient for Malcolm, who lived in Ealing). Burford, its celebrated high street lined with olde worlde tea shops (Malcolm, tenderly wiping jam from her chin). Its antique market filled with unusual gifts and cherishable collectibles (Malcolm, goosing her as she climbed the steps to the first floor—*More Stalls Upstairs*). Its picturesque rambles in the local countryside (Malcolm, dropping her hand when other walkers appeared. For Christ's sake, they were hardly going to meet anyone they knew!). Its imposing town hall, built of honey-coloured stone (Malcolm in the phone box outside, the furtive hunch of the faithless husband. These were the days before mobiles, the adulterer's friend and—sometimes—enemy).

Four weekends they had spent together in Burford. The first, she had been a business trip to Rouen. The next time she had been a conference in Scarborough. She had also been a visit to his old school chum. And the last time . . . Monica couldn't remember, just that it was the last time.

*   *   *

Monica parked outside the hotel, next to a row of

SUVs and a Porsche. Bay trees in tubs were lined up against that familiar facade. She switched off the engine. Her times with Malcolm, here and elsewhere, each so short, each so intense, were sealed into caskets in her memory like votive objects in a tomb. On many occasions she had taken off the lids and re-examined them but they had remained preserved in formaldehyde. How could she keep that old hotel in her head, inviolate, when faced by a million-pound makeover?

In their day the Yew Tree had been a dowdy establishment smelling of Brussels sprouts, with violently patterned carpets and a barometer in the lobby—the sort of place nobody they knew would ever visit, which was the point. The menu was hilariously old-fashioned, even then—Prawn Cocktail, Black Forest Gateau. It was the last place on earth to still serve Melba toast.

'I designate this an item of archaeological interest,' said Malcolm, picking up a slice.

'So's the waiter,' whispered Monica.

They smiled at each other, their feet hooked together under the table. How staid the other diners looked, blazered men and their lady wives! How stolidly married. And yet they were dear to Monica, included in her love, warmed in its orbit. They were her unwitting co-conspirators.

'I wish I'd known you—' Malcolm stopped. Instead, he broke off a piece of Melba toast, spread it with mackerel pâté and popped it into her mouth. 'Let's talk about them.' He pointed to another diner. 'Think he's a Russian spy?'

Dear God, she had loved him.

And now she was here again. Joe, the manager, ushered her in.

21

'The whole place was totally run-down,' he said. 'A dump, not to put too fine a word on it, riddled with dry rot. People must've been mad to stay here.'

Joe showed her round the lobby. Grey walls, spotlit buckets of lilies, blown-up photos of American convertibles rusting in the desert. The staff, young and comely, dressed in black, moved around as gracefully as gazelles.

Joe said: 'There's a bedroom free if you'd like to look it over before lunch.'

It was one of theirs. It just would be. Bedroom 12, with the view of the church.

'State-of-the-art entertainment centre,' said Joe, pointing to a row of winking lights. 'Bang and Olufsen. Wi-Fi of course, home cinema.'

It was dark—charcoal walls, maroon bedspread heaped with black satin cushions. On the wall was a photograph of a ruined factory.

'We aim for an unusual, voguey, sexy vibe, with our signature palette of colours.' Joe pointed to the photo. 'We're particularly proud of the rust-belt art. Great feedback on that.'

Monica tried to remember how it was. She and Malcolm naked on the disordered sheets, flock wallpaper, a brown stain on the ceiling from an old leak, a fire extinguisher in case they combusted. The church bells calling the righteous to prayer. She remembered drinking wine from their smuggled-in bottle. Malcolm was too mean to use the minibar but she didn't mind, his faults were his wife's concern, and anyway who cared when he was pulling her close and opening his lips against hers, the wine flooding her mouth?

'Seen enough?' asked Joe. He took her into the bathroom—rough limestone bath, Cowshed toiletries, a second flatscreen TV. 'We offer the intimacy of a boutique hotel with the sort of capacity your outfit requires.'

He was waiting for her to make a comment. Monica registered him for the first time— model-boy looks, probably gay, perspiring in his black polo neck. It was a sweltering day. He treated her with a cocky lack of interest. No doubt he considered her a dried-up old spinster, one of those middle-aged career women who lived with her cat and had a gluten-free diet. Who only drank herb tea. If he considered her at all.

She replied something or other. He took her on a tour of the spa, the therapy rooms, the conference centre. They had lunch on the terrace and discussed the various packages and room rates. A waiter refilled Monica's glass. She thought, for the thousandth time: Had Malcolm ever intended to leave his wife?

The trouble was, it was always the wrong time. Over the years crisis followed crisis. Hilary, his wife, had a breast cancer scare. His daughter was sent down from university for drug-dealing. His son was diagnosed bipolar—the word had just come into fashion. Then Malcolm was briefly made redundant and she had to be supportive. Finally, just when he promised to extricate himself, his mother got Alzheimer's and the whole family was convulsed with guilt about whether or not to put her into a home.

Monica lived these lives at one remove. They were in the sunlight while she dwelt in the shadows, year after year of snatched copulations in hotel rooms around England and Europe; brief lunches in riverside pubs where she and Malcolm stroked

23

each other's fingers, sweethearts in their sealed bubble; candlelit dinners in her flat when she wore fancy underwear and pretended she didn't notice him sneaking a glance at his watch. Their affair remained in stasis while his family moved on, his daughter getting married, how could he bail out then? She felt she was watching a TV soap—nine years passed and by that time she had collected the bloody box set. *Malcolm and his Family.* And her life remained the same, she stayed the same for him for all those years, trussing herself up like a turkey in her crippling corset, knowing the only power she had over him, the power of the mistress. Not for them the drudgery of domestic life, the naggings about car insurance and household repairs. The breakfasts, the crosswords.

Domestic life with Malcolm. Christ, she had longed for it. Sometimes she longed for it so much she felt she would explode.

The waiter refilled her glass. Monica was not the sort to cry in public. Besides, she was here on business. She put on her spectacles to inspect the dessert menu. She remembered that last weekend and her sudden realisation. *He wants to have his cake and eat it.* They were sitting here, on the terrace, and as he looked down at the menu he scratched his head. By now his hair was thinning. She thought, quite clearly: *I'm his bit on the side.*

How painful it was to apply the words to him! Surely their relationship was different from the others, she was the love of his life, those clichés didn't apply? But the words had been buried like shrapnel, deep beneath her skin, and it had taken them years to work their way to the surface.

It was all so long ago. Apparently Malcolm and

Hilary had retired to the Dordogne—so seventies of them, almost as dated as Melba toast. Monica imagined one of those shuttered French villages with amputated plane trees. The high spot of Malcolm and Hilary's day would be trundling their trolley around the local Carrefour, sited in an industrial estate surrounded by fields of blackened sunflowers. They would spend their evenings getting sozzled on *vin de pays*, rereading paperbacks swapped with the other Brits and Facebooking old acquaintances who out of desperation they would invite to stay, anything to relieve the boredom.

Does he ever think about me? Monica wondered. How he stole nine years of my life? That last day in Burford, the showdown outside the gift shop. The sign said *All Breakages Must Be Paid For*. He hadn't, had he?

'Sure you're OK to drive?' Joe asked.

Monica got to her feet. 'Of course!' she snapped, carefully replacing her chair.

They parted company in the lobby. She felt Joe's eyes on her as she made her way to the car. Look! She was fine. Unlocking the door, starting the engine.

Burford's celebrated High Street was clogged with coaches. They disgorged hordes of the undead—elderly ladies in pastel cardies and beige footwear. Burford was full of them, their white hair freshly set, some with sticks, some on mobility scooters. They shuffled around the antiques arcades, blocking the aisles; they peered through the bow windows of Country Casuals, endlessly deliberating, never going in; they clogged up the post office, turning postcards over in their arthritic hands, photos of lambs gambolling among the

25

daffodils; and always, always, there were lines of them at the public toilets, queuing for a wee. She and Malcolm had giggled at them.

'Imagine *her* giving someone a blow job,' he whispered.

The two of them, sated with sex, chortled at the old dears—there were a few men among them, with bowed legs and fawn anoraks, but they were mostly old dears. Monica had thought: Catch *me* ending up like that.

I have to get out of here. Monica hooted the van in front. She drove up the hill, round the roundabout and pulled onto the A40. Putting her foot down, she swerved around a dawdler and overtook a Sky Broadband van. The driver honked his horn but she didn't care. She was still young, sixty-four-years-young, she wasn't finished yet. The car ahead, a souped-up Mini, had a sticker across its back window: *GET IN. SIT DOWN. SHUT UP. HOLD ON.*

That was her kind of guy! Monica accelerated. Fuck the cauliflower-heads, fuck Malcolm, fuck the lot of them.

The Mini slowed down. This mildly surprised her. She pulled out and passed it. Then, glancing in her mirror, she realised why.

A police car was drawing closer, its light flashing.

It was only then that Monica admitted she was drunk. In an instant, her future flashed before her eyes. She would be pulled over and breathalysed. Public humiliation would follow. She would lose her licence; she would lose her job. She was an ageing woman whose work involved travel; she would be finished. What then awaited her but loneliness and death?

Behind her, the siren wailed. Monica slewed onto the verge, bumping over the grass, and came to a standstill.

The police car sped on.

She switched off the engine. The police car disappeared, its siren fading. Traffic whizzed past. She sat there, slumped against the steering wheel, and started to shake with laughter.

After a while she got out of the car and ducked under a barbed-wire fence. She thought: I shall have a little lie-down and sober up. She was in a meadow, the traffic a distant hum. *O why do you walk through the field in gloves?* She must look odd, in her business suit, but there was nobody around. A hedge screened her from the road.

Somewhere, a bird sang. Heaven knew what it was. Birdwatching, like reading hardback biographies, was something people only did when they retired. She remembered a hot afternoon like this, she and Malcolm making love in a field. When they returned to the hotel a couple of ornithologists had chatted to them in the lobby. 'I saw some great tits,' said Malcolm.

Though funny at the time, in retrospect this remark struck her as vulgar. There was a touch of the used-car salesman about Malcolm, it was one of the things she had found attractive. But would you buy an old banger from him?

Monica lay down on the grass and closed her eyes. *Fat white woman whom nobody loves.* She thought: I'm not going to die alone. Tomorrow I shall log on again. Surely I can do better than a toothless quantity surveyor?

How long she slept, she didn't know. Her dreams came thick and fast. At one point she seemed to be on a cycling holiday with Harrison Ford. They spent the night in a B&B and now he seemed to be kissing her forehead, her eyes. 'Blossom,' he murmured, his tongue wet on her skin.

Monica woke with a start. Something was licking her cheek.

'Blossom!' said a man. A face swam into view. He was gazing down at her.

Groggily, she tried to focus.

'Blossom, you naughty girl!'

A dog was licking her face. The man grabbed its collar and yanked it away. 'So sorry,' he said, 'she's just a puppy.'

He was out of breath; he must have run across the field. Monica sat up and wiped the drool from her cheek. Her limbs ached; there was a chill in the air.

'Are you all right?' he asked.

'It was just such a lovely day,' she muttered. She stood up, brushing the grass from her skirt. Avoiding the man's eye, she stroked the Labrador. It wagged its tail and gazed at her with its moist brown eyes. Strings of saliva hung from its jaws.

The man clipped on its lead. He was joined by a woman, presumably his wife, and two small children.

'We thought you might have had an accident,' said the woman. She laced her fingers through her husband's. The two children looked at Monica with their frank, direct gaze.

One of them said: 'Why was that woman lying in the field?'

Buffy

Bridie's Welsh town was, indeed, a long way from Soho—176 miles to be precise. But then Soho itself was a long way from Soho. Buffy's old watering ground had changed out of all recognition; it was now filled with young people bellowing at each other and vomiting in the gutter; Buffy had no place there any more. He remembered, once, digging up potatoes—those firm, white young tubers—and among them the original seed potato, brown, wrinkled, surplus to requirements.

For once, however, Buffy felt no self-pity. Fate had presented him with the possibility of a new life, if he cared to take it. And now he had arrived on a recce. He had booked into the Knockton Arms, in the centre of town. Though moribund—he appeared to be the only guest—the hotel welcomed dogs, and he discovered, in the bar, that the Scotch egg wasn't entirely extinct.

He had arrived late, only bar snacks available, and found himself chatting with the manager, Dafydd, who was polishing glasses to the far drone of a vacuum cleaner. Buffy mentioned Bridie.

'She was a game old trout,' said Dafydd. 'Could she knock back the Baileys. I believe she had connections in the acting profession.'

Buffy told him that he had connections himself.

'I thought I recognised the voice.' Dafydd stopped polishing. 'You're Uncle Buffy! My little 'uns used to listen to you on the radio.'

Buffy nodded, modestly.

'Uncle Buffy and his Talking Hamster,' said Dafydd. 'What was its name?'

'Hammy,' said Buffy. 'Don't blame me, I didn't make it up.'

'There was Voley too, with his squeaky voice.' Dafydd's voice rose. *'Fancy meeting you here, my furry friend!'*

'I didn't do him,' said Buffy. 'That was the other chap.'

'Bless my whiskers, let's have some jolly japes together!'

'Voley didn't last, they wrote him out.'

A thin girl appeared, dragging a vacuum cleaner.

'Edona my lovely, we have a famous actor in our midst!' cried Dafydd.

The girl switched on the Hoover.

'Don't mind her!' Dafydd shouted over the noise. 'She's from Albania!'

Buffy felt heartened. It was nice to be remembered. Despite what Dafydd said it had always been Hammy's show; the other parts were mere walk-ons. And it had been a good little earner, bless it. His mellifluous tones had sent generations of children to sleep. Probably their parents too.

The next day was gloriously sunny. A rarity, apparently, in these parts. After a greasy and largely uneatable breakfast—no competition there—Buffy and his dog sauntered down to the high street.

Now it was daylight he could see that Knockton was surrounded by hills. The brochure said that its unspoilt countryside was *ideal for ramblers and rich in wildlife.* Knockton itself was a thriving market

30

town with plenty of independent shops; it boasted *several noteworthy buildings and a fine fifteenth-century church*. Buffy, however, wasn't simply a tourist. His interest had a keener, more personal edge: could he live there? He was like a visitor to a commercial art show rather than the National Gallery: not just here to gaze, he could actually take possession of one of the canvases.

It was Saturday morning and people were out and about. How blameless they looked in the sunshine! They greeted each other across the street. A pimply youth—a *smiling* pimply youth—carried an old lady's shopping to her car. Buffy spotted a butcher's, a greengrocer's and—good God—a gents' outfitter's. He had no idea such places still existed. A boy actually leaned his bicycle against the wall instead of leaving it, wheels spinning, sprawled in a doorway to trip people up. No attack dogs, either, with their bowed legs and bulging scrotums. Here, a Border collie courteously sniffed Fig, welcoming him to his town and its smells, and trotted on. And the postman was whistling.

Buffy thought: Maybe people have been living like this all the time and I didn't know. He stopped at the baker's. Fig lapped from a bowl of water, thoughtfully left at the door. The window was stuck with notices for the Green Man Festival and amateur dramatics. Could this be the community Buffy had been yearning for, all these years? A place where *he* would have a place? Would one of these middle-aged hippy women, with their *Keep Knockton Green* shopping bags, be the next love of his life?

No, he was finished with all that. Besides, who would have him? He was a used car with too many previous owners, each with their own special complaints about his parts and performance. No, those days were over but he was not on the scrapheap yet. Bridie had liked this town enough to move here. He wished he remembered more of what she had told him in her letters.

Buffy had not yet seen her house. *His* house. Myrtle House, Church Street. He was meeting the solicitor there in an hour.

Buffy's heart pounded. He wished he had someone with him, for moral support. It was too early to fortify himself in the promising-looking King's Head pub. *Tonite: Jethro and the Dreamers.* He pictured jovial hayseeds strumming banjos. Already he saw his own trusty mug hanging from the beams. No gastro-bollocks here. And no bankers either. The only Land Rover in sight was spattered with mud, and appeared to have a sheep on the back seat.

4

Buffy

Several months had passed. The legalities had finally been sorted out and the house was his. The upheaval of packing up his past had left Buffy traumatised; he had presumed he would never have to do it again. Since his last divorce his living conditions had slid downhill—yes, he could admit it now—into a condition of borderline squalor. This was partly due to sloth, and partly to his reluctance to throw anything away.

This had been a cause of friction in the past. 'It's so anal, darling, to hoard,' said Penny, his last wife. 'It's not as if you're an immigrant, or Jewish, or something.'

Every cupboard and drawer in his flat was stuffed with cardboard boxes and carrier bags; the spare room had become so crammed that the door wouldn't open.

So many memories had been unearthed. A stool, spattered with paint from his and Popsi's youthful attempts at homemaking; a mincer that had belonged to his mother—when did anyone last eat a rissole? Board games, with the obligatory missing pieces, that his children had argued over. A pair of roller skates—Bruno hanging on judderingly to his older brother . . .

The whole process was painful, not just because it brought back the past. Exposed to the cold light of day, the stuff had reverted to junk. It *was* junk. Why on earth had he bothered to keep them all, these dusty souvenirs of events he could hardly remember? He'd have trouble shifting them at a car boot sale.

The trouble was that most of the classier stuff had gone. Jacquetta, his second wife, had nicked it. During their marriage she had had an airy disregard for possessions—she was a painter, a woman ruled by the moon, a creative spirit who lived on a higher plane than the mass of humanity who spent their Saturdays trailing around World of Leather. Buffy had suspected that Jacquetta included himself in the shuffling hordes but it wasn't fair, he was just as impractical when it came to worldly goods—for instance, he had never discovered how to work the microwave, which he now found shoved under the bed.

Though he had, of course, bought it. That he had supported Jacquetta for years as she produced unsaleable painting after unsaleable painting was something she took for granted and which seemed to coexist happily with her feminist beliefs. Logic had never been her forte. She even implied that there was something squalid about the whole subject of finance. And yet, when their marriage broke up, how suddenly she had swung into action, hiring a jungle beast of a City lawyer who had proceeded to divest Buffy of his assets, including his Ivon Hitchens painting which Jacquetta implied only she was sensitive enough to appreciate.

Moments like these brought Buffy to a standstill. No wonder it took him so long to pack. They weren't all bitter memories, of course, but the happy ones were just as time-consuming. And then there were all those decisions. What about his children's gifts to him, long-since collapsed objects made out of toilet rolls and coat-hangers? How could he bear to throw them away? And boxes full of dusty cassettes, recorded by his various loved ones, their spidery writing now faded to sepia, condemned to silence forever due to his new machine only playing CDs.

*   *   *

'Wow, Dad, it's fucking enormous,' said Bruno, coming downstairs. 'Six bedrooms, fucking hell.'

'They've all got washbasins, did you see?' said Tobias.

'If this B&B thing doesn't work, you could always turn it into a brothel,' said Bruno.

'Great idea, bro,' said Tobias. 'The locals would love it. Make a change from shagging the sheep.'

Tobias and Bruno chortled. Though both in their thirties, when together they regressed, jabbing each other with their elbows and making infantile jokes. They had come to help Buffy move in. Surrounded by packing cases, the three of them sat down in the kitchen and unscrewed a bottle of whisky.

'Are you sure about this B&B thing?' asked Tobias. 'You are seventy, you know.'

'So was my friend Bridie,' said Buffy.

'Yeah, but your heart, your back . . .'

'Your prostate,' said Bruno.

'Don't worry about that,' said Tobias. 'There's three toilets.'

Buffy, filling their glasses, gazed fondly at his sons. They were going to spend the night together, something they hadn't done for years. During the upheaval of the past few weeks, his children had rallied round. Celeste had even come over from France to shove his stuff into bin liners. Whatever their motives, they had been surprisingly helpful. He remembered when he had had that suspected heart attack and they had all come running. It had been worth all the pain and terror.

'The point about a B&B,' said Buffy, 'is that you kick them out after breakfast and then you have the day to yourself.'

'But who's going to cook them breakfast?'

'Me, of course.'

His sons sniggered. Actually, Buffy was an expert at fry-ups. Like many divorced dads, it was his way of wooing his children when they came to stay the night.

'What about the laundry and stuff?' asked

Tobias.

'There's a girl who did that sort of thing for Bridie,' said Buffy. 'I'm sure I can get her back.'

Faced with reality, Buffy's resolve had weakened. He was determined, however, to persevere. Running a B&B would be company, and an income. Both things were vital for his declining years. Nyange had offered to do the accounts; she had checked places online and discovered that prices in the more upmarket B&Bs were hardly less than those charged by hotels.

'Upmarket?' Tobias raised his eyebrows. The three of them sat there, gazing at the nicotine-stained ceiling, the strip light spattered with flies, and the monumental, baffling Raeburn. It was a chilly evening but they had failed to light it and had plugged in an electric blower, which barely warmed their ankles.

'They won't see the kitchen,' said Buffy.

'Yeah, but what about the rest?'

Buffy had to admit that the place had seen better days. Though imposing from the outside—double-fronted, with a pillared porch—the interior did present a challenge.

'Nothing that a lick of paint won't cure,' said Buffy. His cheerful tone didn't even fool himself. Bridie's belongings had been cleared out—a process even more melancholic than sorting out his own. Her furniture remained, some of it familiar from the Edgbaston days. But taking over a house of this size, on his own, in a strange town, struck Buffy as so impossibly daunting that, now he had sat down, he couldn't imagine ever getting out of his chair.

It was early spring. Buffy had been in residence now for two weeks. When he took his constitutional he noticed the catkins hanging from the trees, whatever sort of trees they were, and in the fields lambs wobbled around on pipe-cleaner legs.

Now he was seventy he called it his constitutional. Moving to the country had jolted him a notch onwards. In Blomfield Mansions he seemed to have stayed sixty for years but this new environment had given him a *coup d'age*. He found this surprisingly invigorating. He could start again, beholden to nobody, the baggage of his past sloughed off. People humoured seventy-year-olds. He would buy a tweed suit and become a country gent, sexually unthreatening, jovially waving his walking stick at passers-by and chucking babies under the chin.

Already he felt at home. His first impressions were spot on—Knockton was a friendly place. Even the somewhat bovine cashier at Costcutter's, a stout young woman in a tabard, called him *my love*. People seemed to know that he had moved into Bridie's house. She had been a popular member of the community, particularly with the publicans, and the goodwill seemed to have spread to himself. That she had bequeathed him her property raised few eyebrows. Buffy was to discover that stranger things happened hereabouts—*hereabouts* being another word he intended to use.

Contrary to what he told his sons, he had decided to do nothing to the house at all. He was hopeless at DIY. If it was good enough for Bridie it was good enough for him. Her guests had liked it well

37

enough; he had read their remarks in the Visitors' Book. Doug and Jenny from Potters Bar had described it as *our favourite refuge, a haven from the hurly-burly of the city.* Heinz and Gudrun, from Salzburg, wrote that *despite the inclement weather, the warm welcome and generous hospitality has made Myrtle House, as always, the high spot of our British tour.*

People spent large sums of money to create the shabby-chic look that Bridie had effortlessly achieved by doing nothing at all. Nowadays, of course, everyone was in thrall to the makeover but in Buffy's youth one just moved into a place and saved all that trouble. Time could be spent more enjoyably than arguing over colour charts or shuffling around that Circle of Purgatory, Ikea. Besides, he had no money for renovations. If he had learned one lesson, it was that once you started prodding around, in relationships as well as houses, dry rot would be discovered and one would end up faced with a crippling bill.

The house was charming as it was. Large, draughty, but charming. Wide, stone-flagged hallway, gracious fanlight over the front door. The dining room had fancy cornices and a bay window overlooking the street. At the back, the sitting room opened onto a veranda, decorated with coloured glass. Both rooms had massive marble fireplaces, blocked with hardboard panels. When Buffy removed them he was hit with a blast of icy wind and hastily jammed them back. However, the man who had done the house clearance, Barry, had showed him how to work the Raeburn and the radiators were now, intermittently, lukewarm. Faced with a plethora of choice, Buffy had chosen the smallest bedroom; with two blowers full blast and an electric fire he managed to work up a fug. It overlooked the tangled garden—horticulture had never been Bridie's forte—and next door's shed where the neighbour, Simon, repaired lutes. He too had made Buffy feel welcome and on moving day had passed a plate of vegan cupcakes over the fence.

'I heard you were an actor,' he said, 'but I'm afraid we don't have a TV.' His greying hair was tied back in a ponytail, not a look that Buffy usually admired, but he was willing to give the chap the benefit of the doubt.

Simon's partner, Jill, came out. She was huddled up in a man's overcoat, bent against the wind. 'We lived in London once,' she said. 'It did our heads in.' It turned out that she ran the eponymous Jill's Things in the high street, which sold vintage dresses and joss sticks. Buffy had assumed that joss sticks, like Scotch eggs, were now museum specimens but this town seemed to exist in a time warp.

Buffy, to his regret, had pre-dated the sixties. He had been born just too early and was already married to Popsi, his first wife, with a baby on the way, when people started smoking dope and tearing off their clothes. In his teenage years he had worn a polo neck and listened to Juliette Greco but in retrospect this seemed a timid stab at rebellion in a world still drab and exhausted by war. However, time was a great leveller and the once-youthful flower children of Knockton looked nearly as decrepit as he was himself, their skin flayed by the elements.

How did people in the country stay warm? And what did they do when darkness fell and the endless night loomed? By nine o'clock the town had gone to sleep. The only signs of life were the lit windows of the chippy and the pubs.

Buffy already considered himself a regular at his local, the King's Head. Barry, the house-clearance chap, had accompanied him the first time, like a kindly prefect with a new boy, and introduced him to various fellow boozers who were huddled round the fire.

'Haven't I seen you somewhere before?' asked a bearded man whose name Buffy hadn't caught.

'He's been on the telly,' said Barry.

'You were in that thing with what's-her-name . . . she was in that thing about the vet . . .'

'What was it called? That bloke was in it . . .'

'I know the one. He played Doctor Who.'

'He never did. You're thinking of what's-his-face. Little slitty eyes.'

'No, the one before him.'

'What *was* her name?' said the bearded man. 'It's on the tip of my tongue. Big tits. She was in that thing about the cook.'

'Fanny Cradock.'

'*No.* The other one.'

'Who's that soap star who lives in Llandrindod Wells?'

'Order, order!' said Barry. 'The point being, we have a celebrity in our midst.'

The bearded man turned to Buffy. 'What was the name again?'

'Russell Buffery,' said Buffy.

They looked at him in silence.

'Anyway, he's moved into Bridie's old house,' said Barry.

The conversation moved on. Though hardly the

Algonquin Round Table, Buffy had enjoyed the cut and thrust of the banter. Since then he had spent several convivial evenings in the pub, and joined the team for the weekly quiz. Catch this sort of community spirit in London! The barman, an amiable alcoholic called Reg, nowadays began to pull his pint as Buffy walked through the door.

*   *   *

'Good man,' said Buffy, pulling out his wallet. 'One for yourself?'

It was a few days later. Buffy had come in to ask the whereabouts of Voda, the young woman who had cleaned for Bridie. She was apparently a stalwart of the darts team but he hadn't yet found her in the pub.

The trouble was, the house was slipping into squalor. Buffy hadn't even finished unpacking and already the place was covered with dust. He had hardly stepped into some of the rooms. The cellar, for instance—he had glimpsed into the abyss, pitch black and stinking of death, and closed the door with a shudder. The prospect of sorting it all out, let alone running it as a B&B, seemed increasingly remote. What had he been thinking of? Some days, especially when it rained, he was plunged into doubt about the whole enterprise. People had been so encouraging but it was easy for them. He himself had urged adventures on friends without considering the consequences. The future always seemed sunlit and full of possibilities until one actually waded in.

Buffy asked about Voda. 'You're in luck,' said Reg. 'She's sitting over there with Aled. He's her

41

brother.' He lowered his voice. 'Don't mind the squint. It's the brucellosis; he got it off the cows.'

Buffy went over and introduced himself. They were a stocky couple, with ruddy cheeks and dreadlocks. Despite the cross eyes, it transpired that Aled too was a champion darts player. He went outside to smoke a cheroot, leaving Buffy and Voda to talk business. She was a capable-looking young woman; apparently she lived in a remote cottage and had been lambing all week. Her sleeves were rolled up. Buffy looked at her hefty forearms resting on the table and thought: She'll sort me out. She was drinking a pint, too—another promising sign.

'I expect you need plenty of stamina for that house,' said Buffy.

'No problemo,' she said. 'I can do the paperwork too, if you want. I did Bridie's. Want me to set you up a website?'

Buffy was no longer surprised at this multitasking. Everybody seemed to be at it. Barry, the Man with a Van, also sold organic dogfood and played the drums in the local band. Buffy, still in the honeymoon stage, considered this admirable. How different from the average Londoner, lounging around in their tracksuits, emerging only to collect their benefits and slag off Muslims!

Voda came round the next day and set up her computer in the utility room, next to the washing machine. She couldn't work at home, she said, because her boyfriend had installed a solar panel to generate electricity.

'Electricity, my arse! I told him it was a stupid idea, the daft bugger.' She plugged in her laptop. 'There's no bloody sunshine, see. I'd be sitting there, working away, and suddenly the power cuts out and I'm staring at a blank bloody screen.' She sighed. 'That's Conor all over. Still, I do miss him.'

'Where is he?'

'Shrewsbury Prison.'

'Heavens,' said Buffy. 'What did he do?'

'Only went and set up a bloody skunk farm.'

'But skunks aren't illegal—' Buffy stopped. Voda looked at him. 'Only joking,' he said quickly.

'Stonking great polytunnel,' sighed Voda. 'You could see it from Llanelly. I told him to put it behind the shed but would he listen?' Her eyes grew moist. 'His mother spoilt him, see. Thought the sun shone out of his bottom.'

'Glad it shines somewhere, round here.'

'Thinks he's Prince Charming, nothing can touch him.' She shrugged. 'Anyway, that's why I need all the work I can get, now the lambs are born, bless their cotton socks.'

5

Amy

Amy met Neville when he rang her doorbell, canvassing for the Lib Dems. She was jet-lagged and still in her pyjamas.

'What local elections?' she asked.

He looked at the pile of unopened mail, heaped on the floor. 'There's probably a polling card in there somewhere.' It wasn't a rebuke—he looked a mild man—just an observation.

'I've been away,' Amy said. 'I'm all over the

43

place.' When she had left it had been midwinter and now the trees were heavy with blossom.

Amy worked in the movie industry; she was a make-up artist. They had been filming in India, in various unpronounceable places. She had never even looked them up on the map. That was film crews for you. When away on location you surrendered up that sort of curiosity. Rising at dawn, lolling half asleep on the bus, closeted all day in the trailer, you could be in Outer Mongolia. Even in England, when working on a set, nobody read a newspaper. In fact, it took her a moment to remember the name of the Prime Minister.

'Just vote Lib Dem then,' he said.

'OK.'

He laughed. 'If only they were all like you.'

He leaned against the door frame, exhausted. The yellow rosette drained the colour from his face. Amy hadn't seen a man in corduroy trousers for God knew how long. He said his name was Neville.

'I suppose I should do the people upstairs,' he said.

'Don't bother. The first floor's empty and at the top they're illegal immigrants.'

'Good-oh.' He remained slumped. Amy wished she could offer him something but she hadn't been to the shops yet. Besides, her flat was a pit.

Neville straightened up, tucking the clipboard under his arm. 'Better crack on.' He turned to go, and then stopped. 'Would you mind if I picked some mint?'

'What?'

'There's some here.' He pointed to a tangle of weeds beside the dustbin. 'Just a sprig. I'm cooking some new potatoes.'

44

Amy looked at him with interest. Unable to cook herself, she was charmed by the idea of a man in an apron. 'Help yourself,' she said.

In India she had gone down with Delhi belly; they all had, at one point or another. Food and bowel movements had been their main topic of conversation. Two days' filming had been lost when one of their stars had succumbed to a rare intestinal parasite. A plate of boiled potatoes was just what they longed for during their lengthy sessions on the Portoloos.

She felt the stirrings of hunger. 'What else are you cooking?'

'Sea bass in a herb crust.'

Neville's voice was reverential. She wondered if he was gay. He looked sensitive, with that limp sandy hair. Most of the guys she worked with, in make-up and wardrobe, were gay. They swapped recipes with the actors, speaking with their mouths full of pins.

He said: 'After a day at this game I need a proper dinner.'

'It must be crap, knocking on people's doors and nobody interested.'

Neville looked taken aback. 'Some of them are.' He paused. 'But they're usually the loonies.'

He said he bought his sea bass at the local farmers' market. Amy didn't know such a thing existed but that wasn't surprising. Acton was just the place in which she came to rest, briefly, between jobs, the floor of her flat strewn with unpacked clothes, her fridge empty but for a mouldy yogurt. Planes flew overhead, rattling the windowpanes; sooner or later one of them would whisk her away again to God knew where.

As Neville turned at the gate to wave goodbye, he said he was at the farmers' market every Saturday, helping out his friend who had a bread stall.

Later, lying in the bath, Amy mused about her love life, that disaster zone. In India she had had a fling with a grip called Craig. Already she could hardly remember his face. No doubt she too was a distant memory—or, to be more accurate, forgotten the moment he returned home to his family. If he *had* a family; she had no idea. Camera crews were a blokey bunch, they didn't talk about relationships. Besides, filming existed in its own perma-climate. Being on location sealed a person off from their other life, the life back home. Copulations were snatched and feral; you grabbed your pleasures where you could, like an alley cat.

Amy loved the camaraderie of life on set. It was hard work but she was part of a gang. After the wrap party, however, her temporary family vanished into thin air and now here she was, towelling herself dry in her empty flat, aged thirty-one and with nobody in her life except a few mates who never phoned because she was always somewhere else.

Amy realised she was crying. This gave her such a shock that she found herself sobbing harder, great shudders shaking her body. She buried her face in her towel and thought: I'm all alone with nobody to love.

The next Saturday she went to the farmers' market to buy a loaf; and so it began.

*　　　*　　　*

46

Neville had been living with her for three years now. He did indeed bring an apron with him, and oven gloves. It took him a while to sort out her flat but Amy just let him get on with it; domesticity didn't interest her. For years she had lived a gypsy life. On location, of course, everything was on tap. You wanted your hair cut? Your car fixed? Your computer sorted out? No problem. There was somebody at hand for every contingency.

Back home she was helpless but Neville didn't seem to mind. He seemed to find it endearing, but that was love for you. Sometimes he joked that *he* was the wife. He cooked, he cleaned. He was a keen recycler and despaired for the planet. She laughed when she saw him refilling his plastic bottle from the tap but he took these things seriously and found the profligacy of filming insane. The waste! The carbon emissions! The madness of blanketing a landscape in fake snow for a scene that ended on the cutting-room floor!

'But it's a movie about global warming,' she said. 'Doesn't that strike you as somewhat ironic?'

She kept quiet about the fact that every day a 4×4 was dispatched to London to collect lunch for their star, some gluten-free vegan nonsense cooked by the chef at the Meridian, a round journey of 120 miles. Or that one of the actors was flown in from LA to speak a single line. Nowadays she hardly talked about her work. Besides, Neville knew none of the people involved and celebrity gossip didn't interest him.

This was a shame. Her hot, stuffy trailer was a confessional. All actors were insecure; under the pitiless glare of the mirror lights they were at their most vulnerable. For hours each day she was

47

closeted with them in perfumed intimacy, powdering and painting, making them beautiful, making them younger. On set she was their ally. Between takes she sprang into action, her belt stuffed with brushes, darting around the stars' faces like a hummingbird, a dab here, a dab there. Nobody in the camera crew talked to the actors; they lit them, they shot them, but they were busy and they were blokes. It was Amy and her colleagues who heard about the marital problems, the tantrums on set in some previous movie, and which film star was secretly gay and supplied with a beard—some decoy female to be snapped canoodling with him as they emerged from the Ivy.

'They roped me in once,' Amy said, over supper. She told Neville about a Hollywood star. 'There had been rumours, see, and it would've killed his career. He was having a thing with one of the sparks and somebody got wind of it. The sparkie was sworn to silence because if he went public he'd never work again. So the publicist takes me aside and tells me to ditch the jeans and scrub up. Next thing I know I'm in some swanky nightclub and this guy's all over me, tongue down my tonsils, horrible thing like a slug, God knows where it had been, and someone's popping the old flashbulb and next day it's all over the papers. My fifteen minutes of fame.'

Neville passed her the broccoli. 'Do you think we ought to have a baby?'

Sometimes Amy felt she didn't know him at all. They were in coracles, if that was the word for them, frail vessels anyway, tossed around in the sea. Occasionally they stretched out their hands and touched and then the waves swooshed up and they were lost.

48

'What, now?' she asked.

'What do you mean, *what, now*?' Neville put down the dish. 'We're not getting any younger. Well, you aren't. In biological terms.' He gazed at her across the table. 'We love each other. We're here. Isn't this what we do?' He reddened. 'I'm sorry, I'm saying this all wrong.'

'It's me who's sorry.'

She had no idea what she meant. They both inspected the tablecloth.

'Don't you want to go into politics?' she blurted out.

'What difference would that make?'

'I don't know.'

She didn't know anything. Her life was a mess and she had thought Neville would solve it. She knew that he had been lonely too, she had sensed it on her doorstep. Suddenly she longed to pack her bags and hightail it out of there, arriving at some unit base in fuck knows where, with its joshing and joking and bacon butties and its punishing schedule that stopped you thinking. Could she really have a family with this man?

'My dad once hit me with a frying pan,' she said. 'Did I ever tell you that?'

Neville frowned. 'What's that got to do with it?'

'I don't know.'

'Look at me, Amy. Concentrate for once.'

'You sound like a schoolteacher.'

'For God's sake, this is important!' Neville leaned over and touched her fingers. 'Do you want to get married? Is that it?'

Hurt, she snatched back her hand. 'You *so* don't know me!'

Proposals weren't supposed to be like this. Even

49

she, as a child, had dreamed of moonlight and roses—even she, a tomboy.

'We could go the whole hog if you liked,' Neville said. 'It would be nice to see you in a dress.' He smiled, trying to make a joke of it.

Amy, confused, turned away. She stared at the wall. Neville had painted the room yellow when she was away working on *Kiss Me Again*. It was a romcom about a mismatched couple who, surprise surprise, really loved each other.

'I'd go mental,' she said, 'stuck here with a squalling brat.'

'It wouldn't be a brat if it was ours,' he said. 'Anyway, I would help.'

'Oh yeah? They all say that.' Why was she being so hard on him? She had no idea. 'What about my work?' she asked. 'You can't take a child on set.'

Neville stood up and collected the plates. 'Forget it,' he muttered.

That night, in bed, he turned away from her and lay there, hunched. She cupped herself against his backbone. She knew she had upset him, but then he had upset her. Everything they said, recently, came out wrong. She reached down and cupped his curled, defeated cock in her hand. It filled her palm, as soft as a marshmallow. He didn't respond.

A moment passed. Her hand felt embarrassed, so she removed it. Neville's body seemed unknowable to her. Outside, people shouted in the street; a car door slammed.

A little later Neville's breathing deepened. She thought he had fallen asleep but he was just taking a breath to speak. He said: 'They've made me redundant.'

'What?'

He spoke into the pillow. 'I've lost my job.'

Amy tried to pull him round to face her but he wouldn't move.

'Oh, Nev.'

'The council's slashing the libraries budget so bang goes my career.'

She laid her hand on his hip. This seemed friendlier than clutching his penis. He was a thin man; his backbone was knobbly against her breasts.

'This country's in bloody meltdown,' he said. 'Know what services the council's cutting? Respite care, youth clubs, home visits. Know how much the CEO of Barclays took home last year? Want a guess?' He flung himself on his back and stared at the ceiling.

Amy hadn't a clue. The whole economic thing had rather passed her by. 'When's it going to happen?' she asked.

There was a silence. 'Last month,' he said.

She sat up. Neville cowered, flinching. 'Last month? What do you mean?'

'I stopped work last month.'

She switched on the light. 'Why didn't you tell me?'

'You were away.'

'But I came back a week ago.'

'It never seemed the right moment.'

'But you went off to the library every morning.'

'Yes . . . well.'

'Well what?'

'I didn't go, did I?' he said.

'What did you do?'

'Mooched around,' he said. 'Had coffee. Helped out at the Bengali drop-in centre.'

Amy's head reeled. She was shocked, of course.

51

And hurt that he hadn't told her. And sorry for him, that he had lost his job. All those things, plus it was so weird, so unlike the person she thought she knew. But she didn't know him. They were strangers, lying in bed on a stifling summer's night. Ridiculously, she felt a small stirring of desire. Neville—dear, mild Neville—had been living a secret life and he suddenly seemed interesting to her.

She nuzzled his neck. 'Give us a kiss.'

He pushed her away and stumbled out of bed. 'Don't you see, my life's in ruins? I had such high hopes of everything. You. Me. The Lib Dems.' He ran his hands through his hair. 'You blazed into my life—'

'Blazed? I was in my pyjamas.'

'So feisty and independent, striding around in your jeans, knocking back the Diet Coke. I thought *here's a girl.* You wouldn't have believed how humdrum my life was till I met you.' Neville stood there, naked in the lamplight, hands hanging by his sides. 'You and your glitzy life.'

'*Glitzy?* What, getting up at five in the morning? We're the first on set, did you know that?'

'All those film stars.'

'I'm only covering up their spots. I don't know them.'

'I haven't a clue who they are. And they certainly interest you more than I do.' He paused. 'Even when you're here, you're not here.'

Was that true? She had no idea.

'Let's face it,' Neville said. 'You weren't that fascinated by the library.' He sat down on the bed. 'You haven't even got any books.'

'I do!'

52

'Well. One or two. But they're not exactly . . .'

'Not exactly what?'

He sighed. 'Never mind.' He leaned across her and switched off the light. 'Let's go to sleep. Big day tomorrow.'

'Big day?'

'It's what my mother used to say, before a birthday or something.' He tapped her nose. 'I meant it ironically, sweetheart.'

*　　*　　*

As luck would have it, another job came up the next month—an adaptation of *Mansfield Park*. There hadn't been a lot of work around, the recession had hit the film industry, but bonnets came to the rescue and Amy found herself on location in various country mansions across Britain.

'Haddon Hall, Burghley House, Wilton Place, I'm telling you, duckie, it's like a blooming NADFAS tour.' Eldon James, an elderly actor who played Sir Thomas Bertram, sat on the steps of his trailer smoking a cigarette. 'And I've filmed in them all. In fact, I've owned Haddon Hall three times.' He indicated one of the runners. 'Who's that nice young man?'

'Son of the director,' said Amy. 'Don't even go there.'

Her mobile rang. It was Neville.

'The washing machine's flooded,' said Neville's voice. 'I'm waiting in for the man from Bosch. When does *a.m.* stop, do you think? Twelve or one?'

It was hot. Amy gazed at a group of extras, perspiring in their costumes. They sat outside the catering wagon, playing cards and chattering on their mobiles. The women flapped their skirts to cool their nether regions. Extras were the lowest of the low but Amy had a soft spot for the underdog. They were always going through some emotional crisis, or had a relative with an obscure terminal disease. And the amount they ate! She even felt sympathy when they elbowed each other aside to get in shot.

'Nothing else much,' said Neville's voice. 'The printer's jammed again and it seems to have forgotten how to scan. I do miss you.'

Amy didn't miss him. The truth was, she hadn't thought about him all morning. *Even when you're here, you're not here.*

The third AD was rounding up the extras. They got to their feet and dusted themselves down. Amy felt flooded with love for all of them—the cast, the crew, the extras who were shuffling off for their big moment. She loved the way they pulled together, how each and every one of them was part of a team. She loved the loyalty that grew up between them, the way they created their own world, sometimes just yards from passers-by but corralled off by walkie-talkies, how they were all busting themselves to make a movie that might be rubbish but hey, who could tell? Besides, most of them would never see it.

She could tell Neville none of this. She didn't want to rub his nose in the fact that she was working, and though he liked movies he could never remember the names of the actors. 'Couldn't you ask some of your friends to dinner?' he asked once. But her life wasn't like that, the only time her mates got together was at the wrap party and the next day they were scattered to the four winds.

And somewhere, deep down, she suspected that Neville considered her job trivial. He was a serious man with a social conscience. He was campaigning against the closure of the local hospice and the opening of a Tesco. All day he sat at his laptop firing off emails. He said he was as busy as ever, God knew how he had ever found time to go to work.

Neville tried to make a joke of it but she knew he was humiliated—so humiliated that he had kept it a secret all those weeks. 'I'm redundant,' he said. 'All men are redundant. You don't even need our sperm any more.' Not that there was any danger of that; his libido seemed to have died away completely. Amy blushed to think of her attempts to arouse him. Nowadays he often stayed working at his desk when she went to bed; she could feel him, through the wall, willing her to fall asleep. Or he would yawn theatrically and say how whacked he was. 'And those lentils, don't you feel bloated?' he asked her as they undressed. 'Do we have any Rennies?'

Amy stubbed out her cigarette and went back to work. Nowadays Neville even slept in his T-shirt and underpants, his personal cordon sanitaire. He had become her house husband, bitter and desexed, and it was all the fault of the recession. *Those fucking bankers*, he said. *Spawn of Satan*. He had gone on a march and even sprayed a building with graffiti, that's how angry he was. Even insects had suffered from his fury. In their early days he had charmed Amy by helping a spider out of the bath with his flannel. Now he squirted fly spray around willy-nilly, as if he was targeting hedge-fund managers, or whoever it was who had got them into this mess.

She rubbed foundation into Eldon's skin. It was ravaged by decades of smoking; Polyfilla would be more appropriate. 'Remember my old mucker Russell Buffery?' he asked her. 'You were working on *Miss Marple* with us, you were practically in nappies. Big fat beardy bloke. He played a master of hounds. Just a small part. He called it a cameo, of course.'

Amy thought for a moment. 'Oh yes, and it turned out he couldn't ride.'

Eldon chuckled. 'He kept quiet about that, the old rogue.'

'I remember,' she said. 'They had to use a stunt double for the action scenes, the producer was well pissed off.'

'Anyway, I bumped into him last week. Turns out he's running a B&B in the wilds of Wales. Now that's something I would pay good money to see. Chap can't open a tin.' He paused. 'Gave up the acting, or should I say the acting gave up on him. Bit too fond of the old Cab Sav.' He leaned forward, inspecting his face. 'Still, pots and kettles. I'm bloody lucky to get this gig, we're none of us getting any younger. And to tell the truth, I miss the old tosser.'

At the time Amy was hardly listening. She was thinking about Neville. No, she wasn't. She was thinking about one of the extras.

*   *   *

They were filming in Stamford, a town somewhere near Peterborough. Amy left the unit base and

56

arrived on set. The high street had been transformed, its tarmac spread with earth and horse droppings, its shops dressed as haberdashers and whatnot. They were filming a big, complex scene and the place was the usual mixture of order and chaos, rare-breed pigs milling around, the megaphone booming. Amy spotted the extra straight away. He looked great in breeches—tall, skinny, brown curly hair. No doubt that was the reason he was playing a toff, strolling past the Assembly Rooms.

Do you want to get married? Is that it? She thought: Catch Jane Austen writing something like that. No wonder people flock to her movies. In Jane Austen films it was guys who looked like that dropping on bended knee. *Would you do me the honour of consenting to be my wife?*

She remembered that night in the bath, when she had burst into tears. Did she really want to die childless and alone? Would Neville do?

'Coming to the bar tonight or are you going home?' asked one of the grips. Tomorrow was a free day and Amy was planning to drive back to London.

At that moment the guy in breeches, leaning against a wall, caught Amy's eye. He grinned.

Amy said: 'I'm staying here.'

NCOL. Not Counted On Location.

The extra's name was Keith. He ran a record shop on the high street. Its frontage had been dressed as a butcher's emporium, the window hung with rabbits. When Amy snuck in that evening, however, she found that behind the carcasses the interior was unchanged. Keith now wore drainpipe jeans. He looked younger now, a scattering of

57

pimples on his chin.

'They're always filming here,' he said. 'Last time I was a Yokel with Cow. Don't know how you stand all the hanging about, it would drive me mental. Afterwards I had a drink with the focus puller.'

She recognised his small-town swagger, having grown up in Leamington Spa herself. She warmed to him simply because he wasn't Neville and her heart didn't sink when he walked through the door. How quickly it was all unravelling!

The laughter went first; that had disappeared a long time ago. She remembered their early days, driving past a cenotaph. Its sign said *Polish War Memorial.* 'Should have brought my duster,' said Neville. Last month she had driven past it again and tears had sprung to her eyes; he would never joke like that now. Nowadays in the car he was tense and abstracted, only breaking the silence to groan when a Tory Cabinet minister came on the radio.

Amy thought: Why does he listen to Radio 4 when it only irritates him? Why not bellow along to the tunes on Radio 1, like I do when I'm alone? Why not have some fun?

Keith had brought in some beers. He cracked open a couple of cans.

'I recognised some of them,' he said. 'That actress, she was in that thing on the telly. Do you get to talk to them?'

Amy told him about her job, about which stars had nips and tucks, about the backstage dramas.

'This is just between ourselves,' she said. 'Don't you dare tweet.'

Keith's interest pleased her; it had been a long time since she had explained her work. He seemed to find it glamorous; not trivial at all. She longed to touch him; to feel the voltage of a strange body.

He drained his beer. 'What tunes do you fancy?'

'It's your shop, you choose.'

He jumped up and put a record on the turntable. *Wild thing, you make my heart sing.*

'Come on, you.' He pulled her to her feet. 'Let's have a dance.'

*　　*　　*

'But I thought it was your day off.' Neville's voice on the phone. 'I've bought a guineafowl.'

'I'm sorry, Nev, it's a pain in the arse. We had all these retakes and then we lost the light, so we've got to finish the scene tomorrow, the schedule's shot to pieces.' Amy could feel the blush rising.

'Poor you,' he said. 'Well, get a good night's sleep.'

Amy slept, with Keith in her arms, in her room in the Peterborough Heritage Lodge. It was yards from the ring road but no sound penetrated its perma-sealed windows. She lay in a timeless, airless capsule, clothes strewn across the floor, closed off from the outside world; closed off even from the other members of the crew who slumbered in nearby rooms. *NCOL.*

Keith whimpered in his sleep. It felt intimate, to hear these mewlings without the knowledge of their owner. More intimate than the sex. Keith had been an energetic, workmanlike lover, making her come twice and then turning her over, her face buried in the pillow, for his own shuddering climax. She was warmed with erotic gratitude as she lay there sniffing his sweat. It had been years since she had

59

fucked a man she knew nothing about, not even his surname. She had forgotten how affectionate two bodies could be when they were cut adrift from their lives and owed each other nothing. Why couldn't it always be this simple?

The next day Keith fetched her a helmet and loaded her onto his motorbike. It was a molten September morning; sunlight bathed the car park.

'Ever seen one of these before?' He stroked the flank of the machine. 'Thought not. It's a Triumph Speed Triple, see. They only made a few hundred of these babies—low-weight, fantastic torque and as much roadholding as any headbanger could want. Plus, of course, she's black.'

They rode into the fens, along empty roads leading nowhere, roads straight as rulers, the distant tarmac dissolving in a mirage. Amy yelled into his helmet: 'My boyfriend's got a pushbike!' But the wind snatched her words away.

Keith stopped beside a canal. She flung herself on the grass while he rolled a joint.

'The sky's so *big*, somehow,' she said.

'Yeah, everyone says that.'

'I love this time of year.' Suddenly she sat up. 'Shit. I've just realised what day it is.'

'What?'

'September 11th.'

He looked puzzled. 'What?'

'September 11th,' she said. 'Twin Towers?'

'Oh. Yeah.' He lit the joint and passed it to her. 'That was a bummer.' He indicated the road. 'I got busted along here. Hundred and twenty miles an hour, I was doing. It was on the Honda CB 900. Fast as fuck but it had no soul. Plus, the alternator kept frying.'

60

Amy's heart sank. They should have said their goodbyes after breakfast. She suddenly missed Neville, alone with his guineafowl and his dashed hopes. She felt a lurch of guilt. How could she race around the countryside, quite apart from the other thing, when Neville was miserable and jobless?

Keith was talking about his shop. 'There's no money in vinyl any more, the internet's killed it. And I've been paying an arm and a leg for the lease, £12,000 a year, would you believe that?'

And at least Neville was interested in world affairs. Most of it had gone over her head, but at least he wasn't boring.

'To tell the truth,' said Keith, 'I'm thinking of packing it in.'

Amy took a final drag and stood up. 'Shall we go?'

They rode a few more miles. They had a burger in a café and some perfunctory sex in a wood, but then it clouded over and this gave them an excuse to return to the hotel. Pulling off the helmet, she shook her hair loose. She was so relieved at leaving Keith that she kissed him warmly.

'It was fun last night,' she said. 'I think that every day people should have a dance. Keep them out of mischief.'

He grinned. 'Not in your case.'

Just for a moment she fancied him again, and then he was gone. Listening to the roar of his bike fading, she thought: I bet he's as relieved as I am.

*   *   *

It all unravelled that autumn. She and Neville had been tied by a slender thread—sexual attraction,

61

loneliness. In her heart of hearts she knew they had little in common. During her long absences they reverted to their former selves; on her return it took them a while to readjust to each other. This time, however, the thread had snapped. Neville had closed himself off; he no longer made the effort to discuss anything except the need for more Hoover bags. Depression had made him elderly and irritable; now he disliked all the presenters on the *Today* programme, instead of just two.

In the old days lovemaking would have restored them to each other but that had petered out. Her guilt about Keith disappeared—would Neville even have minded?—and she stopped shaving her legs. Did this always happen, sooner or later? She had no idea; none of her previous relationships had lasted this long.

The final unravelling happened fast. She had brought home some shopping from Tesco's, a shop he hated.

'Well, I was in a hurry,' she said, glancing at his laptop, open on the kitchen table. He had been playing chess. *Chess.* He had told her he was sending off a job application.

'What's this?' He held up a plastic packet.

'Rosemary. You said you were cooking a lamb thing with rosemary.'

He held it close to her face. 'Read that.'

'What?'

'The price.'

She looked. '£1.25.'

He grabbed her hand. 'Come here.'

Her heart jumped. Was he going to drag her to bed? But he swung round the other way, yanked open the kitchen door and bundled her into the garden. He pointed to a bush.

'What's that?' he asked.

'How should I know?'

'*Look*, woman!' He broke off a branch. 'It's *rosemary*! Here, in your fucking garden! A huge fucking bush of it.'

'I didn't realise,' she said. 'Does it matter?'

'You haven't a clue, have you?' Neville stared at her wildly. The wind whipped the hair across his face. 'Oh, I give up. What's the point of it all? It's all a bloody waste of time, we're all fucked.'

'What do you mean?'

'When even a bright woman like you, after all I've told you—when even *you* go to Tesco's, *Tesco's*, and spend £1.25 on something that's growing right under your nose.'

'It's my money,' she said. 'Can't I spend it how I want?'

'Thanks for reminding me!'

'What I meant was—'

'How do you think I feel, spongeing off you?'

'You don't sponge. Anyway, you've got your redundancy—'

'I'm useless. Go on, say it!' He stared at her, distraught, the branch trembling in his hand. 'I'm useless, I can't even get it up any more, no wonder you don't want to have my baby, I'm a useless snivelling hopeless failure banging on about things nobody gives a toss about and I'm not surprised you don't want me because nobody else does either!'

He flung the branch over the wall and slammed into the house.

It started to rain. Amy stood there, stunned. The guy was mad. Yet the whole scene had had an awful inevitability to it; she knew, at that moment, that it

63

was over.

The next day Neville moved out to his sister's house. He took everything with him. All that remained was a half-empty bottle of mouthwash and a DVD of *Brokeback Mountain*, free with the *Mail on Sunday*, a newspaper of which he disapproved.

That evening the boiler broke down. Amy sat huddled in the kitchen, eating a takeaway pizza. She had lit the gas rings but it was still freezing. She pushed her chair closer to the oven, which had never been clean in the past and would never be so clean again. Misery rose in her throat, like nausea. She thought: A herb brought us together and a herb drove us apart.

*   *   *

Two months passed. Amy stood at the carousel at Heathrow, waiting for her suitcase. She had been in Johannesburg, working on a Bacardi ad. The rest of the crew had retrieved their bags and gone. Only the cameraman remained, talking on his mobile.

'Who's a clever boy,' he said. 'You can do it all by yourself now? What did Mummy say?'

Just a few bags were appearing now, trundling into view. A black couple loaded a vast suitcase onto their trolley and wheeled it away.

'How many puppies?' asked the cameraman. 'Did you get to stroke them? . . . Mmm, well, we'll see about that. Maybe if you're a *really* good boy. Ah, here's my bag.' With one hand he heaved it off the carousel. Still hunched over his mobile he walked away, swallowed up into his other life.

Amy stood alone; around her, voices echoed

from afar. It was late and most of the carousels were stilled. She scratched the mosquito bite on her wrist. For some reason she thought about her brother, who had died at six months and was never mentioned. He would be thirty now, with children of his own. She pictured herself as their spinster auntie, spoiling them. Maybe she would have bought them a puppy. His wife, a woman he would never know, who had another family now, would baulk at this gift but would finally welcome this new addition to the family.

The tannoy boomed. *Please keep your luggage with you at all times.* Finally Amy's suitcase nudged open the flap and hove into view. It looked so solitary. Red and brave, vastly travelled, but alone in the world.

*   *   *

Midnight, and Amy lugged her suitcase from the Tube. It was January, and bitterly cold. Bent against the wind, she trudged past the closed library, past the glare of the kebab shop. Back home, mail was heaped on the doormat—*While You Were Out* cards for undelivered parcels, a flyer for the Conservative Party. The kitchen remained in the same state of chaos in which she had left it, though the smell was more powerful now; she hadn't been able to locate it and had hoped it would have disappeared by the time she got home. Why should it? She had no idea.

Amy sat down and lit a cigarette. What a relief that Neville wasn't around! She needn't shiver in the garden. She could do whatever she liked—stay up all night, stay in bed all day watching YouTube stuff on her computer, let the flat sink into deeper squalor with nobody to tut at her, read celebrity gossip, have her old mate Josie around whom Neville found annoying . . .

It was two o'clock. Amy had been sitting there for a long time. Stiffly she rose to her feet. The thought of washing seemed too laborious so she lay down on the bed fully-clothed and pulled the duvet over herself. She could fart in bed, too; just another of the many advantages of living alone.

The next morning she could bear it no longer. Her eyes were sore from crying. She splashed water on her face and tried to pull herself together. At nine o'clock she finally plucked up courage and dialled the number of Neville's sister.

After some pleasant chit-chat she asked: 'Er, is Neville around?'

'Didn't you know?' said his sister. 'They're in Tenerife.'

'What?'

'Just for a week.' There was a silence. 'Oh heck, have I put my foot in it?'

'No, no, of course not.'

'I thought you knew.'

Her name was Alice. She and Neville had met while mucking out the pigsty at the City Farm. It turned out that they were saving up for the deposit on a flat.

6

Buffy

'Still pouring with rain.' Frieda stood at the window.

'Absolutely bucketing,' said Iris.

Buffy was still in his apron, though breakfast was long since over. He stood beside his guests, gazing into the street. Rain lashed down. A hunched figure ran to a car and jumped in, slamming the door. In the Coffee Cup opposite, disconsolate figures could be seen through the steamed-up windows, killing time in their cagoules.

'Looks like it's settled in for the day,' he said.

Frieda and Iris were schoolteachers, both retired. Buffy presumed they were lesbians, they shared a twin-bedded room, though they might have just been saving the pennies. They were both squarely built, however, with no-nonsense haircuts. Their hiking boots waited by the door.

'We'd been planning on tackling Hergest Ridge,' said Iris.

'Then a pub lunch,' said Frieda.

'Just our luck,' said Iris.

There was a silence.

'You can't go out in this,' said Buffy.

'But . . .' The word hung in the air. It was half past ten, they should have been out of the house by now.

'Come on,' said Buffy. 'I'll make us some coffee.'

After some half-hearted protestations they moved to the back room, the sitting room which

67

was vaguely Buffy's, though he hadn't quite laid down the boundaries. Where did his life end and theirs begin? He had been sharing his home for a month now with various guests but hadn't got round to staking out his own territory. This was mainly due to sloth. Bridie had apparently been stricter about her own space but then she had been a professional.

Besides, he was a gregarious chap. It had been the rainiest May on record, and, on many occasions, guests had been trapped in the house all morning because he hadn't the heart to kick them out. This had resulted in some surprisingly revealing chats with the random collection of strangers who found their inhibitions loosened by the knowledge that they would never meet again. It reminded Buffy of life on tour, but with a constant change of cast. And if he needed to retreat there was always the kitchen, the warmest room in the house, where he had installed his own TV and a rack full of bargain bottles from Costcutter, his wine merchant of choice.

Buffy put on the kettle. Voda was talking on the phone in the utility room. 'Yes, sir, we do have a vacancy then but it's filling up fast,' she said. 'I suggest you make a firm booking.'

It was a lie, of course, but it often did the trick. The girl was a marvel; he had become pathetically reliant on her. In fact, without Voda the whole business wouldn't have got off the ground at all. She had cleaned the house from top to bottom and got her brother to fix the lethal electrics. She had emailed the previous guests and informed them that Myrtle House was reopening under new management, dogs welcome. She had set up a

68

website, with a link to the tourist board and various cycling and rambling magazines. And now that the guests were arriving—in dribs and drabs, but these were early days—she laundered the sheets and cooked the breakfasts. At first Buffy had taken command in the kitchen but as black smoke poured out of the Raeburn Voda had elbowed him aside and done the job herself. 'It's not like cooking for your kids,' she said. 'Our customers are actually paying for this, you know.'

So he had taken on the less taxing role of skivvy. After all, he was used to receiving orders from a director; as long as he hit his marks the two of them worked amicably as a team. And he remained mine host, meeting and greeting, serving at table and generally running the show. He liked a house full of people, it reminded him of the old days of his marriages.

He could admit it now; the bachelor years at Blomfield Mansions had been bloody lonely. Now, when he locked up, he could almost feel his customers slumbering upstairs, warm mammals safe for the night. And though there were occasional complaints, for example the erratic hot water in the bathroom, so far these had been voiced in a mild, apologetic manner as if it were all the guests' fault. How simple such complaints were, compared to the complex, passive-aggressive guilt trips laid on by his wives, or the strident accusations of his children!

'I was saying to Iris, weren't you in that thing?'

'What thing?' asked Buffy, pouring out the coffee.

'That thing set in an old people's home.'

'No, silly,' said Iris. 'That was Michael Gambon.'

It turned out that they were keen theatregoers.

They passed a pleasant hour listening to Buffy's reminiscences. How his old mate Eldon James, well in his cups, had gone to see a show only to realise, when the curtain went up, that he was supposed to be in it. How he himself, in his final public appearance, had played a bedridden patriarch and during one performance had fallen asleep.

'Not that it mattered,' he said. 'It was a deathbed scene anyway. That's the problem with being old, one gets the snuffing-it roles. Johnny Gielgud must have died fifty times before he finally shuffled off this mortal coil. At least he'd had some practice.'

Outside the rain was still drumming on the veranda roof. Far off, the church clock struck twelve.

'Time for a snort.' Buffy got to his feet. 'Glass of Pinot Grigio, anyone?'

'Oh no, we couldn't . . .'

'Come on, keep me company.'

The two women looked at each other. 'We don't usually drink in the middle of the day.'

'That's what they all say,' said Buffy. The other one being *I don't usually have a proper breakfast.* Those were always the guests who packed it away— sausages, black pudding, the full monty.

'But don't you have anything else to do?' asked Freida.

'No,' said Buffy.

'It's very kind of you,' said Iris. 'And, well, we are on holiday, I suppose.'

They all said that, too. Buffy returned with a bottle and glasses. Those who protested the most, he had discovered, always knocked it back the fastest. They settled down for a natter. It turned out that Iris had a brother who was going through a midlife crisis.

'Earring, ponytail, the lot,' she said. 'And now he's joined his son's band, he plays the guitar . . . he wears this little waistcoat, and his *tummy* . . . Oh, the young are so forgiving.'

'Not in my experience,' said Buffy. But then he could hardly blame them. And in fact, as time passed things had improved between him and his offspring as they found themselves stumbling through the same mistakes that he himself had made. Frieda and Iris were good listeners; lesbians often were, in his experience. He found himself talking about Celeste, the daughter who had suddenly appeared in his life, popped up from nowhere, aged twenty-three.

'You can't mean nowhere,' said Iris. 'Who was her mother? Who were you with, all those years ago?'

'Well, I was vaguely with Lorna,' said Buffy.

'Not that vaguely,' said Iris, emboldened by the wine.

'It was just an on–off thing, she never told me she was pregnant, and then she got a job in a show and I didn't see her again.'

The two women listened, wide-eyed, as he told them the story of how Celeste tracked him down, how she had got a job in his local chemist's shop and finally revealed that she was his long-lost daughter. Frieda's eyes filled with tears. My God he was enjoying himself! A glass of wine, an appreciative audience—what more could an old performer want?

Voda put her head through the door. 'Just popping out.' It was visiting day in Shrewsbury Gaol. Glancing at the bottle, at the two women who looked settled in for the duration, she caught Buffy's eye. *You old softie.*

*   *   *

Then there were the couples. Lance and Janet Pritchard hogged the only bathroom until half past ten one morning. Giggles and splashes could be heard in the corridor where the other guest, a timid geologist, reappeared at intervals clutching his towel. Though there were two showers, one was broken and the other attached to Buffy's bedroom. Buffy had to finally scoop up his clothes from the floor and usher the chap into his sanctuary. At eleven, an hour after the official kicking-out time, the Pritchards appeared in the dining room, smug and flushed. Word seemed to have got around that the rules were somewhat relaxed at Myrtle House; perhaps people were Facebooking or something. Buffy didn't have the heart to make a fuss; instead, he felt a pang for the past, for creaking beds and the raised eyebrows of proprietors less tolerant than himself.

Besides, it was raining again. In fact, a gale was blowing. Though Knockton was only a mile from the English border its weather was unmistakably Welsh. Buffy kicked Fig into the garden and shut the door with a shudder. There was no question of a constitutional that morning and, fond though he had become of his town, it offered little by the way of diversions even on a Saturday. Shopping and a gossip were unappealing prospects in the pouring rain, and the lure of a Yes You Can Sing session at the British Legion wasn't powerful enough to get him out of the house.

72

The geologist, undaunted, had disappeared for the day. The Pritchards, however, stood side by side at the dining-room window, a stance with which Buffy was only too familiar.

'We could go on that tour of eco homes,' said Janet.

'In this?' said Lance, staring at the rain.

'Or that model railway museum,' she said. 'In that place I can't pronounce.' She looked at him. 'You like model railways, don't you?'

'Yeah, when I was six.'

She looked at the brochure. 'There's a Kraft Fayre in the Assembly Rooms.'

Lance didn't reply.

'Look!' She pointed to the page. '"Shiatsu for People, Dogs and Horses"! Isn't that funny?'

'Very funny.'

There was a silence.

'We could go to Aberystwyth,' she said.

'Why the hell would we want to go to Aberystwyth?'

'It's beside the sea.'

'Or we could go home,' said Lance.

She froze. 'What?'

Buffy, who was squirting Pledge on the tables, paused.

'This isn't working, is it?' said Lance. 'I'm packing. You coming?' He strode across the room, bumping into a table, and briefly glanced at Buffy. 'Sorry, pal, I'll pay for tonight.' And he was gone.

Janet sat down on a chair and burst into tears.

*　　　*　　　*

An hour later the three of them were in the sitting

73

room, working their way through a second bottle of Rioja.

'He's always up a ladder doing something or other,' said Janet. 'He never talks to me.'

'You're the one who wanted the maisonette,' said Lance. 'I told you it needed work.'

'We used to have a laugh,' she said.

'You sounded happy enough this morning,' said Buffy. He was going to add *in the bath*, but stopped.

'I do crack jokes,' said Lance. 'You just don't find them funny any more.'

'This weekend, it was going to be our second honeymoon,' she told Buffy. 'Lance had a terrible childhood. His stepfather used to lock him in the boot of the car when he went to play golf.'

'Bloody hell,' said Buffy.

'Thanks, Jan,' said Lance. 'Anything else you want to tell the world?'

'I'm just trying to explain our problem,' she said.

'We don't have a problem.'

'That's the problem,' she said. 'You've put your finger on it.'

'What are you babbling on about?'

'Why can't we talk?' She indicated Buffy. 'He understands, he's had lots of problems, you heard what he said about his wives—'

'Ex-wives,' said Buffy.

'Whatever you and I are going through, he's gone through them too. You can tell, just looking at his face.'

'What's wrong with my face?' snapped Buffy.

'You've *lived*,' she said. 'It's written all over you. And you like talking about it—the stuff you've told us, it's fascinating. None of Lance's friends talk, you see. They go to the pub, they go to the footy. They don't know how to *talk*.'

'I do talk,' Lance said. 'Problem is, you're not interested.'

'You don't talk about feelings,' she said. 'You're still locked in that boot.'

'Strewth, woman, give us a break.' Lance pulled out a packet of cigarettes.

'You can't smoke in here,' said Janet.

'It's all right,' said Buffy, 'everyone else does.'

'That's why he went into the army,' she said. 'No danger of talking to women there.'

'No,' said Lance. 'Just getting my head blown off in Helmand.' He gazed at a damp patch on the wall and turned to Buffy: 'Should get that seen to, mate, or there'll be trouble later. Ten to one it's a leak in the downpipe.' He stood up. 'Got a ladder? I'll check it out if you want.'

Janet burst into laughter. The sun had come out. It blazed through the stained glass, patterning the room with Spangles.

For some reason, Buffy didn't know why, peace was restored. Had he helped? Maybe it was the booze. The Pritchards disappeared upstairs. Buffy thought: They treat this place like a hotel. He didn't mind; the chap had risked his life for his country. Exhausted, he lay down on the sofa and buried his face in a cushion. Was it his imagination or did it still smell of Bridie's cats?

That afternoon the Pritchards went for a walk. Buffy watched the two of them strolling down Church Street, pausing to look in the shops. The puddles glinted in the sunshine; people had emerged and were nattering on doorsteps. The town had the rinsed innocence of a Frank Capra movie, the look that had made him fall in love with the place all those months ago.

Buffy thought about Janet's complaint. He himself had had many problems with women, but talking wasn't one of them. He thought: I could run a course in it. He looked in the *What's On in the Marches* brochure that the Pritchards had left in the dining room. Its two pages of workshops listed the usual stuff—yoga, acupuncture—but also 'Shamanic Soul Retrieval' with somebody called Clare, and Qigong, which seemed to be internal martial arts, whatever that was, with Nigel in Hereford. With so many beardies around, this sort of thing didn't surprise him. He presumed, however, that these classes took place in silence. Indeed, with 'Metamorphic Therapy', he read, *unwanted behaviour patterns from birth and before are released without having to utter a word.* None of them taught the art of conversation, that was for sure. And yet women had always complained about men's lack of communication.

He already saw the notices. They were pinned up in those bastions of blokeiness, the local pubs. 'How to Talk to Women, with Russell Buffery'. It might bring in a few quid; this B&B business was not the money-spinner he had imagined.

It didn't turn out quite like that, but the seed was sown.

7

Harold

'What, exactly, is your novel about?' Pia leaned against the door frame, looking at Harold as he sat at his desk.

'Novelists aren't supposed to tell,' said Harold. 'Or it's all spoilt.'

Pia raised her eyebrows. What a handsome woman she was! Tall and rangy, a racehorse of a woman; high cheekbones, taut dry skin, now tanned from gardening. Flat dancer's stomach. After all these years, her looks still gave Harold a jolt of pleasure.

Pia shrugged, and walked past him to water her seedlings. There were rows of them, jammed on the window ledge. Harold hunched himself over his computer, like a child hiding his work in an exam. Behind him, she puffed at the plants with her puffer thing. A haze of water drifted onto his open notebook, which lay on a chair nearby. It was a page of jottings about one of the characters. He watched his handwriting dissolve, and the character with it, but didn't protest. Pia would somehow imply that it was his fault, for leaving it there in the first place.

'I think you're shamming,' she said. 'I think you sit there downloading porn.'

'All right, I'll tell you.' Harold took a breath. 'It's a comic novel written by Mary Pickford's cat.'

'What?'

'Movies and cats, it's a cast-iron best-seller.'

'But cats can't speak,' said Pia.

'Nor can silent movie stars.'

'Of course they can,' she sighed. 'You just can't hear them. Anyway, did Mary Pickford have a cat?'

'Everybody has a cat at sometime or another.'

'OK, OK,' Pia said, suddenly bored. She rubbed her nose with her finger, leaving a smudge of earth. Looking around the room, she said: 'You really should let the cleaner in here.'

'Not till I've finished the book.'

The words hung in the air—*And when might that be?*

Harold suspected that Pia was only mildly interested in his novel. Though she ran an arts centre she wasn't an intellectual; dance and drama was her thing, and the more foreign the better. She was just vaguely curious about how long it was taking.

So was he. After years of teaching the novel he had imagined that he knew the rudiments of how to do it—after all, his Introduction to American Fiction had been the most popular module at Holloway College. He could quote whole pages of *Humboldt's Gift* by heart; surely some of it must have seeped into his unconscious, or wherever it was that his creativity lay. But how, exactly, did one get started? He felt like a newly trained pilot sitting in some vast, empty jumbo jet, stuck on the runway; he knew every button on the control panel but had no idea how to take off. *Fear of Flying*, he thought; another of the books on his set list.

He had, in fact, started his novel many times. But the moment he had written a paragraph his inner critic kicked in and he began to deconstruct his words so ruthlessly that the whole thing fell to

78

pieces. And where exactly *did* one start? With the birth of the cat? Mary Pickford's first movie? How was this fucking cat supposed to speak anyway, with a few *miaows* here and there? For months Harold had sat at his desk, frozen with low-level panic; Sellotaped to the wall, photographs of America's Sweetheart, kiss-curls and all, smirked down at him. *You really think you can mess with me, you talentless little runt?*

'I'm off,' said Pia.

'What, now?'

'Why not?'

'I thought we were having lunch.'

Pia flushed. 'No, sweetie, I told you. I've got to go to a meeting about the Arts Council cuts.'

'On a Sunday?'

'It's the only time we can all get together.'

He was going to say *but you're together all week*, and stopped. Why had she called him *sweetie*? Pia stood there, rubbing her eyebrow with her thumb and gazing around his study in a vaguely distracted way. He could tell she was longing to leave but didn't want to look too eager. She was caught in a shaft of sunlight—a Nordic goddess with her fair, flyaway hair and evasive blue eyes.

'It won't take long.' She kissed the top of his head and was gone. Downstairs, the front door slammed. For some reason Harold leapt to his feet and hurried across to the bedroom. Out of the window he saw her striding down the path, zipping up her leather jacket. A cough of the engine and she was off, a helmeted Valkyrie on her Piaggio scooter.

Recently Pia had, indeed, become somewhat distracted. He presumed it was her anxiety about

79

the impending cuts. The banking crisis was hitting the arts and the future of the Hackney Fudge Factory, where she worked, was looking increasingly dodgy. He had his criticisms of the place; its recent Menopause Season seemed unlikely to appeal to the local populace, but he had kept his thoughts to himself out of loyalty to his wife. No, out of fear. In twelve years of marriage he had learned that any criticism, however amiably murmured, would result in hair-tossing contempt for the very fact that he was a man—surely the reason she was attracted to him in the first place. It wasn't worth the fight.

The doorbell rang. Harold roused himself from the bed, where he had fallen into a stupor, and ran downstairs.

A woman stood at the doorstep. 'Is Mrs Cohen here?' A cardboard box sat at her feet.

Harold explained that his wife was out. In the road a car waited, its engine running.

'You'd better take them then,' she said. 'We're late as it is.' She wore a floral dress and cardy; there was the air of a geography teacher about her. You didn't see many women like that in Hackney. She looked at him, eyes narrowed. 'You do realise these hens are severely traumatised?'

'Oh God.' Harold stared at the box. 'I thought they were coming on Wednesday.'

'Today was more convenient, as we were passing,' she said. 'We're on our way to a wedding in Sandwich.' Out in the road, the car hooted. 'They've been wormed and deloused, but remember they're ex-bats.'

'What?'

'Ex-battery,' she said patiently. 'So don't be

80

shocked by their appearance. The feathers should grow back in a couple of months. I do supply knitted jackets, very cute. There's some in the car, ten pounds each.'

'I'm sure they'll be all right.'

'You haven't seen them yet,' she said.

A faint clucking came from the box, which shifted on the step.

'I have to warn you that some of them never recover, they've been kept in such terrible conditions, but with any luck these girls will soon be scratching around like nobody's business.' She knelt down and spoke to the box. 'Bye-bye, sweethearts.' She got to her feet and dusted down her dress. 'What's the best way to the Blackwall Tunnel?'

Harold carried the box into the back garden. It was surprisingly heavy and struggled in his arms. Needless to say, this hen business was Pia's idea; he preferred his chickens stuffed with fennel, red onion and pancetta, his favourite recipe in the River Café cookbook. The cage was ready; one of the stagehands from the Fudge Factory had knocked it up. Inside the cage sat the henhouse, roofed with faux-gingerbread tiles from last year's panto.

There was a squawk from the box as he lowered it onto the ground. That bossy suburban woman seemed to think that it was she who was doing *him* a favour. What the hell was he supposed to do now? Why wasn't Pia here?

A beak pushed up through the flap. He remembered his mother's chicken soup with knaidlach, he could smell it now. The family gathered round the table as his father lifted the lid ... the steam, the exhalation of breath. *What do you say? Thank you, Mother.* His parents had worked day and night to get out of this place and into Golders Green and here he was, full circle, only half a mile from where he was born. Pia had urged him to buy a house in Hackney because it was near her work. She also liked the ethnic diversity but it was fast becoming gentrified—in fact, the people who sold them the house said, 'This is an up-and-coming area. We're the only black family and we're moving out.'

Harold heaved the box into the pen and pulled open the flaps. Three hens struggled out; clambering over each other, they ran off with a rolling gait, like drunks, and huddled in the corner of the pen. My God, they were completely bald! No, worse than that, they were bald everywhere except their heads and necks, which were tufted with half-hearted eruptions of feathers. Just a fleshy stump, where their tails should be. He had never seen anything so repulsive in his life.

Harold shut the gate with a shudder. Heads tilted, the hens stood watching him malevolently with their tiny yellow eyes. No hint of gratitude, of course. Did they realise how silly they looked? He had a suspicion that Pia, like that awful woman, might call them *girls*. Grounds for divorce, in his opinion.

He knew that he should be more supportive of his wife's recent fad. The thing was, would it last? Her previous craze for keeping fit had resulted in a house crammed with discarded equipment, including an exercise bike that jabbed his ankle whenever he tried to get into the downstairs loo. This smallholding business was worse, particularly now it was the growing season. Every window ledge

82

was crammed with seedlings. They lolled out of their little pots, parched and needy; they seemed to multiply overnight—wherever he looked there seemed to be more of the buggers, all clamouring for his attention because of course Pia was out at work all day. It was like running a bloody orphanage.

'Why don't you like gardening?' asked Pia.

'I'm a Jew,' said Harold. 'We're desert people.'

'Grow cactuses then.'

'Cacti.'

'Don't be a pedant.' She sighed, and started again. 'Isn't it satisfying, to eat our own vegetables?'

Harold kept quiet. He didn't like to mention the potatoes filled with slugs, the tomatoes covered with warts or the fact that, the moment their meagre crop was ready, the shops were filled with exactly the same thing but much more delicious and a fraction of the price if one factored in all the effort involved. Plus the fact that there was no room to sit in the garden any more because it was filled with rotting cabbages. And now, a hen run. 'Do stop moaning,' Pia said. 'Why do you have to be so negative all the time? We're rescuing them from a life of misery. And think of the eggs.'

The hens were still eyeing him from their corner. Harold thought: Why not save the trouble and eat them now? After all, they were oven-ready. He picked up the shit-spattered box and shoved it into the recycling bag, squashing it down with his foot. Pia accused him of moaning but she herself was no slouch in the complaints department. The impending cuts were threatening the Fudge Factory and they had already lost two of their staff. She was working longer hours, meetings on Sundays, emergency powwows; no wonder she was stressed and distracted, muttering into her mobile and sitting up late at her computer. Harold had every sympathy but at least she had staff, whereas all he had was a houseful of seedlings and—now—three hostile chickens.

Harold suddenly realised: no wonder they were looking at him like that. They had nothing to eat. Pia had ordered some hen food online but it wouldn't be delivered until the next day.

Harold stomped into the kitchen. What the hell was he going to do? He stopped in the doorway. Earth was scattered over the floor; the cat had used one of the seed trays as a toilet. He ignored it and opened the larder. What did hens eat—bulgar wheat? pasta? Should he cook it first? Standing there, he cursed the Arts Council. No, he cursed the bankers. If they hadn't been such greedy bastards his wife would be here, sorting out the poultry. His Sunday was in ruins, the whole of the country was falling to pieces and did they give a flying fuck?

Harold grabbed his wallet and slammed out of the house. No chance of getting any work done today. He would have to buy some birdseed—peanuts, that sort of thing. There was a garden centre off Dalston Lane.

Despite it all, his spirits rose. They always did when he escaped from his computer. It was a gloriously sunny day in early May. He walked round the corner, past the parade of shops—the Jamaican patty takeaway, the Afro hairdresser's with its display of wigs, the ill-named Elite Minicabs. Soon they would be gone; the block was earmarked for development. Property prices had shot up since the

Olympics and the City boys were moving in. Harold gazed with affection at the leprous, doomed shops. Though he had never felt the need for hair extensions he would miss them when they were gone. The whole neighbourhood was being regenerated—out with the patties, in with the pesto. There was even talk of a Waitrose.

In fact, the Waitrose was being built on the site of the garden centre. Harold stopped, and cursed. He hadn't been to Dalston Lane for months and the place was unrecognisable. Traffic thundered past as he gazed at the skeletal supermarket. Beyond it stood a brand-new block of executive apartments wrapped with a banner proclaiming *Only Six Remaining*. Across the road, a new hotel seemed to have sprung up overnight.

And out of its revolving door stepped Pia. She carried her helmet and was accompanied by a Japanese woman. They were talking so intently that they bumped into a group of businessmen who were entering the hotel. Harold waved at Pia but she didn't see him. He stepped off the pavement but a lorry blared its horn and he jumped back.

Through the traffic he could see Pia bending down to unlock her scooter. The Japanese woman opened the seat and took out the second helmet. She was tiny, and dressed in black. She slung her leg over the scooter and they sped off, bouncing over the speed humps in the car park, swerving round the newly planted trees and disappearing through some far exit.

*   *   *

Pia didn't arrive home until nine o'clock. She flung

85

herself on the sofa and pushed her hand through her hair, shaking it loose like a dog. Her nose was sunburnt.

'Christ, what a day,' she groaned. 'I'm so sorry, darling. Blame it on this crap Bullingdon Club Tory philistine crap government. That Arts Minister should be shot.'

Harold told her about the hens. She jumped to her feet and rushed out. He joined her at the pen. Dusk had fallen and the hens had put themselves to bed; through the window of the henhouse he could see the glimmer of their bald bodies as they sat side by side on their perch.

'Night-night, girls,' said Pia. 'You're going to be very happy here.'

He told her about the food situation, how he had ended up buying the chickens some bar snacks at Londis—sunflower seeds and peanuts.

Pia smiled. 'You are a dear.' She put her arm around his waist as they stood there, looking into the pen. *A dear?*

'By the way, what were you doing in that hotel?'

She paused, her hand on his hip. 'What?'

'I saw you with a Japanese woman.'

'Oh, her.' Pia moved away and walked towards the house. 'She's that director I told you about,' she called over her shoulder. 'She's rehearsing *The Scream*. From the Munch painting.'

He followed her into the kitchen. She was rummaging in the cupboard.

'Do we have any Ovaltine?' she asked.

'*Ovaltine?*'

'I just feel like some.'

Harold gazed at her back view. She was squatting on her haunches, examining the tins and jars.

'So what did you do with her?' he asked.

'Who?'

'The Japanese woman.'

She took out a jar and inspected it.

'That's marmalade,' he said.

'I took her to the meeting. She was bored stiff in that hotel.'

Harold was puzzled. 'She was bored stiff, so you took her to an eight-hour meeting about Arts Council cuts?'

'They're having the same problem in Japan.' Pia shut the cupboard and stood up. 'No Ovaltine.' She looked around the kitchen, and sniffed. 'There's a funny smell in here.'

'The cat crapped in the seed tray, but I cleaned it up. I'm afraid the seedlings are a goner.'

Pia sat down suddenly. Her eyes filled with tears.

'Oh God, is it that bad?' Harold was alarmed; Pia never cried. 'Can't you plant some more?'

Pia sat at the table, shuddering, her face in her hands. The cat came in and rubbed itself against her leg.

'Pia, what's the matter?'

She looked at him through her fingers. 'We didn't go to the meeting. We went for a walk on Hampstead Heath.'

'But how . . . I mean—did you just sneak out?'

She muttered something but he couldn't hear, her hands were in the way.

'What?'

She removed her hands. 'There wasn't a meeting.'

Harold was confused. 'Why not?'

'There just wasn't.'

Harold gazed at her sodden face, her sunburnt

nose. 'So you went to Hampstead Heath? For the whole day?'

She nodded.

'Why didn't you tell me?' he asked. 'I could have come. It was such a beautiful day, and to tell the truth I'm having a few problems with this novel. To be absolutely honest, I haven't really entirely started . . .' His words trailed away. He suddenly pictured the familiarity with which the woman had strapped on the helmet.

'That wouldn't have been a good idea,' Pia said.

*　　　*　　　*

By midsummer the Fudge Factory had closed, a victim of the cuts. Pia, too, had gone. She had moved to Amsterdam with Kasuko, the tiny Japanese woman. Apparently they were living in some sort of collective.

How could he have been so stupid? His sister Maureen was a lesbian, he should have recognised the signs. But what *were* the signs? Pia had always worn baggy trousers and no make-up. Besides, she said she wasn't a lesbian, she just happened to have fallen in love with a woman. She had said it in a dreamy, excluding way, as if he as a mere man couldn't possibly understand. Harold had resisted the temptation to say that of course he understood, he loved women too.

For weeks he was sunk in depression. He felt disembowelled, the stuffing pulled out of him; he could hardly drag himself out of bed in the morning. He felt utterly deserted—not just deserted as a husband, but as a member of the male sex. Would it have been worse if she had left him for a man? That would have been understandable—horribly hurtful, but understandable; he might even have fought back. He had been there before, he knew the rules of engagement in the battle between the sexes. But Pia had moved out of the familiar arena into an unknown world, leaving him alone in the wreckage of his marriage, picking through the rubbish and looking for clues. Acid had seeped back through the years, corroding even the happiest times. Had Pia really desired his hairy, middle-aged body; those unlovely giblets between his legs? Looked at objectively, he could see her point. No wonder she had fallen for a woman. In fact, as time went by, he felt a surprising bond with his wife. He pictured Kasuko's body, smooth as a seal and sort of boneless, like all the Japanese. She would have a neat black triangle of pubic hair, silkier than an English person's. Imagining this, Harold felt a jolt of desire. How perverse was that?

Working on his novel was now out of the question. He was an abandoned husband, he had every excuse. In his heart of hearts this was a relief; he could surrender to self-pity. Mary Pickford simpered in the photo that had started to curl on his wall. Hang on, did she become a lesbian too? He knew nothing about her, the whole thing had been a *folie de grandeur*. Just because he taught something didn't mean he could do it himself. When his friends enquired he kept it quiet, like a cot death.

For his friends had rallied round. The break-up of his marriage had opened its curtains to the world; they all weighed in with their honest opinions of Pia, opinions they had kept to themselves all these years. He agreed with most of them, of course—*she was so blooming right-on . . . humour bypass . . . so Scandinavian . . . banging on about women's rights . . . making you look a twat.* There was a sense of male solidarity in this, and a sort of uneasy hilarity. A lesbian! In a weird way, it was a relief. After all, it was no reflection on Harold.

'I always thought she was a muff-diver,' said Dennis, one of his less reconstructed friends. 'That's why she was so bloody rude.' In fact, she was rude to Dennis because she thought he was an arse but Harold kept quiet; he was fond of Dennis, they had been to primary school together, and though they had little in common they would have laid down their lives for each other.

Some of his women friends were simply sorry for him.

'How are you going to cope?' asked Annie. 'The garden. The hens. She always did everything.'

'I did pull my weight, you know,' said Harold irritably. 'I did all the financial stuff. And her computer, and the remotes, she never got the hang of SkyPlus. And I shopped, she hated shopping, and, oh, all sorts of things. I'm not completely useless.'

'No.' Annie looked at him, her head on one side. 'Not completely.'

They burst out laughing. It was refreshing; he hadn't laughed for weeks. Annie was an old friend, a big, warm woman; they had taught together at Holloway College. Her lovelife had been a series of disastrous affairs with men who had turned out to be manic-depressives, or shits, or both. He and Pia used to give her advice from the safety of their marriage; now he had joined her in the wilderness.

It was a terrifying prospect; he had thought he'd been safe for life. At some point, would he have to start *dating* again? Such a stomach-churning word. What did one do: meet women in wine bars or something? Take them to the cinema and drape one's arm casually around their shoulder? He was far too rusty—if, that is, he had ever known how to do it in the first place. When he was young people just got drunk or stoned and found themselves in bed with somebody, whether they liked them or not. And then he had somehow tumbled into marriage with his first wife because that's what one did, then. Now he was fifty-six and the thought of getting to know a woman all over again filled him with a panic-stricken desolation.

'There's something wrong with that hen,' said Annie.

They were standing in the garden, gazing into the pen. One of the chickens was hunched in the corner.

'She's just depressed,' said Harold.

'That's projection,' said Annie, who went to a Jungian analyst. 'Forget about yourself for a moment.' She cooed through the fence, 'You poor girl.'

'Why does everybody call them *girls*? They're fucking hens.'

'Don't take it out on me,' snapped Annie. 'I'm not your wife.'

Harold apologised. 'The trouble is, she's left me with all these *things*. The hens, the cat. It's got some infection in its eye, it's gone all sticky. And look at the weeds.' He gestured around. 'Why do they grow faster than plants?'

'They're not *things*,' said Annie. 'They're animals

91

and vegetables. You just have to look after them.'

In fact Harold had done some weeding in the past. When *Jazz Record Requests* was on he had weeded around the back door, where he could hear the radio from the kitchen. But Pia had accused him of pulling up her camomile so he had stopped. And now the garden was choked with what even he could see were thistles. Her seedlings had long since been engulfed.

'Nowadays everything in the garden either pricks me or stings,' he said. 'Symbolic or what?'

'You poor dear.' She put her arm through his. 'But she really was a pain in the bum. I can say that now.'

'What happens if she comes back, her tail between her legs? Imagine how embarrassed you'd be.'

But Pia wasn't coming back. After she had unburdened herself in the kitchen, after the tears and recriminations, the whisky-drinking into the small hours, she was a woman transformed. Relieved of her secret she was flushed with love, she looked ten years younger. As his wife packed up her belongings she had hummed—*hummed*. He had heard her through the door. A woman had done that, a slippery Japanese seal dressed in black. Hens and vegetables were forgotten, evaporated in a sapphic haze. Pia had treated him with the sort of offhand kindness she treated the cat, a bowl of Whiskas left out for him as she canoodled upstairs on her mobile. In a matter of weeks their marriage had vaporised as if it had never existed.

And she had wanted nothing. This had made it worse. Her passion existed on a rarer plane than mere possessions. The house was full of her stuff—the exercise bike, a Moroccan tagine that wouldn't fit into the dishwasher, a dinosaur-era Polaroid camera, folksy tourist rubbish from holidays, a breadmaker, stuff, *stuff*, cupboards full of stuff. And all he wanted was her naked body in his arms.

'I'll help you if you want,' said Annie.

Harold jumped. They were looking at the garden; sunlight shone on the leathery leaves of the ivy that smothered the wall. 'I've got the time, now it's the holidays,' said Annie. 'And my daughter's off to Durham, did I tell you? She's going to study marine biology, so that's my little bird flown.' Her arm was around his waist; she kneaded his flesh between her thumb and finger. 'I could bring round a spade and get stuck in.'

*　　　*　　　*

The next day the phone rang. It was Melanie, another single parent, who lived a few streets away. 'How are you doing?' she asked. 'Need any help with the garden? I've only got a balcony, I hate being cooped up in this weather, and my son would love to see your hens.'

She appeared that afternoon with a bottle of wine in her hand. She wore denim shorts and a vest top.

'Sorry about my little one, I forgot he had to go to a birthday party. Maybe I could bring him back an egg.' Melanie's hair, newly washed, swung around her shoulders as she walked down the path. 'Is that an apple tree? And what are those long purple things? I'm hopeless, I'm *so* not a gardener but I'm longing to learn, your wife was so clever, it's

like another world out here, a little bit of paradise.'
Harold followed her. The cheeks of Melanie's
buttocks moved from side to side in the tiny shorts.
'God, you're so lucky,' she said over her shoulder.
'I'd kill for a garden.'

Harold's mobile rang. It was Allie, the ex-wife of
his squash partner. 'I've researched weedkillers,'
she said. 'What you need for the nettles is
glyphosate. I can bring some round, you just paint it
on the leaves, it's totally harmless. And if you like, I
could stop at Marks on the way and bring us
something to eat?'

*　　　*　　　*

'Didn't take long, did they?' Dennis spluttered with
laughter. 'I knew it. Couple of months and they're
crawling out of the woodwork, panting for it.'

Harold wished he hadn't told him, it seemed
disloyal to the women concerned. 'They're only
trying to help,' he said.

'Yes, dear.' Dennis patted his hand.

'With the garden. It's all got a bit beyond me.'

'And have we got our leg over yet?'

'Is that all you think about?'

'Yep.'

They were sitting in a pub on the Essex Road.
Dennis was halfway through a hair transplant and
had to keep his head covered. Though it was a
sweltering day he wore his son's hoodie; in it, he
resembled a porky, middle-aged mugger caught on
CCTV.

He sighed. 'You're a lucky fucker, Harry.' He
was the only person who called him Harry. 'A
pussy-magnet at your age. *Our* age. But then you've

always pulled the women, being an intellectual. A bit of the old T. S. Eliot and they're creaming their pants.' He drained his pint. 'Should've finished me A levels. And you've kept your hair, you sod.'

'I don't want women. I want my wife.'

'Have mine!' Dennis laughed. 'Actually, I'm fond of the old girl. Well, she's had to put up with *me*, hasn't she, for thirty years? Seen me through some ups and downs, as you very well know.' Dennis was a wealthy property developer. At various low points, however, he and his family had been reduced to living in a caravan in Gravesend. 'She sends her regards, by the way.'

'Any gardening tips?'

'Ha ha.' He paused. 'It's just that sometimes a bloke wants to be let off the leash.'

'I wouldn't recommend it.' Harold frowned at him. 'Don't scratch your hood.'

'My scalp itches.' Dennis stood up, to get more drinks. 'Us Jews aren't supposed to lose our hair. We're a hairy race. It's one of the reasons people resent us.'

Harold eyed his head. 'How much did you pay for that?'

'Don't ask. But it was the top guy in the business, little Indian bloke. Only the best for my beloved.'

'What do you mean?'

'So she can remember me when we were young, childhood sweethearts and all that.' His shy smile both surprised and moved Harold. Good God, the man really loved his wife.

That night Harold lay in the big double bed, listening to glass smashing down in the street. He hoped it wasn't his car. Soon the crime would disappear; Dennis and his fellow developers would see to that. But in a strange way Harold would miss it, just as he missed the fireworks of his marriage. What was the point of getting up in the morning without the friction and the chats, the resentments and sudden, swooning intimacy, the everything else, even the bloody seedlings, of life with Pia? As he lay on his back, gazing at the ceiling, the cat walked over him. She trod on his testicles, as she always unerringly did, and settled down next to his face.

Her sticky eyes gazed at him in the gloom; she purred, exhaling toxic breath. Harold flinched but he didn't turn away, it would only offend her and then it would be sulks the next morning.

8

Buffy

Voda was an adventurous cook; it was yet another of her talents. Apparently she had just perfected her sushi, using crayfish from the local stream, when Conor was arrested. That he was now languishing on a prison diet was one of the few things that upset her. Sometimes, when there was a darts match, she cooked supper for herself and Buffy before repairing to the pub. Sometimes, in fact, she stayed the night, sleeping in one of the unoccupied bedrooms. He suspected she was lonely in her cottage. She told him that her nearest neighbour was a recluse called Taffy, who lived in a caravan where he watched porn all day and made hooch by hanging marrows in ladies' stockings to drip into a bowl.

96

Buffy was glad of the company. He was fond of his sturdy helpmate with her flaming cheeks and spicy casseroles. Voda seldom asked about his past; like many country people she was only concerned with the here and now. He had presumed it was some rural survival instinct until he discovered that in fact she was born in Loughborough; her parents, lured by some cult, had moved to Wales where she and her brother had been brought up in a bender. Nobody was quite what they seemed, in Knockton as in life, and few of them turned out to be Welsh.

Tonight she was cooking chicken in saffron for themselves and Nyange, who had arrived to help with the accounts. They sat in the kitchen. Curtains of damp sheets hung from the ceiling; the tumble dryer had broken.

The account book lay open on the table. Nyange ran her finger down the page. Her nails were long and metallic green. 'This place is haemorrhaging money,' she said. 'In fact, you're hardly breaking even.'

'Tell me about it,' sighed Buffy.

Voda, stirring the sauce, said: 'We can't charge more, we don't have the facilities.'

Nyange closed the book. 'You've got six bedrooms, right? Two singles, three twins, one double and only two en suites between them.'

'And one's mine,' said Buffy.

'It's not what people expect nowadays,' said Nyange.

'Ah, but we make up for it with a warm Myrtle House welcome,' said Buffy. 'The people who come here love it.'

'That's because they hang about all day getting pissed with you,' said Voda. 'Honestly, it might as

97

well be a hotel. We could charge more then.'

'Yes, but then I'd have to be here all day,' said Buffy.

'But you are.'

'Only because it's always raining,' said Buffy. 'Anyway, what about regulations and inspections and whatnot? Don't hotels have to have all that? The point about a B&B is that it's nice and amateurish.'

'You can say that again,' said Voda, carrying the pot to the table.

Nyange shifted the papers to one side. 'Your problem is that you're empty all week. People only come at weekends, and then just for a night or two. It's very labour-intensive. You need them to stay for a week or more. And you have to sell them meals and especially drinks. That's where the money is, the mark-up on alcohol. You can reckon on 500 per cent.'

Buffy gazed at his daughter. 'How do you know all this?'

'I did some work for Wetherspoon's. Profits have gone through the roof—people drink more in a recession.'

Voda lifted the lid off the pot. 'Where does she get all this from?' Through the steam, she raised her eyebrows at Buffy.

'Not from me, that's for sure,' he said.

'Grandad worked for Credit Suisse,' said Nyange, 'in Accra.'

'Did he really?' asked Buffy. His blood relation, and he knew nothing.

Nyange, in her black trouser suit, sharpened the air in the chaotic kitchen; Voda looked woolly beside her as she plonked down the plates.

'We can bumble on as we are,' said Buffy.

'Honestly, Dad! Where are you going to find the funds for a new roof? People don't pay good money to find buckets in the bedrooms.'

'Only the Bluebell Bedroom,' said Buffy. 'And we charge less for that one.'

Nyange looked at him pityingly, her head on one side. With her metallic talons she looked like a bird of prey inspecting some roadkill and thinking better of it. 'Forget it,' she said. 'Mmm, this smells good.'

'Nyange's right,' said Voda. 'This house has got to wash its face.'

It was a balmy evening; the back door was open. Bessie Smith drifted out from Simon's workshop next door. Buffy gazed fondly at the two young women, such surprising allies so late in his life. The hanging sheets gave them a theatrical air, as if they were in a production together—*Myrtle House: The Soap Opera*, with its changing cast of characters. He remembered his sons sitting at this table and how disorientating it had felt, as if he had landed in a show without learning his lines and the packing cases were filled with props. *We strut and fret our hour upon the stage.* But he was here, this was reality, this big draughty house whose every inch had become familiar to him. It was his past that now seemed weightless and blurred; what exactly had he *done* all day? London felt increasingly irrelevant; he hadn't been back since he had moved to Knockton.

And yet the distant past could suddenly swoop close; he could smell it and touch it. This same kitchen table, back in Edgbaston . . . Bridie stubbing out her fag and calling him *dearie*. He could see her now, her smudged mascara and bravely hennaed hair. He could feel her big, soft arms around him, under the eiderdown. She always undressed in the dark; he realised, now, that she was shy about her body. Had he never told her how beautiful she was? When she died he discovered that she had lied about her age; she was eight years older than she had let on. This had made his heart ache for her.

'It's funny,' he said, 'but I still feel this is Bridie's house, that I'm just borrowing it for a while. I keep thinking that she'll come through the front door and say *you wouldn't believe where I've been*—'

The doorbell rang. They all jumped.

Voda pushed back her chair and hurried out. There was a murmured conversation in the hall. For a mad moment Buffy thought he recognised Bridie's voice. When Voda returned, however, she was accompanied by a young Indian woman.

She wore a Glastonbury T-shirt and Converse boots. 'I'm so sorry,' she said. 'I'm supposed to be in Blandford Forum.'

'Have you eaten?' asked Voda. She turned to Buffy. 'She wants a room for the night. I told her she could take her pick.'

'I didn't mean to intrude—'

'Sit down and have some supper, you poor thing,' said Voda, pulling out a chair. 'You look as if you could do with a meal.' She had come over all motherly. Apparently she longed for a baby but Conor was still resistant. Fifteen months in jail, she hoped, would make him come to his senses.

'I've got a rubbish sense of direction,' said the young woman. 'So I bought a satnav and what did it do? Dumped me in the middle of nowhere. Thanks a bunch, satnav. Mmm, this smells great.'

100

Voda ladled chicken onto her plate. 'It's Moroccan fusion.'

'I thought I must be lost because the signs were in a funny language.'

'Welsh,' said Buffy.

'So I ended up in this yard full of dogs. An old bloke lived there, he said he was a blacksmith.'

'That'll be Gruffydd,' said Voda. 'He used to do horses but now he makes bondage frames for the S&M market.'

'The what? Anyway, he said I was a long way from Blandford Forum.'

'That's in Dorset, sweetheart,' said Voda, patting her arm.

'He suggested I get a room here for the night.'

Her name was Sita. Over the second glass of wine she told them she had just split up with her boyfriend. 'He was heavily into cars,' she said. 'He's a Sikh, they all are, that's why they're taxi drivers. Open a bonnet and they're happy bunnies. I think it was my Toyota that first attracted him. Apparently it's a Celica GT or something, I haven't a clue, my dad gave it to me when I qualified.'

'What as?' asked Buffy.

'A speech therapist.'

Sita certainly knew how to talk. As Buffy had noticed before, something about the house made guests open up; or maybe it was the Shiraz. Conversations became so intimate that it felt odd to take money from his customers in the morning. Soon Sita was telling them about her boyfriend's shortcomings in the sexual department.

'It was all wham-bam-thank-you-ma'am,' she said. 'If I was an engine he'd know what knobs to twiddle.'

'Conor was useless when we met,' said Voda. 'I blame the cocaine.'

'*Provokes the desire but takes away the performance,*' said Buffy.

'Dad!' said Nyange. 'Since when did you take drugs?'

'The Bard was referring to drink.'

Sita stared from Buffy to Nyange. 'He's your father?'

Nyange nodded. 'I know, I know.'

'Oh well, horses for courses,' said Sita vaguely. She burped and clapped her hand to her mouth. 'Pardon me.'

There was a silence. Outside, darkness had fallen; somewhere beyond the rooftops an owl hooted.

'Sounds as if you're well out of it,' said Voda.

Sita nodded but she looked unconvinced. 'He was a nice boy, ever so kind. He was even kind to my guinea pig. But when he died something died with him.'

'Your boyfriend died?' Voda put down her glass.

'My guinea pig. I'd never cried so much in my life. My boyfriend didn't get it, he'd never had a bereavement, you'd think he would with all his relatives.' Sita cut herself a wedge of cheese.

Nyange said: 'Charlie felt threatened by my love for my cat.'

'Who's Charlie?' asked Buffy.

'You wouldn't know.'

She was right; there were gaps in his daughter's life that Buffy knew nothing about. But where did he start? Tonight he had hoped to have a real conversation with Nyange but events had conspired against it; they always did. He remembered the last

102

time, and their fruitless search for a parking space. Nyange, however, didn't seem to mind; she seemed more interested in their visitor.

'Thing is, I'd got to rely on him doing things,' said Sita. 'Like fixing my car. I'm so crap at that sort of thing. That's why I'm going on this course in Blandford Forum, 'Basic Car Maintenance'. I need to feel empowered, you know? My self-esteem's at rock bottom.'

'With Charlie it was DIY,' said Nyange. 'I hadn't a clue. Like, what's a Rawlplug?'

'I've never heard of this Charlie,' said Buffy. 'Tell me about him.'

'It doesn't matter,' said Nyange. 'It was over long ago.'

'But—'

'Dad, it's history.'

Sita was chattering on. 'See, I need my car for my work. I can't take the Tube, I've got boundary issues.'

'Boundary issues?' asked Voda.

'She means being near other people,' said Nyange.

Buffy, brooding on his inadequacies as a father, hadn't been listening. It was only now that something Sita had said snagged in his mind. *I need to feel empowered.*

It was getting chilly. Voda got up and closed the back door.

'Coffee, anyone?' she asked.

Buffy's skin prickled with the boldness of it—the probable madness of it. 'How to Talk to Women' . . . 'Basic Car Maintenance'. He said: 'I've got an idea.'

9

Andy

Andy had earache. Possibly it was a brain tumour. He leaned against the kitchen unit and gazed at his reflection. The mortal man gazed back, spectral against the dark garden. Soon he would be forty, a word that filled him with dread. Already he noticed a faltering in the stream when he pissed. Prostate, no doubt. He wasn't usually gloomy but there had been a pile-up that morning on the North Circular—two cars overturned and wailing ambulances. It brought it home to a man; all day he had felt as frail as an invalid. He couldn't confide in Toni, she would pooh-pooh it, tossing her hair.

Shrill laughter came from the lounge. Tonight it was out of bounds. Toni was plotting a hen party for one of her girlfriends; obeying orders, he had snuck in through the back door. Judging by the shrieks, they were well into the white wine.

Andy felt both excluded and relieved. It sounded like there were quite a few of them; he was surprised they hadn't woken up Ryan. What were they finding so hilarious? Men and their inadequacies? Men, with particular reference to himself? Surely not, in his own home. And why did Toni never laugh like that when he and she were alone together?

Toni had left his dinner on the microwave—a cling-filmed plate of something or other. There was beer in the fridge. The problem was, he had left his *Angling Times* in the lounge. No way could he sneak

104

in and retrieve it. He could imagine, only too well, the women's stifled chortles when he left the room. *Angling Times*! Toni herself treated his hobby with indulgent pity, a boys-will-be-boys thing. She had once actually patted his bottom when he was leaving the house with his rods.

Andy rubbed his ear. Maybe he'd caught dengue fever. Three days ago a mosquito had bitten him at the Ruislip reservoir. He pictured himself on his deathbed, sodden with sweat, surrounded by Toni's heartless teddy bears. When they had set up home together he had hoped she would leave her soft toys behind—indeed, he had hinted that his furry audience, their glass eyes following his every move, had an inhibiting effect on his performance. No such luck. And she called *him* immature.

The kitchen was spotless. Once in her apron, Toni was a human dynamo. The efficiency of the woman! Andy felt, as he so often did, that he was an intruder in his own home—too large, too hairy, too male. He cracked open a beer and stepped into the garden. It was blessedly quiet; the only sound was the far hum of traffic and the trickle of the water feature.

The rooftops of Wembley rose up against the suffused sky. Even in the suburbs, nothing was safe. This particular accident, for some reason, had upset him. Maybe it was the pot plants, their earth scattered over the dual carriageway. Somebody had looked forward to a blameless day of gardening, a mug of tea . . . He lit a cigarette. Toni believed he had given up but what the hell. One nanosecond and your life was obliterated—there on the North Circular, with drivers gawping.

Andy was by nature a cautious man. Toni had

105

laughed, the first time they met, when he had buckled himself up in the back seat of the minicab. On her profile she had put *adventurous and fun-loving,* which was what had attracted him—to be honest, she wasn't that great-looking. But the woman bungee-jumped! And the next weekend, she told him, she was going zorbing. Apparently this entailed rolling about in a giant ball. This seemed a strange thing to do but he had to admire her pluck, and it was this, rather than lust, that prompted him to ask her out on a second date, and his fate was sealed.

'There you are!'

Toni grabbed his arm. Andy jumped, and flicked away his cigarette.

'They're just going,' she said. 'Come and say bye-bye.'

Toni led him into the lounge. Eight female friends, some of whom he recognised, stood around in various stages of departure.

'This is my man, Andy,' said Toni, her grip tightening. 'My lover and my best friend. Most of you know him, don't you?' She turned to Andy. 'Us girls have got it sorted. First we're going to pamper ourselves big time, we've got a deal at the Marriott, spa treatments, San Trop, the works . . .'

She babbled on. They were going to Prague, hen-party central. Andy caught the words *Karlovy Lazne Club . . . cocktails . . .* As he stood there, however, he felt strangely disembodied. Was this really his home?

Of course he recognised various items of furniture as his own, the settee and so on, but how come he was living here? It had all happened so fast. One moment he was a single man and now he was a couple, he was a lover and a best friend, a year had passed in a blur and all of a sudden he was living in Wembley with a hefty mortgage and a sort of stepson, Ryan.

Women, in his experience, always took an age to leave. Finally, however, they had gone and he was eating his dinner while Toni cleared up.

'Vicky's a lucky girl, we're *so* pulling the stops out.' Toni paused, a plate in her hand. 'Wonder if she'd do the same for me.'

'What?'

'Nothing.' She sighed, and bent to the open mouth of the dishwasher. As she stacked the plates, Andy gazed at her back view. Leggings weren't ideal for a woman of her proportions, but of course he said nothing. Every woman he had ever met was touchy about her weight.

'You fancied Jodie, didn't you?' Toni said.

'*What?*'

'Couldn't keep your eyes off her tits.'

'I haven't a clue who you're talking about. Which one was she?'

'You men, honestly!' Eyes twinkling, Toni stepped over to him and kissed the top of his head. 'What are we going to do with you?' She wagged her rubber-gloved finger. 'You and your one-track minds.'

Andy gave her his plate. 'There was a pile-up on the North Circular today.'

'Don't change the subject.'

'Makes you think.'

'Elbows!'

He lifted his elbows. She wiped the table beneath them. 'She's going to wear white,' she muttered. 'Bit of a joke, isn't it, when they've got two kids?

Still, it's the romance, I suppose.'

There was a silence. He could feel her looking at him, the heat of her expectation.

'Don't you think?' she said.

'Think what?'

'Andy!'

She turned away abruptly. What did she want? More and more often, he felt the weight of something heavy between them. He would catch her looking at him through narrowed eyes. A small sigh and she would turn away, as she did now, and squeeze out the sponge.

He yawned. 'I'm off to bed.'

In the bathroom he stood at the mirror, brushing his teeth. Toni's footsteps ascended the stairs. The bedroom door opened and closed, with a click. His ear still ached. Maybe a parasitic worm was burrowing into his brain. Could he use it as an excuse? *Sorry, sweetheart, I can't have sex tonight because I'm dying.* He paused, toothbrush in hand, and listened. Not a sound. Maybe, if he stayed in the bathroom long enough, Toni might simply fall asleep.

Were all women like this? It wasn't a question he could ask his mates; men didn't talk about such things, not once a steady girlfriend was involved, and besides they would laugh in his face. *She wants THAT MUCH sex? Blimey, and you're complaining, you lucky sod?*

Andy rinsed his mouth. Of course he had had girlfriends in the past but he had never actually lived with one. Moving in with Toni had placed several demands on him but he hadn't predicted this one, nor its result—the mixture of dread and incipient exhaustion as night approached. He loved her but the woman's stamina was astonishing, as indeed was the frequency of her orgasms; they were like the London Tube, a rumble in the tunnel announcing the arrival of yet another one in three minutes' time.

Andy realised that he was sitting on the edge of the bath, his head resting against the wall. How cool the tiles were . . . he could almost nod off now. The trouble was that he desperately needed to sleep. He was a postman, he had to get up at five in the morning.

'Hey, you.'

Toni, eyebrows raised, head on one side, smiled at him. She wore her blue satin dressing gown.

'Time for beddy-byes,' she said, taking his hand.

She led him into the bedroom, shrugged off the dressing gown and swung round to face him. Her midriff was encased in a black lace corset thing that pushed up her breasts; she wore fishnet stockings and high heels.

'Wow,' said Andy.

'Went a bit mad at Brent Cross.' She pulled him down on the bed and unbuckled his belt. 'Let's get these off, big boy.'

Night lights flickered among the teddy bears; it gave them a conspiratorial air. Two dolls leaned together. Andy felt, as always, that he was interrupting something. The soft toys had been talking about him before he came and they would talk about him when he left. The whole bunch of them had it in for him. He had blundered into this girly, pastel room; he had stolen their mistress's affections and he would be punished for it.

Toni peeled off his socks. For a while, after reading an Indian manual, she had been into tantric sex. He had never quite got the hang of it—nor, he suspected, had she. In fact, at one point he had remembered the plumber joke, *you stay in all day and nobody comes*, and had snuffled with laughter, which had killed the whole thing dead.

Toni was straddling him now. She was a heavy girl; they had sunk down into the mattress and she had to steady herself on one knee.

'That's so good, so good,' she moaned, flinging her head back. He tried to concentrate on giving her pleasure, it *was* good, but his mind drifted to the River Lee, to the shady bank he loved and the soft plop as the weight sank into the water . . . And now he was back in his childhood, standing on the beach at Dawlish, skimming pebbles . . . his father, who would soon be gone forever, laying his hand on his shoulder . . .

'Cockee want suckee?' whispered Toni. She lay on top of him, nuzzling his ear and rotating her hips from side to side.

'Not yet,' he panted. He must concentrate on not coming too soon. They were both sweating; their skin, as they moved, made soft little farts.

'Yes . . . oh yes,' she moaned.

Suddenly the desire drained out of him. An image rose in front of his eyes; it was himself, being led around like a prize bull by Toni. She was a competitive girl; there was something grimly determined about her lovemaking, something of the look-at-me about it. She was performing like a porn star not for her teddies but for her girlfriends. *We were at it all night.*

'What's the matter, love?' Toni rolled off him.

'Sorry. Got earache.' This was a lie; his earache had gone.

110

She looked at him, her hair tangled. One of her breasts had popped out of the corset.

'Don't you love me any more?' Blushing, she stuffed the breast back in.

It rose up in a rush—pity for her, for himself. Andy wanted to say: I was thinking of my father, how I don't even know where he lives, whether he's alive or dead. Maybe it was that accident, I don't know. I feel both strange and very tired tonight. He wanted to say: You don't have to prove anything to me. I love you, I'm here, isn't that enough? He wanted to tell her that he admired her, that she had pulled herself out of poverty, out of a family even more dysfunctional than his own, that she had shown more courage and guts than he would ever possess.

'Say something.' Toni lay beside him on the duvet, staring at the ceiling. Now that desire had evaporated, he knew she felt ludicrous in that outfit.

'You seem to have more fun with your girlfriends than with me,' he said, 'nattering away six to the dozen.'

'Yeah, because they *talk*.'

'What do you want me to say?'

'Anything.'

'What do you mean, anything?'

'Oh, I give up!' She heaved herself off the bed. Grabbing her dressing gown, she slammed into the bathroom.

Ryan started crying. Andy heard the muffled wails and then Toni's footsteps. Through the bedroom wall he could hear her crooning to her son. For years it had just been herself and Ryan, alone in the world. She spoilt him rotten but then what did Andy know about being a parent?

Her Snoopy clock said 12.55. Andy's body longed for sleep but his mind was whirring. He knew, for some reason, that he was at a crossroads in his life. He lay there naked, sweating in the heat. Outside this stuffy little house, a house he shared with a large young woman he barely knew, lay a dangerous world where a human being had been snuffed out that very afternoon. Each click of the clock took him nearer his fortieth birthday and the blurred, alarming years beyond it. Here he felt safe. He wasn't an intruder, it was his home too. He shared it with this makeshift little family, whose murmurs he could hear through the wall. A year ago he hadn't known they had existed but a click of his computer had brought them into his life, had brought Toni into his bed. How weird was that?

A breeze blew through the window; one of the night lights guttered and died.

Toni came in. 'He'll be all right now.' She turned her back to Andy and started undressing.

He couldn't bear it. 'I'm sorry,' he said. 'I just feel ...'

'Feel what?' She was bent over, peeling off her stocking. He felt her humiliation, and his failure.

'A lot of things, I guess,' he said. 'Do you mind if I have a cigarette?'

'What?' She straightened up.

His jacket lay on the floor. He rolled over, fumbled inside it and took out his cigarettes. He flung himself against the pillow, exhaling smoke. It was strangely exhilarating, to pollute their boudoir.

'Tell me what's the matter,' she said.

The words came out in a rush. 'I'm not up to it, love. I feel like I'm on display, I feel like you're measuring me up against other blokes. Like Ryan's dad, for instance.'

'Ryan's dad?' Toni sat down, one stocking around her ankle. 'Why?'

'Him being black.'

'What's that got to do with it?'

He sucked in a lungful of smoke. 'You know what they say about black men.'

Toni stared at him. 'You blokes, honestly! Listen, I hardly knew him, he worked out at my gym, we went on a few dates. He wasn't even that great in the sack if you really want to know, it was all over in, like, one nanosecond. Is that really what's been bothering you?'

Andy blushed. 'I guess I've been feeling . . .'

'What?'

'I don't know.'

Toni came over and sat on the bed. She had washed off her make-up; in the flickering light her face looked plainer and more honest. 'Talk to me,' she said.

He could smell her face cream. Suddenly he felt close to her—truly close. He took a breath. 'I just feel—like, I'm not up to scratch. I'm doing this boring job—well, you think it's boring. I'm useless around the house. You've got everything spotless, you're a great little homemaker, and I just get under your feet.' He inspected his cigarette; there was nowhere to stub it out. 'And sometimes . . . you know, *here* . . .' He nodded at the duvet. 'Well, I'm just too bloody tired. But I've got to—like, well . . . you know. But to tell the truth, sometimes I just fancy a mug of Horlicks.'

Toni took his cigarette and squashed it into a night light. 'Why didn't you tell me?'

113

'I thought you'd be hurt.'

She pointed down to her corset. 'This doesn't turn you on?'

He shook his head. 'To be honest.'

She snatched away her hand. 'Now you tell me!'

'It doesn't do you any favours, love.'

'You mean I'm fat?'

'No,' he lied. 'I just like you looking natural.' This seemed the right thing to say but she picked up her dressing gown. He watched her put it on again, her eyes glittering with tears. 'Where are you going?'

'To sleep with Ryan.'

He jumped off the bed and grabbed her. 'Don't be an idiot.'

She shook him off. 'You don't fancy me, do you?' she hissed. 'I'm too fat, aren't I? Think I don't look at myself and think—what on earth does he see in me, good-looking bloke like him? Think my girlfriends aren't mad with jealousy? Nobody thought I'd pull someone like you, I couldn't believe it myself, I still don't believe it, I thought I'd never find anybody, I'd never have a steady boyfriend.' She threw her arms around him and sobbed into his shoulder. 'I know I'm not gorgeous like Jodie and Vick, I know you're going to leave me.'

Andy pushed her away. 'Why would I do that?'

'Cos I'm ugly.'

He looked at her. 'You're not ugly, you're gorgeous.'

She wiped her nose. 'That true?'

'I wouldn't be here otherwise.'

'You never said it.'

'I'm saying it now.'

114

She astonished him, this vulnerable girl who was suddenly revealed to him. Her blunt, naked face gazed up at him as blindly as a puppy.

'Don't cry.' His heart swelled. 'I'll look after you.'

'Will you?' she whispered.

He kissed her damp eyes, one then the other. 'You're safe with me.' He was her man, her protector. It was such a novel sensation that he felt dizzy. She needed him. Her arms tightened around him.

Outside, thunder rumbled. A chill wind blew through the window; the last night lights flickered and died.

'Promise you'll never leave me,' she muttered into his chest. 'Ryan loves you too, he thinks of you as his dad now. He's had a tough time, he'd be gutted if you dumped me.'

'I won't!' he blurted into the darkness. 'I'm here for you. Why don't we get married?'

She froze in his arms. 'You mean that?'

'Of course!' he said, inflamed by his own recklessness. He, Mr Caution. Look at me now!

Toni still hadn't moved. In the silence he could hear the far hum of the North Circular. His life was shifting beneath him.

'On one condition.' Emboldened, he spoke into her hair. 'You get rid of those fucking teddy bears.'

*   *   *

Later, Andy looked back on that night. The curtain between them had lifted and they were revealed to each other. There was a thunderstorm, he remembered that; the summer's heatwave had broken. Afterwards they had climbed into bed, exhausted, and had made love like true lovers, openly and deeply. In the morning he had walked into the sorting office, his eyes stinging from lack of sleep, his limbs as heavy as sandbags. He was filled with a kind of numb exhilaration.

I'm going to get married. He slotted the letters into their pigeonholes, his mates' banter echoing from far away. He was both sealed off and yet somehow united with the human race. This is what blokes did: they got married, they had kids. He told nobody; big with his secret, he joked with his mates as if it were a normal day. Later, as he trudged the streets, he looked at the *Mr and Mrs* on the envelopes. Credit-card bills, boring stuff like that, nobody wrote real letters any more. But even the junk mail felt potent. *Mr and Mrs*; he had cracked the code, he had joined the club. After the storm the streets smelt fresh, even the streets of Neasden, their front gardens concreted into car parks, their rubbish heaped on the kerb. A blackbird sang for him.

Four years had passed since then. The curtains had opened and closed so briefly; that moment of naked honesty had never quite been repeated. They moved into a larger house, in Cricklewood, and spent eighteen months on renovations, the air bedimmed with plaster dust. Toni had revealed herself to be a shrewd businesswoman. Since the crash, property prices had slumped; she had given up her hairdressing job and bought three buy-to-lets in Stratford, near the Olympics, prices were already rocketing. She worked out at the gym, she hired a private tutor for Ryan, who was getting poor grades at school. She was an achiever.

'Why don't you give up your job?' she said. 'The

116

pay's rubbish, you're always exhausted. You could come in with me and project-manage. I'm exchanging on Calthorpe Road next week and it needs a lot of work.'

Andy didn't reply. When she told people *my husband's a postman* she gave a titter. Was she ashamed of him?

Toni looked at him with narrowed eyes. 'Or maybe you like flirting with the housewives.'

'Don't be daft.' He delivered in Neasden; most of his customers were Punjabi. 'Some of them don't even speak English.'

'Who said you have to *talk*?'

Andy shrugged. She hadn't a clue. He pictured the bashful, sari-clad matrons taking delivery of their sons' Amazon parcels and wanted to laugh. He wasn't a flirt; he was a postman, and proud of it. Toni would never understand his feelings of loyalty towards his customers, his knowledge that he played a small but essential role in their lives. In fact, he loved his job. Despite the heavier loads and longer shifts, despite the meddling from management, the targets and directives and corporate bollocks, despite the imploding chaos that was Royal Mail, there was still a sense of camaraderie in the sorting office. He enjoyed the magic of dawn, the suburban streets coming to life. He liked the curious mixture of the solitary and communal that was a postie's working day. He told none of this to Toni. Besides, she had never asked.

'Now you're sulking,' she said.

'I'm not.'

'Ha, you're going all red!' She nudged her son. 'Look, Ryan, Daddy's getting cross.'

'I'm not.' He wanted to say, *I'm not his daddy.*

117

'Here we are.'

They had arrived at the park gates. It was a Saturday and he was taking them on a jaunt.

'Where are we going?' asked Ryan.

'I told you. There's something I want to show you.' Andy led them along the path. 'One of my mates told me about it. It's called Postman's Park because it's near the main sorting office.'

Office buildings reared up around them. Beyond them stood St Paul's Cathedral, unseen but immense.

'There's nothing here,' said Toni.

'Yes there is.'

He led them past the flower beds to a wall of china tiles, sheltered by a roof. They were alone among the plane trees in the hushed little park.

'I thought we were going to the new shopping centre,' said Toni. 'The one by St Paul's. I thought that was the surprise.'

'No. This is.' He pointed to the tiles. 'They were put up in Queen Victoria's time. Go on, read one.'

'What?'

'Read one. They're amazing.'

Toni looked at him, puzzled. She stepped closer and peered at a tile. '*Frederick Alfred Croft, aged 31, saved a lunatic woman from suicide at Woolwich Arsenal Station but was himself run over by the train.*'

'Gross,' said Ryan.

'Look, this boy's your age,' said Andy. '*Henry James Bristow, aged 7, saved his little sister's life by tearing off her flaming clothes but caught fire himself and died of burns and shock.*' He looked down at Ryan. 'They're just ordinary people, like us, who did really brave things. These are their memorials.'

'What a twat,' said Ryan, rummaging in his

118

nostril.

Toni sat down on a bench. 'I don't believe this. You sick or something?' She shook her head wonderingly. 'You brought us all the way here to look at *this*? Know how weird that is?'

'I just thought—it was kind of inspirational—'

'Look at Ryan! You've *so* totally freaked him out.'

They looked at Ryan's bent head. He was sitting on the grass, playing on his Nintendo DS.

'He looks all right to me,' said Andy.

'He'll be having nightmares for weeks.'

Ryan looked up. 'This is boring. I want to go home.'

'See?' Toni got to her feet. 'He needs to get out of here, it's cree-eepy.' She grabbed Ryan's hand. 'Come along, darling. Let's go and find an ice cream.'

*   *   *

Mrs Enid Price lived at 12 Arnos Drive, Neasden. Andy had been delivering her mail for years. She was an elderly widow, racist and testy, but he was fond of her. She was lonely, her neighbours had left, one by one, to be replaced by multi-occupancies and by Indian families with whom she had little in common; sometimes Andy suspected that he was the only person she spoke to all day. In the way of postmen, he was intimate with her life. He knew about her old schoolfriend in Wigan (shakily written address), the state of her finances (final demands), her love of birds (RSPB magazine). Sometimes she grabbed his arm with her ruthless fingers. 'I need your help, young man,'

119

she said, and propelled him into her lounge to swat a wasp or shift a piece of furniture. She told him about her late husband, how he had been a medical auxiliary in the war, pulling out bodies from the rubble, how he had never truly recovered. Sometimes Andy would stop by, at the end of his round, and have a cup of tea.

And then Enid broke her hip. She returned from hospital diminished and confused. Every morning she was sitting at the window, waiting for him. 'They seem to have put me into some sort of hotel,' she said.

'It's not a hotel, love. It's your house.'

Her finger kneaded his arm. 'Get me out of here, I want to go home.'

As the weeks passed she grew more and more disorientated.

'There's a man upstairs in my bed,' she whispered. 'And there's another one in my wardrobe. I've never believed in threesomes and I'm not going to start now.'

That night, Andy repeated the remark to Toni. He thought they could have a laugh; she was always complaining that he never talked to her enough.

Toni looked at him thoughtfully. 'Gaga, is she?'

Andy nodded. 'The nurse arrived when I was there. They're going to put her into a home.'

Toni paused, spatula in hand. She was frying chicken thighs. 'Pass me the tarragon, will you?'

Andy thought no more of it. He was used to these mild disappointments, these disconnects. More and more he felt lonely in his own home. Maybe if they had a baby things would change, but she was still on the pill and it seemed too intimate a topic to bring into the conversation. When did one broach the subject? He hadn't a clue.

It was a week later. Snow had fallen during the night. The streets were hushed with a lunar stillness; his footsteps crunched as he walked up Enid's path. He was thinking about Postman's Park and whether he was capable of an act of selfless heroism. Enid's husband had pulled strangers from burning buildings but how could a man be tested now? Was he really so weird, to find the plaques affecting?

Enid opened the door. 'A nice lady visited me yesterday,' she said, taking her letters. 'We had a cup of tea. She wants to buy my house.'

He thought no more of it. For all he knew, it might have been one of her delusions. Later, however, when he arrived home from work, he heard Toni's voice in the kitchen. She was on her mobile, her voice raised in excitement. He paused in the hallway.

'She's a batty old bag, she's no idea what it's worth. I said to her, *you don't need an estate agent, they'll cost you an arm and a leg and they're all rubbish—*'

She must have heard him arriving, because she closed the door.

*   *   *

He remembered now: he had told Toni the address. She must have sneaked out to Arnos Drive; she hadn't told him, she knew it was wrong.

That night, as he lay beside his sleeping wife, Andy knew that his marriage was over. He and Toni were strangers who happened to be sharing a house. In an odd way it was a relief, to put it into

121

words. In fact, he felt a curious exhilaration. It was like feeling vaguely ill and finally being diagnosed with cancer. Painful as it was, he could now admit the problem and do something about it. Funnily enough he was almost grateful to discover—to *confirm*—that Toni was a ruthless young woman who could take advantage of a senile widow.

He hadn't tackled her about it; he hated confrontation. Besides, what would be the point? The house business had just made clear to him something which, deep down, he had known all along. Andy lay there staring at the ceiling, the Snoopy clock ticking the minutes—no, ticking the countdown. For he knew, as more snow fell silently outside the window, that this was the beginning of the end.

He dreamed he was sitting in an aeroplane that wouldn't take off. It bounced through the streets, its wings banging against the houses on either side. He could hear the houses collapsing and people wailing. Children were buried in the rubble but all he could do was sit helplessly strapped into his seat as the plane lurched along on its trail of devastation.

Andy woke drenched with sweat. Snow bathed the room with light. It was Sunday; he heard Toni downstairs, rattling around in the kitchen, her murmurs as she spoke to her son. Last night's certainty had disappeared; he lay there, rigid with dread and confusion. Could he really bail out? That's what his father had done—packed up and buggered off. Men did it all the time. He pictured himself pulling down his suitcase from the top of the wardrobe, bringing with it an avalanche of teddy bears from their place of exile. How could he

122

do that to Ryan? The boy would feel that it was his fault, just as he himself had done at his age.

Andy rolled over and buried his head in the pillow. Did he really have the courage to tell Toni that their marriage was over? Did he really believe it himself, in the cold light of day? Could he walk downstairs and, in one sentence, drop the bombshell? He pictured Toni collapsing onto the floor, screaming with fury, her face streaming with tears. Perhaps she would attack him, pummelling him with her fists while Ryan wailed from the sidelines. How could he be responsible for such misery? What had she done to deserve it? People rubbed along, after all. He himself was probably not the easiest person to live with; she was always complaining that he only talked about football and fishing. The thought of dismantling their life together filled him with terror. He would grow old alone, living in a bedsit overlooking the North Circular, a man beloved by no one. Perhaps he should forget the whole thing and take the two of them out tobogganing.

Andy got up. He showered, shaved and went downstairs. Ryan was in the front room, playing on his computer. Shouldn't a boy his age be outdoors throwing snowballs? Toni was sitting at the kitchen table, working on her laptop.

Andy stood with his back to her, spooning coffee into the Gaggia machine. Toni had bought it at John Lewis the week before. She was a serious shopper but then she was making serious money nowadays, she was a businesswoman with a property portfolio, she had hauled herself up from nowhere by sheer determination. The TV makeover shows had inspired her, aspirational couples

123

gasping over colour schemes and tripling their investment. And why not? This morning Andy felt strangely tolerant—indeed, he rather admired her for it. How weird was that? Was that because he was going to leave her?

Andy thought: I must speak now before I change my mind. He said: 'I don't think this is working.'

With a sigh, Toni scraped back her chair and joined him at the machine. 'I told you, you have to push down that knob.'

'No,' he said. 'I mean us.'

There was a pause. Toni walked across the room and closed the door. She stood there, leaning against it.

'I know,' she said.

Andy was astonished. Outside, the great snowbound world lay silent around them.

'*I'd* better make the coffee,' she said, and came over. She unscrewed the metal cup. 'Look, I'll show you. You fill this up, here, and screw the lid down like this.' She stopped. 'Actually, what's the point?'

'What do you mean?'

'You don't need to know how to work it, do you?' She busied herself with the machine. 'Not now.'

'I didn't say—'

'Yes you did. We can't go on like this. You're right.' She wrenched the lever tight. 'You don't even try any more.'

'Try what?'

'To show an interest in what I've been doing. To say nice things. You did a bit, once, but that stopped long ago. I could be wearing a bin bag and you wouldn't notice.'

'That's not true—'

124

'Yes it is!' The machine started to hiss. She glared at him through the jets of steam. 'It's like I'm not even here, you hardly talk to me, we never do anything together, I might as well not exist. You don't even have the decency to use the air-freshener when you've been to the toilet.' The cups rattled as she put them in their saucers. 'You want froth?'

'Black's fine.'

The door opened and Ryan came in.

'Go away!' she snapped. 'Mummy's talking.'

Ryan backed away. Andy closed the door.

Toni put the cups on the table. 'Got a cigarette?' she asked.

Andy stared at her. 'You want one?' He reached behind the microwave, where he had hidden the packet.

'I used to smoke,' she said, taking a cigarette. 'I gave up when I was pregnant with Ryan.'

'I didn't know that.'

'You don't know anything, do you?'

'You never told me.'

'You never asked.'

He lit their cigarettes. She inhaled deeply and blew out a plume of smoke. It made her look like an unknown woman, like an actress.

Andy had no idea what to say; the room expanded around him.

'You've never really loved me, have you?' she said.

'Of course I have!'

She shook her head. 'That's why I didn't want a baby. I knew you'd dump me, like Ryan's dad did.'

'No I wouldn't.'

'Oh yeah?' She looked at him, her eyes glittering with tears. 'So what the fuck do you think you're

125

doing now?'

'We don't have to break up,' he said weakly.

'Don't be stupid. Of course we do. I've seen it coming for months.'

*   *   *

Over the next few days the strangest thing happened. Now they knew their marriage was over the tension lifted; the words had been said, the decision made, and there was a curious sense of release in the air. They treated each other gently, like invalids. They stopped snapping at each other; they weren't angry, just fathomlessly sad. And suddenly the floodgates opened; they found themselves talking late into the night, like passengers on a long-haul flight, strangers who had sat next to each other for twelve hours but who only start chatting when the plane begins its descent. Toni told him how she had been bullied at school because her mother was in the nuthouse. Andy told her about his fruitless search for his father, his fury and drinking, his botched relationships with girls. And more, much more. Why had they never talked like this when they faced a lifetime together?

So, now their marriage was over, they finally became friends. No, not friends—intimates in sorrow. They took Ryan tenpin bowling and told him that Andy was moving out but that he wouldn't go far and would still take him to the football. Toni and her son closed ranks, reverting to their previous survival mode; though Ryan was already overweight she stuffed him with pizza and let him play on his computer until the small hours. How could Andy blame them? Financial arrangements were made;

Toni took out a loan to repay him the meagre amount he had put into the house. She was brisk and businesslike, working out the sums on her computer in a fug of smoke, for she was back on the fags.

Whether she bought Mrs Price's house was no longer his concern. Royal Mail went through another lunatic spasm of reorganisation and he was transferred to Harrow; in the throes of removals his customers slipped forgotten into the past. Toni helped him pack up his belongings, her pale, doughy face naked, her hair pulled back in a rubber band like a chavvy single parent. She *was* a single parent. This desexed woman broke his heart. He thought how strange it was that the curtains between them had parted only twice, once at the beginning and once at the end of their marriage.

On the eve of his departure Toni cut his hair, as if preparing him for a long journey.

'Property's effing lonely,' she said. 'All the builders are from Ukraine, they talk even less than you.' She sighed. 'I miss the salon. We had a laugh, me and the girls.'

'What did you talk about?' He remembered her girlfriends gathered in the lounge, the shrieks and giggles, the silence when he entered. 'What *do* women talk about?'

Snip-snip went her scissors. 'Blokes like you, of course.'

10

Buffy

For once it was warm. Buffy sat in the garden drinking wine with his sons, Tobias and Bruno. The two young men lay slumped on the grass—a matted expanse of dandelions, now gone to seed, it could hardly be called a lawn. They had stopped for the night en route home from the Crazy Sheep Festival, where it had poured with rain for three days. Needless to say, the sun had appeared just as everybody was packing up. This seemed to be the norm, with festivals.

They had arrived matted with mud and stinking of trench foot. Reverting to their younger selves, also the norm with festivals, they had consumed copious amounts of drugs and, upon their arrival at Myrtle House, had gone to bed in a catatonic trance, sleeping for fourteen hours surrounded by the disgorged contents of their rucksacks. Luckily the only other guests were a young family who left a similar trail of destruction behind them. Through the open window of the utility room Buffy could hear the grunts of the tumble dryer as it coped with the mountains of washing.

'Mum came too,' said Bruno. 'God, it was embarrassing. She *danced.*'

India joined them, collapsing on the grass. 'Nobody should see their mother dancing,' she said. 'Specially after she's had a couple of spliffs.'

'We had to hide in our tent,' said Tobias. 'Luckily she couldn't face the toilets so she went home.'

Buffy remembered how Jacquetta danced, swaying in her loose, ethnic layers, jewellery swinging, her eyes closed in showy self-absorption. In the early days he had found it mildly erotic but as time passed her exclusion of everyone else, himself included, had drained away his lust and he had stopped joining her on the dance floor. He doubted that she noticed.

'It's embarrassing watching *anyone* dance for the first time,' said India. 'It's like hearing them speaking French.'

She rolled over and held out her glass. Buffy, who was sitting in a chair, leaned down and filled it. He was very fond of India, though in fact she was just his stepdaughter, the product of Jacquetta's earlier marriage to a man called Alan and named to celebrate the place of her conception, an ashram in Bangalore. Buffy pitied India; a name like that, and its explanation, seemed a good deal more embarrassing than dancing, and would last a lifetime. The sixties had a lot to answer for.

'So what's the big plan, Dad?' asked Tobias.

Buffy gazed down at his long, lean son, his bare feet protruding from his jeans. He had mentioned something the night before but he presumed they were too stoned to listen.

'I'm going to run residential courses for people who're just divorced,' he said.

Bruno sat up. 'What?'

'Or just broken up,' said Buffy. 'Split up. Something I'm a bit of an expert in.'

'Courses?' asked India. 'What sort of courses?'

'Where they learn the skill the other person had. Say, gardening or DIY. I got the idea from somebody who had lost her way trying to get to

129

Blandford Forum. She was going to a course on basic car maintenance. She said her boyfriend had always taken care of that side of things but now she was alone she needed to feel empowered.'

'Empowered?' Tobias raised his eyebrows. All three of them were now sitting up.

'Your stepmother Penny, for instance,' said Buffy. 'She knew how the boiler worked, and the video, and all sorts of stuff around the flat. When she buggered off with that photographer I was as helpless as a baby. If it had happened now I could've gone on one of my courses and not been such a pathetic wreck.' His voice rose in excitement. 'There'll be courses on all sorts of things—Household Finances—'

Tobias burst out laughing. '*You*, teaching Household Finances? But you live in total chaos, you file everything under M for Miscellaneous.'

'Not me,' said Buffy patiently. 'Other people; I'm already asking around. I'm only going to teach one of the courses.' He remembered Janet Pritchard's complaint about her husband. Indeed, Sita's complaint about her boyfriend. 'It'll be called "How to Talk to Women".'

The three of them were now doubled up with laughter. Tobias clutched his stomach as if in physical pain.

Buffy, offended, said: 'Voda thinks it's a marvellous idea. We'll have full occupancy throughout the week. There's room for five guests here, more if they share, and if we're oversubscribed there's other B&Bs nearby.'

'Everyone'll be shagging!' Tobias chortled. 'Rebound sex—wow, it'll be a total fuckathon.'

'No, that must be against the rules.' India looked

serious. 'People will be feeling very fragile when they get here—'

'Heartbreak Hotel!' said Tobias, humming the tune.

'—I know I did when Guy dumped me.'

'Who's Guy?' asked Buffy.

'It doesn't matter,' India said. 'It's all over.'

Buffy felt the familiar lurch of melancholy. How much was he missing, stuck out here in Wales? But then how much had he missed throughout the lives of the three people at his feet, now humming together tunelessly? After all, in the eyes of the world they were grown up. Bruno, who worked in IT, lived in Shepherd's Bush with his pregnant girlfriend; Tobias did graphics; India made jewellery. Buffy only knew the bare bones of their lives but maybe this would have been the case if he had stayed married to their mother. Divorce skewed a man's perceptions and poisoned them with guilt.

'Since my baby left me, I've found a new place to dwell . . .' They swayed side by side, singing in unison as the dandelion clocks floated around the garden. Buffy felt a surge of optimism. The sun was shining; the more he spoke of it, the more his idea gained weight and conviction. Why had nobody thought of it before?

They ate lunch in the kitchen, which still smelt of the morning's fry-up. Buffy told them his catering plans—a simple midday meal but a full sit-down dinner, cooked by the 'Basic Cookery' class. He pointed out of the window. 'And the "Gardening for Beginners" can sort that out. Cunning or what? Set the students to work! What could be a neater way of utilising labour?'

131

And a necessary one. The problem was, he had to make some money, and fast. The roof was leaking, the window sashes were rotting. Maybe he could set up a course in 'Basic Home Repairs'! Nyange's visit, a few weeks earlier, had faced him with the grim reality. Of course he had owned houses before, but none as vast or ramshackle as this—the gas bill itself was jaw-dropping. Besides, in the past he had earned some sort of income—a fluctuating one, to be sure, but in his prime his mellifluous tones were much in demand; his voice-over for Dyno-Rod had redecorated his house in Primrose Hill. And, oh the joy of the returning series! Though First Usher in *Crown Court* was by no means a major role, that old sod Andrew Cruikshank having nabbed the part of Judge, it did fund his sons' progress through the private schools that Jacquetta had insisted they attend, even though they emerged with a cannabis habit and Estuary accents.

Fig's yapping announced the return of Voda from the cash 'n' carry. India jumped up and helped her unload tins of paint. The two young women had taken an instant liking to each other, and as he watched them Buffy noticed their physical resemblance—both stocky and purposeful, with unruly dark hair. India, however, had a Londoner's pallor while Voda's cheeks were even redder than usual. So, in fact, were her lips. Was it possible that she was wearing make-up? There was a skittish air about her, too, which was unusual—the way she giggled at something India said and clapped her hand to her mouth. Did she have the hots for one of his sons? Hopefully not for Bruno who had a girlfriend already and a pregnant one at that. His girlfriend's resentment at his skiving off when she was seven months gone had surfaced in a series of texts which had briefly beeped to life when his mobile got a signal on the way to Knockton, and disappeared again.

Buffy told them about the front room, which he was going to convert into a bar and lecture theatre for his students. This was situated on the other side of the hallway from the dining room; until recently it had been used as a storeroom by a friend of Bridie's who collected railway memorabilia—boxes of timetables and assorted junk.

'He's an old boy called Lenny,' said Buffy. 'I think she had a thing with him.'

'Nobody has a thing with a railway enthusiast,' said Bruno. 'That's why they're railway enthusiasts.'

'Bridie wasn't too picky, bless her,' said Buffy, hoping that this hadn't applied to himself. 'Anyway, I let him keep the room for old times' sake but he's had to sell the lot off to pay for his care home. We're going to tart it up with a lick of paint.'

His sons were driving back to London that afternoon but to his surprise India offered to stay on and do some wallpaper-stripping. Buffy helped Tobias and Bruno gather up their vast collection of clothes, some of which were draped over the bushes in the garden, bade them goodbye and padded off for his snooze.

When he emerged, promptly at the cocktail hour, he heard shrieks of laughter coming from the room downstairs. He paused on the landing. The evening sun shone through the fanlight. Already he could imagine the convivial clink of glasses, the rapt silence as he shared his wisdom with rows of blokey, unreconstructed men who'd only spoken to women in monosyllables, the burst of applause as he finished with a flourish. There would be amusing anecdotes from his own past—even humiliating ones (plenty to choose from, there)—and of course he'd crack some jokes to break the tension. *I don't think I'll get married again. I'll just find a woman I don't like and give her a house.*

Buffy went down to the front room. India and Voda were sitting side by side on the floor smoking roll-ups. He looked at Voda in surprise; he had no idea she smoked. One wall was half scraped; strips of paper hung down, lolling like tongues.

'I was telling her about my stepfather,' said India.

'Not me, I hope,' Buffy.

'Of course not you. I wouldn't slag you off in your own home. We were talking about Leon.'

'He sounds a right tosser,' said Voda.

Leon was the celebrity shrink to whom Jacquetta had confided her marital woes—in other words, Buffy's hopelessness as a husband—and with whom she eventually absconded, taking his Ivon Hitchens with her.

'I was trying to explain our family,' said India. 'Who was married to who, and who had children with who, but she's got a bit lost. In fact, so have I.'

'One really needs a paper and pencil,' said Buffy.

'No,' said India. 'A bloody wall chart.'

'Wish my parents had got divorced,' said Voda, stubbing out her cigarette. 'Then I wouldn't have had to hear them shagging in their bender.'

'Or them hear *you*,' said India.

'And the *rows*,' said Voda. 'Even worse than Conor and me.' She sighed. 'He's such a moody bugger. Like, he even gets irritated by the way I wash up. He can sulk for weeks, long after I've

134

forgotten what it was all about.'

'Like a child who stomps off with its suitcase and nobody notices it's gone so it has to crawl back home,' said India. 'I did that once.'

'Did you?' asked Buffy.

'But then Mum never noticed anything. I could've been away for months.'

Voda sat there, deep in her own thoughts. 'It's ever so peaceful with him in prison,' she said. 'No temper tantrums when the van doesn't start, no fag ends in the loo. And he would have made me drown the kittens. To tell the truth, I'm dreading him coming out.'

Buffy raised his eyebrows. Voda had never spoken so openly before. But then Buffy was her employer, and a bloke—doddery, portly, unthreatening, but still unmistakably a bloke. It was India who had loosened her inhibitions.

The two women carried on stripping the wall. They looked so companionable together; they even seemed to be scraping in unison. He was glad they were getting on so well. Voda was telling India about her brother's squint, and how the commune briefly tried to cure it with their cult chant—to no avail, surprise surprise. How Aled had found solace in cows, the only creatures that had given him real affection. From there they segued seamlessly, as women so often did, onto the subject of their disastrous love lives, with particular reference to India's hopeless exes.

Buffy heard this with interest; they seemed to have forgotten that he was there. He thought: Funny, isn't it, that no woman needs a course called 'Talking to Women'. They just do it all the time.

A makeshift bar was installed in the corner of the room. It was a battered mahogany counter that Voda had found in a skip outside a community hall when playing a darts match in Brecon. A stack of plastic chairs was purloined, following a tip-off that, due to the cuts, the local drop-in centre was closing down. The room was taking shape. To add a personal touch, Buffy hung the walls with framed playbills which he had found stacked in the cellar. They included a production of *The Rivals* in which he had played the lead. His younger, slimmer self, bewigged with corkscrew curls, gazed out from the photograph. The raised eyebrow, the insolent smirk—what a swagger there was to him then! For the first—and last—time, he had seen his name in lights on Shaftesbury Avenue. Now, however, damp had crept beneath the glass; a tea-coloured stain corrugated half his face, like a birthmark.

Gazing at his image, Buffy thought of the characters he had played, from Sir Anthony Absolute to Hammy the Hamster. They belonged to another life. Actors might strut and fret upon the stage but they were basically children dressing up in costumes. He was now the proprietor of a guest house with a licence for alcohol to be consumed on the premises. At long last, indeed at the ripe old age of seventy-one, he almost felt like a grown-up.

His plans were taking shape; the search was now on for tutors. Later that day he was meeting a chap called Nolan in the pub. Nolan, like the drop-in centre, was a victim of the cuts; until recently he had worked as a labourer for the local council but had now been made redundant. His passion, however, was cars. Apparently he had two lock-ups near the bypass that were charnel houses of dismembered vehicles; this, and a sunny disposition, made him a possible candidate for the car maintenance course.

There was also the question of advertising. Buffy was pondering this as he walked around the bedrooms replenishing the freebies—shampoo miniatures, tea bags, biscuits. Needless to say they were always pocketed—even, pathetically enough, the sachets of sugar.

Should he put an ad in a lonely hearts page, an upmarket one like the *London Review of Books*? Were lovelorn bluestockings his core clientele? More to the point, did he want to fill his house with them? Penny would know what to do. Standing in the Pink Room, Buffy suddenly had a pang for his ex-wife. She was a journalist, a hack to her core, with a wily lateral mind that had proved useful in the past. Not always, it had to be said, to his advantage. Particularly not, when it concerned her adultery. He remembered Penny's 'press trips' abroad, how she returned suntanned, how she amused him with stories about her fellow freeloaders while unpacking gifts of exotic foodstuffs. How in fact she had simply gone to ground in her lover's Soho flat, hastily slapping on the bronzer and buying pasta from Camisa's before breezily returning home in a taxi 'from the airport'.

One had to admire her chutzpah. He hadn't then, of course. But it was all so long ago, the years had passed and it all seemed like a dream. Buffy stood there, watching a spider lowering itself from the ceiling. It did it with such insouciance; did it really know where it was going, and did it really

137

want to get there?

Penny did. She was smart and ruthless, with a nose for a story. When some friend burst into tears, confiding some childhood trauma, she would stiffen like a fox scenting a rabbit—could she write a piece about it? Nothing was wasted, from sexual abuse to a dropped hem. Penny could always cobble together a thousand words, and bung it off to anything from the *Daily Mail* to one of the glossies. One had to admire her for it. She was also fun—a lot more fun than her predecessor Jacquetta, of whom she was furiously jealous. Buffy remembered Penny's first visit to his country cottage, where the cesspit was being cleaned out. 'Thank God,' she had said. 'I don't want any old wife's droppings in there.'

'Lunch!' Voda yelled up the stairs. Buffy jumped. Was it really that late? How long had he been standing there, clutching a box of UHT milk pots? This happened more and more often nowadays. Voda called him a lazy old sod but he was just ambushed by the past. There was so much of it, waiting to immobilise him in a sunlit bedroom.

As he walked downstairs Penny's voice was still in his head. *Don't waste your money on an ad, silly. Get someone to write a piece about it.*

*   *   *

Roy was a raddled old hack who worked for the *Radnorshire Echo*. Buffy had bumped into him some months earlier, when their respective dogs were relieving themselves in the churchyard. He knew where to find Roy—in the bar of the Knockton Arms Hotel, at the far end of town. Buffy

138

usually avoided the place due to Daffyd the barman's insistence on addressing him in the squeaky voice of Voley, a joke which had long since run out of steam, if it had had any in the first place. Today, however, a monosyllabic Latvian was on duty. The place was empty except for Roy, who sat at the bar attempting to engage the chap in conversation.

He turned, relieved, when Buffy came in. 'Hello, old cock! What brings you to this den of iniquity?'

They sat down in the snug with a couple of sharpeners. In his youth Roy had been a Marxist firebrand, firing off rabble-rousing polemics in the *Manchester Guardian*. Moving to London, and to the right, he had worked for the red tops in the good old days of Fleet Street, propping up the bar at El Vino's and picking up gossip for the showbiz pages. Buffy had glimpsed him at various watering holes and indeed been interviewed by him when cast in a *Morse*, a cameo that had subsequently hit the cutting-room floor. Roy had long since retired to Wales with his wife, a tough old bird whose skin was kippered by the fags and with whom he dined at four-star hostelries in exchange for shameless puffs in the local paper.

Buffy told him his plan.

'I'll see what I can do,' Roy said. 'It's the silly season after all, they're gagging for stories. You want one of the nationals, of course—big readership, someone might bite. Nobody round here would be stupid enough to pay for one of your courses.' He thought for a moment. 'The *Daily Express* owes me one. Managed to blag my way into the green room at the Hay Festival and fed them a very tasty little item.' He chuckled. 'Caught one of the PM's aides in the khazi, stuffing Bolivian marching powder up his nostrils.'

'Do I want *Daily Express* readers?' asked Buffy.

'You old snob. Anyway, you'd be surprised who reads it. They all say it was lying around at the doctor's, of course.'

Roy was right; it had to be a national. Buffy suspected that nobody read the local paper unless their runner beans were up for a prize. News items ranged from 'Mystery of the Mobility Scooter' which had been spotted in someone's front garden, the only clue to its ownership a pair of gentleman's gloves, to the rumour of a panther roaming the countryside under cover of darkness. A reporter, wearing night goggles, was dispatched to lie in wait, only to discover after a week of staking it out that it was an overweight tom. This story, apparently, cropped up every summer.

So Roy wrote a piece for the *Daily Express*. It was accompanied by a photo of Buffy, bearded and beaming in his panama hat, standing outside Myrtle House, a *No Vacancies* sign displayed prominently in the window.

> Viewers of a certain vintage might remember him as the gaff-prone landlord in TV's *Bed and Board*, shamefully pulled after one series. Now, however, retired actor Russell Buffery, 71, has taken on the role for real. A year ago a dear friend bequeathed him her B&B in the picturesque town of Knockton. 'It was a bolt from the blue,' says Russell 'Buffy' Buffery, relaxing in the garden of the period property. 'But I was ready for a new challenge, away from the hustle and bustle of the city.'

Swapping the greasepaint for the paintbrush, he set about restoring the handsome Georgian building to its former glory and it was soon up and running as a thriving business. 'Every actor likes to play to a full house,' he jokes, 'and I was set for a long run.'

However, never content to rest on his laurels, the energetic thesp has hit on a novel idea. Himself no stranger to the marriage-go-round—'Shame there are no repeat fees,' he jokes, 'or I'd be a rich man'—he has now set up Courses for Divorces. 'So you've split up,' he says. 'It happens to the best of us. But marriage is a division of labour and chances are you've relied on your better half for something you can't do yourself—fixing the house, sorting out the finances. When they've gone, you're as helpless as a baby. Enrol at Myrtle House and in a week you'll be able to stand on your own two feet. This, plus the beautiful countryside and three-course dinners with locally sourced products, will set you on the road to recovery.' The first course, 'Basic Car Maintenance', starts on 15 September. 'It's cheaper than therapy,' he adds, with his trademark chuckle. 'And who knows? Maybe it won't just be the spark plugs that ignite.'

11

Amy

'I've never read the *Express* before,' said Rosemary. 'I happened to see it at the dentist's.'

'Me too,' said Amy. 'At the doctor's.'

The two of them had checked in at the same time. It turned out they were sharing a twin-bedded room.

'Our host looks vaguely familiar,' said Rosemary. 'Perhaps I've met him somewhere before.'

'He's an actor,' said Amy. 'I did his make-up once, for a *Miss Marple*. I've only just realised.'

'Is that what you do? How glamorous!'

'Not really.'

'I adore *Miss Marple*. Especially when what's-her-name plays her.' Rosemary unzipped her suitcase and started pulling out her clothes. 'I haven't shared a room with anyone but Douggie for forty years,' she said. 'Still, I don't mind if you don't. As long as you don't snore.'

'I don't think I do,' said Amy. 'Nobody's complained.'

'Douggie did, like a warthog in labour. Had to jab him with my elbow.' Rosemary pulled out her sponge bag. 'At least we've got our own sink.' She looked at the washbasin. 'Haven't seen avocado since Edward Heath was PM. Before your time, dear.'

Amy was relieved to have a room-mate of senior years. Some willowy creature in a thong would make her feel even more inadequate than she felt already. Rosemary was a big-boned woman from Aldershot; she wore a navy skirt and floral blouse. Her husband had apparently been in some regiment or other before he had retired and promptly decamped with the waitress at his golf club. 'What an utter ass,' Rosemary said. 'No fool like an old fool. God knows what she sees in him.' All this Amy had gathered before they had dumped their suitcases on the beds.

In truth, Amy was glad of the company. The recession had hit the film industry; she hadn't had a job for six months and had been spending far too long alone in her flat. Worse still, the illegal immigrants upstairs had disappeared and been replaced by a couple with a baby. At night its wails morphed into the cries of her own dream-baby, newborn and snuffling at her nipple. A tiny Neville, it gazed up at her with such love that her insides melted. And then she woke up to the desolate reality. She was thirty-five, with no boyfriend and the clock ticking.

'I've brought my gardening trousers,' said Rosemary, carrying them to the wardrobe. 'I presume we'll get covered with oil, fiddling under a bonnet or something. They've already been demoted from my going-to-the-shops trousers, they're pretty disgusting.'

Amy had just brought another pair of jeans. This was lucky as there were only four mismatched hangers in the wardrobe, and Rosemary had bagged three. She had, however, brought along a couple of spare jumpers as Wales was rumoured to be cold. It *was* chilly; the sash window seemed to be jammed, slightly open, at an angle. Rosemary had found a blow heater which blasted out a smell of

143

singed fur.

The room must once have been gracious. Now, however, a piece of hardboard blocked the fireplace and the floral wallpaper had faded. On the wall hung a photograph of John Gielgud as Prospero (studio lighting, plenty of slap), signed with a flourish to *dearest Bridie*. It was on the top floor; she could see over the rooftops to the hills, where the sky was heaped with bruised, mutinous clouds.

Amy's spirits lifted; she felt the alert buoyancy of the new arrival. It was good to get out of London. Though she had travelled all over the world she had never been to Wales and the first sight of the mountains, seen from the M5, had thrilled her, despite the ominous rattle in the engine of her Punto. Still, this Nolan Evans, whoever he was, would surely be able to identify the problem and sort her out. He was the course tutor. And already, as the sky darkened, she could smell the promising aroma of dinner cooking.

Buffy

Buffy found it hard to believe that it was actually happening. Despite all the planning, an air of unreality still hung over the whole enterprise. It had failed to disperse, even with the arrival of six strangers who were now thudding around in the rooms upstairs, getting ready for dinner. He had imagined it for so long that his dreamed guests floated like a hologram over the solid human beings, he couldn't connect them up. Still less could he visualise a five-day course on car maintenance actually materialising. He was filled with panic. The

144

whole idea was insane. What happened if Nolan didn't turn up and he was left with a houseful of people shuffling around like penned cattle, the rain streaming down the windows? What could he do with them—play racing demon?

But then, eighteen months ago, he couldn't have imagined running a guest house in a small town in Wales. How unlikely was that? It still felt odd to be in possession of a credit-card machine. More often than not, his guests had become his friends. He remembered a pleasantly inebriated afternoon with a brass-rubber called Mavis. The heating had broken down; she lay curled in a blanket on the cracked leather sofa and told him about an affair she had conducted with a long-distance lorry driver, how she had crouched in a roadside ditch to insert her Dutch cap and got stung with nettles. He had told her about his breezily uninhibited first wife, Popsi, how she used to sit on the lavatory, squirting cream on her diaphragm with the skilled insouciance of a *pâtissier* anointing a tartlet. They had moved on to disastrous sexual encounters, a conversation which had become increasingly competitive and which they had finally agreed a tie. The following morning it had felt weirder than usual to trouser her cheque.

'Fuck off, Fig!' India kicked the dog away and turned to Buffy. 'Can't you lock him up somewhere?'

The kitchen was filled with steam. She and Voda were furiously chopping and frying, India acting as sous-chef. India had volunteered to help for the five days. Buffy was deeply touched; it warmed the cockles of his old heart, that she had driven all the way from London to support her stepdad. 'No worries,' she said. 'I needed a break.' Besides, she had fallen in love with Knockton, with its jovial butcher, its thrift shops run by raddled hippies, and Audrey's dusty emporium, with its tottering cardboard boxes of bedroom slippers. 'Is this what it's like everywhere?' India had asked. 'When it's not London?' She was staying at Voda's cottage as—for the first time—all the bedrooms were occupied.

Buffy gazed fondly at the two young women, their faces damp with sweat; at the nicotined ceiling, the strip light bespattered with flies; at the sink heaped with pans. If this wasn't real, what was? And now the doorbell was ringing with a late arrival; it would soon be time for him to pull off his apron and take charge behind the bar.

Amy

'I'm *so* not a beach person,' said Lou, spearing a carrot. 'I mean, what's the point of lying around in the sun? I like to learn something on my holidays.' Munching, she ticked off the courses she had attended—Scuba-Diving, Spanish for Beginners, the Courage to Sing. 'Actually, I'm not that interested in cars—if mine goes wrong I just call the AA. But this was the only course with any vacancies left.'

Lou worked in a secretarial position for a law firm in Droitwich. She had sallow skin, pitted with acne scars. For a small person she could certainly pack it away, but then the food was delicious— tomato 'n' basil tart followed by Welsh lamb and roasted vegetables, with plum syllabub for pudding.

146

Her eyes flickered around the room. Amy recognised a fellow lonely heart—the ruthlessly straightened hair, the eager perusal of the assembled company, the chronic disappointment.

'Silly me,' Lou sighed. 'I should have realised it would all be women.'

There was, in fact, one bloke. Amy had chatted to him over the welcoming drinks. She hadn't caught his name and it was too late to ask now. Otherwise, Lou was right. There were nine women of various ages sitting at the two tables, eating dinner in the candlelight. Some of them were staying elsewhere; they had the faintly wistful, excluded air of day pupils at a boarding school. For the residents had already bonded, chiefly in the queue for the bathroom.

'Not quite the facilities I expected,' said Rosemary, who was sharing their table. 'But that's part of its charm. Douggie would have kicked up a fuss but he's not here, is he? Rather a relief actually.' She snorted with satisfaction. 'Now *she's* got to put up with his grumbling. And his snoring. Serves her right, the conniving little cow.' Douggie had tried to take the car but she had hidden the keys. 'I can just see them, shivering at the bus stop in the rain. Love's young dream or what?' She drained her glass. 'I give the whole thing three months.'

Rosemary had enrolled on the course in a spirit of rebellion. Apparently Douggie had patronised her, along with women drivers in general; he was forever rolling his eyes when watching one attempting to park. When Rosemary herself drove he would sit rigid beside her, drawing in his breath sharply, and, when she braked, jamming his foot on the floor and theatrically slumping forward.

'Actually, I'm a much better driver than he is. He's one of those crawlers who slows down when he's talking. Sometimes he'll come to a complete standstill in the middle of the road. So maddening. And he parks about a hundred miles from the pavement. But I've always kept quiet to save his stupid pride. That's what you do when you're married.' Rosemary's voice shook. 'And look where it's got me.' She averted her face and wiped it with her napkin. 'Bloody hot flush.'

Amy wanted to put her arm around Rosemary's shoulders; she looked so large and abandoned. But Rosemary was an Englishwoman of a certain generation and a military wife to boot; she wouldn't welcome such a show of affection. Instead Amy said: 'I bet he comes back. He's just having a midlife crisis.'

'Bit late, at sixty-five.'

Amy thought of her own ex, Neville, whose girlfriend was now pregnant. She wished nobody had told her; it felt like a knife through her heart. She remembered that terrible evening: *Do you think we ought to have a baby?* Why had she taken such offence? Neville might have put it clumsily but she had loved him and now she had lost him forever.

'My boyfriend's never coming back,' she said. 'I've got to stand on my own two feet. Car-wise and everything-wise.'

'I'm sorry, dear.' Rosemary patted her knee. 'I'm sure you'll find somebody else, a pretty girl like you.'

'Actually, he wasn't much help with the car. He didn't drive, you see. He rode a bike. I relied on people at work—crew members—to sort me out.'

148

'Are you an air hostess?' asked Lou.

'She works in films, dear,' said Rosemary.

'But I haven't had a job for months,' said Amy. 'It's made me realise how dependent I was. That it's time I grew up.'

'Have you met any celebrities?' asked Lou.

'She's met our host,' said Rosemary. 'He used to be quite a well-known actor.'

'But he's so fat,' said Lou. 'And old.'

'He wasn't, once. In fact, he was quite the matinee idol.' Rosemary looked at their host, who was sitting at another table. 'I seem to remember him in some Noël Coward thing at Guildford. With what's-her-name, you wouldn't know. And of course he has such a wonderful voice, so deep, like molasses.'

A glass tapped. Silence fell. Their host rose unsteadily to his feet.

'Welcome to you all,' Buffy boomed. Florid, bearded and portly, he wore an embroidered waistcoat and green velvet jacket. 'Just a few housekeeping rules.' He paused, surveying the room. Amy, who was familiar with actors, settled back in her chair. You could trust a real performer to make a drama about anything, even tampons down the toilet.

Having done this, the dog yapping in excitement, he outlined the course. Their tutor, Nolan Evans, would meet them at ten o'clock the next morning in the garage behind the house. These sessions would last three hours, with time for questions. A buffet lunch would follow. Afternoons would be taken up with individual tutorials for those who had brought their own cars; otherwise students would be at leisure to explore the surrounding countryside or

149

sample the local attractions. After dinner various entertainments would be on offer—film screenings in the bar, a music gig at the pub. 'Thursdays are Comedy Night,' he beamed. 'This week it's our local stand-up, Falafel George. We make our own entertainments here.'

A voice piped up. 'One evening, could you read us some poetry?'

Heads turned to gaze at an intense, dark-haired woman. Cowed by the attention, her voice faltered.

'I just remember, when I had my hysterectomy, I heard you on the wireless reading *The Faerie Queene*. It was as if you were in the room, smoothing my brow.'

Voda and India had come in to clear the plates. They clapped their hands to their mouths, stifling their giggles.

Nolan

Nolan was using Buffy's car as a demonstration model. It was a clapped-out Citroën CX, 104,000 miles on the clock, and not ideal as a teaching tool due to the Citroën's idiosyncratic hydraulics and electrical system. Buffy, however, had insisted that it be the guinea pig as it would get a good going-over—indeed, a free service—and, besides, the pupils could get their own cars seen to during the afternoons.

Nolan had agreed. He was an amiable chap and Buffy was the boss. Besides, he needed the money. He had been out of work for a year now, having lost his job on the roads due to the council cuts. It pained his heart to see the effects of the recession

150

on his beloved home town. The tarmac had broken up during the harsh winter but the potholes remained unmended. When it rained they filled with muddy water which splashed pedestrians when vehicles drove by. Weeds were choking the playground of St Jude's, his old primary school. It wasn't just him who was redundant, of course. Half his mates were out of work and frying their brains with skunk. And then there were the closures. The youth club was boarded up; the bus service slashed. Even the Old Court House, next to Myrtle House—a noble building, the pride of Knockton—was up for sale.

It was lucky he was an optimist. He had to be, for his mum's sake. They lived together in a council house beyond the bypass and he was all she had in the world.

Nolan carried his toolbox to the door. It was Monday morning. *Hey-ho, hey-ho, it's off to work we go.* He almost skipped along the hallway. For the first time in months, he could feel his muscles working under the skin. Of course there was the dread that he would cock it up but that was part of the adrenalin rush.

'Bye!' he called.

'Don't forget my pills,' Shirley said, heaving herself into position on the settee. She fished under the cushion for the remote.

'I'll try not to, Mum, but they might keep me there over dinner.'

The telly blared into life. Shirley turned her massive back to him. 'That's nice. So I'll be having a panic attack and you won't give a fuck.'

'Don't be daft—'

'I know what you're thinking. That I should get

151

off my fat arse and get them myself.'

He was, in fact, thinking that. 'Sorry. Course I'll get them.'

Nolan went back and kissed the top of her head. As he did so he gazed at her thighs, as vast as bolsters in the grey tracksuit. It was only recently that his mother had ballooned to this size. She had given birth to him at seventeen; photos from that era showed a young girl with stick-insect legs and knock knees. Somewhere, buried in this flesh, was the teenager, with her high spirits and quick wits, with her hopes and dreams, who had danced with him around the kitchen to 'Jumpin' Jack Flash'.

He knew her so well. As Nolan walked towards the pedestrian underpass he could sense her waiting another five minutes, just in case he had forgotten something. By the time he reached the high street she would be getting to her feet and making her way, surprisingly fast, to the fridge.

Amy

'Honestly, it went straight in one ear and out the other,' said Nina, over lunch. 'What exactly *is* an alternator?'

Nina was the dark, intense woman who liked listening to *The Faerie Queene*. She ran a dress shop in Whitstable; her husband had recently died and her daughter had bullied her into enrolling on the course.

'That's not Nolan's fault,' said Amy. 'I thought he was really good at explaining things.'

Nina tapped Amy's plate with her fork. 'You just fancy him, sweetie.'

'That's *so* not true,' lied Amy.

'Well, everyone else does,' said Nina. 'No wonder we can't remember a thing. I thought my libido had died when my darling husband passed away.' She sipped her cranberry juice. 'So dazzling, like a Greek god. And even better because he seems totally unaware of it. That's because he's a country boy, bless his heart. You don't get a compliment from a cow.'

Nina was right, about Nolan's effect on the assembled women. As they clustered around the open bonnet, eyes had flickered from the rusty and incomprehensible entrails of the engine to the whippet-slim loins of their tutor, encased in faded jeans. To his black curly hair and perfect profile; his tanned forearms and grimy fingertips; to his thick caterpillar eyebrows, tenderly raised when one of them asked a stupid question.

Amy didn't want to think about Nolan. Nobody would ever love her again; she was destined to be the tomboy mate, the gooseberry, the good-natured confidante of other people's romances, one of the crew—that is, if she ever worked on a film set again. She would grow old alone, her womb shrivelled to a walnut, surrounded by empty pizza boxes.

Nina was expecting a reply. Instead, Amy turned to the woman on her other side, whose name she hadn't caught, but she was fiddling with her mobile.

'I need to speak to my cat-sitter,' she complained. 'And I can't get a signal.'

Voda plonked a jug of water on their table. 'Depends on your network,' she said. 'If you're Orange it'll work if you stand on the bypass, next to the recycling skips.'

The woman was gazing at Voda. 'You look very festive today.'

Voda's cheeks reddened. Shyly, she touched her earrings. She had several piercings but today the studs had been replaced by dangling silver decorations.

'Do you like them?' she asked. 'India made them. She said I look like a Christmas tree.'

'So India makes jewellery?' The woman pointed to Voda's ears. 'I love these, especially the little teddy bear.'

'Actually, it's a kangaroo.'

The woman put on her specs. Voda obligingly tilted her head. Various other women got up and inspected her earrings. When it was discovered that India had brought along her toolkit several of them expressed interest in watching a demonstration or even having a go at making something themselves.

So that afternoon India took her soldering iron into the dining room and gave an informal class. Other guests disappeared up to the bypass to make phone calls. Amy, however, had an appointment with Nolan for an individual tutorial.

She parked her car in the back lane, next to the garage. There was no sign of Nolan. Bending down, she peered into the wing mirror. She had drunk two glasses of wine at lunchtime and her cheeks—and worse, her nose—glowed crimson. Faint music came from the shed in the neighbouring garden, where apparently a man made lutes. *Love oh love oh careless love* . . . The boughs of an apple tree hung over the wall, heavy with fruit. *It caused me to weep, it caused me to moan, it caused me to lose my happy home.*

Nolan hurried down the lane, breathing heavily.

154

Amy straightened up.

'Sorry I'm late,' he panted. 'Had some errands to run.'

Amy's heart lurched. His gypsy beauty was, indeed, astonishing—tanned skin, blue eyes, curly black hair. And those eyebrows, with a life of their own, speaking from a different script.

'It's my mum,' he said. 'She's not too well.'

'I'm sorry, what's the matter?'

'Angina, diabetes . . .' He ticked them off on his fingers. 'Panic attacks, lactose intolerance . . .'

He paused. She silently urged him to carry on, for them to just stand together under the apples. 'Anything else?'

'Shortness of breath, maybe early emphysema, dropped arches, IBS.'

'What's IBS?'

'Irritable bowel syndrome. She gets constipated, see, with these stomach cramps. Inflammation in the colon or something. Then—let's just say all hell's let loose.' The eyebrows rose up his forehead. 'Basically, she should lose some weight.' He shrugged. 'You don't want to know all this. Let's get cracking on that Punto. Been having any problems with overheating?'

'You bet.'

He opened the door and eased his long, lean body into the driver's seat. Amy gazed at him as he leaned forward, shoving his hand under the dashboard and rummaging around with his fingers to find the bonnet spring. Weak with desire, she leaned against the garage door. A click and the bonnet slid ajar.

'Electrics can be dodgy on this model, too,' he said, climbing out. 'Want me to talk you through your fuse box?' He opened the bonnet and pointed. 'These fuses are called spades, due to its being a Fiat and, like, Italian.'

'Last time it went wrong one of the sparks fixed it.'

'What's a sparks?'

'An electrician.' Amy told him that she worked in the movies, that she was a make-up artist.

'No way!' This response was always gratifying. Nolan's eyes widened with awe, with a new respect; she felt a small shift of power between them. 'You worked on any horror pictures?'

She nodded. *'Bognor Vampires. Swimming with Zombies.'*

'You must be kidding! I got them both on DVD.' Nolan closed his eyes dreamily. 'You know my favourite bit of *Bognor*? When the bloke's in the shed, that actor, what's-his-name, he thinks he's safe, and then the vampire bursts through the door and claws out his eye. All the gore and stuff down his cheek, and his eye's on a string, like, swinging.'

'I did that.'

'You did?' Nolan's look of astonishment was followed by a look of pure devotion.

Any nodded. Never, in her whole life, had a man gazed at her like that. 'It's just prosthetics,' she shrugged.

'How did you do it?'

'First you prep the skin with moisturiser. Then you cover the eye with medical masking tape and lay these thin rolls of wax to make the socket.'

'What about the blood and gore?' he asked eagerly.

'Hang on, we get to that.'

'And pus?'

156

'And pus.'

The car was forgotten. They sat down side by side on the grass verge and talked about horror movies. Somewhere, a bird was singing. Somewhere, a clock struck three. Voices murmured in the garden of Myrtle House; there was a burst of laughter. The high brick wall, however, sealed the two of them off from the ignoramuses. They were alone. The back lane—potholed, weedy, lined with garages in various stages of dilapidation and a few parked cars—was suddenly dear to her. What did she care that her bum was damp? That she had a stomach ache, due to the lavatories being occupied that morning and no chance of a crap? Burrs were stuck to the sleeve of Nolan's jacket but she didn't dare do something so intimate as to pick them off.

At one point his mobile rang. He looked at the name, paused, and clicked it off.

'That was my mum,' he said. 'I should talk to her but, know something? I'm not.' He put the phone in his pocket. 'She's on all these meds—sometimes I think it's *her* who's the zombie. To be perfectly honest, I don't think there's anything much wrong with her. Thing is, she's on the internet all day, spooking herself with symptoms. She's got cancer, she's got Crohn's disease—she works herself up into such a state she's back on the Prozac. To tell the truth, she just needs to get out of the house a bit more.' He stopped. 'Why am I telling you this?'

'You got a dad?'

Nolan shook his head. 'It's just the two of us.'

'Maybe she's frightened. If she got well, you'd leave.'

Nolan scratched at a scab of mud on his jeans.

'Sorry,' Amy said. 'That was out of order.'

157

Nolan looked up at her. 'No, you're right. I'm twenty-eight.' There was a silence. She felt him sucked away from her, swallowed into his own imponderable future. She had to haul him back.

'Want to know how to make up a mummy?' she asked.

'Pardon?' The black caterpillars shot up. 'I don't think she'd let me.'

'Not your mummy. A *mummy.*'

Nolan burst out laughing. They sat there, slumped against the wall, shaking with laughter. She had set this up; she was quicker than him, she had realised this.

'First you paint the skin with gum. Then you layer on these thin strips of gauze—'

She stopped. A car roared down the lane. Gravel spurted as it jerked to a halt beside them. It was a black, open-top sports car; in it sat Bella, one of the students, her blonde hair tousled.

'Wow,' said Nolan. 'A BMW.'

Bella switched off the engine, opened the door and swung round her long tanned legs. 'Am I early?' she asked.

Nolan looked at his watch. 'Blimey, it's four o'clock.' He struggled to his feet.

Bella flashed Amy a smile. 'Sorry. My turn now.'

Bella's family owned half of Wiltshire. No break-up had been involved in her decision to enrol on the course—who could break up with somebody as beautiful as Bella? The reason was that her parents had bought her the BMW for her twenty-first, on condition she learned how to look after it. Amy had overheard this at breakfast, along with a drawling description of the family's Tuscan hideaway where Bella had spent the summer

158

snorting coke and skinny-dipping in the infinity pool.

She turned to Nolan. 'I know fuck all about cars.'

'That's what I'm here for,' he replied, smoothing down his hair. There was something subservient about the gesture. Amy had already lost him.

She snapped shut the bonnet of her Punto. It was acned with calcified bird shit. 'I'll drive this back to the car park,' she said.

Nolan was running his hand along the shiny flank of the BMW with the reverence of a farmer assessing a prize bull. 'Bet it has plenty of poke,' he said to Bella.

Bella adjusted the strap of her sundress, which had slipped off her shoulder. 'Yah. Last week I drove from Wiltshire to Notting Hill in ninety minutes.'

Amy inspected her through narrowed eyes. Posh totty, buffed and polished, glowing with entitlement. Too rich to feel the cold in her skimpy retro-frock.

Amy got into her car and inserted the key. Nolan's face appeared at the window. 'Sorry about your lesson,' he said, squatting on his haunches. 'Got a bit carried away with all that blood and gore.'

Amy thought: This is my only power over him. Suddenly she said: 'Want me to make you up?'

'What?'

'I'll do you a make-up, I've brought my kit with me. You can have a bullet wound to the head. Or how about a road-crash victim?'

His eyebrows shot up. 'You kidding me?'

'No.'

His face broke into a smile. 'You bet. How about

159

after work tomorrow?'

*　　*　　*

Amy had lied. Her make-up kit was in London—
why would she bring it to a course on car
maintenance? Like many honest people, on the few
occasions she blurted out an untruth she did so with
total conviction.

Her heart pounded. What was she going to do—
drive back to London to collect it, a round trip of
over seven hours? She stood immobile in the car
park. A greyhound, its neck tied with a spotted
handkerchief, loped past and raised its leg against a
motorbike. At this very moment Bella would be
moving in for the kill. Amy pictured her bending
over the open bonnet, her breasts two shadowy
globes. Nolan's arm was around her shoulder as,
heads close, they inspected a gasket. Woozy with
petrol fumes, Bella leaned against him . . .
Suddenly, cupping her chin with his grimy finger, he
turned the ravishing trustafarian's face to his, their
lips blindly seeking each other . . .

Amy rallied. *Don't be feeble.* A man wearing a
bobble hat whistled to the greyhound and climbed
into a pickup truck. Suddenly she had an idea. One
of her colleagues, Ellie, lived in Wales. Somewhere
beginning with two Ls; she remembered Ellie
chatting about it to Michael Sheen, who came from
Port Talbot, while doing his make-up.

Ten minutes later Amy arrived at the bypass, the
only place where those on the Orange network
could get a signal. Several of the other guests stood
in the lay-by, next to the recyling skips, shouting
into their mobiles. Among them was Rosemary, the

160

wind whipping her skirt around her sturdy, pallid legs.

'Don't be so pathetic, Douggie!' Rosemary yelled. 'Just bung it in and switch on the cycle for Wool and Synthetics . . . What? . . . How would I know, I haven't seen the blithering machine, have I? It'll have *numbers* on it, on the *front*!' She rolled her eyes at Amy. *Men.* 'What? *What?*' A lorry thundered past. 'Course you have to defrost it first, just stick it in the microwave. *What?* Well, get your little friend to do it, that's *her* job now . . . What? . . . I'm not being sarky. And remember it's Hannah's birthday on Friday, don't forget to send her a card. You do know how to stick on a stamp, don't you?' There was a crash of glass. 'I can't hear you! I'm at the bottle bank, it's a Transition Town, everybody's bloody at it, bottles flying everywhere, they're recycling-mad . . . *What?* You don't know *her address*? Your own bloody *daughter*?'

Rosemary switched off her mobile and turned to Amy.

'He's moved into this bedsit, you see,' she said. 'He's as helpless as a kitten. Well, tough titties—he shouldn't have left, should he? She's got her own flat but there's no room for him there, she's got a child, she doesn't want him cluttering up the place.' Eyes glittering with tears, Rosemary shoved the mobile into her handbag. 'I bet he's not taking his pills. I used to lay them out for him, you see. His blood pressure's probably going through the roof.' She smiled thinly. 'Funny, isn't it? *I'm* supposed to be the helpless one, can't work a car, all that. Hence this course. But it's not me, it's him, the nincompoop.'

Rosemary turned away abruptly and strode

161

across the bypass, holding up her hand like a sergeant major and causing an approaching car to slam on its brakes.

Amy punched in Ellie's number, praying that she would be at home. Nearby, a bearded man fed newspapers into the mouth of a skip. Some item caught his eye; he pulled out the newspaper and sat down to read it.

Ellie answered the phone. Yes, she was at home. Yes, Amy could borrow her make-up kit. Amy arranged to drive to Llandeilo the following morning to pick it up. She would have to miss the lesson—Maintaining Your Vehicle's Bodywork—but too bad.

Amy walked back along the high street. The church clock struck six. Swallows still swooped in the sky but soon they would be gone. She felt a surge of exhilaration. How chancy it all was; how fragile the moment that might change one's life! If Ellie had been away on a job . . . if Neville hadn't spotted a clump of mint growing in her front garden . . . . Already she was racing ahead of herself; nothing might come of this—indeed, it probably wouldn't. And yet she felt flooded with joy, smiling at a pink-haired woman who was locking up the magic crystals shop. Amy strode along the pavement breathing in great lungfuls of the invigorating Welsh air. Even her stomach ache was gone.

At dinner Rosemary, eyes puffy from crying, was knocking back the wine. She said that a man had tried to pick her up when she was standing at the bypass, talking on her mobile. 'So thrilling—at my age, too. He stopped his van and asked me how much I charged.' She gave a shrill laugh. 'They

162

obviously like the older, more experienced woman here.'

Voda, who was collecting the plates, asked: 'What sort of van?'

'Blue, covered in rust.'

'Thought so.' Voda nodded, her earrings swinging. 'That'll be Gareth. He's got brain damage from sniffing the paraffin.'

Rosemary put down her glass. 'Thanks for that,' she said.

Nolan

Something had been unleashed in Nolan. He had never talked about his mother like that—certainly not with his mates. They talked about cars and motorbikes and getting stoned on the various illegal substances that were swilling around the council estates of Knockton and the badlands up in the hills. They used to talk about girls, of course, but various pregnancies, and the ensuing shackled domesticity, had put paid to that. The erstwhile hellraisers could now be seen at the playground, acne still inflaming their cheeks, smoking a furtive cigarette while their toddlers ran amok.

No, mates didn't talk like that. But then this girl appears out of the blue and suddenly the words pour out of his mouth. Until that moment Nolan hadn't even known the words existed. Was that because Amy had spoken the truth? *If she got well, you'd leave.* Now he thought about it, several of his romances had been sabotaged by some medical or emotional crisis in Shirley's life. He remembered a cancer scare putting the kibosh on a weekend in

Aberystwyth with Cath. He had gone out with Cath for six months; to celebrate, she had booked them into a fancy hotel in Aberystwyth—en suite jacuzzi, the works. Instead, he'd had to drive his mother on a mercy dash to Hereford hospital where a contemptuous nurse had diagnosed a mild case of vaginal warts. The ensuing row with Cath—she accusing him of being a mother's boy, he accusing her of being hard-hearted, she demanding he pay the lost deposit, he accusing her of meanness, she accusing him of being a loser, him accusing her of kicking him when he was down, he was busting himself to find a job . . . even now he shuddered to think about it. And a year later she got married to his best mate.

It was six o'clock; work was over for the day. Nolan stood at the kitchen sink, washing his hands with Swarfega. Outside, swallows swooped low over the rooftops. He was exhausted. Teaching was harder work than he had imagined; the trouble was, none of the students had a clue. To them, a car was simply something that got them from A to B. They seemed to have no curiosity at all about what went on under the bonnet. Of course they made polite noises, they were by and large a pleasant bunch, but some of them had already drifted off to join a rival group making jewellery. He had seen them in the garden, heads bent over their work, chattering away as if released from prison. One of them had come over and touched his arm. 'It's no reflection on you, honestly. It's just that we've realised why we weren't interested in the first place.'

There had been no sign of Amy all morning. He had scanned the necklace-makers, of course, but he hadn't expected to see her there—he had never met

164

a girl who took so little interest in her appearance. This was something of a surprise, considering her job; perhaps all her efforts went into making other people beautiful. In fact, she wasn't bad-looking—a round, merry face; freckles; flyaway reddish hair cut into a fringe. But she dressed like a tomboy in jeans and T-shirt, her feet grubby in flip-flops. This was a relief; he didn't have to make an effort. If he had a gang, which he didn't any more, she would be an honorary member.

Suddenly Nolan was weak with a longing for his youth, when things were simple, when his mother danced with him around the kitchen. When he had a gang, as hopeful as himself. When anything was possible—he would be a Formula One driver, he would take the world by storm. He would walk tall; men would look up when he entered the pub.

Now, as he pulled off the kitchen towel, he thought: How can I be a grown man when there's no world for me to be a grown man in? Just now he had a job, just for a week, and then what?

It was a brief moment. Nolan was an optimist, he mustn't think these thoughts. He dried his hands. Amy was due at his house at six thirty. As luck would have it, his mother Shirley had gone out for the evening. She had an appointment with an aromatherapist in Leominster, and was then meeting her sister for a curry. But would Amy turn up? Maybe she had been summoned by a famous film star! *I'm not going in front of the cameras unless Amy does my make-up. Call the girl here!* At this very moment Amy was bowling back to London, her engine overheating due to that familiar Punto problem, a blocked rad—a problem he had meant to address before he was diverted by talk of horror

165

movies. And then Miss Long Legs had arrived in her BMW and it was too late.

At that moment the doorbell rang.

Shirley

Shirley was already in a bad mood by the time they arrived at the Jalalabad. During the massage she had listened to her sister, in the next cubicle, boasting about her children's achievements at school. Julia had then gone on to talk about her relationship with her husband, how they were still besotted with each other after twenty years of marriage, how he had bought her a set of Ann Summers underwear for her birthday. Her voice had sunk to a whisper, then she and the aromatherapist had burst into giggles.

And now they were sitting at a table opening their menus, she and Julia—Julia the slim sister, the pretty sister, the sister who still had great sex with her husband, the sister tanned from her holiday in Thailand. When Julia dropped her napkin, two waiters dived for the floor.

Shirley ordered three poppadoms for herself, for starters.

Julia raised her eyebrows. 'Are you sure you should?'

'What do you mean?'

'Well, you know.'

'What?'

'Nothing!'

It escalated from there. They were sisters; they knew each other's raw spots. Soon they were hissing at each other across the table, ignoring the waiter

166

who was hovering nearby, ignoring the glances of the other diners. Later, Shirley couldn't remember the breaking point; it would be one of three or four, they were always the same. All she remembered was pushing back her chair and saying 'I don't need this.'

She got up with a stagy flourish, a toss of her head—an actress, just for a moment—and stalked out into the street.

Driving home, seething, her stomach rumbling with hunger, Shirley thought: Serve her right if I crash! See her face then! It was only seven thirty but already dark. She opened the glovebox with one hand and rummaged around; as she suspected, she found nothing but wrappers. Panic rose in her throat but she told herself to calm down. Soon she would be home and Nolan would give her a hug. All the pent-up tears would come tumbling out; Nolan would understand, he was on her side, he hated that stuck-up bitch too, he would defend his mother to the death. They would get stuff from the freezer—chicken tikka, rogan josh—stick it in the microwave and have their *own* Indian meal. She'd been mad to visit her sister, it always ended in tears. In fact she'd been mad to go out at all—what was the point when she had everything she needed at home? Besides, she never had anything to wear.

Shirley pulled up outside her house and switched off the engine. A profound feeling of relief spread through her. Lights glowed through the lounge curtains. Nolan was home. How surprised he would be, to see her back so early!

She walked up the path and let herself into the house. A murmur of voices came from the lounge. Opening the door, she peered in.

167

A young woman was bent over Nolan. He sat slumped in the armchair, his head flung back. His face was covered in blood.

Shirley screamed.

'Hi, Ma.' Nolan sat up. His cheeks were crusted with gore; one eye hung down his cheek.

Shirley screamed again. A sharp pain shot across her chest and she fell onto the floor.

Buffy

Buffy gazed fondly at his guests as they sat down to dinner. Several of them wore their new earrings; they glinted in the candlelight. Day two and things were going swimmingly. Who cared if some of them had abandoned car maintenance and taken up jewellery-making instead? Anything to keep them happy and Nolan hadn't seemed to mind. If Buffy had learned anything in life, it was that nothing goes according to plan.

Take India. Until recently she had been a Shoreditch girl, her world boundaried by Brick Lane and Columbia Road. In Buffy's view its inhabitants scored highly on the wanker-ometer but he was an old fart, he would think that. Now, however, his stepdaughter was a breathless convert to the delights of small-town living. Everybody knew everybody! They left their bikes unchained! They left vegetables outside their doors with a sign saying *Help Yourself*. Instead of being spattered with vomit, the pavements were chalked with hopscotch. *Hopscotch*.

Nor, until recently, had India shown the slightest interest in cooking. Her usual meal, he seemed to

168

remember, was hummus, scooped out of the tub with her finger. Now she had become an enthusiastic sous-chef, chopping, stirring, testing recipes and sipping sauces from Voda's outstretched spoon.

This volte-face pleased him hugely, of course, as did her high spirits, especially as his sons had told him how gloomy India had been recently. She was also taking more care of her appearance. Tonight she had brushed her hair and clipped it up with two plastic butterflies. She was also wearing a flowery granny-dress, bought from Jill's Things in the high street, a change from her usual baggy layers and leggings. It was only now, however, that Buffy realised the reason for this transformation. It wasn't the cooking that had brought a flush to her cheeks; it was Des.

Des, the only man on the course. Des, who due to his shyness had been the object of some speculation. He was a sandy-haired chap, a rugby player; BMW Bella had attempted to chat him up on the first evening but had met with little response except for the fact that he had been given a car by a mate of his who had lost his licence for drink-driving. A broken relationship didn't seem to have been involved, but then it hadn't in her case either. Despite having this in common Bella had made little headway with Des, a matter of some gratification to Buffy whose loyalties lay with his stepdaughter.

For now he was recognising the telltale signs. Tonight's starter was artichokes. He watched India squat down beside Des, who was looking bemused at the object on his plate, and demonstrate how to eat it. India even pulled off a leaf and tore at it with

169

her teeth. All the while she was smiling at him, balancing herself against him as she swayed on her haunches. Des said something and she burst out laughing—a shrill, flirtatious laugh that suggested it wasn't that funny but she was giving him the benefit of the doubt because she fancied him.

Buffy smiled to himself as he uncorked the wine. When he had thought up his plan he'd had a vision of battle-scarred veterans like himself, casualties of the war between the sexes, pitching up at his establishment and finding comfort in each other's arms. He himself had retired from the field, a grizzled soldier weighed down with medals for service in dangerous and hostile terrain, but was on hand to give advice. India had not figured in this scenario but then, as he had noticed, nothing goes according to plan.

He walked from table to table, pouring out the wine. How radiant India looked as she carried round the water jugs! From what he'd heard, her love life had been pretty unsatisfactory, involving a high percentage of Hoxton tossers. Buffy looked at Des, who had given up on his artichoke. This chap wouldn't know the White Cube Gallery if it came up and hit him in the face. He was a sportsman, strong and solid. There was something reassuring about his great freckled slabs of forearms, thatched with blond fur. They would encircle India and keep her safe. Buffy's imagination raced ahead. The two of them would marry and buy a cottage in Shropshire—no sense in hanging around, India was nearly forty, after all. Maybe just time for a tow-headed son who would bang his spoon on the kitchen table and demand porridge with his piping treble voice.

'Has anyone seen Amy?' asked Rosemary.

Buffy was jerked out of his reverie. Amy had been spotted briefly during the afternoon but had disappeared again. She had not checked-out or taken her luggage. Here in the dining room her empty seat, next to Rosemary, had a disquieting, Banquo air to it.

'I hope she hasn't broken down somewhere,' said Rosemary, holding out her glass. 'She should have waited till the end of the course, then she'd know how to fix it.'

'She'd phone, if she'd broken down,' said Buffy.

'Don't bet on it,' said Rosemary. 'She's Orange. The signal here's very patchy. Even on the bypass it's touch and go.' She gulped down some wine. 'I got propositioned there yesterday for the first time in thirty years. Shame the chap turned out to be a mental defective.'

Buffy was fond of Rosemary, with her Home Counties separates and hearty laugh. Besides, he always warmed to a fellow drinker; most of the ladies were disappointingly niminy-piminy in this respect, placing their hand over their glass and rolling their eyes heavenwards like a painting of the Virgin in some dim Italian church. Tonight, however, Rosemary seemed out of sorts. She had put a brave face on her misfortune but now the bitterness was breaking out. He had heard her, during cocktails, comparing notes with another female guest of mature years, also abandoned for a younger model.

'Fancy going to bed with somebody who hasn't heard of Cliff Michelmore,' Rosemary had snorted. 'It must be so bloody lonely.'

'Cliff *Richard* even,' said the other woman. '*His*

little tart's barely out of nappies.'

'Douggie's wants *children*,' said Rosemary. 'I can just see him pushing some bawling brat around Sainsbury's, with his gammy leg playing up, missing the cricket and sodden with vomit. A high price to pay for a bit of hanky-panky, if you ask me.'

Now Rosemary had relapsed into gloom. She sat slumped in her chair, rolling her bread into pellets. Buffy, who had sat down beside her, tried to think of something encouraging to say. He hated to see such a sport brought low. Though no stranger to adultery himself, he felt a wave of anger against the errant Douggie. How could the man be such a cliché?

A faint crash came from the kitchen. Silence had fallen in the dining room. The artichokes had long since been dismembered or abandoned; people were waiting for the main course.

A moment later Voda appeared, her face shiny with sweat. She hurried over to Buffy and crouched at his ear.

'Bit of a disaster,' she whispered. 'Do something! Entertain them for twenty minutes!'

She disappeared into the kitchen. Though momentarily taken aback, Buffy rallied. After all, he was a pro. He felt the old instincts rumble into life, like a boiler firing up in the basement. He leaned over to Nina, the widow from Whitstable, who was sitting opposite.

'Would you like to hear a poem then?'

Nina's face lit up. 'Oh, yes please! We've been dying to hear you perform. You're really quite famous. It was a thrill to arrive here and find it was you.'

'I haven't dared say so,' said another woman, 'but

172

I loved your Sergeant Whatsit in *Journey's End.* I saw it in Beccles.' She stood up and tapped her glass. 'Shh, everybody! Our host is going to read us some poetry!'

'Did you know he was Hammy the Hamster?' said someone else.

'I'd prefer *The Faerie Queene*,' said Nina, gazing at Buffy with devotion.

'Afraid I can't remember a word of it,' said Buffy. 'Anyway, it doesn't half go on.'

He got to his feet. At the next table sat the younger guests, who by now had segregated themselves. The ravishing Bella had pinned up her hair and wore a strappy little top. She whispered something in Des's ear and stifled a giggle. Buffy glared at her; didn't she know that Des was taken? Des didn't respond. He was gazing dreamily in the direction of the kitchen. Was he yearning for India or his main course?

'I'd like to dedicate this poem to my stepdaughter India,' boomed Buffy, 'who is at this very moment putting the final touches to your guineafowl or, in the case of the veggies, aubergine bake.'

He took a breath. Suddenly his mind went blank.

A moment passed. Faces were turned towards him expectantly. Buffy broke into a sweat. His brain had literally emptied; the words had disappeared down a plughole, he could feel the hiss. Every actor's nightmare and it had to happen now, with no fellow thesps to bail him out. He had dried a few times in the past, of course; it happened to everyone. But there was always the prompt, or one of the cast, to give one a nudge. Once, in *Who's Afraid of Virginia Woolf?*, he had skipped three pages of dialogue, startling both himself and his stage wife, but the audience didn't seem to notice. After all, they were both playing alcoholics and the odd non sequitur was simply par for the course. He seemed to remember an inspired riff about armadillos that lurched them back onto the page. Albee would have been proud of him.

Several minutes passed. Buffy cleared his throat. Rosemary gave him an encouraging smile. The only line of poetry he could remember was

Celery raw develops the jaw
Celery stewed is more quietly chewed.

Suddenly the doorbell rang. The dog yapped and rushed into the hallway.

Saved by the bell! It must be Amy, late for dinner. Buffy, breathing a sigh of relief, hurried out and opened the front door.

A dishevelled, middle-aged man stood there, wild-eyed under the street light. 'So sorry to disturb you,' he said, 'but is Mrs Rosemary Turnbull there?'

Buffy led him into the dining room. The guests gazed, puzzled, at the newcomer. Was he a late addition to the course?

Rosemary struggled to her feet. 'Douggie!' she cried.

Nolan

Nolan, hurrying down the hallway, saw flashing lights through the glass. He flung open the door. Two paramedics stood there.

174

'Blimey!' said one of them.

'She's in the lounge,' said Nolan. 'We haven't moved her.'

They were staring at him. 'I think you should sit down, sir.'

Nolan looked at himself in the mirror. He had pulled off the dangling eye but there was no denying he looked a mess. He had rubbed the gunk off his face but blood still seemed to be smeared over his cheek, and his eye socket was encrusted with wax. 'It's not me. I'm fine.'

They exchanged glances over the static of their radios. They worked at the sharp end, they had dealt with nutters. With murderers too. With scenes of domestic carnage beyond Nolan's imaginings, and both of them barely out of their teens. He tried to smile but his skin was too tight.

'It's my mum,' he said. 'I think she's had a heart attack.'

He led them into the lounge where Amy sat on the floor, holding his mother's hand. Shirley lay where she had fallen, her head propped against the pouffe.

The paramedics squatted down beside her and set to work. Nolan gazed at the beached body of his mother. She had dressed up for her sister, with whom she had a competitive relationship; there was something pitiful about the tiger-sequinned top, now pulled up to reveal her massive, grubby bra. He averted his eyes from the mounds of flesh.

The paramedics were talking to Shirley, asking her name, asking about her symptoms. Shirley, her chest heaving, replied in a whisper. Nolan met Amy's eye across the body. Amy looked stricken, her face bleached by the glare of the ceiling light.

175

Thrust into intimacy with her, he felt they were two naughty children, caught by the authorities. There was a flash of complicity between them, and then it was gone.

Should he be recording *House Swap* on the TV? It was one of his mother's favourites. Was Amy longing to get the hell out of there? Why hadn't he tidied up the lounge? The place was a pigsty.

How could he think like that? His mother was lying there gasping for breath, perhaps dying, and stupid things kept coming into his head, he couldn't catch up with himself, it was like wading through treacle.

'Would you like a cup of tea?' he asked the paramedics.

They shook their heads. One of them went out and returned, carrying a machine.

How could he have been so thoughtless, to terrify his mother like that? He didn't know she would come home early, of course, but it was all his fault. Nolan stood there helplessly, his hands dangling at his sides. Amy, a girl he hardly knew, was now sitting in the armchair, her arms around her knees, her face inscrutable. He had no idea what to say to her, or to his mother whose eyes were squeezed shut, or to the two brisk medics upon whom her life now depended.

He squatted down beside her. 'It'll be all right, Ma,' he said.

She opened an eye. 'I love you, son,' she said.

Son? Nolan was taken aback. She sounded like one of her afternoon soaps.

'I love you too,' he whispered. He kissed her cheek; her skin was as clammy as putty. It all felt stagy; this wasn't happening, not for real. They

176

were acting in some movie, Amy on hand with her make-up kit. In a moment somebody would shout '*Cut!*' and the two medics would get to their feet. His mother would sit up and crack a joke with them. They would all go off and get something to eat, for his stomach suddenly rumbled so loudly that he blushed.

Shirley was asked what medications she was taking. She rolled her eyes towards Nolan. 'You tell them, love,' she whispered, and turned to the paramedics. 'He looks after me, see.'

'Losartan . . . Buspirone . . .' Nolan said, ticking them off with his finger. 'Aloe Vera Colon Cleanse . . . Dormadina . . .'

As he spoke, he saw the paramedics exchange glances. He knew what they were thinking. *We've got one here—a right old hypochondriac.* Was that a flicker of contempt? *Look at him, Mummy's little helper, has SHE got him by the short and curlies. Get a life, mate!*

Nolan felt a stab of envy for their job. They *had* a job. They saved lives, they were part of a team. Of a gang. They were heroes! They were *needed*. Who needed him? His mother, that was who. Her need was so vast, so all-devouring, that she was eating him alive. *If she got well, you'd leave.* And now *she* was leaving *him*, as if she had overheard Amy's harsh and truthful words, and was offering up her own solution.

He felt a wave of love for his mum, who had cared for him just as he was caring for her, whose life had not panned out as she had hoped. He looked at her lime-green toenails, so bravely painted. Nowadays she could no longer reach her feet; her friend Kath came round to give her a

177

pedicure. It was one of the few occasions when he heard her laugh. Her abandoned sandals, with their diamanté straps, made his eyes sting, as if they were the relics of a road crash.

Nolan knew he should be ringing his Aunt Julia, to tell her what had happened, but he couldn't bring himself to pick up the phone. By putting it into words, he would make the whole situation real. Besides, they were now bringing in a wheelchair.

'I'd better go,' said Amy.

'No, don't,' he blurted out.

'But—'

'Please come to the hospital.'

Amy looked at him in surprise. He wanted to say *you're involved in this, please don't leave me alone*.

She sat there, tearing at a fingernail with her teeth. 'I've got the car outside,' she said. 'I could follow you to the hospital. Then I'd be able to bring you home.'

What, when she's dead? But maybe his mother wasn't going to die, they just said she needed further tests.

'What about your dinner?' he asked stupidly.

'Dinner?' Amy looked at him, equally stupidly. She glanced at her watch. 'It's nine o'clock, I've missed it.' She took out a tub of cream. 'But first I'd better get that stuff off your face, else it's *you* they'll be rushing into A&E.'

The paramedics chuckled. They were heaving Shirley into the wheelchair, waving away Nolan's offer of help. He realised that, for them, this was just a normal evening's work.

His mother, with a sigh, was wedged into the wheelchair. It creaked under her weight. She turned to Amy. 'You met any film stars then?'

Nolan looked at her in surprise. Wasn't she having a heart attack?

Buffy

Douggie, the runaway husband, had joined them at dinner. The main course still hadn't arrived. He sat next to his wife, eagerly tearing at the absent Amy's artichoke.

'There's so little flesh on them, isn't there?' he said, picking a thread of fibre from his teeth. 'All that work, and they leave you hungrier than you started.'

'Been starving you, has she?' said Rosemary.

Douggie flinched. His eyes flickered round the table. How much did the other people know? Judging by the bright air of artificial chit-chat, a lot.

'What a charming house,' he said to nobody in particular. 'And charming town. What I could see of it. In the dark.'

Rosemary was silent. The constraint between them cast its own larger silence. A burst of laughter came from the next table, where the young people seemed unaware of the situation. To them, middle-aged passion would have been a repulsive thought, if they ever thought about it at all.

Nina cleared her throat. 'Rosemary said you were in the army,' she said. 'I expect the two of you have been to some fascinating places.'

Rosemary's shoulders twitched irritably.

'Oh yes, we've certainly seen the world,' Douggie said. 'Haven't we, darling?'

He smiled at Rosemary. She gave him a look over her wine glass as she drained it. Douggie ran

179

his hand over his sparse, grey hair. His shirt and sports jacket were both crumpled. It was hard to believe that he had once been a military man.

'So how are you enjoying the course?' he asked the guests.

They nodded energetically, their eyes shifting from him to his wife.

'Our tutor looks like a Caravaggio,' said Nina.

'Actually, some of us are making earrings instead,' said another woman. She tilted her head coquettishly. 'Don't you think they're pretty?'

'Er, very nice,' said Douggie.

Buffy had joined them at the table. He knew he should be investigating what was happening in the kitchen, which was ominously quiet, but a sense of male solidarity had drawn him to the errant husband. Besides, he was curious. Why had Douggie appeared? To make it up? To tell his wife he wanted a divorce? Rosemary was inspecting the ceiling. Her face betrayed nothing. There was a sense, however, of the unspoken words—words of recrimination and fury—waiting to pounce when she and her husband were alone.

Was the chap planning on staying the night? He couldn't drive back to Aldershot, or wherever it was that he had gone to ground. Amy, of course, was sharing Rosemary's room and would no doubt be back at some point, so Douggie couldn't be tucked up there, even if his wife was willing—which, judging by her face, was unlikely. People had expressed their concern about Amy's disappearance but Buffy wasn't unduly worried. He had had long experience of film crews and their sexual habits. Amy had probably picked up some bloke in the pub and would creep back as dawn was breaking.

180

India came in and whispered into Buffy's ear: 'We're ready now. Sorry about the delay.'

Buffy followed her into the kitchen. There was a wet patch on the floor.

'We dropped the aubergine bake,' said Voda. 'Even the dog wouldn't lick it up.'

'It *was* the vegetarian option,' said India.

'Anyway, we scraped most of it up and put some more sauce on top and browned it again, so nobody'll notice the difference.'

Rosemary

It was nearly eleven o'clock and still Douggie and Rosemary had not had a moment alone. After dinner Douggie had suggested, in a low voice, that they pop down to the pub but Rosemary had said she wanted to see the film. So they had sat side by side in their plastic chairs watching *Groundhog Day*, which was being screened in the bar. They had already seen it twice, once in the cinema and once on a video with their children. Appropriately enough it was exactly the same this third time round, though tonight Douggie's barks of laughter sounded forced.

Rosemary knew she was a coward, to delay any confrontation, but part of her wanted him to suffer. After he had caused her such pain it gave her a grim satisfaction to see him so uncomfortable among the other guests, unable to speak to her freely. Besides, she was dreading what he had to say. It broke her heart, to fear being alone with the man she had loved so dearly, but she had no idea what bombshell he was going to deliver. Maybe

181

he wanted a reconciliation. Maybe the girl was pregnant. God knew what was going on in the heart of a man who had once been so familiar to her.

She hadn't seen Douggie for five months and his appearance had shocked her. He looked so gaunt and dishevelled. Nor had he shaved; stubble was all very well on the young, but the middle-aged looked like alcoholics. Maybe he was exhausted by vigorous sexual activity—oh, she mustn't think about it. Anyway, knowing Douggie, it was really rather hard to imagine. Maybe, when retreating to his bedsitter, he had simply reverted to his slovenly bachelor ways. Maybe that awful girl liked him looking like a homeless person. He *was* a homeless person. The girl's flat was just for visits and his bedsitter was rented. Rosemary hadn't seen it. Apparently it was somewhere behind the Aldershot Sainsbury's but she hadn't even driven past to look. She couldn't bear it. She couldn't *bear* it. Nor had the children been there, not to her knowledge. They weren't speaking to him, they were still too angry.

On the screen Bill Murray lived his life again, trying to get it right this time. Rosemary was conscious of her husband's body next to hers, a sliver of space between them. The dog, who had taken a shine to her, sat on her other side, licking her fingers one by one.

Now the credits were rolling. Somebody switched on the lights. Douggie leaned over and whispered: 'Is there somewhere we can talk?'

They left the room, people's heads turning. Rosemary led him upstairs. She closed the bedroom door and sat down on Amy's bed. Douggie sat slumped on the opposite bed, his hands dangling between his knees like an old man outside a betting shop. He did seem years older than when she had last seen him. But then she felt older too. Funny, she thought, how marriage can keep you innocent for so long.

'I'll say what I've got to say and then I'll go,' he said.

'What, back to Aldershot?'

'I just needed to see you.' He raised his head, his eyes rheumy. 'Oh, Rosy, I don't know what to do.'

'Chucked you out, has she?'

He jerked back, as if stung. A burst of laughter came from the lounge below.

'Why are you here, Douglas?' she asked.

The word *Douglas* startled them both. He ran his hands through his hair and gazed despairingly around the room. 'Funny that you're here without me.'

'Not that funny.'

'In this place. When we've done everything together for so long.'

'Actually, I'm having a lovely time,' said Rosemary. 'And I've got very fond of my room-mate, I don't know what's happened to her, I hope she's all right.'

She saw now that Douggie was sitting on her nightie—the pink, brushed-cotton one she had bought after he'd buggered off because it was so cosy. Already she had garments with which he was not familiar. She hoped he hadn't noticed it; there was something of the care home about its Peter Pan collar.

'I miss you,' he said. 'I miss the children. And the grandchildren.' He tried to smile. 'I even miss mowing the lawn.'

183

She didn't reply. Outside, the church clock struck eleven. They waited for the beats.

'We've never really talked about stuff, have we?' he said.

'What sort of stuff?'

'Us.'

'Bit late now.'

'Is it?' he asked, raising his face.

'You threw away everything,' she said. 'All of us, everything you've loved, to go and live with what's-her-face.'

'Agnieska.' He paused. 'Do you want to know why?'

'No.'

He took a breath to speak, and stopped. 'Fair enough.'

Footsteps padded along the corridor. The bathroom door slammed. People were starting to go to bed.

'Let's just say . . .' He paused. 'It's something about being your silly old sausage.'

'Sausage?'

'Part of the furniture.'

'You weren't,' Rosemary said. 'You were the centre of my life. You were the point of everything.' Tears filled her eyes. 'I know you hated Joni Mitchell but it's true. *You don't know what you've got till it's gone.*'

'I don't hate Joni Mitchell. I just think she's a bit lacking in the humour department.' He gave Rosemary a thin smile. 'That's never been our problem, has it?'

Rosemary shook her head. Suddenly she was crying helplessly—great heaving sobs. Douggie reached across to her. She was too far away; he slid

184

to the floor and worked his way across the carpet on his knees.

'Darling, I'm so sorry,' he said.

She heaved him up and now he was in her arms. She smelt his familiar smell, the one thing that hadn't changed.

'I've been such an idiot,' he muttered into her hair. 'Will you forgive me?'

And now he was kissing her keenly, kissing her in a way she had forgotten, if indeed he had ever kissed her quite like this. She thought: Has he learned it from the Polish girl?

Rosemary squeezed her eyes shut, squeezing out anything but the two of them, she and her husband, her beloved. Who cared where the passion came from? They keeled over onto the bed and now he was unbuttoning her blouse. She thought: I hope he's taken his blood-pressure pills.

Douggie clambered to his feet and switched off the ceiling light. Then he was back with her on the bed, kissing her neck, her throat. She pulled up his shirt and felt his dear, soft midriff. Once he had been so firm and muscular. So had she. In army quarters around the world they had battled it out on the tennis court. He had the serve but she had the guile.

Oh God, she thought, what if Amy comes in? Two middle-aged people on her bed, half naked, not a pretty sight. It'll put her off sex for life.

And now Douggie was pulling off his trousers. He flung them on the floor, to join the rest of the strewn clothes. Usually, he hung them on a chair before they went to bed.

She whispered to him: 'I'll have you back if you stop criticising my driving.'

185

'You two go home,' said Shirley, propped against the pillow. She turned to beam at the doctor. 'I'm in good hands here.'

Amy thought: She's enjoying this. Lying there, the centre of attention, a nurse checking her pulse, wires stuck to her chest and, best of all, a handsome young doctor telling her it was nothing life-threatening, a minor arrhythmia, but they would keep her under observation for a couple of days. Amy thought: *She's a pig in shit.*

The colour was back in Shirley's cheeks, her eyes bright. Within the bloated face, she was really rather pretty; Amy could see where Nolan got his looks. There was no denying she had had a shock, but Amy wondered just how much she had played up to her own symptoms. From long experience in her job, Amy could recognise a drama queen and it turned out there had been several such incidents in the past. 'Hello, love, it's you again,' said the nurse as Shirley was wheeled in.

Nolan leaned over to kiss his mother goodbye. She flung her arms around his neck, dislodging the wires, and pinioned him to her.

'Love you,' she said. 'Will you bring in my nightie tomorrow, and my make-up and my iPhone—'

'Mum, I have to teach.'

'I'll do it,' said Amy.

They both looked at her in surprise.

'I've missed one class already, I might as well miss two.' Amy turned to Nolan. 'You can give me a catch-up later.'

As they walked out of the hospital, the doors sliding open, Amy thought: Was it really only yesterday that I met him? It was hard to believe. Yet here she was, thrust into the hot centre of his life. Bella didn't have a chance—in fact, she herself had forgotten that Bella was the trigger for all this. So much had happened that she could hardly catch up with herself; it seemed a week ago that she had made the mad dash to Llandeilo, and yet, unbelievably, it was only that morning.

It was late, eleven o'clock, and the car park was empty. Her Punto looked lonely under the arc lights. 'Do you want to drive?' she asked Nolan.

It felt intimate to give him the keys, as if they were married. He slid his long legs into the driving seat and they set off through the sleeping suburbs of Hereford.

Something had been released in Nolan. On the journey home he talked non-stop. He told her his dreams of opening his own garage, how he'd missed his chance due to the bank's refusal to give him a loan. How he had ended up working for the council repairing the roads, a dead-end job but at least a job until they had made him redundant. How as the months passed he felt the energy draining out of him, that he was on the scrapheap. Many of his mates were in the same position, he said. 'I should be grateful that I don't have any little mouths to feed.'

Amy felt a jolt in her womb. *Little mouths to feed.* She should be used to it by now but every time it took her by surprise. Was she becoming a hysteric, like Shirley? A tree loomed up in the headlights and was gone. They drove through a village, one bedroom window lit. She was filled with despair. Soon Nolan would be gone; she herself would be gone. They were both basically cheerful but life had defeated them. If she ever worked again—and she might not—she was doomed to the occasional, arid one-night stand. A quick grapple with men like Keith, the motorbike bloke, up in Lincolnshire or wherever it was. No roots, nothing. Just a shifting from place to place, bunging on the slap for movies she would never see. Movies that disappeared into the ether, the stuff of nothing.

Nolan drew up outside Myrtle House and switched off the engine.

'What a night,' he said. 'Thanks a lot, you've been a real pal.'

Was he going to kiss her? No.

'How are you going to get home?' she asked. 'Shall I drive you?'

'It's only up the road,' he said. 'I can walk.'

He opened the door. At that moment Buffy appeared, cigarette glowing, walking his dog round the block.

'Hello, stranger!' he said. 'We've been worried about you.'

She explained that Nolan's mother had been taken ill. As she got out of the car Buffy said: 'Er—this is rather awkward.'

'What's awkward?' she asked.

Buffy cleared his throat. 'There's somebody in your room. Rosemary's husband. I think there's a bit of Truth and Reconciliation going on.'

There was a silence. They watched the dog cock his leg against the recycling box.

'I can't go to bed?' Amy said.

'We'd better go and kick him out,' said Buffy, moving towards the door. 'It's your room, he's no business being there.'

'Wait,' said Nolan.

They both turned to look at him.

'Come back to my house,' he said to Amy. 'You can sleep in my mum's room.' Nolan stood there in the lamplight, his thick eyebrows raised. 'Please. I'd be glad of the company.'

So she did.

12

Buffy

'Gardening for Beginners' was planned for early October, before the cold weather set in. Spring would have been preferable, being the growing season, but if this was a success they could always set up another one then.

'I'll concentrate on pruning, weeding, plant identification, autumn sowings, division of perennials, soil types, planning your garden from scratch, plants suitable for shade, for cities, for window boxes, for containers. Plus basic vegetable-growing, of course.' Lavinia Balcombe, the course tutor, looked at Buffy. 'How does that sound?'

'Splendid,' beamed Buffy. By God, the woman was terrifying. She was an Hon., the owner of some vast pile over the border in Shropshire whose grounds were open to the public under the National Gardens Scheme. Heaven only knew why she wanted to teach the course. Maybe, like many toffs, she was on her uppers. Or maybe she just liked bossing people around.

'Will there be some hands-on stuff?' asked Buffy. 'You could use the garden here as your guinea pig.

So to speak.'

Lavinia didn't smile. Glancing out of the window, she gave a brief nod. Buffy was relieved. This, of course, was part of the original plan. Though he had got the lawn mowed during the summer, the rest of the place was still a shambles. Now he had got his car sorted out it was time to get to grips with the garden. The beauty of it all, of course, was that people paid him for doing it.

And the first course had been by and large a success. It hadn't gone entirely according to plan, but then what in life did? On day three Rosemary had decamped with her husband on a second honeymoon in the Brecon Beacons; Des, instead of falling in love with India, had been found in bed with Bella; Amy had decamped to Nolan's house, reappearing each morning sated with sex and tenderly stroking his bottom when nobody was looking. Then there was the breakaway jewellery group, who had given up on the course altogether and who had gone home festooned like Christmas trees. But they had all enjoyed themselves and the course had made a modest profit.

And now he and Voda were preparing the house for the next influx. All the rooms were booked, with the overflow accommodated in local establishments. The alarming Balcombe woman had submitted her teaching plan for the week in spread-sheet form, each topic itemised and boxed into its allotted half-hour slot, with ten minutes for questions. He wouldn't be surprised if she turned up in jackboots.

And India was arriving, yet again, to help. This, of course, was welcome—during the last course they had been run off their feet, she had been a godsend. Besides, Buffy always enjoyed her company. But didn't the girl have better things to do than be a dogsbody to her stepdad? He had actually rung Jacquetta to ask her opinion but his ex had been her usual vague self. 'India has issues,' she had said, and gone on to tell him about her own experiments with driftwood sculpture. At what point, in his marriage, had he realised the depths of Jacquetta's self-absorption? Later than he should, but such is the treachery of desire.

Now India was there, helping Voda make up the beds. Buffy had a bad back, he couldn't perform the heavier tasks. His job was to replenish the tea bags. As he did so, India told him about the imminent arrival of his grandchild.

'The baby's due any day now,' she said. 'Bruno's having kittens.'

It was about time Buffy became a grandfather. Though several of his children were middle-aged, none of them had yet reproduced. Quentin had the excuse of being gay, but what about the others? Had their parents' shenanigans destroyed their faith in becoming parents themselves? Nowadays people were putting it off until later, of course—women like Nyange, with her high-flying career. But the old clock was ticking and though Buffy found Bruno's girlfriend a whiny little creature he was grateful to her for knuckling down and getting on with it.

Buffy fancied himself as a grandfather and had been rehearsing the role for years. Everyone said that it was so much easier than being a parent. God knew he had made mistakes in that department but by all accounts a grandchild would be different. Less responsibility, more fun, that sort of thing. To some extent this was also true of stepchildren. His affection for India was unmuddied, even during her teenage years, by the complex and guilt-inducing relationships he had had with the fruit of his own loins. He exempted Celeste from this. Having appeared in his life aged twenty-three, a fully-formed adult, the two of them had picked up from there with a clean slate, and how delightful that had been.

'They're going to text me if anything happens,' said India.

'I thought your mobile didn't work here,' said Buffy.

'I've switched from Orange,' she said, glancing at Voda. 'I'm on Vodaphone now.'

Buffy chuckled. 'How appropriate.'

'What?' said India sharply. For some reason, she blushed.

He turned to Voda. 'Talking of which, I've always wanted to ask—'

'Don't.' Voda held up both hands, as if to ward him off. 'Mobiles weren't invented then. I was named after some Norse god, but they got the spelling wrong. That's Mum and Dad in a nutshell.'

'Everyone asks her that,' said India. 'She's fed up with it.'

Buffy looked at India in surprise. How did she know? And why take such a proprietorial tone?

Voda frowned at India. Why? There was something going on between them but Buffy was blessed if he knew what.

India changed the subject. 'I'm amazed anyone actually pays for this room.' Arms full of sheets, she was gazing at the dressing table, whose broken leg was propped up with a copy of *Palgrave's Golden*

192

Treasury. They were in the Blue Bedroom, the one that leaked. As it wasn't raining, the bucket was tucked discreetly under the washbasin.

'You sound like Nyange,' Buffy said. 'Anyway, if these courses are a success I'll be able to fix the roof.'

At that moment the doorbell rang. Buffy hurried downstairs to find an early arrival on the doorstep.

'God, I'm sorry,' said the man. He pulled out a crumpled piece of paper and looked at it. *Check-in time 2 p.m. onwards.* 'Shall I go away again?'

'Of course not.' Buffy looked at his watch. Five to twelve. 'Come in and have a drink.'

Buffy still hadn't got over the novelty of having his own bar, where he could pour his own drinks and not pay for them. There was a transgressive thrill to it. One day he would get a proper contraption where the bottles hung upside down; as it was, they were simply lined up on a sideboard.

The man, who had introduced himself as Harold Cohen, was looking at the posters. 'I thought I recognised you,' he said. 'You're an actor, aren't you? I saw you in that thing with Anna Massey. You were a Lebanese pimp.'

Buffy passed him a gin and tonic. 'Not my finest hour,' he said. 'Slight case of miscasting.'

They sat down. 'Pia, my ex, was in the theatre,' said Harold. 'But dance was more her thing, the more obscure and foreign the better.'

'I had a wife like that,' said Buffy. He remembered Jacquetta dragging him along to see Pina Bausch's troupe, where a lot of flat-chested women threw chairs at each other. This was followed by a heated argument in Pizza Express and a week-long sulk, on both sides.

Harold heaved a sigh. 'Bit of a girls' thing,' he said. 'As I found, to my cost.' He had a lugubrious, Jewish face and an unkempt air. Buffy recognised a fellow refugee from the marital battlefield; the frayed cuffs and defeated slope to the shoulders were a giveaway. He was already warming to the chap.

'I'm glad I spotted the article,' said Harold. 'Not that I read the *Express*—I found it on the Tube. But things had been getting a bit out of hand.'

'In the garden?'

He nodded. 'I was sort of inundated.'

'I know. Wait till you see my thistles. I'm hoping you lot can sort that out.'

'I mean, with people.' Harold stirred the ice cubes with his finger. 'I didn't realise there was so much desperation out there. I mean, *I'm* desperate too, of course, in a cosmic sense. But I'm talking about women.'

'Women? You lucky sod.' Buffy inspected Harold. He looked younger than him, late fifties at a guess, but nobody could conceivably call him a babe magnet.

'I know, I know,' said Harold. 'Thing is, I've got a feeling anyone would do, even an old wreck like me. Or maybe they just fancy the house. Or the hens. God knows. But I'm finding it rather awkward, especially with a couple of old friends. Things haven't been the same since they, you know . . .'

'Tried to get into your trousers? Send them down here!'

Harold laughed. 'Anyway, that's why I thought I should learn to tackle the garden myself.'

Buffy made them both a sandwich and uncorked

a bottle of wine. Time seemed to be pleasantly slipping away, as it did on a soporific Sunday afternoon. The dog lay slumped in the sunlight, twitching with rabbit dreams. Buffy knew he should be helping the girls but, after all, Harold was a customer. It turned out that the chap was a blocked writer—another reason for the cuffs and the shoulders. He hadn't written a word for months.

'You'll find plenty of material here,' said Buffy, refilling their glasses. 'The town's heaving with drama. London is too, of course, but nobody knows their neighbours so who can tell? Here, the post office queue's straight out of *The Decameron*. Then you've got the people on the course—'

The doorbell rang.

'Talk of the devil,' said Buffy, heaving himself to his feet.

He opened the door to three guests, smiling expectantly. They had vast suitcases, as if arriving for a month. At the same moment India thundered down the stairs, waving her mobile.

'I've just got a text from Bruno!' she cried. 'Becky's waters have broken!'

Lavinia

Lavinia, the course tutor, had joined the guests for dinner. When Buffy came round with the bottle, she put her hand over her glass. 'None for me, thank you, I've got to give my talk.'

'Er, what talk?' Buffy asked.

'My introductory talk. Nine o'clock, in the bar.' She paused, feeling her face heating up. She took a breath and said: 'You know, you're to blame for me

195

becoming a magistrate.'

'Goodness, are you one?'

'When I was young, I was a fan of *Crown Court*. I used to watch it in the school holidays. You were in it, weren't you?'

He nodded. 'First Usher, for my sins. Well, fancy that!' He paused. 'Er, what exactly were you planning for this talk?'

'I call it "Roots and Shoots". Just basic plant structure.'

'Are you sure they'll be in the mood for that? After dinner?'

'We might as well get cracking. There's an awful lot to get through in five days.'

Appropriately enough, Buffy was wearing a floral waistcoat. Lavinia recognised the distinctive leaves and drooping, bell-shaped flowers of *Dicentra formosa*. Though he had put on a lot of weight since the *Crown Court* days—*every button doing its duty*, as her mother used to say—she had felt a small *frisson* when they met. A real actor! She didn't meet many—indeed, any—in her circle. In fact, this had been one of the reasons she had volunteered to run the course in the first place. Had she sounded too syrupy?

India brought in the starters. Several people, leaning back and plucking her sleeve, asked, 'Any news?' That Buffy's daughter-in-law was labouring, at this very moment, to bring his grandchild into the world seemed to have caught the guests' imagination.

Lavinia herself had never liked children and certainly didn't want one now. Her husband Teddy had once or twice mildly raised the subject but she had stopped that nonsense with one of her looks.

196

Now she was forty-eight and any danger of that was long since past, even if she and Teddy were at it hammer and tongs, which was most certainly not the case.

Besides, her job as a magistrate had put her off any idea of procreation. Why? Need one ask? People seemed to think that the judiciary were old fuddy-duddies but nothing could be further from the truth. The things she heard would make a normal person's hair stand on end, such was the Sodom and Gomorrah of modern family life. Emerging from the court she felt like a coal miner covered in filth; only a good wallow in the bath could wash it off.

No, her plants were her children. After all, babies looked exactly the same as each other but each plant was different. No contest. She gave life to them by sowing the seed. She nurtured them through their frail, early weeks, then potted them on like teenagers leaving home. But they still needed her, even when settled into the big wide world of her mixed borders. Every day she walked around checking up on them, checking them for pests, for blight, for all the blows that life might fling at them. Their suffering was her suffering; the sight of a dahlia consumed by slugs gave her physical pain. And their flowering was her triumph too.

Not that her husband noticed a thing. Teddy had no interest in the garden at all; it was just a handy site for a blaze. What was it with men and bonfires? Every autumn he waded in, slashing and burning, leaving a trail of destruction behind him. He looked such an inoffensive chap, but then so did most of the men who turned up in front of her bench, guilty of the most brutal abuse.

That's why Lavinia liked opening her garden to the public. At last she had an appreciative audience for her handiwork. She enjoyed standing there modestly, listening to their gasps of awe—at the house, at the grounds—and answering their questions. *Yellow Book* visitors were a nosy bunch, always trying to worm their way indoors on some pretext or other, usually the loo. They also helped themselves to cuttings, glancing around furtively before taking out their secateurs for a snip. Lavinia didn't mind; she did the same thing herself.

And at least they were interested. Lavinia was in the bar now, the chairs arranged around her in a semicircle. She was giving her introductory talk about plant structure but her pupils seemed more eager to hear about the blasted baby. 'How much is she dilated?' they asked India, when she brought in the coffee. 'How many contractions per minute?'

It was mostly women who asked, of course, but then it was mostly women in the audience. In fact, it was mostly women everywhere, and all of a certain age. Wherever one went—to church, to the theatre, to a gallery, to a garden centre, it was wall-to-wall females. The same applied to courses, to cruises, to just about anything. The only place where men outnumbered women seemed to be at the magistrates' court or the Shropshire Agricultural Show. Lavinia had presumed that 'Gardening for Beginners', advertised for those who had recently broken up, would attract an equal proportion of males—more, in fact, as they were unlikely to know much about the topic—but it was the usual ratio of three men to seven women. Several of these had the bright, needy look found in solitary females of advanced years. Pathetic though Teddy was, the thought of abandoning him and joining their ranks was too ghastly to contemplate.

India's mobile beeped. Another text!

'Do give her my love,' said one of the women ridiculously. She didn't know the creature!

Someone else said: 'I know what she's going through, when I had my Benji it was fourteen hours of sheer hell.'

'My first took a day and a night,' said somebody else. 'I had an episiotomy and forceps.'

'Ha, you were lucky,' said another voice. 'I had twenty stitches. Had to sit on a rubber ring for weeks.'

'Can we get back to the matter in hand?' snapped Lavinia. She pointed to her wall chart. 'This is the stamen, with the anther and filament, and this is the pistil—'

'Read us the text!' hissed a voice.

India read: '*6 cm dilated. Contractions stronger.*'

'Stronger!' snorted one of the women. 'That means bloody agonising.'

'You feel you're being split in half,' said another voice.

Lavinia was losing her audience. She felt a pang of sympathy for Buffy. Was this how actors felt, when trying to hold the stage?

India sighed. 'The poor thing,' she said. 'I'm never going to have a baby.'

'You will, pet,' said somebody else. 'You'll forget about it once it's over.'

'Do you have a boyfriend?' asked somebody else. 'Are you in a committed relationship?'

India shook her head and passed round the milk jug.

Lavinia soldiered on with her lecture. As she did, she felt something nagging at the back of her mind. One of the women, the one sitting beneath the poster of Buffy, looked familiar. A mousy specimen wearing a frilled blouse that made her resemble a piper in an Irish band. Where had she seen her before?

When the talk was over, Lavinia took out her list of names. Searching it, she recognised one. *Mary Taylor.*

The woman in question was standing at the bar, where Buffy was serving drinks. Lavinia read the address: *18 Willow Close, Ludlow.* So she was local. Maybe she had just seen her in town. At that moment the woman turned. She glanced at Lavinia, who was gathering up her papers. Was that a flicker of recognition?

It was only half an hour later, when Lavinia was driving home, that she remembered. Mary Taylor. The woman had been brought before her in court, for shoplifting.

Buffy

The next morning Buffy had a granddaughter. A photo had been emailed showing a crumple-faced baby. Like all babies, it bore a striking resemblance to Charlie Drake. He told India this but of course she was too young to know what he was talking about.

Harold did. He and Buffy were discovering that they had a lot in common. They reminisced about the dwarfish, cigar-chomping comedian who they agreed was the least funny man on earth. Norman

Wisdom, they also agreed, ran a close second. It was a beautiful morning. The two of them sat drinking coffee in the lounge. Outside in the garden was a sight to gladden Buffy's heart: the entire class, busy weeding. They were tackling the far border—a row of rumps, bent over, with Gauleiter Balcombe patrolling up and down barking orders. 'They look like pilgrims at Mecca,' observed Harold. He had excused himself from physical exertion; like Buffy, he suffered from a bad back.

'In the old days, of course, a bloke just went to the pub till it was over,' said Buffy, remembering the birth of Quentin. Well, *not* remembering. In fact, he hadn't been present for the birth of any of his progeny. Popsi had laboured alone, while he was getting drunk. Jacquetta had had both Tobias and Bruno by Caesarean section. She had unique complications, apparently—everything about her was both unique and complicated. Buffy still suspected that it was simple cowardice. The boys were delivered in a private hospital too; those were the glory days of voice-overs. Nyange's mother was almost a stranger, while he had had no idea Celeste had even been born.

Sometimes Buffy wondered what his third wife, Penny, would have been like as a mother. Anybody less maternal would be hard to imagine. She was a hard-boiled hack through and through; even puppies and kittens left her cold, unless she had to write a soppy piece about them for *Woman's Own*. Once, sentimental old fool that he was, he had asked her why she never looked at him with the same devotion that he looked at her. She had replied: 'I don't do dote.'

Harold had a daughter from his first marriage,

who lived in Australia. She had recently had a baby, who burbled at him on Skype. 'Talk about a hands-off grandfather,' he said, relapsing into gloom. Pia, his second wife, had shown no interest in children.

'It's not too late,' said Buffy. 'You could start all over again. Plenty of men your age are pushing pushchairs around. Anyone here take your fancy?'

Harold shook his head. 'I'm finished with all that. From now onwards I'm going to devote myself to my writing and my garden. Both are in a total mess.'

The door opened and Voda came in. 'Sorry to disturb you,' she said to Buffy, 'but your BAFTA's gone missing from the bog.'

'What?'

'You haven't taken it off to polish or something?'

'Why on earth would I do that?'

She looked at him. 'No. Silly question.'

Buffy followed her into the downstairs lavatory. His BAFTA had indeed disappeared from the windowsill.

'You think it's been stolen?' asked Voda, wedged in there with him.

'Who on earth would steal a BAFTA?'

'It's gold, isn't it?'

'Shouldn't think so.'

'It felt heavy enough.' She squeezed past him back into the corridor. 'I always said you should put it somewhere safe.'

The question was: where? The bedroom cupboard would certainly have been safe, but then nobody would know he had won it. On the other hand, pride of place in the lounge would have seemed too ostentatious. The lavatory had seemed the solution—lightly ironic, even humorous, yet there for everyone to see. Due to the shortage of bathrooms, the downstairs cloakroom was heavily patronised. Besides, if various interviews were to be believed, the more stylish Hollywood stars kept their Oscars in the toilet.

Buffy had won it for Best Supporting Actor in *Read My Lips*, a BBC drama about a deaf Holocaust survivor. Disability always cleaned up at the BAFTAs and the Auschwitz element clinched it. He had played a kindly speech therapist, sporting, for some reason, mutton-chop whiskers.

'I remember that,' said Harold. 'You had an old Land Rover and a practice in Harley Street.'

'Never quite got to grips with my backstory. I think I'd had a sheep farm at some point but they'd sacked the original writer so I never found out. There was also a puzzling reference to twins.'

'Still, maybe the best performances are based on ambiguity.' Harold paused. 'Wish I'd thought of that to tell my students.'

Buffy gazed thoughtfully out of the window. 'Do you really think one of them nicked it?'

Harold looked at the figures toiling in the garden, weeds heaped up around them. 'Hard to believe, isn't it? They look so middle class.'

'They're the worst.'

'Maybe one of them's a fan and wants a little piece of you.'

'A big piece, excuse me. BAFTAs don't grow on trees, you know.'

'Maybe you should say something at dinner.'

'I don't want to poison the atmosphere,' said Buffy. 'Everyone's getting on so well.'

They did seem to be a harmonious bunch. The

birth had given a zip to things and bound the group together. Smartphones had been passed round at breakfast by those who had already been blessed with grandchildren, and photos exclaimed over. One of the ladies had even produced her laptop, whose screensaver featured her son's triplets. It seemed a shame to introduce an element of suspicion.

And there was already a marked improvement in the garden. By lunchtime the bed had been cleared and, according to Lavinia, several rare shrubs had been revealed. The group tramped in, ruddy-faced and perspiring, and attacked the buffet lunch. A morning in the fresh air, they all agreed, had done them a power of good. Buffy had still not got to grips with all the names. He had got a little squiffy the previous evening and had lost his concentration. He didn't usually touch the stuff, of course, but it wasn't every day one celebrated a grandchild's arrival. Whether they had all joined the course as a result of some marital break-up was not a question he felt he could ask, and besides, who cared? They were here, they were tucking in, and though it had started raining that didn't matter as Lavinia was setting up her seed boxes in the bar, for the afternoon's tutorial.

He was starting to warm towards Lavinia. She was one of the plainest women he had ever met and this, he thought, explained her bossiness. After all, beautiful women didn't have to assert themselves; doors opened, barriers melted. Underneath the head-girl exterior, however, the turtleneck jumper and pearls, he sensed a women riven with insecurity. Even her lack of humour could be excused as a form of deprivation. All that wealth, you would think they would loosen up a bit. But then he had never understood the upper classes; he preferred to pity them. All that entitlement, all that privilege, those beautiful homes with their herbaceous borders, and yet Lavinia looked no happier than Connie at Costcutter's.

So his heart ached for her when he snuck into the bar that afternoon and found half her audience asleep. And in those plastic chairs too! The morning's weeding had exhausted them; Lavinia's demonstration on pricking-out was accompanied by a snuffling chorus of snores. However, she was soldiering on. 'I would recommend John Innes Number 2. Thoroughly soak the compost before you plant the seedlings.'

Buffy tiptoed to the bar counter, notebook in hand, to check the stock. Scanning the shelves, he noticed a gap. A bottle was missing—a full bottle of Jamaican rum. It had been there for months because nobody drank rum nowadays. Though, apparently, somebody did. He opened the honesty box—just a couple of pounds. Besides, that was for drinks, not for a whole bottle.

Buffy gazed at the snoozing guests, lolling in their chairs. Could there really be a thief in their midst? It was a horrible thought. He ran the place on openness and trust—my home is your home, read my books, play my CDs. His early plan to close off the lounge for his own use had never materialised; he liked people wandering in and out for a natter, and he could always retreat to the kitchen or his bedroom if he wanted to escape. Nothing had been stolen before, as far as he knew. In fact, the opposite seemed to be the case. People were always leaving things behind—scarves, brollies, books, sunglasses, body lotion, even a waxed jacket whose owner he had been unable to trace and which he had finally appropriated for himself. One could even say he made a modest profit in this respect.

Lavinia said: 'These little chaps will produce their first flowers in early April and provide some much needed colour in your garden. At Tite Hall we plant them among the tulips, an idea I stole from Chatsworth.'

Buffy frowned at her. Perhaps *she* was the kleptomaniac. Everyone knew that the aristocracy had the morals of polecats, that's how they became aristocrats in the first place. Perhaps she was prey to uncontrollable urges like Lady Isobel Barnett, famous TV personality and shoplifter!

India and Voda wouldn't know about the Barnett woman, of course; she was before their time, like Charlie Drake. He had better tell them, however, about this latest theft.

Buffy left the bar and went down the corridor to the kitchen. It was empty except for the dog, asleep on the rag rug. There was a delicious smell of baking.

Harold

Harold had wandered into the kitchen for a chat. Voda was making a cake. After she had poured the mixture into the cake tin she let him lick the spoon, something he hadn't done since he was a boy, back in Golders Green. He also discovered that she kept hens. He told her about his own chickens, now fully feathered but repulsive in a new way.

206

'They've developed very unattractive scaly legs,' he said.

'That'll be scaly leg,' she said.

'It's called that, is it?'

She nodded. 'It's caused by the scaly leg mite.'

'Fancy that. So what do I do about it?'

'You need some scaly leg mite powder. They sell it at Bob's Poultry Supplies.'

She said that Bob's Poultry Supplies was situated on the industrial estate beyond the bypass, and offered to take him there.

'You'll never find it, and I need a break.' She slid the cake into the oven and wiped her hands. As they walked along the hallway, Lavinia's plummy voice could be heard in the bar. Harold was playing truant again, but what the hell. He was an adult, he could do what he liked. Whatever pricking-out was, he didn't know and he would never discover. After all, he'd managed without it up to now.

Voda, square and sturdy, wore a striped poncho thing and sequinned trainers. Her dreadlocks were tied up in what looked like a duster. He considered the nostril stud ill-advised, it resembled a bogey, but there was something satisfying about Voda's looks—an autumnal wholesomeness, like a russet apple. Apparently her boyfriend was a tosser and currently banged up in prison. Harold already felt protective of this plucky young poncho-wearer. Buffy said she worked like a navvy, was always cheerful, and could be depended on in a crisis. And the woman ran the darts team! Was there no end to her talents? Harold learned this as they walked past the pub, where she was waylaid by a cheery old drunk who congratulated her on their latest win.

'That's Walter,' she said as they walked on. 'He

207

used to breed shire horses. Once he was doing a ploughing contest with one of his mares, who'd just foaled, and he got so thirsty that he stopped her, bent underneath and had a drink from her teat.'

Voda was full of such stories. How Connie, who worked at Costcutter's, had once been a man. How Robbie, who ran the deli, had a secret second family in Plymouth. How Dafydd, the barman at the Knockton Arms Hotel, had decamped to Goa with a busty Russian, where he had set up a diving school and partied the nights away on the beach. 'Then one day his arm was paralysed by a jellyfish sting, and while he was in hospital she scarpered with his savings, so he crawled home, tail between his legs, and begged his wife to take him back. But she'd changed the locks and become an MP.'

And all this before they had even reached the high street. Harold was riveted, not just by the stories but by the number of people who greeted Voda and stopped for a chat. He was surprised anybody got anything done at all. Back in Hackney he knew practically none of his neighbours.

The rain had stopped; in the road, the potholes glinted in the sunshine. Voda said that all was not what it seemed; beneath the bonhomie, the town was in a terrible state. Services were being run down or cut altogether. They walked past the recycling centre; black bags were heaped around the skips; she said that refuse collections had been reduced and people were driving there in desperation and flinging out their rubbish. Half the kids were unemployed.

'Stuff's happening now you wouldn't believe,' said Voda. 'Friend of mine's husband topped himself because he'd lost his job. They found him hanging in the woods. I blame the wankers in the banks.'

Voda showed no interest in Harold's own life but he didn't mind. This was far more fascinating. By the time they reached the industrial estate he was starting to feel a curious sensation. His skin was prickling and his face heating up. At first he thought it was the beginnings of flu.

Harold's heart thumped. As he paid for the mite powder he noticed that his hands were trembling. It was only then that he realised the cause for this turbulence. Deep down in his body's engine room, the rusty old boiler was rumbling to life.

Mary Pickford's cat. What an asinine idea that had been. The couple of notions he'd flirted with since then hadn't been much better. Here, in front of his nose, lay all the material he needed for his novel. Knockton was heaving with drama—farcical, tragic, duplicitous, touching. The light side; the darker side.

And little did he know there was more to come.

Buffy

India came into the kitchen and dumped the shopping bags on the table.

'Cor, that cake smells good,' she said. 'Where's Vody?'

'Popped out, I think.' Buffy looked at his stepdaughter. She was wearing Voda's long fringed skirt. 'You and she are looking more and more alike.'

India pulled out a bundle of leeks. 'Well, I'm staying with her, aren't I? We like trying on each other's clothes.' She sighed. 'It's so beautiful at her place, isn't it? Hens clucking round, lovely view. Even in the rain.' She emptied a bag of potatoes into the sink. 'Do you ever miss London? Theatre? Old mates?'

'Strangely enough, hardly at all.' Throughout his adult life Buffy had been unnerved by how easily he sloughed off the past. Serial marriages had something to do with it. Each one brought its new location, its new set of friends. With each marriage one became a subtly different person. Besides, he was an actor, acquiring and then losing a series of close-knit families, always moving on, calling them *darling* when he bumped into them again because he had forgotten their names. Impermanence seemed to be the only permanent element in his life.

India was washing the potatoes. 'It's just . . . I was wondering what it would be like to live here. What one would miss.'

Buffy stared at her. 'You're not thinking about it, are you?'

Under the strip light, India blushed. 'The thing is . . .'

'The thing is what?'

'Nothing.'

'India?'

'*Nothing!*'

Far off, the front door slammed. Voda came into the kitchen.

'Where have you been?' asked India.

'Buying mite powder with Harold.' She opened the oven. 'How's that cake coming on?'

An hour later the course members gathered in the dining room for tea. The cake was to celebrate the new baby. Buffy, however, couldn't concentrate. What had India been trying to tell him? There was something thrumming beneath the surface, something unsettling about the whole day. After they had raised their cups for a toast he beckoned Lavinia into the hall.

'I thought I ought to tell you,' he whispered, 'there's things going missing. My BAFTA and a bottle of rum. I was wondering if any of the class has mentioned—you know—if anything's disappeared. Personal items, stuff like that.'

There was a silence. Bridie's grandfather clock struck five.

'I wasn't going to say anything,' said Lavinia. 'After all, it was a long time ago and she's paid her debt to society.'

'What?' asked Buffy. 'Spit it out, woman.'

She looked at him, startled.

'Sorry,' he said. He'd forgotten she was an Hon.

Lavinia took a breath. 'One of the ladies here, Mary Taylor, is a convicted shoplifter.'

*　　　*　　　*

Buffy knew who she was talking about—a shy, inoffensive creature who wore vaguely inappropriate clothes—shirtwaisters, frilly blouses; the clothes of somebody who was playing the part of a woman and not getting it quite right, like a transvestite. She was occupying the Honeysuckle Room, up in the attic.

After tea, they all trooped off to their next class. When he was sure the coast was clear, Buffy made his way upstairs. His heart was heavy. He dreaded finding proof of her crime; what was he going to do

211

then? Call the police? He hated confrontation. He also hated the idea that somebody was taking advantage of him under his own roof. He ran this house on trust. On generosity too. Voda thought he was mad to throw in the wine with meals, but it seemed too complicated to mark each person's bottle or tot up what they had drunk. Besides, he was getting the stuff at rock-bottom prices, having abandoned Costcutter's for a cash'n'carry near the M5 motorway junction, a peeling prefab in a no-man's-land of lorry containers and abandoned shopping trolleys.

The Honeysuckle Room was tiny, home to generations of lonely housemaids. It had a sloping ceiling and doll's-house fireplace, speckled with soot. Sunlight shone onto the single bed.

Buffy closed the door behind him and looked around. A laptop lay open on the chair. A pair of chaste white knickers hung drying on the bedpost. On the chest of drawers sat a small jug, purloined from the kitchen, in which Mary Taylor had arranged a bunch of Michaelmas daisies, probably picked from his own garden. He couldn't decide if this was touching or rather a cheek. On the bedside table sat a copy of *That Takes Ovaries! An A–Z of Female Empowerment* and a saucer, also purloined from the kitchen, with two cigarette stubs in it. A secret smoker! It made the woman more interesting. Did it also make her a thief?

In fact, it was *he* who felt the criminal. Buffy cocked his head, listening for footsteps, but all was quiet. A search through the chest of drawers revealed nothing except an astonishingly large vibrator, nestling beneath her underwear. There was nothing in the wardrobe, or her suitcase. He even, with difficulty, crouched down and peered under the bed. Nothing there but fluff and hairpins.

Buffy got to his feet, his joints cracking like pistol shots. He suddenly felt a pang for Bridie. She would have found the whole thing hilarious. They could have compared notes on running a guest house; they could have spent a convivial evening in the pub, talking about the good old days in Edgbaston—Sir Digby Montague, naked except for his monogrammed socks! Buffy missed her. He missed the person he was, in her company. Both those people had gone. Just for a moment his real relationships felt as insubstantial as the roles he had played. Odd, really, that one of those had resulted in something as solid as a BAFTA.

Where the hell *was* his BAFTA? It was his prized possession, the crowning glory of his career. Buffy, exhausted by his exertions, went down to his room and lay on the bed. Fig jumped onto the counterpane and tenderly licked his face. Dozing off, Buffy dreamed that he had grown donkey's ears and that Titania was softly covering him with kisses. They were on a stage, the audience sighing and rustling like leaves in the forest. Titania was played by Lorna, his long-lost love—Lorna, who had given birth to Celeste, the child he never knew he had . . . and now the audience was bursting into thunderous applause—

Buffy jerked awake. Outside, a storm was brewing. The wind battered at the window, rattling the panes. Across the landing, a door slammed shut. By God the house was draughty! Buffy sat up and switched on the light. Through the wall, he heard a thud.

Buffy heaved himself to his feet and went out.

He tapped on the door of the next bedroom but there was no reply. When he entered the room the cold air hit his face; somebody had left the window open. The standard lamp had fallen over.

It was then that he noticed the wardrobe. Its hinges had perished with rust; due to this, and the slope of the floor, the door normally hung ajar.

Not now, however. Jamming it shut was Buffy's BAFTA.

*   *   *

At six thirty they all gathered in the bar for drinks. Outside, the storm was raging. Everyone seemed to be in a high good humour, as is sometimes the way with groups.

'I think we're still a bit tipsy from your lovely cake,' said one of the women to Voda, who was bringing in the ice bucket. 'You must give me the recipe.'

'I use double the amount of rum,' said Voda. 'The book says one cup but I use two, that's what makes it so moist.'

Buffy spun round and looked at the shelf. The Bacardi bottle was back in place, some of its contents gone.

'What's so funny?' asked Harold, who was waiting for his gin and tonic.

'I'll tell you later,' said Buffy.

Lavinia

Lavinia had meant to leave before dinner but she phoned home and told Teddy she was staying on.

214

He could make himself beans on toast. There was bound to be a cricket match on somewhere in the world if he could work out how to use the new TV.

The thing was, she was having too good a time to leave. To talk about gardening all day was her idea of heaven, and the responses she'd had so far were gratifying. She didn't realise she knew so much; one thing led to another and lo and behold an hour had whizzed by. One lady had even called her a born teacher. No wonder the prospect of dinner was so appealing. The choice between such appreciative company and Teddy's grunts was, as they said, a no-brainer.

She was also developing a bit of a crush on Buffy. This seemed ridiculous when he was far too fat and at least twenty years older than herself, but there was something raffish and twinkly about him, a whiff of the greasepaint, that was mildly intoxicating for someone from her background. Bohemians had a lot more fun than the county set, where the men were such dry sticks. Besides, judging by the photo in the bar, he had once been quite a dish. And the chap *chatted*. She was so unused to this that she felt like someone going to the first talkie—they opened their mouths and words came out! She also felt a certain complicity between the two of them, bound together as they were in their roles as course tutor and host. They had had an enjoyable little huddle in the hallway when he'd told her about his 'stolen' goods. Fancy somebody using his BAFTA as a doorstop! And the rum going into the cake! She had come over all giggly; it reminded her of her pashes at school.

As they took their places for dinner, however, she found herself sitting next to Mary Taylor. Her

215

heart sank. Tonight Mary resembled a Ryanair stewardess in a red suit and white blouse. She frowned at Lavinia.

'I'm sure I've seen you somewhere before,' she said. 'I've been trying to work it out for the past two days.'

'Maybe you've visited my garden under the National Gardens Scheme,' said Lavinia shortly.

Mary shook her head. Her blouse was fastened at her throat with a fancy brooch. Were those real diamonds? Jensen's the jewellers had reported a spate of thefts, it had been in the local newspaper. 'I wasn't interested in gardening till recently,' said Mary. 'That was my husband's domain. He didn't like me helping, he said I pulled up the wrong things. But now he's gone I thought I'd better get to grips with it. That's why I'm here.' She paused. 'You weren't in the Christmas panto, by any chance? In the scouts' hall?'

'Good God no,' said Lavinia.

'I'll work it out in a minute,' said Mary. 'I can feel it coming.'

Lavinia hastily turned to Harold, who was sitting on her other side. 'Where were you this afternoon? I noticed you weren't in the class.'

'Sorry,' Harold said. 'I was buying stuff for my hens. Then I stopped at the bypass to listen to my messages. You can get a signal there.'

'Everything all right?' Lavinia asked. She didn't have the least interest, of course, but had to keep the conversation going.

'Had some good news, in fact. My daughter, who lives in Australia, has decided to move back to London. She's arriving in a couple of weeks, with her family. So I won't be rattling around the house,

216

alone.'

They talked for a while about Harold's life in Hackney. Anything to avoid the prospect of facing Mary, who was struggling to remember where exactly they had last met. Besides, Lavinia liked Harold; he had something of Buffy's rumpled charm, though younger and more Jewish. She had never seen a man less resemble a gardener, but that's why he was here.

Voda, Buffy and India appeared, carrying in the food. At that moment two things happened. Next to Lavinia, there was a sharp intake of breath. Mary had remembered! And the doorbell rang.

Lavinia sprang to her feet. Saved by the bell. 'I'll go!' she called to their hosts, who were burdened with plates. She was one of the team, one of the bohemians. She wondered: Should I tie up my hair in a duster, like Voda?

Lavinia hurried into the hallway and opened the door. It was still pouring with rain. A drowned rat of a man stood there, carrying a plastic bag.

He stared at her, and then recoiled. 'What the fuck are you doing here?'

She peered at him. He did look vaguely familiar.

'Where's my Voda?' He pushed past her, reeking of alcohol, and strode down the hall. She followed him into the dining room.

'Voda!' he cried.

Voda froze, plate in hand. 'Conor! What are you doing here?'

'What do you think, woman? Why weren't you there? I had to take the fucking bus!' He stumbled towards her, banging against the chairs.

'Good God,' said Buffy. 'It's Douggie all over again, I'm having a déjà vu.'

'You're not out till next Tuesday,' said Voda, putting the plate on a table.

'It's *this* Tuesday, stupid cow!' He grabbed her. 'Give us a kiss.'

She pushed him away. 'Not here!' The diners watched, glasses raised halfway to their mouths.

He grabbed Voda's arm. 'Let's go home.'

'I can't! I'm dishing up dinner.'

'Fuck dinner!' He glared at her, his hair plastered around his face. 'Get the car, we're going.'

'Please, Conor! Wait for me in the kitchen.'

'So that's where I belong, is it? In the fucking kitchen?' He grabbed her again.

'Stop it!' hissed Voda. 'Everyone's looking.'

'Oh, *everyone's looking*!' He put on a mincing voice. 'Mind more about that, do you? Thanks for the welcome, bitch.'

Lavinia strode over to him. 'Don't talk to her like that. I'm a magistrate.'

'I know, you sour-faced cunt. I remember you.'

'So sorry, everyone!' Buffy boomed to their audience, transfixed in the candlelight.

Voda took her boyfriend's hand. 'You're drunk, Conor. Let's go and sit down somewhere quiet.'

He shook her off. 'I think they should be told, don't you?' He turned to the guests. 'Look at her, all mimsy-wimsy, butter wouldn't melt in her bloody mouth—well, don't you be fooled. She's got a heart of fucking stone—'

'Don't talk about her like that!' blurted India.

Conor looked at her, and turned to Voda. 'Who's she?'

India said: 'I'm her girlfriend.'

'Whoever you are, keep your fucking nose out of

218

it—'

'I'm her *girlfriend*,' said India, her face crimson.

Voda hissed: 'Not now, darling—'

'It's too late,' said India. She turned to Buffy. 'I love her, we're lovers, oh, it's just so marvellous to say it out loud at last.'

'You're what?' Buffy's mouth dropped open.

India's blush deepened. 'We were going to tell you . . . we were going to tell him, when he got out of prison. We were going to tell the *world* . . .'

Suddenly Conor burst into tears. A small, ferrety man, his denim jacket stained by the rain, he seemed a pitiful specimen. Round his neck hung a string of what looked like rodents' teeth. Voda put her arms around him; Conor slumped against her, shuddering with sobs. 'Don't leave me, babe. I dunno what she's talking about. Don't leave me, I'll mend my ways, I'm going to be a good boy from now on.'

India touched Buffy's hand. 'I'm sorry,' she said. 'It didn't go quite as I planned.'

'No, I expect not,' he said, smoothing down her hair. 'But then, what does?'

13

Buffy

Only five men had signed up for Buffy's own course, 'Talking to Women'. He was no stranger to the humiliation of the empty hall. He remembered a matinee performance of *Sleuth*, in Harrogate, when the audience consisted of two old dears who

219

had come in from the rain and a blind man and his guide dog. For some reason the man had brought in a bowl of water, from which the dog lapped noisily during the second-act reveal. It hadn't bothered the old dears, however, who were fast asleep.

And the lack of numbers didn't surprise him. Most men wouldn't admit they had a difficulty in this department. Buffy remembered Lance and Janet Pritchard, all those months ago—*We don't have a problem*, said Lance. *That's the problem*, said his wife. *You've put your finger on it.* That five men had admitted their deficiency was, in a sense, half the problem solved. And he would teach them the rest.

He had it all planned out. Whether it would stretch to five days was doubtful but with any luck they would all chuck it in and go to the pub. He was looking forward to some male bonding. Now India was part of his household the oestrogen levels had risen—giggles as she and Voda made the beds; swaying in unison as they cooked; mutual hair-grooming sessions, like female gorillas. He was happy, of course, that she was in love, but their few B&B guests since the course had all, for some reason, been female too and so he could do with an injection of testosterone.

Two weeks had passed since India had come out in such spectacular fashion—how seldom, in his professional career, had he triggered such an audience reaction! Conor had disappeared a few days later, to God knows where; India had given notice on her flat in London and was preparing to move into Voda's cottage. Buffy had rung Jacquetta to discuss this turn of events in a *cor, how about that?* manner but as usual his ex had squelched him.

220

'You really are hung up on gender, aren't you?' This was followed by a small, patronising sigh. After all these years, Jacquetta could still make him feel vulgar.

It was Sunday afternoon. Last night's B&B guest, an Oxford bluestocking who had come for a concert, had long since departed. The house was ready for its five pupils. Buffy and Voda were sitting in the kitchen, working out the menus for the week.

'Poor Conor,' Voda said. 'How's he going to find another woman when he's got my name tattooed on his back?'

'In big letters?'

She nodded. 'With swirls and a dragon.'

'Bit of a hostage to fortune, one would think.'

'It's ever so painful, apparently, to have it removed.' She sighed. 'India and I are planning to grow vegetables in his polytunnel. Well, *my* polytunnel. It's all mine, he never paid a penny for anything, he was such a sponge. Funny how you only realise stuff when you've broken up.'

Buffy nodded. 'They do say that love is blind.'

'And he never talked, not really. He just *told* me things.'

'He should come on my course.' Buffy chuckled. 'Just kidding.'

'India and I talk all the time.'

'It's lovely seeing you both so happy,' he said. 'I knew something was up when she started calling you *Vody*.' This was untrue; he hadn't a clue. He thought he was an observant man but then one often didn't notice things when they were right under one's nose. Jacquetta and her shrink, for instance—her flushed cheeks when she returned

221

from her 'therapy sessions', and her subsequent need for a shower. He couldn't tell Voda this. After all, Jacquetta was her lover's mother; blood was thicker than water, even at one remove.

Buffy suddenly felt lonely. Voda was so young and so female. Once or twice they had talked about her problems with Conor but now she had disappeared into a sapphic world in which Buffy could not venture with his big hairy insensitive male feet. He wished Harold were here. Harold understood; he too had been battered by life, by women. They were singing from the same song sheet. The trouble with lesbians was that they made men feel irrelevant; all men had were their puny little dicks which were obviously, so very obviously, surplus to requirements. Harold and he had talked about this at length with reference to Harold's ex-wife Pia, also a turncoat lesbian, who bore a certain resemblance to Jacquetta though without the punitive sting-in-the-tail of hideous, hideous alimony. The Ivon Hitchens still rankled.

'Where are they all?' said Voda, looking at her watch.

It was half past five. The pupils should have been arriving by now.

India came in and gave Voda a kiss. She had only been laying the table in the dining room, for God's sake! Buffy felt a lurch of exclusion. 'Where is everyone?' said India.

'Search me.' Voda turned to Buffy. 'Has anyone phoned to say they're going to be late?'

Buffy shook his head. The two women started to chop vegetables. Gazing at Voda's broad back, her loose trousers patterned with stars, he wondered if she had ever been a lesbian in the past. Now she was out, she definitely looked like one. Harold had said the same thing about his wife Pia, though she was apparently bonier. There was something vaguely intransigent about Voda that he had never noticed before, something a little contemptuous in her attitude to men. He hoped she made an exception for him. He was old and fat and hardly a man at all by now.

Buffy, suddenly consumed with self-pity, left them to it and took the dog for a walk. It was a grey, blustery afternoon; the church bells were tolling for evensong. On the road lay a slab of stucco. It had fallen off the Old Court House, next door. The place was up for sale but there had been no buyers yet; the council couldn't afford to maintain it and it had fallen into a state of delapidation. Somebody could have been killed! Another victim of the cuts! Only the week before, the postman had broken his leg tripping over a crack in the pavement.

In the churchyard he met Roy, the Fleet Street hack, walking his standard poodle. 'Fancy a sharpener?' asked Roy, looking at his watch.

Buffy reluctantly declined, saying he was expecting guests for his course, 'Talking to Women'.

'You mean, how to chat them up?' said Roy. 'Mine never failed. I'd give them tuppence and say *Phone your mum and tell her you won't be home tonight.*'

'Tuppence? Good God, when was this, the Stone Age?'

Roy nodded, suddenly gloomy.

'Anyway, it's not about chatting women up,' said Buffy. 'It's about how not to talk about your car.'

223

'But I thought you've just done a course in that—talking about your car. Anybody shag anybody?'

'Not the ones I expected, with the ones I expected.' Buffy watched their ludicrously mismatched dogs—vast poodle and tiny terrier—sniffing each other's bottoms. 'And it turned out some of them weren't on the rebound at all. They came for all sorts of reasons.'

'But I bet they all said they never read the *Daily Express.*'

Buffy left Roy at the Knockton Arms and walked his dog round the block, down the high street with its shuttered shops, down Church Street where, in the pub, they'd soon be sharpening their pencils for the quiz. Lights glowed behind the curtains. He remembered that first day, the postman whistling, how he had thought *I could live here.* And he wasn't alone. Recently he had bumped into Nolan at the post office; Amy had apparently decamped from London and moved in with him and his mother. India, too, had upped sticks. And only that morning Harold had phoned to say he was thinking of renting a room in Knockton to write his novel, leaving his daughter to look after his house in Hackney. Who could have predicted any of this when he, Buffy, had dreamed up his plan? His courses were, indeed, having unforeseen results.

Still nobody had arrived when he got home. Seven o'clock came and went; dinner bubbled on the stove. Voda went into the office to look at the computer.

'Do you think they've chickened out?' asked India.

Voda, returning, said: 'I've looked at the emails. All but one are from the bloody ex-wives. *They're* the ones who signed them up.'

'No wonder they're not coming!' cried India. 'Oh God, what are we going to do with all this food?'

'And what about their fees, thank you very much?' said Voda. 'They've only paid their deposits.'

'And what about my course?' said Buffy. 'I've been planning it for weeks.'

At that moment the bell rang.

Buffy hurried down the hallway and opened the door. A tall, pleasant-looking man stood there, wearing a waterproof jacket. He introduced himself—Andy Jeffreys—and Buffy helped him in with his bag. 'I've left the other stuff in the car,' the man said.

What did he mean? Buffy shrugged and ushered him into the kitchen. 'Snuff out the candles, Voda, we'll eat in here.' He turned to Andy. 'I'm afraid nobody else seems to have turned up.'

Andy blinked in the strip light. He looked around, bemused. 'I didn't know an evening meal was included. I was going to dump my stuff here and go to the pub.'

'Good Lord, man, it's all part of the package.' Buffy looked at the array of pots. 'I hope you're hungry.'

It turned out that Andy was a postman. He lived in Neasden and, after some prodding, revealed that he had recently split up from his wife. He didn't say much, but then he wouldn't, would he? That was why he was here. The four of them sat around the table eating beef and chorizo stew. He said that his ex, Toni, was into doing up houses.

'She likes a building with potential,' he said, looking around at the kitchen. 'She'd go bananas

225

about this place. Must be expensive to heat, though.'

'Did you talk about it together?' asked Buffy.

'Pardon?'

'Her interest in doing up houses?' He might as well start the course now; there was no point in doing the housekeeping speech about sanitary towels.

'Not much.' Andy relapsed into silence.

'What *did* you talk about?'

Andy looked at him, mildly surprised. 'I don't know. This and that.'

'Let him eat his dinner,' said India. 'The poor bloke's driven all the way from London. Can't you start all that tomorrow?'

'Tomorrow?' Andy's eyebrows shot up.

'She's right,' said Buffy to Andy. 'Though it's going to be a bit strange, just the two of us.'

Andy looked puzzled. No doubt he had been forced to come, against his will, and was now feeling the fear. Maybe he would do a runner in the night! Men could be such cowards. Though, if he were in his shoes, Buffy would probably do the same thing himself.

Voda came to the rescue, talking to Andy about the local attractions. As he listened politely, Buffy tried to size up the man. Good-looking, though he seemed unaware of it. Thick hair springing surprised from his head; tanned skin, from his job in the fresh air. A blokey bloke, that was for sure. He had already told them how he had taken the A40 rather than the motorway due to the roadworks at Coventry, a sure sign of a chap out of touch with his feelings.

'Have you been to Wales before?' asked India.

226

Andy nodded. 'Though the last time was a bit of a disaster.'

Buffy's ears pricked up. 'Disaster? In what way?'

Andy paused. 'A bit of an emotional roller coaster, to be honest.'

The three of them leaned forward, their eyes bright. 'What happened?' asked India. 'Share it with the group.'

Andy said: 'England lost 64 to 8. They only scored a try in the last minute.'

They leaned back in their seats, with a sigh. *We've got one here. Men, honestly!*

After dinner Andy went up to his room to unpack. Nobody else was coming now, that was for sure. The two lovebirds disappeared to Voda's cottage. With his plans shot to pieces, Buffy decided he would take Andy to the pub. The quiz would be over but they could have a pint together with the old soaks.

The problem was, how could he teach the course with only one pupil? He had planned some role-playing; that was now out of the question. So was his multiple-choice panel game, created for light relief. As he waited for Andy to come downstairs the whole enterprise struck him as ridiculous. No wonder only one person had turned up. How could he set himself up as an authority on relationships when his own track record was so rocky? Granted, among the litany of complaints from the various women in his life, blokeish taciturnity was the one shortcoming that hadn't been thrown at him. He loved a natter; he was interested in clothes and always noticed what a woman was wearing; he liked weepy films; he had no interest in sport or cars; he was thoroughly domesticated and liked nothing

227

better than sitting around chatting—though this, now he thought of it, had been condemned as sloth. Above all, however, he loved discussing all the emotional stuff that really was the basis of everything—so fathomlessly interesting, so endlessly absorbing. Why did anybody talk about anything else?

Andy came downstairs. 'It's going to be a funny five days, just the two of us,' Buffy told him. 'I should give you some sort of refund.'

'Refund?'

'Perhaps we could just watch some DVDs. *When Harry Met Sally* is spot on when it comes to the battle of the sexes.'

'You mean in the evenings?' Andy was looking at him oddly. 'I'll be out all day, of course, but I've got nothing planned for when I get back.' They walked up the hallway. Andy, deep in thought, paused at the front door. 'You really don't have to entertain me, honest.'

'But, dear chap—' Buffy stopped. There seemed to be some missed connection somewhere.

They left the house and walked up the street. Perhaps the man was a mental defective, or had Asperger's. He really hadn't got the hang of the situation at all. Perhaps—oh God—his ex hadn't told him about the course! She had enrolled him as an act of revenge. Or perhaps—a more charitable thought—she had had his best interests at heart, and wanted to give his next partner a better chance of happiness. The course was like those starter packs one found in a holiday flat—bread, eggs, sachet of Nescafé—to get one going. On consideration, this seemed too saintly to be true.

Andy stopped at a car, parked under a street

228

lamp. 'I was just wondering if I *should* bring my stuff in,' he said. 'Don't want it to get nicked.'

Buffy peered into the back seat. In the lamplight he could make out a long, bulky object and a pair of waterproof waders.

Andy peered in with him. 'It does look pretty tempting,' he said.

Buffy's head spun. The man was some kind of lunatic. 'What do you want waders for?' he asked.

'Fishing, of course,' said Andy.

There was a silence. A burst of laughter came from further up the road, where the smokers were huddled around the doorway of the pub.

'When are you going to go fishing?' Buffy asked faintly.

'Tomorrow morning, bright and early. They say it's twenty minutes' drive to the Wye. I was going to ask, what time's breakfast?'

Buffy laughed—a high, hysterical laugh. 'Skiving off, are you?'

'That's what my wife used to say. She said I only did it to get out of the house—like, to escape her. She said all anglers were miserable bastards but that's so not true. There's a great camaraderie. And she said we never talk. We *do* talk. We talk about fishing.' Andy paused for breath.

Slowly, it was sinking in. The fellow hadn't enrolled on his course at all. He had come for a week's fishing. Buffy said: 'I do apologise. You must have thought I was mad. There seems to have been a bit of a mix-up with the bookings.'

Once that was cleared up, they went to the pub for a restorative pint. Talk of fishing had loosened the poetry in Andy's soul. As they sat by the fire he waxed lyrical about salmon migration. Apparently they swam all the way to Greenland to grow up, and then swam back again to spawn in the same spot of the River Wye. He didn't seem to mind that after all their trouble he was standing there waiting to murder them.

'You feel the tug on the line,' he said. 'There's something underneath the water but you don't know what it is. Then it's tugging stronger and then bugger me! Up comes three feet of silver!'

He said that his father had taught him to fish; it was the only occasion he had had his dad to himself. It was a time of the purest happiness; they would take sandwiches and stay out all day. On the way home his father would stop at a caravan park where he had business to attend to. Andy would play on the swings. Only later, when his dad had disappeared for good, did he discover his father's mistress had lived there.

'My wife wanted us to get a caravan but I couldn't, could I? They were, like, tainted.'

'What did she say when you told her the reason?' asked Buffy.

Andy thought for a moment. 'Don't know. Don't think I ever did.'

'You never told her? Good God, man! Think of all the sympathy you could have stored up, for when times got rough.'

'Never told anyone.' Andy gazed into the embers. 'Not till now. I suppose nobody's asked.'

Buffy gazed at him with fascination. What a shame Andy wasn't taking the course! If it had existed.

Sitting by the fire, Andy felt the strangest sensation. He was finding himself saying all sorts of things—things he didn't even know he knew. It was partly the effect of two pints of Ludlow Gold, not to mention the wine at dinner. But it was also caused by his host. He had never met anybody like Buffy. It wasn't like talking to his mates—one certainly didn't have this kind of conversation at the sorting office. This bearded old gent seemed to have seen it all before, with his rheumy eyes.

'What do women want?' Andy asked.

'They want a woman with a dick.'

Andy pondered this for a moment. 'I don't want to be a woman. I want to be a man. I want to rescue people from burning buildings.' He told Buffy about Postman's Park with its touching tales of everyday heroism. 'There seems no opportunity for that sort of thing nowadays.'

'Thank God for that,' said Buffy.

'My wife was much braver than me. She went bungee-jumping.'

'The woman was insane!' said Buffy.

'You could rupture your spleen doing that.'

'That true?' Buffy asked with interest. Andy recognised a fellow hypochondriac.

'Something nasty, anyway,' Andy said. 'Thing about being a postie is the pay's rubbish but it's safe work. Unless you catch a chill.'

'Don't be so sure,' said Buffy. 'Our postman broke his leg last week. Saw him in the high street, hobbling about on crutches.'

Buffy was right; nothing was safe. Disaster was waiting in ambush in the most ordinary places—the

231

North Circular, even the lounge. Just now, however, in this cosy, convivial room—the roaring fire, the bonhomie—Andy felt that nothing terrible could happen. This was a proper pub, the kind you didn't find in London any more, where they were either rammed with yelling kids drinking themselves senseless or else smartened up into gastro eateries with stuff drizzled with *jus*, whatever that was, costing a bloody arm and a leg. And ahead of him lay a week's angling, a prospect as near to rapture as he could imagine. When Ryan was older he would bring him along and teach him to fish, as his own father did before it all went wrong.

He told Buffy about his life with Toni nowadays, how he dropped by to take Ryan to the football, how there was a new companionship between them. 'Thing is, I'm better friends with my wife now that we've separated,' he said.

'Know that cartoon? A couple saying to each other *We were happy until you wanted a relationship.* Spot on, in my experience.'

'There was all this, like, *pressure.* To perform, you know? To be a bloke. But she was the big achiever, she was making the money. Bit of a ball-shrivelling experience, to be honest.'

Buffy told him about one of his wives, Penny, who was a journalist and wore power suits. How she strode through life with a breezy self-confidence, glossy hair swinging; how, when his work dried up, he became the house husband and shadowy plus one in her restaurant column. '*My companion had the turbot,* that sort of thing. I didn't mind, at least it was a free meal. But then she started this column for *Antiques Monthly* called "Him Indoors". House hubby's funny little foibles and general incompetence. You can imagine how *that* affected the old hydraulics department.'

Andy was cheered by this. He wasn't alone! He gazed at the men leaning against the bar, sharing a joke. They looked pretty happy to him. Maybe in Knockton men really could still be men. There was wood to chop, homesteads to fortify against the storm, tractors to be driven through the mud and slurry. He pictured himself arriving home and pulling off his boots, his woman—his woman!—throwing her arms around him and tenderly removing a twig from his hair. *Welcome home, boyo*, she would say in her sing-song Welsh voice.

'What's so funny?' asked Buffy.

Andy swallowed his beer. 'Nothing.' He indicated Buffy's glass. 'Fancy another?'

Buffy

Myrtle House felt palpably empty. Now the course was cancelled, its unknown pupils could almost be felt by their absence. Who were those ghostly men Buffy would now never meet? Did they even know that their rooms had been prepared for them? Buffy's annoyance at the lost income gave way to a more metaphysical loneliness as he rattled around the empty house. Voda had taken a few days off to settle India into her cottage; Andy was out all day fishing. Buffy was alone with only Fig for company, and even the dog was restless and whiny, scratching at the bedroom doors as if willing their occupants into life. The rain lashed at the windows; now the clocks had been put back it seemed to get dark soon after lunch. Once, after his nap, he had made

233

his way downstairs in the gloaming and heard a sound in the kitchen. He was still groggy, his head full of dreams. As he paused at the door he knew, he just knew, that Bridie was in there. She was shuffling around in her kimono, putting on the kettle for their tea.

When he switched on the light, the kitchen was empty. He suddenly missed Bridie, painfully. The jokes, the whisky, the love so freely given. *We were happy until you wanted a relationship.* Bridie had never expressed any desire for such a thing, and he had believed her. Could they both have been wrong? Could she have been the love of his life? Maybe a larky companionship and tender sexual gratitude added up to the same thing.

Buffy stood there, immobilised yet again by the past. Who could he talk to? Voda, his most constant companion, was not the most curious of women. Besides, so many of the people he had loved were dead. Why should Voda be interested when he himself could hardly remember some of their faces?

But what could he do with all this stuff in his head? Without the distraction of guests it swilled around until he felt dizzy. Talking about Penny had made *her* swim back into focus. He hadn't spoken to her for a year or so; apparently she had moved to a remote village in Suffolk. This seemed so unlikely that it made her unknown to him all over again, as if they had never met. Was she still with that foetal-aged photographer? He had no idea; with no children to bind them together she had disappeared from his life.

The bitterness had long since gone; now he remembered their years together with fondness.

234

They had certainly lived high on the hog—meals out, trips abroad, all on expenses. Penny had been something of a legend in this respect, even among her fellow hacks. One had to admire her chutzpah; he remembered how she had got the flat in Blomfield Mansions redecorated top to toe for an article in the *Sunday Times* that only ran to four hundred words. Buffy wouldn't have been surprised if she had claimed *him* against tax.

Those days of the freebie were long since gone, for Fleet Street as well as for himself. But it had been fun. For the first time in months Buffy felt a pang for the bright lights of London. He imagined himself leafing through *Time Out* and circling movies with his Pentel. After a saunter through Soho he would partake of a raspberry tart in Maison Bertaux, whose decor had been unchanged for the past thirty years and where that nice bloke, what's-his-name, Belgian, would greet him as if he'd never been away. Maybe a stroll through Chinatown and down through Leicester Square, sneering at the tourists stupid enough to eat in the Angus Steak House, then back for a couple of pints at the Coach & Horses with some of his old cronies. Finally a show or a movie, ending up at a large, noisy table at Joe Allen's, preferably with somebody else picking up the tab.

If Buffy were honest, however, this vision of his life as a *flâneur* bore little resemblance to his recent existence in London. A large part of his time, in fact, had been taken up with visits to the osteopath, the podiatrist, or the sickbeds of friends, followed by trips to their memorial services in appalling places like Penge. Seething, too, took up a good part of the day, the list being almost endless (pavement cyclists, the government, mobiles on trains, that shameless old ham Digby winning an Oscar, and so on and so forth). So did lengthy and maudlin brooding on the past, which was exactly what he was doing now.

It was Harold who came to his rescue. Late on Friday the phone rang. Harold told him he was moving to Knockton—his daughter would hold the fort in Hackney. He had rented the flat above the gents' outfitters in the high street and would be arriving in a week's time.

'Might as well strike while the iron's hot,' he said. 'It's all thanks to you, old pal. Knockton's got the old creative juices flowing—there's something about the place; I felt it when I was buying the mite powder.'

Buffy was ridiculously pleased by this news. Harold was a man after his own heart and would bring a welcome whiff of the metropolis with him. Though Buffy had grown fond of many of his fellow Knocktonites he had yet to meet a soulmate among the old lags and sandalled beardies in the pub; besides, Harold's marriage to Pia bore such a strong resemblance to his own fractuous union with Jacquetta that he felt their bond was forged in blood.

*   *   *

Dai Jones's Outfitter's stood between the chippy and the magic crystals shop. Its window display was celebrated for its continuity. Headless mannequins, dressed in an assortment of sports jackets, corduroys and cavalry-twill trousers, leaned at a drunken angle season in and season out. It had

236

clothed generations of farmers and their sons; indeed, generations of Joneses had come and gone. Apparently Connie from Costcutter's had worked there as a young man before changing sex and crossing the street to work at the supermarket.

Buffy told Harold this as they sat in the flat above the shop, drinking a celebratory bottle of Prosecco. It was Saturday morning; sunlight blazed through the window. Harold's luggage—a laptop and a suitcase—sat on the floor.

'I shall live like a gypsy until my work is done,' said Harold. 'As Virginia Woolf so rightly pointed out, all one needs is a room of one's own.'

'But you've got a whole house back in Hackney.'

'Don't nit-pick.' He told Buffy about a novelist he knew who lived in a mansion in Dorset. 'Every day he solemnly walks across the garden to a freezing little shed, littered with dead wasps. It's the only place he can write.' Harold got up and flung open the window. 'And look! All human life is here! I love these people, they're stopping to chat to each other, it's like Brigadoon!'

Buffy joined him at the window. 'I felt that, when I first came here. The dogs are friendlier too.'

'Look down there.' Harold pointed. 'Even the postman's whistling.'

Buffy stared. 'Good God, it's Andy.'

It was, indeed, Andy. Red postman's jacket, parcel in his hand. Despite the street noises his whistling could faintly be heard as he delivered the parcel to Jill's Things and emerged a few moments later. He climbed into a Royal Mail van and drove off.

What on earth was Andy doing in Knockton? He had left for London the week before. Was he filling

237

in for the regular postie who had broken his leg?

'Who's Andy?' asked Harold.

Buffy started to tell him. As he got to the bit about the fishing he noticed a commotion down in the high street. Somebody was walking along the middle of the road. He was naked, except for a pair of grubby underpants. As he walked, he raised his arms and twirled round to display himself.

People stopped and stared. Behind the cavorting figure was a procession of cars. Somebody honked their horn.

It was Conor. Now he was nearer, Buffy recognised him. Even from this distance, he could see that Conor's puny chest and back were covered in tattoos. A scruffy chap, who looked like one of his mates, skipped along beside him, holding up his mobile to take his photo.

'Blimey,' said Harold. 'Is this normal, for Knockton?'

People came out of the shops to watch. Kids cheered. Conor, who looked unsteady on his feet, was shouting something incomprehensible. 'Get off the road, you twat!' a motorist yelled. A dog broke through the crowd and bounded up to Conor, barking.

Buffy and Harold hurried down the stairs and through the shop. The assistant was gazing out of the window. 'He's been at the wacky baccy again,' he said.

By the time they were out in the road Conor had given up. Shaking with cold, he sat slumped on the kerb outside the newsagent's. His friend tried to haul him to his feet but he shook his head. Burying his face in his hands, he burst into tears.

'Poor thing, he really is the runt of the litter, isn't

he?' The woman who ran the charity shop stood beside Buffy, shaking her head. 'Should have been drowned at birth.'

'What's he up to?'

'Did you see he's had *phone* tattooed on his back?' she asked. 'Next to *Voda*?'

'Why on earth would he do that?'

'Apparently he fancies himself as a walking advertisment for Vodafone. He thinks they'll pay him when they see the photos and he can do it around the country.'

Even Buffy, for a moment, was lost for words.

Harold pulled a notebook out of his pocket. 'Talk about material. And I only arrived last night.'

'I wonder if he's run that past the people at Vodafone,' said Buffy. 'I'm not entirely sure that a deranged skunk dealer is the best endorsement of their product.'

*   *   *

On Monday morning, alerted by the frenzied yapping of his dog, Buffy hurried down the hallway. Fig tore at the letters as they spewed onto the floor. Buffy, kicking him aside, opened the front door. Andy stood there with his red plastic cart.

'I got you to thank for this,' he said, grinning.

It turned out that the relief postman, called in when the regular postie broke his leg, had himself fallen ill. Andy had heard about this in the pub and the next day had offered himself as a stopgap.

'But you don't live here,' said Buffy. 'You don't know the route, or whatever it's called. How did you swing it?'

'Used your address as my residence, sorry about

239

that. Boned up on the walk and Bob's your uncle.'
He said he had fallen in love with Knockton and
taken unpaid leave from his job in London. There
was no time to talk as he had to get a move on.
Which he did, whistling.

As he pottered around that morning Buffy
ruminated on the unintended consequences of his
courses. Who could have predicted, for instance,
that his gardening course would have germinated a
novel? Then there were the love affairs, never the
ones he had expected. Later that morning he was at
the chemist's, buying cream for his haemorrhoids,
when Amy walked in. She told him she had just
come from the doctor's surgery.

'I'm pregnant,' she whispered. 'You're the first to
know—after Nolan, of course. I haven't even told
his mum yet.'

So now a baby was added to the list!

'His mum's a right royal pain in the bum, to be
honest,' Amy said. 'But I've given her a makeover.
Amazing what you can do with a bit of shading and
highlighting, takes pounds off a face. She's going to
go on the internet and find love. Then she can
move out and we can have the house.'

Business was quiet that week—in fact, they had
no bookings at all. It was early November, the most
miserable month of the year, and the weather had
turned freezing. Talk of babies prompted Buffy to
remember his own grandchild, whose photos had
been emailed to him on a regular basis but who he
had never actually seen. What better time than the
present?

That afternoon he looked up the train times to
London. Already his heart was beating faster. Not
only would he meet his grandchild, he could also

talk to Nyange about her tutoring a course on personal finance and, even more enticingly, revisit the bright lights which in these dark days beckoned so seductively from all those miles away, from a world away.

Andy

A storm raged on the Wednesday night but Andy was unaware of it. He was staying at a Travelodge outside Leominster and his room was sealed from the elements. When he emerged in the dark, early the next morning, he found branches littering the puddled tarmac of the car park. Driving to the sorting office he had to swerve round a fallen tree.

Why wasn't he staying at Myrtle House? It was a lot friendlier than a Travelodge. But basically it was a B&B; Buffy had been generous during that holiday week but Andy didn't want to presume on the man's hospitality. As his headlights probed the darkness he knew, however, that the answer lay somewhere deeper. He needed the sanitised silence, the total absence of any human contact, to clear his head. He was in limbo, suspended between one life and another, and what better place could a chap float weightlessly than in a Travelodge? As he drove through the darkness he suddenly realised: *I'm going through a midlife crisis.*

It was a relief to have the sentence deliver itself up to him, fully formed. It had been lurking at the back of his mind but until now he had only applied it to other people. *I'm having a midlife crisis, I've joined the club.* The symptoms were there: he had bailed out dramatically; he had bailed out so

241

alarmingly it turned his bowels to water; he had bailed out, and he didn't know what the fuck he was doing. That pretty well summed up a midlife crisis, didn't it?

The sun rose in a clear blue sky and now he was making his deliveries around Knockton, walking up garden paths littered with twigs, edging his way around spilled litter bins. The air was as sharp as a knife; he felt a surge of mad optimism. Later he felt it was some sort of portent. A cat streaked across the road; schoolkids jostled each other as they made their way towards St Jude's, a school with which he was becoming familiar. He felt, weirdly, that he was living intensely in the present, and yet far memories—memories he thought he had forgotten—drifted into his head . . . A song they sang in his teenage band, when he played the drums: *Take me down, baby, take me where you go.* He was still a virgin then, he hadn't a clue about anything. And yet the words whispered urgently in his ear, they whispered across the years as if they had some significance, and his life between those days and now, the great mass of his adulthood, disappeared as if it had never been. It was odd, this sense of dislocation, and yet it was strangely invigorating.

And now he was walking up the drive of the Powys Camper Van Centre, his last delivery. It was on the edge of town—a fenced car park filled with vehicles, bunting fluttering in the wind, and a bungalow-cum-office. Among the mail was a recorded-delivery letter for *Mr J. Walmer.*

Andy rang the bell. The door was opened by a young woman, her face streaming with tears.

'You all right?' he asked.

'I'm fine,' she said, wiping her nose on her sleeve. She looked at the letter. 'That's for Dad. Have you got a pen?'

'Sure you're all right?'

She looked at him and shook her head. 'No.' She was thin, with sallow skin and lank brown hair. 'A tree's smashed into his greenhouse. He's going to go ballistic.'

She said her father had gone away for the night and would be back later that day, that she was holding the fort. 'Not that we'll have any customers. Nobody buys camper vans in November, do they? I mean, would you?'

'Want me to have a look?'

She led him through the bungalow and out the back door. He saw a lawn, littered with glass, and half a greenhouse. A tree had buckled the other half.

'It's not your fault,' said Andy. 'It's an act of God.'

She stood beside him, pulling her jumper over her hands, rocking to and fro in her misery. 'You don't know my dad.' She looked so small, so freezing and defenceless. He thought: What the hell!

'You got a saw?'

Andy pulled off his jacket and set to work. In an hour he had chopped up the tree—more of a sapling, to be honest—and stacked the branches against a coal bunker. She sat huddled in a blanket, watching him. How manly he felt! His arms ached but he wasn't letting on.

'When your dad comes home he won't have such a shock,' he said, his chest heaving. 'It's just to show willing.'

243

'You're a champ.' She suddenly smiled—a radiant smile that lit up her pinched little face. His heart shifted.

Her name was Ginnie. *My name is Virginia.* Andy remembered the snuffle of laughter, from his schooldays. *Virgin for short, but not for long.* He felt his face reddening. He and Ginnie cleared up the glass together and then she made some coffee. They sat in the chaotic office, warming their hands on the mugs.

'Funny thing is, I've never been in one of them,' she said.

'A camper van?'

'There's a big wide world out there and I'm stuck here. I want to go to Tabriz.'

'Where's Tabriz?'

'Search me.'

They laughed. Ginnie scratched her arms. She said she had eczema, and that it flared up when she was anxious. Andy caught her looking at the clock. Her father was a bully, he could sense it. In a weird way, he felt he knew her life. And yet they had only just met!

And now he was telling her about his mother, who also had eczema, and about his sister who had run away to Hull with a travelling salesman. And Ginnie was telling him how she was good at drawing and wanted to be a fashion designer but then her mother had died in a car crash and her dad had needed her in the office and to tell the truth she didn't know one end of a camper van from the other. And he told her how he nicked his mother's nail varnish to paint his toy soldiers and what a bollocking he got. For some reason this led on to the neurotic women he had met on the

244

internet, how they all seemed to be in mourning for their cats. And he knew he should be returning to the depot but now it was one o'clock and still thank God her father hadn't arrived, nor had a single customer.

Outside the front door stood his mail cart, forgotten. As Ginnie refilled the kettle he told her about his father, how he had found love in a caravan park, and as he spoke he felt a tingling sensation in his scalp—Christ, was history repeating itself? But now he was telling her how he made up limericks while he tramped the streets and she told him a rude one about the Bishop of South Mimms, and as she made them yet more coffee he realised: my throat is dry; my voice is hoarse. I've been talking for two hours non-stop.

14

Harold

The 'Basic Cookery' course was planned for the last week in November. They had a full house again; hopefully this time people would actually turn up. Voda, who was doing the bookings, said that all the students appeared to be women. This had surprised Buffy, who presumed that the vast majority of useless cooks would be male. He had pictured abandoned husbands fumbling around with tin-openers. Voda told him that this was old-fashioned; nowadays most women were so busy working that they hadn't a clue about cooking, it was neither taught in school nor did girls learn it at their mother's knee. Boiling up some penne and slathering it with a jar of pasta sauce was about their limit. Besides, as had become apparent, it was mainly women who came on the courses in the first place.

Harold, however, was going to join them for dinner each evening. This was partly for male solidarity and partly because the writer's life was a lonely one and by six o'clock he was desperate for company, let alone a drink.

He told Buffy that the novel was forging ahead. Andy the postie had now joined his cast of fictional characters. This had been prompted by the sight of Andy's mail cart parked outside the Camper Van Centre, spotted by Harold on his lunchtime stroll. This, in turn, had resulted in a whole new plot line where the local postie, Alec (new name!), had fallen for the manager's wife while delivering a parcel; stealing one of the camper vans they had driven off together to start a new life in the Scottish Highlands. A telling detail, the sort of detail that only a novelist could conjure up, was the sight of the abandoned mail cart as the months passed . . . blanketed with snow during the winter and—inspired touch!—nested in by a robin when spring arrived. Prompted by this, Harold wondered if he should develop the robin theme: the youngsters leaving the nest as a symbol of hope and renewal? Maybe flitting in and out of scenes as a feathered accompaniment to the action? For a while he played with the idea of some metatextual deconstruction—an unreliable avian narrator? This, however, reeked too strongly of Derrida, the French semiologist with whom Harold had baffled generations of students at Holloway College.

Somewhere within him, within the warm-blooded body of the novelist, there still lurked the dry bones of the academic.

Buffy himself was an invaluable source of material. Novelists were all thieves and liars, of course—the subject of one of Harold's modules, in fact: They Lie to Tell the Truth—but Buffy was a friend and Harold would have to ask his permission to plunder his past. The visit to the newly born grandchild, for instance, was full of possibilities. Within that story lay a rich web of relationships. Relationships between people, of course, but also between themes and images (another module). *Only connect*, said E. M. Forster, himself no stranger to the straitjacket of academia.

Maybe Harold could use the image of hands as a symbol of mortality. Buffy had met his ex-wife Jacquetta beside the crib of their baby grandchild. 'I looked at her old-lady hands—liver spots, knotted veins,' said Buffy. 'And next to them this little miracle, little fingers, tiny little fingernails. Then I looked at my old paws, purple like an old colonel's, and tears sprang to my eyes. Our hands, that had once caressed each other with love . . .' Buffy had broken off, his eyes moistening. Admittedly it was closing time and he had sunk a few, but the emotion had touched Harold and he had hurried back to his room above the shop and pounded away on the old laptop.

All these images swirled around but the trouble was, he hadn't yet got the main plot. Not as such. He was just letting it flow, in the way he had taught his creative writing students to let it flow, and the results were just as hopeless. In fact, he would give himself a B minus. His writing was like a dog in the

247

park, bounding after one scent, sniffing another and chasing after that, sniffing another one and shooting off in the other direction, crashing through the undergrowth. Harold the professor stood there holding the lead, vainly calling the dog to heel.

There were just too many characters jostling for space. Sometimes he sat in the Coffee Cup with his notebook, watching passers-by and making up their stories. After he had sent them off on their (often improbable) journeys, it gave him a jolt to see the real live person cycling past, innocent of their bigamous marriage or rediscovered twin. There was Andy, for instance, delivering the post. Shouldn't he be in the Scottish Highlands? The dislocation was giving Harold nausea.

And then there was the larger theme. What was it? Everyone was always moaning that the British novel was parochial; he'd moaned about it himself. What was needed was a state-of-the-nation book, the sort that the big American jungle beasts wrote. Was he the man for the job? He'd thought the Welsh element would give him some breadth but in fact Knockton hardly seemed Welsh at all. Most of its inhabitants seemed to have come from somewhere else; that seemed to be the case with everywhere nowadays. Indeed, perhaps he could make that one of his larger themes, along with the breakdown of the community, the greed of the bankers, the global recession, the riots—maybe even set up an al-Qaeda training camp at Offa's Dyke?

Harold's head reeled. Luckily it was six o'clock; time to switch off the computer and head down to Myrtle House. It was Sunday and the cookery students would be arriving. He was looking forward

248

to the evening; not just to the slap-up dinner but to the possibilities of new material. Residential courses, as he had discovered, were a hotbed of emotional revelations. With luck there might be another showdown that would trigger some sort of plot.

As he made his way through the darkened shop, past the shadowy drawers of ties and socks, he remembered his first wife Doris. She had been a volatile woman—Jewish, working class, blowsily tarty—and when it came to histrionics she was in a league of her own. My God the rows! The plate-smashing was on an epic, Greek-restaurant scale. He could look back on it now, however, with the detachment of a historian reflecting on the Second World War. Maybe he could work their marriage in somewhere? So many years had passed that he could surely shape it into fiction. Nowadays Doris was a matronly housewife, living in Twickenham with a B A pilot; the result of their tempestuous union was occupying Harold's home in Hackney, with her husband and child. However, though the passage of time had long since healed the wounds he knew he couldn't make sense of it, nor of his marriage to Pia. His own life, with all its treacherous inconsistency, slithered through his fingers like mercury; there was no way he could catch it and work it into a narrative.

A Plot At Last: the writer's headstone. He thought: Please God, don't let me die before I find one.

Monica's heart sank. She stood there, glass in hand, and gazed at her fellow students. A cookery course—a cookery course for people whose partners had done the cooking, a cookery course for total incompetents—and they were *all women*. For a mad moment she thought she had come to the wrong place. A week's precious holiday; several hundred pounds; a four-hour drive . . . all to spend five days with nine females. What a fathomlessly depressing prospect.

Their host, admittedly, was a man: Russell 'Buffy' Buffery, an actor. She recognised him from the TV. She also remembered him playing Falstaff when she had been staying in Birmingham, years earlier, organising a conference. He still looked like a man who could carouse the night away with a cask of sack. She could recognise a fellow boozer at a hundred yards. A bit over the hill, of course. But then so was she.

Her frozen forehead fooled nobody, least of all herself. Monica had a horrible suspicion, too, that her pubic hair was thinning—not that there was any danger of anybody discovering this. The missing hairs, however, seemed to have migrated to her chin. She had only spotted this recently, after purchasing a magnifying mirror. Now she had to put on her reading specs to tweezer them out. And then there were the sudden eruptions of wind. Was there no end to the indignities of ageing?

And now another man had joined them— a writer, apparently, called Harold. Crumpled-looking, not unattractive, but his eyes had flitted past her, round the room. There were younger women in the bar, that was why—younger women, sipping their drinks; Monica was, to all extents and purposes, invisible. *Get used to it.* But it was hard, so hard. She had never been a beauty but she was stylish and striking—she was *chic*. Malcolm had said, 'You look like the manageress of an upmarket Parisian department store. Or'—fondling her breast—'a high-end brothel.' But Malcolm had been married.

'Have some tapas.' Voda held out a plate. She was an androgynous-looking creature, stocky and forthright, wearing a lime-green boiler suit. She had a nose stud and multiple earrings; apparently she was a top chef and was going to be running the course.

Monica remarked in a light-hearted manner on the lack of men. 'Maybe I should smoke in my room and get all those nice firemen round.'

'What?'

'I mean—oh, it doesn't matter.'

The girl looked bemused, and moved away.

Now Monica thought of it, there probably weren't any smoke alarms anyway. The whole place had a hilariously dated, ramshackle air. Her own room looked like the set for some 1950s farce—powder-blue washbasin, bamboo-patterned wallpaper, Bakelite light switch. *Bakelite.* She mentioned this to Buffy, who was refilling her glass. 'I keep thinking that Terry-Thomas will jump out of the wardrobe.'

Buffy laughed. 'I bet you and I are the only people here who remember *him.*'

'Thanks for that,' Monica snapped.

He clapped his hand to his forehead. 'Oh God, I'm sorry, I didn't mean—'

251

'That's quite all right,' she said coldly. 'And since we're on the subject of decay, some sort of mushrooms appear to be growing out of my skirting boards.'

'I know, I know. I keep meaning to do something about it.'

'I must say, this hotel doesn't bear much resemblance to the website.'

Buffy nodded. 'They say that about my photo in *Spotlight.*' He sighed. 'Anyway, it was just an exterior shot, and taken on one of the rare occasions when the sun was shining. I'll give you your money back if you like.'

'Don't be mad. I'm here now. Not that I usually read the *Express*, but I saw a copy in Caffè Nero and thought, I really ought to learn to cook.' She drained her glass and said: 'My husband was a marvellous cook but I'm afraid his recipes died with him.'

Buffy stared at her. 'Heavens, I'm so sorry.'

'That's all right.' Monica sighed. 'He spoilt me, I'm afraid. Every evening when I got back from work there would be this marvellous smell coming from the kitchen, he'd be singing in there along to Radio 2, the soppier the song the better, he was such a softie, bless him. And then this delicious candlelit dinner.'

Buffy's eyes were glistening. 'Why isn't marriage always like that?'

'We were just lucky, I guess.' Ridiculously enough, Monica's own eyes filled with tears. What on earth was she talking about? She'd only had three glasses of wine. For some reason, she resented Buffy for believing her. 'Anyway,' she said irritably, 'it's all over now.'

252

But it wasn't. During the evening this phantom marriage refused to disappear. Far from being dead, her husband was thickening up into a retired accountant called Phil, who was holding the fort back in Clapham. He was missing her, of course, but sent her jokey texts ending with *xxx*s and was using her absence to redecorate the lounge. Phil was a homebody; he spent his time looking after her, whisking the telephone bill out of her hand, seeing off the tea-towel sellers when they harangued her on the doorstep. Though balding, in her eyes Phil was still the handsome man she married thirty-five years ago. And my goodness, how they still made each other laugh!

Monica said nothing about this to her fellow diners, of course; she didn't want to entangle herself still further in lies. But just for now she believed in it herself, it was her own warm secret. So this was how married women felt, when they were away from their husbands!

For a moment she even pitied her fellow diners, who were enthusiastically slagging off their exes. A woman called Tess said she had been married to a control freak who barred her from his kitchen. 'It was like an operating theatre in there,' she said. Recipes were stored alphabetically and meals were eaten in holy silence. 'Just his sharp intake of breath when a drop of gravy fell on the table.'

A handsome black woman said: 'Me and my ex-boyfriend couldn't cook for toffee, we lived on takeaways. But now I've got together with Martin and he expects a meal on the table.' This was greeted with groans. 'He's got a busy job,' she said.

'That old excuse,' said Tess. 'How busy, exactly?'

'He runs the Foreign Office.'

253

Somebody else wanted to learn how to bake cakes as therapy for a broken heart. As the women regaled each other with stories of their disastrous love affairs Monica thought how different this was from a tableful of bankers. None of the City boys confessed to failure; in fact, none of them talked about anything emotional at all. The size of their bonuses was no longer discussed in public, for obvious reasons, but there was still some subtler competitive bragging—moaning about their jet lag, about the wind turbines ruining the view from their country cottage, about their hangover from some Russian crook's birthday bash. The few women at these events usually joined in, out-machoing the males. They had to be tough, to survive.

Buffy sat at the next table, a bull surrounded by cows. Anybody who bore less resemblance to a banker was hard to imagine. He really was a frightful old ruin but he seemed to be making those ladies laugh. Maybe some of them could even find him attractive. Monica herself was not that desperate. She still didn't understand why she had lied to him. To get his attention? His sympathy? To make him believe she had been loved with such devotion? She felt so confused that she decided not to speak to him for the rest of the week. After all, he had plenty of other women to talk to. He wouldn't even notice.

*   *   *

Next morning the women gathered in the kitchen. There were nine of them on the course—some had stayed the night elsewhere—plus a latecomer who was apparently arriving at lunchtime.

254

Voda, her dreadlocks tied up with string, stood in front of the oven. 'Today we're going to make a lasagne, a meat one and a veggie one, which we'll serve for dinner. You'll learn how to make a cheese sauce, the basis of all béchamel sauces. You'll also learn how to make a rich tomato sauce and how to make a bolognese, which can be used in many other dishes—cottage pie, spag bol, stuffed marrow and so on.'

Her aproned assistant, India, was grating cheese. She too was stocky, with unruly dark hair; they looked like two little tugboats. Monica, who had a hangover, sat on one of the plastic chairs that had been brought in from the bar. This morning she felt brittle and vulnerable. She'd had a restless night, disturbed by violent dreams and the flushing of the lavatory, which was next to her bedroom. Coming downstairs she had tripped over the dog and nearly fallen headlong. She imagined herself splayed in the hallway, her knickers showing. Life nowadays seemed full of minor indignities and traps for the unwary; for a horrible moment she remembered lying in a field beside the A40, a Labrador slobbering over her face. *O why do you walk through the field in gloves, fat white woman whom nobody loves?* Why am I here? she thought. I should have turned round and gone straight home.

Voda was weighing out the butter and flour. 'Twenty-five grams butter, thirty grams flour,' she said.

The young girl next to Monica muttered: 'I hope I'm going to take all this in.'

'Oh, it's easy,' said Monica.

The girl looked at her curiously. 'You know how to do it?'

255

Monica remained silent. Tess, on her other side, was writing down measurements in a notebook. 'I think he's rather irresistible,' she whispered.

'Who?' asked Monica.

'Buffy, our host.'

'Good God.'

'Don't you think so? Apparently he's had lots of wives. I know he's awfully old, but I can sort of see why.'

'Really?'

Monica got up and joined the women who had gathered round the oven. Voda was stirring the butter and flour into a creamy paste while India stood by, holding a bottle of milk. Monica thought: They should warm the milk first.

Buffy was nowhere to be seen. So he'd had a lot of wives, had he? She wondered what had brought him to this little town. Was he still an actor? If she had brought along her laptop she could look him up. Maybe he just donned a costume once a year to play Father Christmas, a role for which he seemed eminently suited. She remembered those women gathered around him last night; the shrieks of laughter. They looked like eager children—glowing faces, sparkling eyes—waiting for their presents. They *were* practically children, of course, compared to her.

Buffy's remark still smarted. Of course she could remember Terry-Thomas but he needn't have pointed it out. Besides, it was unfair. Though she was the oldest woman there, she wasn't as old as Buffy—he was over seventy, she had worked it out in bed last night. He had appeared in a film, playing Susannah York's brother, when Monica was still a teenager. She would tell him this when they next

256

met.

'Close your eyes, veggies,' said Voda. 'I'm going to cook the mince.'

Far off, the phone rang. India hurried out to answer it.

Monica tried to remember the last time she had heard laughter in her flat. Whistling she could recollect—it was when the man came to fix the boiler. But laughter? Once or twice she had laughed out loud when her cat, who grew portly towards the end of his life, had difficulty squeezing through the catflap, but the sound had startled her. A madwoman, her cackles echoing in the silence! At least she didn't talk out loud, she only muttered under her breath.

India rushed back into the kitchen. 'It's Conor!' she gasped. 'There's been an accident!'

Voda tore off her apron. Muttering an apology, she ran out of the room.

There was a silence. India looked at the students. 'I'm so sorry,' she said.

The front door slammed as Voda left the house.

'Oh God,' said India. 'What shall we do now?'

'You tell us,' said somebody.

'*I* can't take the class,' she said. 'I can't boil an egg.'

'Great,' muttered a voice.

Suddenly the young girl piped up. Pointing to Monica, she said: 'She knows how to do it.'

Heads turned.

'That true?' asked Tess.

Monica shrugged. 'I'm hopeless at cooking in general,' she lied. 'But I can make lasagne.'

She got to her feet. India passed her the apron.

The secret of a good lasagne? Plenty of cheese, more than you think, preferably mature Cheddar with grated Parmesan on top. Plenty of garlic, more than you imagine. Fry the mince until all the liquid has evaporated and it starts sticking to the pan, this will make it dark and rich, we don't want it flabby and grey, do we? A glass of red wine flung in, so it hisses.

The students were clustered around her. As Monica stirred and fried, talking and even joking, she felt an unfamiliar sensation—happiness. She used to be known for her dinner parties but she hadn't cooked one for years. The equipment was somewhat dated—a sluggish Raeburn and a grease-spattered electric stove—but she was coping; she even demonstrated how to mix a perfect vinaigrette for a salad. 'The secret? You stir together some mustard, salt, sugar and balsamic vinegar first, then add the olive oil, ratio three to one. Here, have a taste.'

At midday Buffy came in, well muffled up in overcoat, scarf and beret. Apparently he had been at the dentist's in Hereford and knew nothing of the morning's drama.

As India explained what had happened, Monica pulled off her apron and furtively wiped her face with a piece of kitchen towel. Sweat was trickling down her armpits. And now Buffy was walking over to her, making his way through the chairs.

'You've saved our bacon,' he said, unwinding his scarf. 'What a star you are!'

'It's nothing,' she shrugged.

The students were leaving, filing out of the door.

258

India was taking food out of the fridge, for lunch. Buffy pulled off his beret and sat down heavily.

'Blimey, it's hot in here.' He looked up at her, his brow furrowed. 'I didn't know you could cook.'

'I can't,' she said. 'I just know how to make lasagne.'

It was a lie, of course. Yet another lie. How could she admit to him the depths of her desperation, that she had enrolled on the cookery course with the sole intention of meeting a man? That she presumed that this course, of all courses, would be crammed with them? Of course she could fucking cook. Maybe all the other women here could cook too! Maybe they had come for exactly the same reason!

'Are you all right?' he asked.

'I'm fine.'

'I owe you,' he said. 'Let me take you out for lunch.'

*   *   *

'Isn't it fun playing truant!' said Buffy.

They were sitting in a restaurant called Chez Adele, a chintzy establishment in a cobbled alley off the high street. Buffy had told her that the eponymous Adele was an ex-model, now run to fat, who had once walked out with Mick Jagger. *Walked out.* Monica wondered if he had used this quaint phrase in deference to her age.

'Now, what shall we have to drink?' he asked.

'Just water for me, thanks.'

'Don't leave me alone. I've just been to the dentist's, I need the consolation of alcohol.'

'What did you have done?'

259

'He cleaned what remains of my teeth.'

Monica raised her eyebrows. 'Traumatic, was it?'

Buffy nodded. 'He said there was a lot of staining.'

'Oh, you poor thing,' she said.

'Red wine and so forth.'

'Now you mention it,' she said, 'maybe just a glass.'

Buffy ordered a bottle of Rioja. He was only giving her lunch out of gratitude. And pity, of course—for her age, for her widowhood. Monica still resented him for believing her lie. How on earth was she going to wriggle out of it? She would have to keep her wits about her during lunch, and after that avoid his company. There were plenty of other women for him to flirt with.

Not that he was flirting with her, oh no chance of that. He liked a chat, he was a sociable fellow, and obviously found more in common with someone her age than some bimbo of forty, but this was hardly one of those pre-seduction lunches she remembered fondly from her dim-distant past. Anyway, in the City nobody had lunch any more, it was all a Pret sandwich at one's desk. An afternoon's fornication had become an extinct activity, like clog-dancing. Besides, Buffy was far too decrepit, even for her. That women apparently still found him attractive—*irresistible*—just proved the terrible unfairness of life. As if she needed reminding.

They both ordered pasta. Her hangover had made her ravenous. As she tucked in Buffy said: 'I do like a woman who eats.'

'Doesn't everyone?'

'There's nothing more irritating than someone

260

picking at their food.'

'What else do you find irritating?' she asked.

'People who drink a mug of tea with the bag still hanging from a string.'

'Nothing wrong with that.'

'Oh yes there is,' he said.

'Anything else?'

'Pavement cyclists. People who say *five-and-twenty past twelve* instead of twenty-five past. People who say *twenty-four-seven*. People who glug from water bottles in the street.'

'Goodness, you must be permanently in a bate.'

He nodded. 'Joggers. People who say *love you* when they're finishing a mobile phone call. People having any sort of conversation on their bloody mobile. Car stickers saying *Keep Your Distance, Baby on Board.'*

'You really are bad-tempered, aren't you?'

'And dachshunds,' said Buffy.

'Why dachshunds?'

'They're too small,' he said.

'But your dog's small.'

'Mine's got longer legs.'

'Only an inch or two.'

'So what irritates *you*?' he asked. 'There must be something.'

Monica drained her glass. The wine had gone straight to her head. 'All right then. Elderly couples holding hands.'

'Totally agree.'

'Striding along with their Ordnance Survey maps, fit as fiddles.'

He nodded. 'Striding along Offa's Dyke. I've seen the bastards.'

She spoke in a rush. 'Living forever, hoovering

261

up their children's inheritance, going on cycling holidays together, being each other's bloody best friend. I think they should be culled. They've had their fun, it's time for them to go. I think there should be trained marksmen stationed at National Trust properties, ready to shoot. And along the South Downs Way, and Hadrian's Wall.'

Blushing, she stopped. Had she really said that out loud? But Buffy was nodding. 'And don't forget Tate Modern,' he said. 'And grandchildren's nativity bloody plays. You find plenty of them there, the smug buggers.'

'Withered hand in withered hand.'

'Golden wedding celebrations!'

'Cull the lot.'

They laughed. Buffy was wearing a frayed green shirt and spotted neckerchief. He looked like the aged owner of a fairground ride. Tipsily, Monica pictured the roller coaster of his own rackety past— no chance of *him* being a Smug Married. How many wives had he actually had? Her life seemed so sterile compared to what she imagined his had been—wives and actresses and greasepaint and fun. Bankers weren't any fun unless they were pissed. Even then it was simply a bunfight. They were such emotional retards; she blamed the public schools. And when did they ever step into a theatre?

'I shouldn't be laughing,' he said. 'Not after what you've been through.'

Monica froze. 'I don't want to talk about it,' she said.

'Let's not, then.' He gazed at her, his eyes moist with sympathy. 'My first wife, Popsi, died five years ago. It wasn't like your situation, we'd been divorced for decades. And Bridie, the woman who left me the house, she had been a dear friend . . . But I didn't realise how much I would miss them. It must be much, much worse for you. So I'm just very sorry.' He passed her the menu. 'Now, how about some pudding?'

Monica shook her head. 'Shouldn't we be getting back?'

What an idiot she was! Despite herself, she had been warming to Buffy. Of course he wasn't interested in *her*—how could anyone be?—but it was a long time since she'd been treated to a non-business lunch, and a very long time since she'd laughed out loud. There was something companionable about Buffy; she herself felt more amusing in his company. Wasn't it Falstaff, appropriately enough, who was not just witty in himself, but the cause of wit in others? And she had ruined it all; the whole thing was based on a falsehood. Who said one grew wiser as the years passed? *They* were the stupid ones.

Buffy helped her on with her coat. As his hands brushed her shoulders Monica felt a small, electric jolt. My God, she was a tinderbox! Any man's touch could ignite her. Four years—*four years*—had passed since she'd had what could even vaguely be described as sex: a drunken fumble with the functions manager at the Royal Thistle Hotel, Harrogate, which had lasted all of ten minutes and had ended in humiliating failure. The image swam up of herself, lying half clothed on her bed as he stumbled from the room.

'Are you all right?' asked Buffy, holding open the door.

'Fine.'

'You had a sudden, haunted look.'

263

'It's nothing!' she snapped.

She thought: Maybe I have an atrophied vagina. The functions manager couldn't get it in, but then he couldn't get it up. And who could blame him?

They walked along the alley. A tractor clattered down the high street, its tyres scattering mud. Buffy pointed out people to her; he seemed to know half the town. It was a raw, blustery day, the air stinking of manure, but suddenly Monica felt exhilarated; she had a mad desire to put her hand through Buffy's arm, to saunter down the street like a couple. Like Smug Marrieds! He looked so large and reassuring, bundled up in his Rupert Bear scarf. She had a ridiculous picture of herself and Buffy cosied up on the sofa in front of the TV, pot of tea, nights drawing in. And laughing. *Laughing.*

Monica walked slowly, relishing the fantasy. She dawdled at a shop window; in fact, she was gazing at herself and Buffy, reflected in the glass. She stopped him in the street, her hand on his arm, and pointed out a passer-by. 'Tell me about him,' she whispered. Anything to delay their arrival at Myrtle House. Just for the moment she had him to herself. Maybe they could sit next to each other at dinner.

As they walked down Church Street she thought: What would happen if I told him the truth? If I said: *I'm so lonely I could scream.*

Buffy opened the front door. 'Back to class,' he said. 'Tell teacher it was all my fault.'

He helped her off with her coat. Her happiness drained away. Back to school, the summer holidays over. She thought: How did I suddenly get so old? It seems like last week that I was packing my homework in my satchel.

She had so much to tell Buffy and now it was too

late. Voices and laughter came from the kitchen. As they walked down the hallway Monica thought: I *can* tell him anything. He would find it all interesting; *I* would find it interesting—silly things that had happened in the past, things I thought I'd forgotten. I've never met a man who conjured up words in my head, not even Malcolm, the so-called love of my life.

She had a mad urge to grab Buffy's arm and say *Let's go back and have that pudding.* But the moment had passed; they had reached the kitchen.

The students were clustered around Voda, who was kneading a lump of dough.

'Conor broke his collarbone, the twonker!' she called out to Buffy. 'Fell into a skip.'

But Buffy wasn't listening. He was staring at a woman who was standing at the edge of the group. Monica didn't recognise her; she must be the late arrival—slim and glamorous, glossy bob of auburn hair, a certain age but beautifully groomed. She looked equally astonished.

'Penny!' said Buffy faintly. 'What on earth are you doing here?'

'What are *you* doing here?' she gasped.

'I live here,' said Buffy.

Voda stopped pummelling. There was a silence as everybody turned to look.

Buffy gestured towards her. 'This is my ex-wife, Penny.'

Penny gave a short laugh. 'Well, one of them,' she said.

15

Penny

Penny was addicted to property porn. In fact, she
had contributed to it. Articles about dream houses
had been a nice little earner during the boom years.
If she'd had a pound for every lifestyle piece she'd
penned, accompanied by a photo of a smug couple
in their barn conversion . . . In those days the
appetite fed on itself; property supplements sprung
up in every newspaper, extolling the joys of market
towns, of seaside cottages, of penthouses in old
blacking factories. In between the estate agents' ads
there were column inches to be filled and Penny
was there to fill them—articles about whacking in a
loft conversion; articles called 'To Deck or Not To
Deck?'; lists of tips to sell your home (baking bread,
fresh flowers, blah blah yawn). She had written
them so often she could do them in her sleep. Every
publication wanted a property piece. She fondly
remembered her *Blissful Bathrooms* series for *The
Tablet*, rubbish pay but it ran for years. So did her
column for the Qantas in-flight magazine, 'My
Rural Bolt-Hole', where minor—sometimes very
minor—celebs posed outside their Cotswold
retreat, accompanied by their soon-to-be-divorced
wives. Then there were the more personal pieces
in which she ruthlessly exploited her own
experience—in particular, weekends in Buffy's
country cottage during their marriage. By cunningly
altering the tone, she had managed to spread these
over several outlets, from the local paper to the

266

national Sundays—decorating mishaps, amusing locals and so on. Those were the days.

For the world had changed. The internet had killed off many periodicals on which she had relied and her contacts had vanished as if they had never existed. When she rang, the phone was answered by some infant to whom she had to spell her name. She was a has-been, her glory days behind her. However, like a drug dealer, she had become addicted to her own product. Alone at her computer, she found herself downloading property websites. Each house or cottage was a new life, a *tabula rasa*, with its inglenook fireplace and vegetable garden. By writing for others, she had finally convinced herself. She would move to the country! She would live the dream she had created for her readers! The pub, the duck pond, the sense of community, the village idiot.

After all, she had been brought up in the country—well, Godalming—but she remembered a golden childhood romping through fields and swishing at things with her stick. In later years there was Buffy's cottage—long since sold—where she had pleasant memories of quaffing Chardonnay on warm summer evenings. Admittedly, they had never gone there during the winter, but no doubt they could have enjoyed bracing walks followed by cosy evenings around the fire. And she had friends who lived in the country and seemed happy enough— crowingly happy, in fact. Infuriatingly happy. *How can you stand London? We wish we'd done it sooner.*

But the main trigger was her break-up with Colin. It was a miracle, really, that they had lasted five years, what with him being so young and—to be perfectly honest—boring. Needless to say, her friends had realised this long before she did. But in the early days, when he droned on she had just gazed at his mouth, and in later years she had simply been grateful she had a man, and such an astonishingly handsome one, when so many of her female friends had been abandoned. Besides, they were often apart—Colin photographing celebs all over the world, she herself off on assignments. Weeks went by when they hardly spoke. And then she had discovered that Colin, a man not known for his originality, had been banging one of his models.

Their break-up had coincided with her sixtieth birthday. These two traumatic events had made her reassess her life. Why not kick over the traces and make a fresh start? She told herself that she'd grown sick of the brittle media world of PRs and press junkets; the truth was, it had grown sick of her. She'd had a good run for her money but now she was a dinosaur. Anyway, soon there wouldn't be any magazines at all. God knew how the young were going to cope, but too bad, she was off. Off to the country! Strangely enough, it was Buffy's announcement that had given her the final impetus. She had bumped into him in Wardour Street one afternoon and he had launched into a diatribe against parking wardens, something about having to eat biscuits in Nyange's car, and said he was fed up with London and thinking of moving to the sticks. During their marriage Buffy had frequently surprised her. Nothing, however, had astonished her as much as this.

'You won't last a week,' she had said. 'Do you realise it's outside Zone 2? It was enough of a heave-ho to get yourself to the Chelsea Arts Club.'

'That's what my children said. Have you no

faith?'

'No.'

'But I had a cottage for ten years.'

'Only because Jacquetta made you buy it. When *we* were married I had to drag you down there by your hair. By Sunday lunchtime you were itching to get back to London. And we never went there after September.' She had paused thoughtfully. 'It was like a mistress rather than a wife.'

'I know that look,' Buffy had said. 'Thinking of an article, are you? *Weekend Cottages: A Bit on the Side*? I'm sure you've done that one already.'

'Since when has that stopped me?' She had shrugged. 'Anyway, *I'm* thinking of moving to the country.'

It had been Buffy's turn to look astonished. *'You?'*

'It's no odder than you.'

'Where do you want to go?'

'Some little cottage somewhere,' she had said.

'Where?'

'Some little village.'

'Some little village?' he had said. 'But there won't be a Harvey Nicks.'

'I've changed, Buffy. I'm not the woman you knew.' She had added bitchily: 'Or thought you knew. Maybe you didn't know me at all.'

Why had she said that? Just to unsettle him. Buffy had raised his eyebrows. But it did unnerve her, that whenever they met they slipped back into their old intimacy, as if nothing had changed.

'Maybe I'll take up birdwatching,' she had said. 'Bye.'

Her lips had brushed Buffy's beard. Did he have another woman? If so, she wasn't keeping that beard in trim. Penny herself used to cut it, the hair scattering on his towelled lap—greyer hairs as the years passed. The sudden smell of him had jolted her. She had stepped off the pavement, nearly colliding with a cyclist.

This meeting had hardened her resolve. If Buffy could do it, so could she. London was too full of memories; bumping into Buffy was like stepping back into the past, it couldn't be healthy.

So her friends thought she was mad? She would show them. Besides, once she had found somewhere they would come to stay for the weekend, they promised. She had visions of them all slopping about in their jim-jams, munching toast and reading the Sunday papers before tramping across the fields in their wellies. Social life in London was a staccato affair—phone calls, the occasional lunch or dinner, punctuating the long periods of solitude. People never just mooched around, chatting. It would be like marriage but without the rows.

Within three months Penny had sold her flat and bought a cottage in Suffolk, in the village of Little Haddon, twenty miles from Buffy's old place. It was a charming cottage—beamed ceilings, uneven brick floor—and a charming village, its thatched dwellings painted pink, its manor house mentioned in Pevsner. It even had a shop, selling jars of boiled sweets.

*   *   *

'So then what happened?' asked Harold.

The two of them were drinking coffee in the lounge. Everyone else was in the bar watching a

270

DVD of *Babette's Feast*, which both Penny and Harold had already seen. Foodie films were on offer every night as an after-dinner entertainment.

'Well, I bought it in the summer, of course,' said Penny.

'Of course,' he said.

'By November it was not only freezing cold and pouring with rain but it seemed to get dark as soon as I'd had lunch. Eight hours of darkness to kill before one could reasonably think of going to bed. What on earth do people do?'

'They drink and commit adultery,' Harold said.

'But there was nobody to do it with.'

'Nobody in the village?'

She shook her head. 'It goes dead in the winter. They're all second homes and nobody's there. Or they're retired people who go to Florida. Or they're local people and very, very old. Do you know, they have their own Mobility Scooter Formation Trophy Team?'

'Good-oh,' said Harold. 'Formula One or Two?'

'Nothing happens. Nothing happens! I was walking to the shop holding a mug of tea, because I was still drinking it, and an old dear stopped and gasped and said, *"Now I've seen everything."*'

Harold laughed. 'What about your friends coming to stay?'

'They don't. They're busy, you see, they *have* a life. And grandchildren and weekend cottages that *they're* always trying to lure *me* to. I'm thinking of bribing them but who in their right mind would want to spend a weekend in a sea of mud, in the dark, when they could be having fun in London?'

'But they'd come to see *you*,' said Harold.

'No they won't. I've become so boring. The high

spot of last week was going to Halesworth to get my lawnmower mended.'

'Tell me all about it.' Harold leaned forward, eyes bright. 'What sort of lawnmower? What was wrong with it?'

Penny laughed. She was warming to Harold even though he wasn't her type—too scruffy, too neurotic. Too short. There were moth-holes in his jumper and his wrists were as hairy as a monkey's.

'It's not so thrilling in this place either,' he said. 'Though I hear there's a Museum of Sheep Droppings in Llandrod.'

'Excellent. Do let's go.'

Apparently Harold had hunkered down in Knockton because he was writing a novel. He and Buffy had become friends and she could see why. They had a lot in common—both liking a natter, both somewhat battered by life and both washed up in what looked like a dead-end town for reasons she couldn't quite fathom.

She was glad to have escaped her ex all evening. Buffy seemed to find it amusing but she still felt disorientated by the whole thing. She'd no idea he had moved to Wales, or indeed that he was—of all hilarious things—running a hotel. She had simply heard about a cookery course and thought that as the nearest M&S was thirty miles away she ought to learn the rudiments of making a meal, something she'd seldom had to do after a lifetime of freeloading and shopping at Selfridges Food Hall. Besides, as the nights drew in she was going stir-crazy and thought a week among other people might restore her sanity.

'Why didn't Buffy know you were coming?' asked Harold.

She shrugged. 'Our surnames are different, and I guess that girl with the funny name—'

'Voda.'

'—made the booking.'

'Well, I'm glad you're here. I've heard a lot about you.'

Penny coloured. 'Really? What has he said?'

They were interrupted by the murmur of voices. The door opened and people shuffled in from the bar, where the film had ended. India came over to Penny and kissed her goodnight. She wore a plastic hibiscus flower in her hair. So did Voda, for reasons best known to themselves.

'We're just off, see you tomorrow,' said India.

Penny nodded. This had been another shock, of course: to find her ex-sort-of stepdaughter at Myrtle House—and not just there, but a lesbian to boot! India's heavy features were radiant with happiness. Penny was glad for her; India had had a rocky time in the past—hardly surprising, with a mother like Jacquetta.

India leaned closer and whispered in Penny's ear: 'Buffy's a bit sozzled.'

'That makes a change,' said Penny.

'Maybe you should keep an eye on him.'

Penny gave her a tight smile. 'Sweetie, he's not my responsibility any more.'

Monica

Later, Monica couldn't remember how she had ended up in Buffy's bed. They were both drunk, of course. She remembered them becoming maudlin about the film, saying nobody like Babette would

273

cook a feast for *them*. She remembered the two of them drinking whisky in the sitting room, everybody gone, the ashes dead in the grate. She remembered the animal presence of Buffy's ex-wife lying in bed upstairs, a woman with whom he must have made love a thousand times. Christ, she hadn't actually put that into words, had she? What else had she told Buffy? That she was as lonely as hell?

She was woken by the dog jumping onto the bed. Buffy lay beside her, snoring into the pillow, one arm flung across her waist. She was still wearing her (mismatched) bra and knickers, and thank God her tights. Buffy seemed to be clothed, though minus his trousers. The bedside lamp was still on, though grey light glimmered through the window.

Monica eased herself from under the duvet and picked up her clothes. The floorboards creaked as she crept out of the room, as furtive as a teenager. It was half past seven. On the landing she paused, listening. The house was silent. Back in her room she poured herself a glass of water, her hands trembling. Her head pounded and she had a raging thirst.

She dreamed she was lying trussed up and naked in a field. Wolves were nibbling her face. Her father stood by, watching. She had a horrible feeling that he was sexually aroused and woke with a jerk, drenched in sweat. It was five to eleven. There was a faint smell of fish.

Down in the kitchen Voda greeted her cheerfully. 'We're making a fish pie. And a bouillabaisse with the stock. I've been talking about soups in general but I'm sure you'll catch up.'

Nobody looked at Monica oddly. India made her a cup of tea and some toast. There was no sign of

274

Buffy.

He appeared at lunchtime, however, when she was sitting down with her plate of food. Standing in the doorway, he caught her eye. Monica felt herself reddening. He scratched his head and gave her a puzzled grin. How unreal it was, to have spent the night lying next to this man! He looked a shambles in his crumpled yellow shirt. Though he had changed his clothes, he still appeared to have slept in them.

Penny was sitting opposite her, looking cool and observant. Did she know that something was up? She wore a *Virgin Airlines Maiden Voyage* T-shirt; there was a healthy, Home Counties glow to her, though Monica suspected a nip and tuck. Probably a tennis player. Anybody less like Buffy was hard to imagine.

Penny was telling one of the women about moving to the country, how it wasn't what she had expected. She said she was writing a column called 'Rural Moans' for the *Grocer*, the only publication that took her stuff, she said, beggars couldn't be choosers. Apparently her cottage was next to a field and when winter arrived an encampment of Ukrainian vegetable pickers was revealed beyond her hedge. 'I'm sure they weren't there in the summer, when I bought it,' she said. 'Their sex wagon's right beside my potting shed. The noise they make, honestly! Like cats being strangled. I wrote a column about it, rather amusing I thought, but they considered it unsuitable for grocers and I had to write about the cuts to the local bus service instead.'

Monica was only half listening. Buffy sat at the next table, gazing pensively at his plate of cold cuts.

275

For once he wasn't being the life and soul of the party. Was it a hangover, or the realisation that he had spent the night with her half-clothed, ageing body?

After lunch the students trooped back into the kitchen to make fairy cakes. Monica announced that she had a headache and was going out for some air. She left Myrtle House and walked down the street, willing Buffy to have overheard what she had said, willing him to follow her. She suddenly, ridiculously, felt sick with longing.

And then the dog was yapping at her heels and she heard Buffy's footsteps.

'Monica!'

She stopped. Buffy wheezily caught up with her and put his hand on her arm.

'I'm so sorry,' he panted.

'What for?'

He frowned with the effort of remembering. 'We didn't do anything, did we?'

She shook her head. 'Not as far as I can remember.'

Buffy let out a sigh. 'Thank God for that.'

Monica shook off his arm. 'What do you mean, *thank God*?' She glared at him, her eyes glittering with tears. 'Such a repulsive thought, is it?'

'I didn't mean—'

'Leave me alone!' She pushed past him and hurried off down the street.

'Monica!' he called.

The dog danced around her feet, whining. 'Fuck off!' she snapped.

'Wait for me!' Buffy shouted.

Monica, stumbling over the dog, turned up an alley and broke into a run. Buffy called out, faintly.

She found herself in a back lane, behind the houses. A man was mending his car so she veered away and turned left. She hurried along the gravel, the dog nipping her ankles. Suddenly the bloody animal was under her foot. She tripped and fell heavily.

'Are you all right?' Buffy helped her up.

'I'm fine!'

He brushed some leaves off her skirt. 'Listen, Monica, I didn't mean it like that. You know I didn't.'

'I don't want to talk about it,' she muttered, pulling away.

He pulled her back. 'I just didn't want you to be lumbered with my drunken advances, really too revolting for a woman of your calibre.'

'My age, you mean.'

'No! calibre. I had a horrible feeling I'd taken advantage of you—if I was capable of such a thing, which I rather doubt.' Holding her hands, he searched her face. 'Especially after all you've been through.'

'What do you mean?'

'Well, with your bereavement.'

'I'm not bereaved,' Monica blurted out. 'I've never even been married.'

Buffy stared at her. 'What?'

'I made it up.' She shrugged carelessly, her heart pounding.

'Why?'

'I just felt like it. You're an actor, you do it. I just felt like trying something else out. New place, new people. I'd be a different person.'

Why had she said that? She hadn't a clue. Buffy gazed at her, his chest heaving. Beyond the wall

277

she could hear the sound of a lute playing. She suddenly felt hopelessly, swooningly, intimate with him.

'I think I ought to leave,' she said.

'I'll walk back with you.'

'I mean, go home.'

He jerked back, as if he'd been slapped. 'Why?'

'I've made a total idiot of myself.'

'It's not you, it's me.'

'See? You thought the whole thing was ridiculous.'

He searched her face. 'Was it?' He rubbed his beard thoughtfully. 'I thought it was rather nice.'

Monica's heart lurched. The lute plucked her own unsaid words out of the air. Maybe Buffy was thinking that too because neither of them spoke.

'Who's that playing?' she asked at last.

'Simon, my neighbour. A hairy, good sort of person. His wife runs a vintage clothes shop that smells of mothballs.'

'I've never understood why people want to look like their grannies.'

'We're in a bit of a time warp here,' he said. 'It's one of its charms.'

Up the lane, the engine spluttered into life. They heard it revving, over and over.

'Don't go home,' said Buffy. 'Sit with me at dinner.'

Penny

'Do you think there's something up with Monica and Buffy?' asked Penny. She was sitting with Harold in the Coffee Cup.

278

'I wouldn't be surprised.' He pointed to the young woman pouring tea. 'Romance seems to blossom at Buffy's establishment. That's Amy, she's just started work here. She copped off with the tutor on her course. And another bloke found love at a camper-van outlet.'

Penny's eyes narrowed. 'There's something going on, I just know it. I've got a sixth sense, you see. At school I hired myself out as a lie-detector.'

'How much did you charge?'

'Threepence a time. I was always right.'

He raised his eyebrows. 'I'd better watch out, then.'

Penny liked Monica. There was something brittle and defensive about her but beneath it Penny could sense, with her sixth sense, a woman trembling with insecurity. Monica might not be Buffy's type but then who was? When it came to female companionship he was catholic in his tastes. Dim, daffy, intense, feminist, glamorous, dowdy . . . they came in all shapes and sizes, though, to do Buffy justice, he remained faithful to each one as long as it lasted. The man was just a hopeless romantic. And no doubt he was lonely here, miles from the bright lights of Soho. Who could begrudge the chap a bit of love?

Penny could, of course. She was his ex-wife, for God's sake. Any subsequent liaison could stir up a rich brew of feelings. Resentment, that this time round it could be more of a success. A patronising pity for the woman about to embark on that dubious adventure called Life With Buffy. Curiosity, of course. A complex sense of sisterhood, muddied by various emotions she preferred not to analyse. Surely not envy—surely not. She wouldn't

279

take Buffy back if he begged her on bended knee. It would be like picking up a dead walrus.

'What's so funny?' asked Harold.

'Nothing. Good luck to her, she'll need it.'

'How long were you married?'

'Seven years.'

'Were you happy?'

Penny considered this for a moment. 'I was never bored, I'll give him that. And we did have fun.'

Suddenly she felt dizzy with loss. How she had adored him! She remembered their early years, the physical pain when they were apart. She remembered how Buffy's very possessions—a pair of espadrilles, the book he'd been reading—were irradiated with her passion for him. *O happy horse, to bear the weight of Antony!* She must have been mad.

'He really was hopeless,' she said. 'Drunk, self-absorbed . . . he was an actor, for goodness' sake! He lived in total chaos. And then there were all those children crawling out of the woodwork.'

'Only one, surely. He knew about the other ones.'

'It just seemed typical, somehow,' she said. 'He was always forgetting where he left things.'

'Well, he seems to be making a go of it here,' said Harold, stirring the froth in his cup.

'Yes, because he's got two women to do all the work.'

'Rather a cunning plan, though, to get people to pay him for fixing his car and sorting out his garden and whatnot. He's going to get the DIY course to do all the repairs on his house.'

Penny paused thoughtfully. 'So that was his idea? And cooking the dinners too? Bloody brilliant.'

Harold's spoon stopped. 'Don't you dare,' he said. 'Buffy told me about that look.'

'What look?'

'That look in your eyes. The *is-there-a-piece-in-it* look. Well, you can't have it. I've bagged it for my novel.'

Penny blushed. 'I wouldn't touch it with a bargepole,' she lied.

Harold's eyes narrowed. 'That'll be threepence.'

Penny laughed. Outside it was pouring with rain but here in the café, with its steamed-up windows and hissing espresso machine, it felt cosy and confidential. Harold was good company, she had to give him that. Colin had been great in bed but he'd had no sense of humour at all. It had taken her a while to admit this, just as it had taken her a while to admit that moving to the country had been a disaster. Could she really face a second winter there alone?

Harold, sipping his coffee, was gazing with interest at the other customers. Beneath his moth-eaten cardigan he wore a Fudge Factory T-shirt. His ex-wife must have given it to him. By now Penny knew a little about Pia. Just for a moment, startling herself, she felt the same stab of jealousy she had felt about Jacquetta. The two women sounded so similar—arty, self-absorbed. Pia had once been a dancer. She would have a flat stomach and strong vaginal muscles. It didn't bear thinking about.

'What are you thinking?' asked Harold.

'Nothing.'

Luckily, Amy came to the rescue. She was passing their table and paused to chat to Harold.

'Nolan's mum's going speed-dating tonight,' she

said. 'I'm giving her another makeover. She's going to look a million dollars.'

Penny said: 'When the speed-dating craze started I signed up for one; I was going to write a piece about it. Then I discovered that all the other people were doing exactly the same thing. We were all journalists, speed-dating each other.'

Harold laughed. Then a gleam came into his eye, a gleam she recognised.

'Don't you dare use it,' she said. 'It's mine.'

Harold sighed. 'We'd better make a pact. You don't use me and I don't use you.'

'OK.'

They shook hands. His hand was dry and warm, the same size as hers. Something shifted in Penny's stomach. She removed her hand and inspected the sugar bowl.

Amy moved off, to serve another customer. Harold looked at her, writing in her little notebook.

'What were you like at her age?' he asked.

'Ambitious,' said Penny. 'I would have got out of this place like a bat out of hell.'

'Amy's done the opposite. Given up her job, everything, to come and live here. She says she's never been happier in her life.'

A dead-end town. That was Penny's first impression. Now she wasn't so sure. She watched the people in the café leaning back in their chairs and chatting to each other; she watched someone greeting a woman as she came in. Never in her life had she been part of a community.

She turned back to Harold. 'So what were *you* like, when you were her age?'

'A nice Jewish boy married to a nice Jewish girl.'

'Of course. Doris.'

'She turned out to be a plate-thrower but I probably deserved it.' He scratched his head. 'I'm a lot easier to live with now. So, I suspect, is she.'

They both fell into a thoughtful silence. Penny returned her attention to the bowl, patting the sugar flat with her spoon.

'What do we do about it?' Harold said at last. 'All this history?'

'I don't know,' she said.

'Do you feel that great swathes of your life have happened to somebody you hardly recognise?'

Penny nodded. 'It's called being sixty, I guess.' She stopped. 'Oh gosh, you're not yet, are you?'

He raised his eyebrows. 'What's a couple of years, between friends?'

'That's what we are, aren't we?' she said. 'Such a relief, not fancying each other.'

He nodded. 'Such a relief.'

She stood up. 'Back to your book then.'

'Back to your cooking.' He got to his feet. 'Same time tomorrow?'

She nodded. 'You really should do something about that cardigan.'

Monica

Monica missed the pre-dinner drinks so she could have a bath; it was the only time the bathroom was guaranteed to be free. She had bought herself a screw-top bottle of wine so she poured some into a tooth mug and sipped it while she lay soaking in the meagre bubbles squeezed from her sachet.

Sit with me at dinner. There was something startlingly erotic about that sentence. It was like

May I have this dance? She knew she was being foolish. Buffy was probably just being polite. Besides, he wasn't her type—his eyes were watery and he had split veins in his nose. Anyway, he was an actor and who could trust one of those?

But who *was* her type? Nowadays, to be perfectly frank, it was anybody who would have her. The slightest flicker of interest and she was theirs. Or would be, if such a thing happened at all. Monica watched a lonely wasp, a relic from the summer, drag itself along the windowsill. I'm just a sex-starved old hag, she thought.

And yet . . . and yet. There was something about Buffy that put a skip in her step. The lunch with him had been so larky; it reminded her of being with Malcolm—the complicity, the jokes.

How many women had Buffy entertained at lunch? There was a handrail beside the bath, installed by the previous owner who had apparently reached a ripe old age. The woman must have been madly in love with Buffy, to leave him her house. And she wasn't even one of his wives.

Monica climbed out of the bath without the help of the handrail; she could manage *that*. The mirror, thankfully, was too steamed-up to reflect her naked body. She dried herself, returned to her room and fished out her Janet Reger underwear. This time she would be prepared—if, indeed, anything were to happen, which she doubted. But her stupid heart was pounding. *If I was capable of such a thing,* he had said. But failure could be bonding. Naked in each other's arms, they could have a giggle. She was a woman of experience; she would understand. Maybe none of his wives or lovers had understood him. Maybe his life had been a series of false starts.

284

She despised romantic fiction but that was the point of it, wasn't it? The right person coming along, when one least expected it.

The whole thing was insane. *She* was insane, fantasising after a couple of tumblers of wine. Sitting on the bed, her tights bundled in one hand, she caressed the heel of her foot. How cracked it was, how dry and neglected! Like her mother's, in her last years. Monica remembered the ruthless grip of her mother's hand—her *claws*—on her arm, as if she were drowning, and she thought: I don't want to grow old alone. I want to sit by the fire eating crumpets with Buffy. I don't mind about all those other women who had him when he was young and slim and successful, whizzing off to premieres and whatnot. I'll be happy with what I can get.

Monica descended the stairs with caution, due not to the wine—God forbid—but to wearing high heels. Voices came from the bar, but when she looked in, there was no sign of Buffy.

Just then she heard a bellow of laughter from the kitchen. She made her way along the corridor and peered in through the doorway.

Buffy sat on a chair, a towel around his neck. Penny sat beside him, cutting his beard.

She saw Monica and called out: 'I couldn't bear it any longer. Soon he'll be getting little bits of food stuck in it.'

Buffy tried to turn but Penny jerked his head back. He rolled his eyes heavenwards.

Voda stood at the stove, stirring the bouillabaisse. 'Great time to choose,' she grumbled. 'Just as I'm dishing up.'

'He looked like Old Father Time.' Penny stood

285

back and inspected Buffy, her head tilted. 'Anyway, it's done now.' She bundled up the towel. 'I know it's hard to believe, but he used to cut quite a dash. Quite the boulevardier.'

'Hard to boulevard in Knockton,' he said, brushing hairs off his cardigan.

'I don't know,' said Penny. 'I'm growing rather fond of the place.'

'Coming to live here, are you?' he said. 'Join the club.'

'Everybody seems to know everybody else,' said Penny. 'It's not dead, like where I live, and it's not lonely like London. There's something to be said for small-town life.'

Buffy laughed. 'Never, ever, in my wildest dreams, would I imagine those words coming out of your mouth.'

'In fact I rather adore it.' Penny shook the towel out in the sink. 'It's never too late to fall in love, don't you think, Monica?'

*   *   *

There was no question of sitting next to Buffy at dinner. Tess and another woman patted the empty seat between them and he sat down without a glance at Monica. He had obviously forgotten his earlier words.

And a good thing too. The trim beard had made him a stranger. He looked natty, no doubt about that, and slimmer, but in his mustard cardigan and striped shirt he resembled a jazzman from the Acker Bilk era, a sartorial look Monica had never found arousing. Besides, that glimpse of domestic intimacy had undone her. He and Penny had

286

looked as if they were still married—teasing and needling each other, familiar with each other, the currents between them too deep to be understood by a mere onlooker like herself. A spinster; an outsider. She was beaten. And to add to it all, her knickers were digging into her crotch; she could hardly shift onto one buttock and pull them out.

Her neighbours—an Indian girl whose name she hadn't caught, and another girl, ditto—were discussing the fish pie and their part in its creation, ending each sentence with a question mark, like Australians. Why did kids do that nowadays? Didn't they realise how annoying it was? Harold sat on her other side, but he was talking to Penny. This was the second night that they had sat together. The two women opposite were slagging off their exes.

'I find it so supportive, being with you all?' said one of them. Christ, they were at it too. 'There's such a feeling of sisterhood here, us all being in the same boat?'

'They should call this place Heartbreak Hotel?' said the other one. 'We've come here to lick our wounds?'

They obviously considered Monica too old to be included in this conversation. Monica removed a fishbone from her mouth. Another thing she had noticed, about getting on, was that food got stuck in one's teeth. Now she knew why elderly people in restaurants jabbed away with a toothpick, sometimes shielding their mouth with a gnarled hand, sometimes not.

Only three days to go until Friday. For the sake of her pride she would stick it out until the end of the course. If she bailed out early Buffy might think that he was the cause, and she wouldn't give him the satisfaction. She would be perfectly pleasant to him, needless to say, but basically she would avoid him. This wouldn't be hard as he was invariably surrounded by females. Who knows? Maybe another of his ex-wives would show up.

Buffy

Off and on, throughout the evening, Buffy tried to catch Monica's eye. He tried to indicate *Sorry, I'm trapped in this seat.* After dinner he tried to indicate *Are you watching the film?* She ignored him and trooped into the bar with the others. He sat in the back row, his view of *Julie & Julia* partially blocked by the abundant hair of Denise, one of his more demanding guests (no gluten, no food with a face). Monica sat in the front row, slightly to his left. She appeared to be absorbed by the film, which struck him as sentimental and girly, not her thing at all. Perhaps she was pretending. Beside him sat India and Voda, fingers laced together. Sometimes they removed their hands and tenderly stroked each other's thigh. Penny and Harold sat together in the front row, whispering and giggling. Somebody leaned forward and told them to shut up.

The presence of Penny was deeply disorientating—her bodily presence in his new home, shifting the molecules in the air; the memories she triggered from the past. Buffy should have got used to her by now but it still gave him a jolt when she appeared wearing the jumper he had bought her when they were married. Of course he had seen her over the years; they had bumped into each other in the street, they had met at parties when she was accompanied by her toyboy Colin, now consigned to history. But they hadn't been together under the same roof for seven years or more. It was so odd to see her in a domestic setting—walking out of the bathroom with her damp hair in a turban, loading her breakfast toast with the usual great dollop of butter (would she have a heart attack? Not his problem now). So odd and yet so familiar. She seemed perfectly relaxed about it; they had slipped back into something resembling their old relationship or a close parallel to it. He had forgotten how she treated him in that fond, vaguely amused way, as if he were the family dog.

Was she gossiping about him to the other guests? The thought chilled his blood. More to the point, was she talking about him to Monica? He had seen no evidence of this but Penny had the sharpest nose in the business and she might have suspected that something was up.

If indeed it was. He really had made a total ass of himself that night. Memories kept rising up, each more blush-making than the last. His self-pitying burblings about *Babette's Feast* and subsequent drooling over Stéphane Audran's beauty, unchivalrous in the circumstances. A sentimental drone about the adorableness of his babies when they were little, equally tactless as Monica was childless. At one point—dear God!—he seemed to remember laying his head in Monica's lap. And then the hopeless fumbling on the landing, his drunken plea that she mustn't leave him alone. Had he tried to unbutton her blouse or had she done that herself? He remembered an attempt at a kiss but the rest was thankfully lost in oblivion.

No wonder Monica had scarcely spoken to him since then. He could hardly blame her. Though inebriated herself, she probably remembered it in all its repulsive detail. How foolish he had been, to think she might have found him as attractive as he found her! Now he thought about it, she had probably fabricated the dead husband to repel any advances on his part. He hadn't understood it at the time but it made sense now.

For he *had* been drawn to her. She was a striking woman—dark, whiplash-thin, with an interesting face that reminded him of Dorothy Parker. Underneath the chic haircut, however, he sensed a seething mass of self-doubt and insecurity. After the years with Penny he was ready to tackle a neurotic woman again. And she had made him laugh.

It was a shame he couldn't ask Penny's advice; she would have something bracing to say, flinging the window open on the fetid room of his psyche. But Penny of course was the last person in whom he could confide.

The next morning Monica was nowhere to be seen. Buffy missed her at breakfast and when he went into the kitchen, where the class had assembled, she wasn't there. He felt a lurch of disappointment. By mid-morning there was still no sign of her. He crept upstairs and tapped on her door. There was no answer, but when he looked into the room, her things were still there. She hadn't packed up and gone, then; but where was she?

Monica

Work was Monica's comfort. After the break-up with Malcolm she had thrown herself into her job, taking on more responsibility, working overtime. Anything to delay returning to her empty flat where grief and madness lurked.

Now she was standing at the recycling centre, the wind whipping her face, phoning her assistant Rupert.

'Any messages?' she asked.

'Nothing I can't deal with,' he said. 'You're on holiday, remember?'

'Are you sure?'

'Don't you worry, I'm holding the fort. You have a great time, wherever you are.' He didn't even know that she was on a cookery course.

Monica switched off her mobile. So now what? She pictured the office, the red plastic chairs around the conference table, the view of Leadenhall Market; she pictured her desk by the window, pictured it with such longing that her body ached.

Traffic thundered past. Mountains of black plastic bags were heaped against the skips; due to the cutbacks, the collections had been discontinued until further notice. She had read this in the local paper, along with news of an anti-capitalist rally in Cardiff. Recently she had felt the rumble of discontent growing louder, the approaching thunderstorm. In fact, her most recent CEOs' shindig had been disrupted by protesters. Acme Motivation were considering increased security at the various hotels they used, something that was due for discussion on her return.

The conference table. The pens and pads laid out at each place. The bottles of water. The problems to be solved, in all their simple complexity. Work was a gleaming city surrounded by a dark, tangled forest filled with snakes.

Now what? Back at Myrtle House everybody else had bonded together, they would be cooking in the kitchen, they probably hadn't even noticed her absence. It was like being at school again, being left out of the team. No doubt they all knew each other's names, while she had been distracted by that humiliating business with Buffy. Oh *God*.

At that moment a battered van slewed to a halt beside her. A man leaned across the passenger seat and wound down the window.

'How much, love?' he asked in a sing-song Welsh voice.

* * *

Monica drank too much at dinner. She knew it at the time, even as she poured herself another glass. And why bloody not? Her relationship with alcohol had lasted longer than her relationship with any man. It wasn't a love affair, or even a love–hate thing; that would be too simplistic. And yet underneath it all it was as simple as simple could be—people might come and go, but a bottle was always there. And she liked the taste, for God's sake!

Buffy hadn't spoken to her all evening. He wasn't even avoiding her. He had simply forgotten about her. Besides, his daughter Nyange had turned up.

Monica had no idea she was his daughter, of course. The woman was black! Big-boned,

292

handsome, with a challenging, stroppy look to her. Only when Penny hugged her, with a whoop of delight, did Monica learn her identity—that she was the product of Buffy's loins. 'He had this thing with a dancer,' Penny whispered.

It was at this point that Monica finally gave up. Buffy was a multi-storey car park crammed with vehicles, its sign saying *No Spaces*. Having circled the block a couple of times, she had to admit defeat and drive home. The whole love thing—with Buffy, with anyone—was too emotionally draining; even her internet dates were little cot deaths. She would give it all up and concentrate on her work.

The night's movie was *The Wedding Banquet*. As Monica sat down she could see no sign of Buffy or his daughter. The wine had made her dozy. After a while she realised that her head was resting on her neighbour's shoulder. Maybe she'd been snoring!

Monica muttered an excuse, got up and left the room, bumping against the door frame. Her head was spinning; she must go to bed.

She went into the lounge to collect her handbag. Buffy, Nyange, Voda and India were sitting there, papers spread on the coffee table. Monica muttered her apologies and looked around. Where had she left the blasted thing?

'We're discussing the appalling state of my finances,' said Buffy. 'Nyange's come down to help. She's an accountant.'

'That's nice,' said Monica stupidly.

'She's been bullying me for months about doing up this place and making it into a proper hotel,' said Buffy.

'I'm not bullying you,' said Nyange. 'I'm just talking sense.'

Monica spotted her handbag on the window seat, underneath a pile of newspapers. She picked it up and clutched it to her chest like a shield. 'I do a lot of work with hotels,' she said suddenly.

'Do you?' Buffy's eyebrows shot up. Now she had his attention! Tonight, in his maroon velvet jacket he looked like an ageing croupier in a washed-up seaside town. He looked hopeless. Monica felt a surge of power.

'Do you want to know what I think?' she asked.

Buffy shifted up on the sofa. 'Come on then, spit it out.' He patted the cushion.

She ignored his invitation. Instead, she leaned against the mantelpiece, a figure of authority.

'This place has masses of potential, none of which you've exploited,' she said. 'Do you want me to be frank?'

'Yes, yes!' said Buffy.

What the hell. Soon she would be gone. Before she went, however, she would give him something to remember.

'Why do people pay their hard-earned cash to go to a hotel?' she said. 'To step into another world, to be pampered, to live in a bubble. There are certain things they expect nowadays, certain standards, and this place just doesn't have them. Myrtle House isn't shabby-chic, it's just shabby. I nearly brained myself yesterday tripping over a hole in the carpet. And I won't even start on the bathroom facilities.' The fire was scorching the back of her legs. Monica moved away and sat on the arm of the sofa, like a teacher addressing a row of schoolchildren. 'What sort of guests do you want? High end? I work with the rich. Even in the deepest recession, they always survive. In fact, they get richer. And what they want

294

is something money can't buy, something that you have here in spades—great countryside and the sort of community that doesn't exist any more. With the right investment this place could be turned around—not just your hotel but the whole town.' Her voice quickened. 'I see Knockton as the new Hay-on-Wye. A Destination Town! Get some celebs down here, get some A-list creatives, set up a photo shoot in one of those retro shops, that hilarious gents' outfitter's, say, place a piece in the *Sunday Times* property pages extolling its charms, plant a story about an actress raising her own pigs and the punters will follow. I promise.'

Monica paused for breath. A log settled, with a sigh, in the fire.

'And this is where they'll stay,' she said. 'Your boutique hotel.'

'Boutique?' said Buffy faintly.

'It's crying out for expansion and I have an idea. Find some investors and buy the Old Court House next door.'

'What?' Buffy stared at her.

'I looked at the details in the estate agent's window,' Monica said. 'It's a fabulous building, masses of potential. Knock through and expand. Create new bedrooms. Convert the cells into a spa—'

'The cells?' said India.

'—treatment rooms—massage, therapies. Convert the courtroom into a conference centre. For various reasons my clients are looking for venues off the beaten track. Nowadays they need somewhere discreet and secure.'

'Who are they, the Mafia?' asked Buffy.

'And Knockton's perfect because nobody's heard

295

of it.'

She shot Buffy a challenging look, picked up her handbag and left the room.

Penny

Overnight the temperature dropped. When Penny looked out, the garden was white with frost. An icy draught leaked through the window sashes; she could feel it even through her Hotel Cipriani dressing gown.

The lavatory flushed. Penny darted out, clutching her washbag, but the bathroom door slammed shut. Somebody had beaten her to it. Through the walls she could sense people in their rooms, poised to make a move. It was like being back in her childhood, the whole family sharing one bathroom as people did then, even in Godalming.

'. . . *the latest government figures reveal that youth unemployment has now reached one million,*' said the news on her radio.

How full of hope she had been, just starting out! And how easy to find work straight from school, as a reporter for the *Surrey Gazette.* One took such things for granted then. Not for the first time, Penny was glad she hadn't had children. A harsh world faced them now, and it was all the fault of their so-called elders and betters. In her youth, bank managers had been avuncular chaps who played golf with one's father. They were there to reassure and help.

These past few days Penny had found herself dwelling on the past, not something in which she usually indulged. The house was dotted with triggers from her life with Buffy, that was why—a stripy rug they had bought together in Greece; various pictures that had been in his possession before she had met him, including one ghastly daub by Jacquetta. On the mantelpiece was a statue of Osiris she had given Buffy after a freebie to Egypt and which she suspected he had never liked; she had bought it on expenses, ah those were the days! And now it was all gone—the days of high living, the days of living with Buffy. Now he was a gallant old wreck with a drinker's nose. She had to admire him for launching out on a new venture this late in life—she had done the same thing herself—but today there seemed to be an air of desperation about both their endeavours. What would have happened if they had both just stuck it out together? Would they have sunk into an undemanding companionship? Would that have been a cop-out, or really rather nice? For she had to admit it: she was dreading the drive home to Suffolk and the cold dark cottage that awaited her.

Just then, gazing out of the window, she saw Monica. She was walking down the garden path, wheeling her suitcase. The door in the wall led to the back lane; she must have parked her car there.

Penny left her room and ran down the stairs. From the kitchen came the smell of frying bacon. The cold air hit her as she opened the back door and strode down the path. And now she was in the back lane where Monica's car stood in a cloud of exhaust smoke, its engine running.

Monica was scraping frost off the windscreen. When Penny called her name she jumped and swung round.

'What are you doing here?' She stared at Penny

in her dressing gown and slippers.

'Where are you going?'

'Back to London,' Monica said. 'I've told Voda.'

'But why?'

'They need me at work,' said Monica.

'Do they?'

Monica turned away and attacked the windscreen with her scraper. Penny tapped the shoulder of her overcoat.

'Can we sit in the car? It's freezing.'

Monica shot her a puzzled look. She nodded, however, and opened the passenger door. They sat side by side, the engine still running.

'Don't leave,' said Penny.

'I told you. There's a crisis at the office.'

Penny gazed at the frosted windscreen. Monica's side, the driver's side, was scraped clean. It reminded her of the specs worn by a girl at school who was blind in one eye—one lens clouded, the other clear.

'I've seen you looking at Buffy,' Penny said. 'The way you look at him.'

Monica sat very still. 'I don't know what you mean.'

Penny took a breath. 'I recognise that look, you see, because I was like that once.'

Monica's gloved hands lay in her lap. There was something touching about her gloves—powder-blue knitted ones, the sort a child would wear.

'He's not such a bad old thing, you know,' said Penny. 'If you wanted, I could give you a reference. In fact, sometimes I wish I hadn't run off with somebody else.'

'Nothing's happened between us.' Monica stiffened. 'Or has he told you something?'

'No.' Penny shook her head. 'I know he likes you, though.'

'Nonsense.'

'I can see it in his face,' said Penny. 'Take my word for it. You see, he used to look at *me* like that.'

'I'm sure he did,' said Monica sharply. 'And all the others.'

There was a silence. 'You can't expect him not to have had a life,' said Penny. 'You have, I have. We all have.'

'Not as much as him.'

'Are you jealous of me?' Penny blurted out. 'Look, feel me, I'm just a normal person.' She slipped her hand into Monica's gloved one and held it tight. 'Just normal flesh and blood.' Monica didn't reply. Penny tried again: 'He and I weren't at it hammer and tongs, if that's what you're thinking. I mean, we had our moments but it was more a companionable thing. Know what our first date was? Buying an orthopaedic mattress for his back—' She stopped. Monica's hand lay inert in hers. 'Listen, Monica, *I* used to feel like that. I used to torture myself, thinking of all the women he'd slept with. I used to think, were they better at it than me? Did they do things I didn't know how to do? Did he find them more exciting? Maybe he thought the same about me but I didn't know, I never asked.' She withdrew her hand. 'It wasn't just the sex. I envied them for knowing him when he was younger and slimmer and livelier. I mean, he and Popsi even rode a *motorbike* together, of all things; she knew a completely unknown Buffy—a racy, slim *man on a motorbike*! I envied her that so much I felt sick.' Penny's voice rose. Now she had started she couldn't stop, even though her bladder was bursting. 'And how could he love someone with such a stupid name? I asked him once and he said it was because Popsi hated her real name. *What was it?* I asked. And he said *Penelope.* That's my name! He'd even slept with my *name* before!' She burst into hysterical laughter. 'And then I met her, and she was just a jolly middle-aged woman with lipstick on her teeth, and I met Jacquetta and some of the others and I realised they were just normal women like me, like you and me sitting here. And he'd loved them just as I'd loved all sorts of men, and what was really upsetting me was remembering the past, and our youth, and how we would never be those people again, any of us.'

She paused for breath. Monica, too, was breathing heavily. Despite the heater, smoke came out of their mouths.

'He doesn't fancy me and I don't fancy him,' said Monica in a flat voice. 'And even if he does, and I did, I can't face it. I can't face being hurt. This man I knew, he was married but I loved him so much I thought I was going mad. He stole my best years, he stole the children I never had, and I can't do that again and that's that.'

'Don't blame Buffy for something that happened to you. He's had his knocks but he's up for it, I can tell. Why don't you just go for it?'

Monica swung round to face her. 'Why don't you?'

'What?'

'With Harold?'

Penny's heart jumped. She picked at the towelling of her bathrobe. 'I don't know what you're talking about.'

300

'I've seen that look. I can recognise it too, you know.'

The heater hummed in the silence. 'I really must go to the loo,' said Penny. 'I'm bursting.'

Monica smiled. 'I'm glad I met you.' She kissed her on the cheek. 'Good luck with that bathroom.'

Penny got out. As she walked towards the house she heard the car drive off.

Buffy

Buffy had a terrible night. Insomnia, palpitations. His back ached; his loose tooth throbbed. He was falling to pieces; he had been for years but in the black depths of the night he felt himself in a state of total disintegration. Even the dog, propelled onto the floor by his tossing and turning, had deserted him and whined to be let out of the room. Buffy was utterly alone in his rotting house. Of course it was full of people but soon they would be gone. Weak with self-pity, he thought: *I come first with nobody.*

Monica lay sleeping on the floor above. In two days she would disappear from his life forever. Her speech the previous evening had thrown him into confusion. That cool, businesslike tone was final proof, if proof were needed, that she felt nothing for him but contempt. And yet her radical plan showed that she had put some thought into his situation. Why on earth had she bothered? Was it just her professional instincts rising to the challenge, or did she really care what happened to him and his establishment? She had looked agitated but that might have just been the alcohol. How

301

handsome she was, though, standing there in her navy-blue trouser suit, metaphorically cracking the whip!

Buffy woke with a jerk. It was a blazingly beautiful day, though freezing cold. At this time of year the garden lay in shadow; only the top branches of the yew tree caught the sunshine. The faint sound of laughter came from downstairs where the morning's class—puddings and desserts—had already begun.

Having no desire to meet anyone, he let himself out of the house and walked across the road to the Coffee Cup. Amy, bringing him a croissant, said: 'If you don't mind me saying so, you look a bit rough.'

'You said that to me on *Miss Marple*.'

'Yes, but then I could do something about it.'

Buffy nodded. 'You and your trusty Polyfilla.'

Amy laughed. She was in love. Everybody seemed to be in love. Andy whistled on his rounds, like the postman Buffy had seen the day he arrived in Knockton; he'd got it together with the girl at the Camper Van Centre. Rosemary and Douggie had rekindled their marriage under his roof. India and Voda had fallen for each other. Even Des and Bella had jumped into the sack. Buffy himself was sort of responsible for these romances. But what about his own happy ending? Morosely, he tore off a piece of croissant and dunked it in his coffee.

It was then that he decided to go for a walk. He would drive up to the hills and stride along Offa's Dyke. That's what people did in this part of the world. They returned to Myrtle House, their cheeks flushed, saying *My goodness, that blew away the cobwebs!* It was ridiculous that in all these months he had scarcely taken the dog further than the

302

recreation ground. Bugger his bunions. Maybe the wind would blow away the cobwebs and reveal the truth as he stood on the summit of somewhere-or-other, three counties spread below him.

Buffy drove two miles up the road, parked at the footpath sign and let out the dog. Yapping hysterically, Fig disappeared into some gorse bushes. A rabbit shot out. Buffy, bundled up in his overcoat, made his way along the path. The sun shone on the frosty, skeletal hedgerows to either side. Ahead of him, sheep were scattered like boulders across the hillside. Idly he wondered where Voda's cottage was; in all these months he had never been invited there; maybe she thought they saw enough of each other at Myrtle House. Nor had India issued an invitation. Nyange, however, had stayed the night with the two of them and would now be on her way back to London. Buffy felt a familiar lurch of exclusion. *I come first with nobody.* He himself was a boulder, people washing up around him and then, at low tide, ebbing away and leaving him alone. Had Bridie felt like this? She had always seemed so cheerful, so generous and accommodating, but had panic gripped her in the depths of the night?

'Lovely day!' A grey-haired couple strode past, hand in hand. The man, repulsively, wore shorts. *Shoot them!* said Monica. *Pick them off one by one!*

Panting heavily, Buffy leaned against a gate. His back ached; his metatarsal throbbed. He was far too unfit for such exertions. But the view was spectacular, hills rising higher and higher into the milky distance, light shining on the uplands. There was no wind, just silence. Silence so vast he could feel it pressing against him.

He remembered a sozzled old boy in the pub, his legs wrapped in fertiliser bags and tied with twine. With surprising erudition he had talked about the Marches, how through the centuries people had fled here and never been seen again, how it had always been wild and lawless country. He had called it the Empty Quarter.

Buffy stood there in the hush. No bird sang. Somewhere in the silence he could hear Bridie's voice. Bridie, the one that got away. The free spirit who had asked nothing of him, and given him so much. She was here, in the hills, in this landscape she must have loved if only he had bothered to stay in touch and find out. *Just go for it, you silly cunt. So it's a disaster. So what? Life's bloody short, you can take my word for it.*

It was then, miraculously, that Buffy's head cleared and he knew just what he had to do.

'Fig!' he shouted.

But there was no sign of his dog.

*　　　*　　　*

It was mid-afternoon by the time Buffy arrived back in Knockton. A good hour had been taken up in searching for Fig. Alerted by the yapping, Buffy had finally run him to ground in the warren among the gorse bushes. Eventually Fig had emerged from a rabbit hole, wriggling backwards and covered in earth. The dog's greeting had been distracted, even offhand, as if he had been engaged in work of great importance. By then it was two o'clock and Buffy had missed lunch.

Had Monica noticed his absence? Now he had made up his mind he felt very close to her and

304

somehow presumed that she felt the same way towards him—that she too had realised they were each other's last chance of happiness, and was punched breathless by the same sudden wave of tenderness. This was ridiculous, of course—mere solipsistic projection. Now he had decided to make a move, however, he needed all the confidence he could muster. Time was running out.

He had a sandwich in a pub, drove into Knockton and parked outside the gents' outfitter's. He would buy some new jockey shorts—had Monica seen his humiliatingly baggy underpants?— and maybe even a fresh new shirt, striped perhaps. As he crossed the pavement he glanced up at the first floor. Harold was no doubt hard at work, otherwise he would go upstairs and ask his advice. Why did love reduce a grown man—a man indeed of advanced years—into a tremulous youngster? For it was love, or the first glimmerings of such a thing, that he felt for Monica. He was a man who, having had no appetite for years, passes an open window and smells bacon frying. Suddenly he feels the first pangs of hunger, a sensation he thought was lost to him forever.

Bugger the guests; Voda and India could look after them. He would take Monica out to dinner and ask her to stay for the weekend, when the others had gone. They would have the place to themselves . . . roaring fire, buttered scones. They would be guests in his own hotel, they would be children when the grown-ups had disappeared. Maybe they'd have a jaunt to the Saturday market in Ludlow and wander around arm in arm, quaffing mulled wine and laughing at the misshapen vegetables. Maybe, just maybe . . . he was getting ahead of himself here . . . maybe the spectre of Christmas would no longer loom, freighted with its burden of loneliness and exclusion, of being the tolerated guest at the various festivities of his various sort-of families . . .

As he walked into the shop Buffy was already flying to Venice—no, to a city he had never visited, with any woman. Caracas, for instance. He and Monica, guidebook on knee, were sitting in the plane, knocking back their plastic glasses of champagne. In their luggage, wrapped in tissue paper, lay their Christmas gifts to each other— slightly inappropriate because they didn't know each other well, but who cared? They were flying across the ocean together. Life was short and they weren't getting any younger, an observation he would wisely keep to himself. *So it's a disaster? So what?*

The gents' outfitter's, as usual, was empty of customers. Behind the counter the assistant was on his mobile, arguing about car insurance. Buffy inspected the glass-fronted drawers of shirts, searching for his size.

Just then, Penny materialised from the back of the shop. Literally materialised, like a ghost. Buffy jumped. She was easing her way past a Barbour-clad mannequin and heading for the door. Spotting Buffy, she stopped dead.

'What are you doing here?' She stared at him, her cheeks flushed.

'I didn't notice you,' he said. 'Were you here all the time?'

'Of course I was!' Penny said sharply. 'I've been looking for Christmas presents, scarves, maybe a nice pair of gloves. It's a marvellous shop, isn't it,

306

all this mahogany, so blissfully *Are You Being Served?* Thank God nobody's turned it into a Gap.' She rattled on, her blush deepening. 'In fact, I might do all my Christmas shopping here in your lovely town, I adore that hippy-dippy place, did you see they still sell dreamcatchers? *Dreamcatchers!* Remember that friend of mine, what's-her-name, the one you couldn't stand? With the cats and the spider plants? She had dreamcatchers dangling everywhere, remember?'

Penny paused, her chest heaving. Buffy gazed at her with interest. That torrent of words meant only one thing—the woman had something to hide. How well he knew her! How well he remembered, on her return home from an adulterous tryst with Colin, the lengthy explanation of where she had been! Poor liars always gave out too much information.

Of course Buffy should have put two and two together. He did later, when he remembered that Harold lived upstairs. Just at that moment, however, as he gazed at the flushed, brazen face of his ex-wife—*go on, challenge me!*—just then the years fell away and they were back in Blomfield Mansions and Penny was unpacking her Selfridges Food Hall bag, unpacking Parma ham, and he was nuzzling the back of her neck, breathing in the biscuity scent of her skin as she abstractedly caressed his head with her spare hand. Their marriage flooded back so powerfully that he felt dizzy. How he had loved her! What good value Penny had been—entertaining, funny and, that rarest of things, a woman totally devoid of neurosis. In fact, one of the pleasures of the past few days was being in her company again.

Penny seemed to have recovered her

equilibrium. She brushed back her hair. Buffy's bracelet—a long-ago birthday present—slid down her wrist. 'So what are *you* buying then?' she asked.

'Oh, just a shirt. Maybe you could help me.'

Penny looked at him, her eyes narrowed. 'If you're sprucing yourself up for Monica, it's too late.'

'What do you mean?'

'She left for London, this morning.'

'*What?*' Buffy felt the blood drain from his body.

'I'm so sorry.' Penny put her hand on his arm. 'I tried to stop her, I really did, but she's gone.'

Harold

Harold, still in a state of shock, lay on his disordered bed. *As Balzac said, bang goes another novel.*

How on earth did that happen? Penny had only brought him an apple crumble. She had cooked it that morning and thought he would like it for his lunch. One thing, as they say, had led to another but now it seemed as unlikely as a dream, especially after her abrupt departure. 'I've got a class at three,' Penny had muttered like a truanting schoolgirl, pulling on her knickers.

He must have fallen asleep because now it was dark. Wrapping himself in his dressing gown, Harold went into the front room. On the table sat the remains of their abandoned meal, ghostly in the glow of the street lamp. He closed the curtains and switched on the light. Good God, it was half past five! He felt nauseous with a kind of jet lag, as if he had woken up in Singapore.

308

Taking the plates into the kitchen, he tried to remember what the one thing had been, that led to the other. He and Penny seemed to have got through a bottle of wine, though the crumble remained half eaten. In his fuddled brain he thought: I must remember to take back the bowl when I've finished. After all, it belongs to Buffy.

So, in a sense, did Penny. Well, she had in the past. Harold's stomach lurched. How on earth was he going to face his only real friend in Knockton now he'd had sex with his wife? Ex-wife, but still, there was something unsettling about it, something vaguely adulterous, with more than a whiff of the homoerotic. After all, the same naked legs had wrapped around them both. In a weird way, a way he didn't care to inspect, it made him and Buffy closer. And yet not close at all, because now he had to keep a secret.

Or maybe he didn't. Maybe—horror of horrors—Penny was going to tell Buffy everything. They seemed to get on pretty well for divorcees. Maybe she had done it as a creepy sort of dare, to make Buffy jealous!

Harold froze, bowl in hand. Now he remembered, Penny had made the first move, almost as if the whole thing was planned. They had stopped, halfway through the crumble, so Harold could fetch his laptop and show her *Old Jews Telling Jokes* on YouTube. Nestled together in front of the screen Penny had said: 'Isn't it sad that after tomorrow we'll never see each other again?' Suddenly she had turned to him. Their noses were so close that it was almost impossible *not* to kiss. And while kissing him she had cradled his face as if it were a precious thing; no woman had done that

309

since forever, and he was so moved that his insides melted, he was hers.

Harold dumped the bowl on the draining board. Maybe—an even worse horror—maybe the two of them had colluded! Buffy had taken pity on him, the abandoned husband, and pimp-like had offered up his ex-wife as a consolation. Penny was a sport. She had also, as Harold had discovered, a healthy sexual appetite. That would explain her sudden appearance and equally sudden departure. Job done.

No, that was too kinky. Truly, his brain was disordered. Penny had bailed out simply because she regretted what had happened. No doubt she had been repulsed by his matted chest hair and thickening waist; he seemed to remember her exploratory fingers pausing thoughtfully at various parts of his anatomy. They had talked at some point about humiliating one-night stands and this was just another one to add to the list, complete with sagging buttocks.

Deep in thought, Harold washed up. Maybe the best plan would be to stay away until Saturday, when Penny would be gone. There was a certain cowardly attraction to this idea, but how could he bear not to see her again?

For he was crazy about her. *Crazy*.

Penny

Before dinner, Penny had a bath. She had found the store of bubble-bath sachets in a cupboard and by squeezing three into the water had built up a decent amount of foam. Every now and then

310

footsteps padded along the corridor and the doorknob tentatively turned. 'Coming!' she called, and sunk back into the water. After all, nobody else had had sex that day.

The whole thing was too hilarious to be true; maybe it hadn't happened at all! She had dreamed up the beige, anonymous flat above the gents' outfitters. By imagining it so many times, during the past few days, she had willed it into reality.

For now she could admit it. She *had* speculated on what it would be like to go to bed with Harold. Was it because he reminded her of Buffy in his younger days, reminded her of herself when they were happy? There were certain similarities between the two men, not least their chattiness during lovemaking. Colin, the last man she'd had sex with, had been entirely silent except for the grunts when he came.

It had been startling, however, to feel the softer body of an older man. Harold was pretty unfit, of course—another thing he had in common with Buffy. But no doubt all men his age were getting flabbier. As of course was she. She wished they hadn't had to undress in broad daylight. Her attempt at slipping under the sheets while still in her underwear was thwarted by Harold's desire to unclip her bra—he said he hadn't done it for years and wanted to see if he still could, with one hand. Maybe Pia, his ex, was too flat-chested or lesbian to wear such a thing.

Such worries weren't an issue, needless to say, if one had lived with somebody for years. You grew old together; each other's bodies were imprinted with the memory of their younger, firmer selves. Two older people, however, meeting as strangers, came slap up against their own mortality, mirrored in the other's wrinkles. If Harold had been shocked he was too much of a gentleman to show it, and it had indeed been gratifying to find she could still arouse a man. But once it was over—clumsy and hasty as it had been—she had felt her confidence drain away. How could she have been so bold? She had practically ravished the poor chap. They had laughed together afterwards, lying damply side by side, surprised by their own exertions, but maybe he had just been embarrassed on her behalf. No doubt he was regretting the whole business, hence her hasty exit.

Penny got out of the bath. As she dried herself she gazed at a print on the wall. Yellowed with age, it showed the ruins of some vast cathedral—gaping windows, crumbling arches; she couldn't read the name of the place without her specs. Had Harold noticed the thread veins on her thighs, or would *he* have needed his glasses? More to the point, was he going to turn up for dinner, as usual?

Penny, heart pounding, dressed and went downstairs. Voices murmured in the bar. She heard a hoot of laughter from Sonia, an amusing and embittered divorcee.

India emerged from the kitchen, carrying a couple of bottles.

'Have you seen Buffy?' she asked. 'Has he been upstairs with you?'

'Why would he be upstairs with me?'

'I want to tell him our news.' India glanced around and lowered her voice. 'Voda and I are going to get married!'

'*Married?*'

'Well, a civil partnership. You know.' She

312

scratched the stud in her nose. 'We haven't told anyone else yet but you're sort of family.'

Penny kissed her. 'How wonderful!'

'I'm so happy, I wish everyone could be this happy. I wish you could be this happy and Buffy could be this happy. I'm going to learn to lamb and everything.' She threw her arms around Penny, the bottles clanking together behind Penny's back. 'There's something about this place. Tobias called it Heartbreak Hotel but that's so not true. Maybe something'll happen to *you*.'

'What, with a bunch of women?'

India disentangled herself. 'There's nothing wrong with women.'

'No. Sorry.'

'The thing about women—'

India stopped. Voda appeared from the kitchen. She waved a piece of paper. 'Buffy left a note,' she said. 'On the dresser, the idiot, I've only just found it. He says he's gone to London and can somebody remember to take out the dog.'

Had Buffy rushed off to find Monica? Penny's interest was only fleeting. She had other, more pressing, concerns.

She walked into the bar and stopped dead. Harold stood there, talking to Sonia. Though he wore his old corduroy jacket he had spruced himself up in a white shirt. He must have just had a shower, because his hair was wet.

Penny's heart turned over. He said something funny. Sonia hooted with laughter and laid her hand on his arm.

Just then Harold turned and saw Penny. He muttered something to Sonia and walked over.

'Thank God you're here,' he said.

313

'Of course I'm here.' Her throat dried up.

'I had a mad vision of you running away.'

She shook her head. 'No.'

He looked at her, his black brows knitted together. 'Still, it wouldn't have mattered.'

'Why not?'

He said, simply: 'Because I would have found you.'

16

Buffy

Buffy drove through the dark, tears streaming down his face. He had put on his CD of Bach's Cantata 82, sung by Lorraine Hunt Lieberson.

> *Schlummert ein, ihr matten Augen*
> *Fallet sanft und selig zu!*
>
> *Slumber now, you weary eyes.*
> *Close softly and pleasantly!*

He was on the M40, in heavy traffic. It was the rush hour, and cars were pouring out of Birmingham.

> *Welt, ich bleibe nicht mehr hier . . .*

Behind Buffy, headlights flashed. He wiped his nose and swerved into the middle lane.

> *World, I will not remain here any longer,*
> *I own no part of you that could matter to my*

soul . . .

His satnav lady had fallen silent for the duration of the motorway. He could hardly say he missed her, not with this playing, but in her own way he found her as soothing as Bach. *At the second roundabout, turn right.* Nolan, knowing Buffy's poor sense of direction, had fitted the satnav as a thank-you for employing him as a tutor. *At the next junction, turn left.* Like Cordelia's, the satnav lady's voice was gentle and low, an excellent thing in a woman. Best of all, she knew where they were going. Which was more than Buffy did.

He must be mad. What was he going to say when he got to Monica's house? What if she wasn't there? What if she slammed the door in his face? He *was* mad.

Yet the drama of it gripped him. He was acting in the final reel, speeding along the motorway in a race against time. On camera was his best (left) profile, his eyes narrowed in the glare of the oncoming traffic like John Wayne's in the Texan sun. Monica was his woman. She knew it; he knew it. As the music swelled she would fling open the door, backlit and dressed only in her negligee. Like the husband in *Brief Encounter*, she would say, in her upper-class voice, 'Thenk you for coming beck to me.'

A car hooted. Buffy jerked to his senses. Christ, he had nearly dozed off! Would Monica be upset? He pictured her switching on the news and seeing the mangled remains of his car. *Well-loved actor dies in motorway carnage.*

Now he was in London and the satnav lady was guiding him to that foreign land called South of the

315

River. *Take the second left . . .* How could Monica live in Clapham? Buffy felt a twitch of irritation. Why couldn't she live somewhere more convenient? He knew that this was a defence thing, to pre-empt his own rejection, but it was true. He had never seen the point of Clapham: those endless streets, straight as rulers, filled with shiny young bankers breeding like rabbits. The dullest common in London. Nowhere to park.

It was a quarter to nine; he had been driving for nearly four hours. His back ached; his haemorrhoids were playing up. His lust—if that's what it was—had drained away somewhere near Droitwich. By now he was too exhausted to be nervous. Really, he was too old for this sort of malarkey. All he wanted was to go to bed. Perhaps he should give up the whole thing and check into the Chelsea Arts Club.

At the next junction, turn right. Was it his imagination or did her voice sound steelier? *Turn right and don't be such a sissy. You a man or what?* And now he was driving down Monica's street, Denning Street, *You have reached your destination*, and of course it was wall-to-wall parked cars. At the end of the road Buffy found himself swept up in a one-way system. *You have missed your turning!* barked the satnav lady, losing patience. The street stretched ahead, pitilessly long, ghostly in the sodium light.

Buffy slowed down but the car behind him hooted. How could a man change his life if he couldn't find a bloody parking space? How did people cope in this world? His eyes filled with tears and this time it wasn't Bach that did it, it was the hopelessness of everything. *Turn right! Turn left! Turn left! Turn right!* What was the difference? It

316

was all doomed. He came first with nobody, not even his dog. Fig would be slobbering over whoever had given him his dinner and soon they would all be dead.

Suddenly Buffy found himself back in Denning Street, purely by chance, and ahead of him a car was pulling out. He parked, switched off the engine and climbed out. It was freezing cold; the other vehicles were already matt with frost. His back was so stiff that he could barely stand up. Number 73 was a few yards away. Outside it, a man was picking up his dog's turd in a plastic bag. Buffy waited until he had moved on and walked stiffly to the gate.

It was a house identical to the others in a street that stretched into infinity. Buffy knew the address, of course, from Voda's computer, but now he had arrived and was faced with the prospect of Monica's bodily reality, somewhere behind those windows— now he was actually standing there, he couldn't catch up with what he was doing. He thought: *I have driven from Wales to visit a woman who might not even like me.* But what an admission of defeat, to turn tail now!

Heart thudding, he walked up to the front door. Putting on his spectacles, he peered at the row of names. *2: M. Kennedy.* He pressed the bell.

Minutes passed. An ambulance sped by, its siren wailing. Finally a shape appeared behind the frosted glass. The door opened and Monica stood there in a blue towelling dressing gown, her face bare of make-up.

She stared at him. 'What on earth are you doing here?'

'I wanted to see if I could still do this sort of thing.'

317

Her face hardened. 'So you've done it a lot, have you?'

'No! I didn't mean that. I just meant—God, I just feel so old.' He sighed. 'Don't look at me like that. I'm not canvassing for the BNP.'

'I'm sorry.' She pressed herself against the wall. 'Come in.'

Buffy followed her up the stairs. She wore backless slippers. With his specs on, he could see the cracked skin of her heels. Suddenly he was overwhelmed with tenderness for her, for the two of them.

And now he was in her sitting room. Spic and span, a few plants, Matisse poster on the wall. The room of a spinster. On the coffee table sat a tray, containing a half-eaten meal. In front of it was an open laptop. Monica hurried past him and closed it.

'What were you watching?' asked Buffy. 'I'm sorry I interrupted.'

'Just something on iPlayer. It keeps freezing, anyway.'

'It's worse in Wales. You're all ready, just about to take a mouthful, and you find yourself staring at that little thing going round and round.'

'Do sit down. Can I get you something to drink?'

Buffy pointed to the bottle. 'That looks nice.'

'It's not really. Tesco's.'

'Anything'll do.'

She fetched him a glass.

'Look, I'm sorry,' he said. 'I didn't mean to barge in.'

Monica swung round. 'Didn't mean to? But you've driven two hundred miles.'

'A hundred and seventy-six actually.'

He smiled at her but she turned away. As she did

318

so, she caught sight of herself in the mirror.

'You look lovely,' he said.

'I don't! I look terrible.'

He spoke to her reflection. 'I'm sorry. I shouldn't have come.'

'I'm not surprised, seeing me like this.'

'Stop it, Monica!'

'I can't give you anything to eat. It's a Serves One. This is all there is.'

'I don't care!' He held out his hand. 'Come here.'

Monica hesitated.

'Please,' he said.

She sat down next to him and poured him a glass of wine.

'I just wanted to see you,' he said.

'I can't think why.'

'Why not?'

She adjusted her dressing gown over her knees. 'I just wish you'd warned me.'

'Why did you run away? You didn't even say goodbye.'

She shrugged. 'There was no point.'

'Why on earth not?'

'Because we both behaved like idiots. Like *teenagers*. And it's best forgotten.'

'But we *are* teenagers, underneath. We're still those people, aren't we?'

They both gazed at the remains of Monica's cottage pie. Next to it was a dollop of tomato ketchup. This touched Buffy deeply. He hadn't pictured her as a ketchup woman. There was so much to learn.

'I can't bear the pain,' she said at last. 'I'm too old for it.'

'*You're* too old?'

319

'Even if we liked each other, which might be true—'

'We do, don't we?'

'Even if we did, we'd have to go through all that rigmarole again.'

'What rigmarole?'

She sighed. 'Finding out things about each other, discovering our foibles, that the person's stingy, or bosses waiters about, or drones on about their schooldays—'

'I'm not stingy—'

'And you know that all those things have been discovered by other people in the past, many, many other people, nice things as well as not-so-nice ones, they've all been delighted over or complained about. It's like exploring a wood and finding it full of footprints and litter.'

'Bloody hell,' he said. 'You really see it like that?' In fact, her woodland imagery had surprised him. *Delighted* him. She was a woman of imagination. This was a discovery and what was wrong with that? No doubt other men had discovered this but now it was his turn.

'It's different when you're young,' Monica said. 'Your heart gets broken but you pick yourself up and fall in love again, there's plenty of people to choose from, but now, to be perfectly honest, there aren't. Not for someone like me. And the ones there are, they're all too entrenched in their ways, we all are, we've all got too much bloody baggage.' She drained her glass. 'Best not to go there. Save ourselves a lot of grief.'

Suddenly Buffy was overcome with gloom. He gazed at Monica's veined ankles in their fluffy slippers. This wasn't going according to plan. But

320

then what had he expected?

'We think we can change people but we can't, not at our age,' said Monica. 'I saw your face last night, when I was suggesting things about your hotel.'

'It didn't sound like *me*. Even if I had the money, which I haven't.'

'I was only trying to help.'

'And I sort of like the place as it is. That's why I'm living there.' He took a breath. 'Everyone tries to change things. Even Marmite. But maybe one should accept things as they are. With all our faults and our funny ways. I know every rotten floorboard in that house but I don't want to tear it up. Everybody's trying to tear things up nowadays and rebrand them and Christ knows what, but isn't that a shame? It's got memories, you see—of the person who lived there and the person before her and before that. It's what's made the house what it is. I know it's an old wreck but I love it.'

Monica was gazing at the gas-effect fire. He looked at her profile—sharp nose; thin lips. People in profile looked so alien; one had to get used to them all over again. Of course, one never saw oneself from this angle.

He wanted to tell her this, and so many other things, but he feared he had lost her. In a funny way he was proud of being so impulsive but Monica hadn't thought so. He would beg a cup of coffee and drive home.

Monica said: 'So you don't think there's any room for improvement, in any of us?'

'Not in my case. It's against the regulations, I'm Grade II listed.'

Monica burst out laughing. 'Not Grade I? You're

321

so modest.' She looked at him, her head on one side. 'Now *that* might be something nobody's ever told you before.'

He nodded. 'There you are. Point proven, whatever it was.' He sighed. 'We do talk a lot of rubbish, don't we?'

'Speak for yourself.'

She gave him a sniffy look. He gazed at her naked face, shiny with moisturiser; at her wide, hungry mouth. God, he loved her.

She said: 'Do you have a cigarette?'

'Heavens! I didn't know you smoked.'

'I gave up years ago.'

She got up to fetch an ashtray. Buffy sat there, weak with longing. Against the wall stood an antique desk with framed photos on it. Some of them seemed to be children—nephews and nieces? The thought of never finding this out, this and so many other things—of her life continuing without him—filled him with desolation.

Monica returned with an ashtray and a bottle. 'Let's have this wine instead of the other stuff. They gave it to me at the office and I've never got round to drinking it.'

Buffy looked at the label. 'Blimey, 1996 Léoville-Las-Cases.' He took the corkscrew and hesitated. 'If we get through this, I won't be able to drive anywhere.'

'I think this deserves new glasses.' Monica crossed the room and opened a cupboard. 'Anyway, where would you go?'

'Not a clue. I can't drive back to Wales.'

'No.'

'My back would go into spasm. They'd have to winch me out.'

322

'We don't want that,' she said.

'No.'

She sat down beside him. Buffy poured the wine. He lit two cigarettes and passed her one. How meltingly sexy it was, how Bogey and Bacall! He hadn't done such a thing for centuries.

Monica inhaled deeply and blew the smoke through her nostrils. They took a sip of the wine.

'We should have let it breathe,' she said.

'Fuck it.'

They smoked for a while in silence. From upstairs came the faint sound of a TV.

'I could make you some toast,' Monica said. 'Or we could rummage in the freezer. I only got back at lunchtime, I haven't been to the shops.'

'Don't worry, I bought a sandwich at Warwick Services.'

'What sort was it?'

'Crayfish and rocket. I've never had one of those before.'

'Nice?'

'Delicious.' He shrugged. 'You see, there are still some things left to discover.'

'What else did you have? A bit of cake? A shortbread biscuit?'

He stubbed out his cigarette. 'Do you really want to know?'

Monica squinted through the smoke. And then she smiled. 'I want to know everything.'

*   *   *

Buffy woke the next morning without a weight on his legs. No dog. Instead, he was lying in a blue bedroom with Monica asleep beside him. Sunlight

323

shone through a gap in the curtains. The room faced the front; he could hear the traffic down in the street.

Monica lay with her back to him. She was breathing so softly it was possible she was awake; she was just lying there, immobilised with the realisation of what they had done. Moles were scattered over her skin; in her dark, disordered hair, the grey roots were visible. He gazed at her bedside table: a blister pack of contact lenses, a pile of *Condé Nast Traveller* magazines. A bottle of water.

Buffy's throat was parched. He tried to reach over her shoulder, to get hold of the bottle, but a spasm shot down his spine. Whimpering, he fell back onto the pillow.

'What's the matter?' she murmured.

'Back's buggered.' He groaned. 'It's all that driving.'

She shifted round to face him. 'Can you move at all?'

'It's pretty stiff.' He tried to sit up and yelped with pain. Easing himself back on the pillow, he lay there staring at the ceiling.

'Has it happened before?' Monica asked.

He nodded. 'I just have to rest it for a bit.'

'How long?'

'I don't know. It varies.'

'You poor thing,' she said without enthusiasm. 'I must warn you, I'm a terrible nurse.'

'Yes, I can imagine.'

She eased herself out of bed. 'I'll make us a cup of tea.'

If they were onstage Monica would fling on a silk wrap in one fluid movement. As it was she had to

324

walk across the room, naked, to pick up her dressing gown. For those of mature years, even filtered daylight is felt to be unforgiving. Buffy turned away and looked at a poster of Botticelli's *Birth of Venus*. Hand shielding her pudenda, Venus returned his gaze with a half-smile.

Suddenly Monica gasped. 'Oh God, they'll be here in a minute!'

'Who, your parents?'

'No, the traffic wardens! It's ten to nine.' She hurried out. He heard her pulling open a drawer and scrabbling about.

'What day is it?' she called.

'Friday.'

'What date?' Monica hurried back in, carrying a visitor's permit. 'Haven't done one of these for ages.'

'Don't know,' said Buffy. 'November the something. Have you got today's newspaper?'

'Of course not. 17th? 18th? I need something to scratch with.' She stared wildly around the room. 'It's one of those scratchcards.'

'I know—it's the 18th. Last day of the cookery course.' How distant that seemed, another world! He hoped someone had walked the dog.

'It says *scratch with a coin*. Where's my handbag?' She rushed out again.

'That's why I left London!' Buffy called out. 'Bloody parking warden vultures!'

'Where're your car keys?' she shouted.

'In my jacket pocket!'

'Where's it parked, what does it look like?'

'You can't go out in your dressing gown!'

But a few moments later she was gone. Buffy slumped back, exhausted. Only nine o'clock and he already felt drained.

Now he was alone he tried to remember the events of the previous night. Again, they hadn't exactly had sex. His feeble erection had been ignored by both of them; their hands had scarcely strayed below their waists. But yet, but yet . . . they had made love. For what seemed hours they had kissed each other, deeply and tenderly. She was a wonderful kisser, that wide soft mouth. Slowly their shyness had melted away. So had their drunkenness. They had tentatively explored each other, their bodies becoming familiar, with that luxuriant holding-back, that promise of better things to come, which he hadn't felt since he was a teenager. No wonder he had expected her parents to walk in.

Now she was back, carrying two mugs of tea. She had brushed her hair.

'Just beat him to it,' she said.

'A small triumph, but a triumph nevertheless.'

She nodded and sat down on the bed. 'It's bloody freezing out there.'

'Nice and warm in here,' he said. 'Come back in.'

She shuffled off her dressing gown and eased herself under the duvet. Buffy put his mug on his empty table. Who had been the last occupant on this side of the bed? How long ago? He hadn't spent the night with a woman since his marriage to Penny.

'What about going to the loo?' she asked. 'I haven't got a potty.'

'I'll try and get up in a bit.' He cleared his throat. 'Talking of getting it up—'

'Shh.' She leaned against him and rubbed her face against his beard. 'I can't tell you how nice that

326

was.'

They sipped their tea in silence. Under the duvet, her foot hooked around his. He trapped it between his own feet and held it there.

'Shouldn't you be going to work?' he asked.

She shook her head.

'I thought there was a crisis.'

'I lied,' she said.

'Fair enough.' He gazed at her face. 'You've changed, you know. When I first met you, you seemed so stiff and tense.' He ran his finger down her cheek. 'Now your face has become alive, somehow . . . it's completely relaxed.'

'You think that's due to you?'

Buffy shrugged modestly.

'To be perfectly frank,' she said, 'it's the Botox wearing off.'

17

Buffy

Four months had passed. Buffy lay awake, listening to the whispers and sighs of the house and its occupants. Monica, his present tense, slept beside him but the hotel was filled with his past. Jacquetta and Leon slept in the room above; Nyange and her mother Carmella slept in the twin room next to his. Celeste and her mother were in the Blue Room; Quentin and James in the Pink Room across the landing. India had moved into the single attic room for the night; it was the eve of her nuptials and she was quaintly following the tradition of staying away from her beloved.

No wonder Buffy couldn't sleep. He listened to the wind rattling the windowpanes. He had half a mind to get up and check that the occupants were actually in their beds. They had lived so powerfully in his memory, for so many years, that the bodily reality of them was deeply disorientating, as if he had dreamed up the whole thing. All they had in common was himself. *House Full.* His hotel creaked with the weight of his history. Indeed, in some weird way the dead were as palpably present as the breathing human beings under his roof. They all dwelt in his memory—Popsi with her magnificent breasts and throaty laugh; Bridie with her hennaed hair and her mugs of whisky, Bridie, who had given him the key to her life. And beyond them, memories of the guests whom that key had unlocked, guests who had slept here over the last two years—the Pritchards; that timid geologist; Rosemery the stoic, abandoned wife . . . and before them, way before them, the ghosts of all the transitory occupants of this shabby old building, of which he was the temporary chatelain.

Downstairs the clock struck three. In a few hours he and his extended family would be gathered together in Voda's cottage for the ceremony. Tobias and Bruno were already staying there, with their partners and the baby. Penny and Harold would join them from his flat above the gents' outfitter's. Buffy's heart raced in anticipation. It was the night before some experimental production starring a motley group of actors, some of whom had known each other before in fraught and humiliating circumstances; hearts pounding like his, they lay in bed preparing themselves for a drama

328

whose lines they hadn't learned, a drama that could explode into a Strindbergian tragedy or an Ayckbourn farce. Still, that was weddings for you.

* * *

'Dad, you're burning those sausages!' Nyange tried to grab the spatula but Buffy shook her off.

He was cooking breakfast. His guests appeared at intervals, ghosts from his past materialising through the haze of frying.

Jacquetta peered into the fridge. 'Do you have any soya milk?'

Her hair was cut short. Buffy had seen this on his visit to London—she had recently had chemo—but the effect was still startling. In all the years he had known Jacquetta her hair had been long, though piled up in various arty arrangements. Now it was streaked with pink. She looked like an ageing punk goddess.

'I could pop out to Costcutter's,' he said.

'It's all right.' Jacquetta sighed. 'I've brought some green tea.'

He had forgotten about Jacquetta's various allergies, in this case to dairy products. Now she was taking blister packs of pills out of her handbag. He felt a lurch of nostalgia. During their marriage, their hypochondria had been something that had bound them together. There had also been a certain competitiveness about who was the most ill. That game was long since over, of course, and anyway Jacquetta had won. She'd had breast cancer!

Now her husband appeared through the smoke, still tall and handsome, still with that great mane of

329

hair. In fact, there seemed to be even more of the stuff. Leon had the buffed and polished look of a TV celebrity, even though he had retired years ago to write his best-sellers. How Buffy had hated the chap! Hardly surprising, since he was fucking his wife. While she was still in transference, too. *And Buffy was paying him for it.* The hatred, of course, had long since vanished. Nowadays on the few occasions they met it was as grizzled veterans, not just of marriage to Jacquetta but as stepfathers to India, who was particularly stroppy during her adolescence.

Leon ruffled India's hair—something Buffy knew she disliked—as she unpeeled the bacon. 'Big day, sweetheart,' he said. 'I'm so proud of you.'

Why? For being a lesbian? For coming out? Leon was no doubt pleased at his own tolerance. No doubt he had intuited it all along, with his shrink's intuition. Buffy suspected, however, that he considered India's intended, Voda, a bit of a rough diamond.

Jacquetta turned to her daughter. 'You're so lucky,' she said. 'I've always wanted to live in this part of Wales.'

Buffy was startled. It was news to him.

'So wild and free,' said Jacquetta. 'Such a pagan vibe. In fact, I went to a happening in a field when I was pregnant with you. Perhaps that imprinted itself when you were in the womb. But Alan was far too straight to live here.' Jacquetta smiled. 'I wonder how he would have coped with today.' India's father, a shadowy figure at the best of times, had died in Australia the year before. 'Not too well, I suspect. A gay daughter would have been a threat to his masculinity. No wonder he emigrated to the

330

most macho country in the world.'

The smoke was clearing as Lorna arrived.

'I've got a terrible hangover,' she said. 'I wasn't used to all that booze last night.'

Lorna, his lost love, had become a little old woman. Buffy could hardly recognise the actress with whom he had once trod the boards; no doubt she was thinking the same thing about him. They were both seventy-two, after all. Crippled with arthritis, Lorna leaned on a stick. The night before, she'd had a long conversation with Monica. Were they comparing notes? Forty years had passed; any notes would be as out of date as old exam papers. Celeste, the daughter they had produced, was now slicing bread and putting it into the toaster.

And now Nyange and her mother appeared, complaining that the hot water had run out. Even in their dressing gowns they looked startlingly exotic. Buffy tipped the sausages onto a plate. How strange it was, that they were all gathered together! And yet no stranger than the assorted guests who had found themselves at Myrtle House. They all had their stories. Under this roof he had been privy to tears and revelations, to the confidences that had been released by the brief occupation of a place where a person had no responsibilities. That was the thrill of hotels.

Buffy remembered the vision of himself when he first saw the house—mine host, exuding bonhomie, his cheeks ruddy with claret. No rehearsals were needed. He hardly had to act the part, for by now he inhabited it.

Monica came in, followed by Quentin and James. She wore a smart green suit for the wedding. Catching Buffy's eye, she gave him a tentative smile.

'Now, who's for eggs?' he asked, beaming.

Monica

'But it's the bankers who've brought this country to its knees,' said Bruno. 'How can you bear to work with them?'

'Somebody has to,' said Monica.

'What sort of future's my little baby going to face?' demanded Bruno. 'It's all their fault, greedy fucking bastards.'

'For God's sake, lay off the poor woman!' said Buffy, coming to her rescue. 'This is supposed to be a wedding.'

'And none of them've been punished, they've all got big fat bonuses!'

'Talking of banks,' said Buffy hastily. 'Conor's just been arrested for holding one up in Llandrod. But he didn't realise the bank's been closed for six years and it's now a reflexology spa. He tried to get the patients to give him their money but they were so comatose they didn't know what he was talking about and then the police came. And it was only a toy gun anyway.'

Monica laughed. The atmosphere eased. Bruno turned to her. 'Sorry,' he said, 'but I feel I can be rude to you as you're sort of family now.'

Monica gazed at the crowd of people. The party was taking place in Voda's cottage. The room was heavily beamed and strung with fairy lights; somebody played the fiddle. This was all so new to her, this being sort of family. During the years with Malcolm, of course, it was the very thing from

332

which she had been excluded. *A bit on the side.* She herself had no children and no siblings; her life had been the solitary one of the professional woman. Now she felt currents pulling in all directions, too deep for her to comprehend. Penny was right; her feelings of jealousy had all but evaporated when faced with Buffy's living, breathing exes, all of advanced years. What remained was far more complicated.

For despite Buffy's best efforts to include her, she felt an alien species in this ramshackle cottage high up in the hills. Was she really more at ease in a roomful of bankers? She couldn't connect the two halves of her life together—her weekends with Buffy, the mess and muddle of it, and her corporate week in hotels where the ceiling didn't leak and there was constant hot water. She watched Voda and India dancing together, bumping into people, daffodils falling out of their hair, and she thought: Both halves have one thing in common—everyone gets roaring drunk.

Yet again, glasses were raised to the happy couple. Despite her confusion Monica was becoming fond of them all. They were Buffy's history, the story of his life. What part was she going to play? She loved him dearly but she couldn't see a place for herself here. Did she really have the courage to up sticks and move to Knockton like Harold, like Penny? Like Andy and Amy who were also jammed in this room somewhere?

Where were they? Monica tried to make out the faces but it all seemed to be getting darker. For a moment she thought that her eyesight was failing. The table lamps grew dimmer; the fairy lights shrank to pinpricks and then disappeared.

The room was plunged into darkness. There was a general murmur of surprise.

Voda's voice said: 'Fuck fuck *fuck*!'

'What's happened?' somebody asked.

'The electricity's run out. It's Conor's *fucking* solar panels.'

Monica leaned against the dresser. It was rather a relief, not having to talk. Her eyes were wide open but she could see nothing. This was curiously liberating and for the first time she relaxed.

Buffy and his family had been swallowed into the blackness. In their place, a vision swam into view—a vision so precise, so exhilaratingly bright in every detail that Monica nearly laughed out loud. Everything fell into place. Why hadn't she thought of it before? It really couldn't be simpler. By the time the candles were lit, her plan was fully formed.

Buffy pushed his way through the crowd, the baby on his hip. 'There you are,' he said. 'I thought I'd lost you.'

'I'm here.'

'In this novel I read, the lights went out and when they came on again somebody had died.'

'I'm not going to die yet,' Monica said.

He gazed at her. 'God, you're beautiful. Please don't ever leave me.'

He wore his blue velvet waistcoat. Even in the candlelight she could see a pale smear of sick down the front. She had never liked babies but for some reason this touched her heart.

'I've got an idea for your hotel,' she said.

'Not the boutique thing. I know it's going to rack and ruin but please not that.'

'No, it's not that. It's something quite different.'

334

18

Acme Motivation is proud to announce their new corporate challenge: 'Surprise' Executive Activity Weekends! Venue: Myrtle House Hotel. Nestling amid the Welsh hills, famed for its locally sourced cuisine and friendly staff, Myrtle House is well off the beaten track and thus offers a high degree of seclusion and security. These weekends, for top-level power brokers in the financial sector, offer a customised series of challenges and bonding sessions. Upon arrival, each participant will be allocated a mystery task guaranteed to be a life-changing experience.

'A life-changing experience'
(Sir Barry Jones, Goldman Sachs)

Over that summer the people of Knockton grew used to the fleet of cars parked outside Myrtle House. Ferraris, 7 Series BMWs, top-of-the-range Range Rovers, spattered with mud from passing tractors.

They also became used to their occupants. A banker is easily recognised in a town like Knockton. Besides, they all wore green boiler suits—'like a chain gang', as Connie from Costcutter's observed.

And like a chain gang they toiled from dawn to dusk. Panting and perspiring, they filled the potholes down the high street, they mended the swings in the recreation ground, they cleared the uncollected rubbish, they renovated the bus

335

shelter, they painted and reopened the public toilets, they restored the flower beds in the municipal garden. As Jill, of Jill's Things, said to her husband: 'We bailed them out so it's only fair, isn't it, that they do the same for us?'

As word got round, people came from far and wide to witness the spectacle. This was more fun than morris dancers. During the weekends the Coffee Cup was crammed with customers; the local shops did a thriving business. 'Watching the Bankers' made Knockton, in Monica's words, a Destination Town. What were they watching—an act of penance? a comedy routine?

For some, the toiling figures were a source of derision; for some, a focus for their anger. 'Give us a mortgage, mister!' young men shouted as they walked past.

Others were kinder, and engaged them in conversation. Old Mrs Bevan-Jones gave a cup of tea to an RBS Divisional Manager who was mending the paving stones outside her house. Her grandson filmed it on his mobile. *Where Did My Pension Go?* became a YouTube sensation.

And for the first time Myrtle House was making a profit. Its lack of facilities was part of the deal. So you queue for the bathroom? Join the real world! As Buffy watched his guests, aching and exhausted, driving off one Sunday night he said to Monica: 'My kids called this Heartbreak Hotel. The lovelorn and abandoned would come here and learn the skill their partners had, but it didn't quite turn out like that.'

'More like Backbreak Hotel now,' she said.

He put his arms around her. 'Do you love me?'

Monica rubbed her face against his beard. 'Of

course.' She paused. 'Besides, at our age one can't be choosy.'

AUTHOR'S NOTE

Want to actually learn something from one of these courses? Go to my website, www.deborahmoggach. com, click on the link to 'Courses for Divorces' and find some short but highly instructive films. You might even meet somebody from the novel.